MW01283635

THE

BUTCHER

OF

LENINGRAD

Tom Hunter

New York
Yasnaya Polyana Press
2011

Printed in the U.S.A.   2.9.9
ISBN 978-1-4507-5648-8

Chapter I

1.

THE child's arm ripped from its rotted body. The Russian sewer worker flung the arm on the pile. By the hair, he dragged the child's one-armed torso to the pile of bodies.

Jack Land, an American reporter who lived in St. Petersburg, stared at the clay-like flesh on the child's face. He decided it was a dead little girl. No blood leaked from her torn shoulder socket. She had been dead for days. Snowflakes drifted from the sky and landed on her face.

The sewer worker went back to the concrete hole and climbed in. Jack stood back on the sidewalk. Another ashen-faced corpse rose from the hole and Jack's heart sunk. So many dead children. Why?

The sewer worker, in his dirty jumpsuit, shouldered the stiff child—a girl from the length of her red hair—clear of the hole. He stepped over the lip and grabbed her by the hair. Her legs had stiffened at an angle. As he dragged her, one toe kept digging in and jerking free, spraying dirt. The worker dumped the girl. He took out a *Belamor Kanal* cigarette—the kind popular among winos—and lit it up. Exhaling, he nodded to Jack and asked, in Russian:

"What do you need."

"What happened here?"

The worker looked down and pressed his tongue to his cheek.

"Nothing," the worker said, angling his head to the side. "Some dead kids."

"What happened to them?" Jack said, crossing his arms in indignation and puffing out his chest to seem more intimidating.

"They just died," the worker said and smiled. "They were homeless and now they're dead."

Jack shook his head and sighed. Jack thought every living, breathing kid was a damn miracle that deserved to be taken the hell care of.

"Happens all the time," the worker said, and flicked away his cigarette. He was about to re-enter the sewer.

"Hold on," Jack said. He saw a triangular stab wound on the girl's stomach. The edges of the wound were black like tar. On the girl's palm, a deep stab wound exposed the flesh under her skin which looked red like salmon. Her pants were ripped open.

The worker stopped with half his body above ground. His face, though frosted in sewer grime, hung slack.

"Looks like this girl was stabbed and *raped*," Jack said. "Looks like she put up a hell of a fight." The sewer worker grunted and resumed his descent. "You don't give a fuck?" Jack asked.

The worker smiled. "What are you, some kind of foreigner pervert?"

"I'm American," Jack said, standing up straight.

The worker smiled and nodded, "Pervert."

"Who would *do* something like this?" Jack said.

"Not my concern," the worker said. "Maybe it's kids, police, Mafiya. All the same—these street kids—they're garbage."

Jack was outraged. The sewer worker looked at Jack with a superior, toothy smirk.

"You're a nobody," said the worker. "What are you going to do about it?"

Jack stared at the ground in anger. He could not fathom why someone would want to kill children. Jack felt angry that somebody thought they could get away with killing all these kids in broad daylight. At that moment, Jack decided he was angry enough to care. He was going to find out who was doing this and stop them. Killing little kids is an outrage. "Who could fucking do this!" Jack yelled to no one.

Jack made his observations of the dead bodies. He took photos of the dead kids but he knew there was no way Sarah Hughes, the Managing Editor of the tourist rag where he worked, would never allow them in *Nevski Novosti*. Still, they documented the evidence and would help him remember what he had seen when he tracked down what the hell was going on.

In the back of his mind, Jack knew he could use this story to get his next gig.

2.

Jack Land arrived in St. Petersburg with no job and no place to live. A man named Andrei Brezhukov met Jack at the airport. In turn, Andrei introduced Jack to a couple who rented Jack their living room for two weeks. That couple handed him off to Octavia, who rented Jack his apartment on Metallistov Prospekt. In that apartment, he lived on his savings like a bum for a month, walking around the city, speaking Russian to everyone he met, flirting like crazy, causing them to wonder where he was from, them trying to place his accent—guessing he was maybe from Estonia.

Jack kept in email contact with his old friend Thor Culpepper, a commodities trader in Chicago. Thor and Jack went to high school together. Thor bought a house, got his first divorce out of the way, got remarried to a hag, and he did not understand Jack's need to go gallivanting half way across the world to Russia, but he did love hearing about what was happening in Russia.

Jack's confidence blossomed in Russia. He felt capable of performing miracles. He had already accomplished his first miracles—learning Russian and getting to Russia on his own. He strolled along Nevski Prospekt with energy and a perpetual smile, feeling connected to Russia, like he belonged there.

He found the Mayakovskaya library, which loaned books in English. Using his blue folding identification card with his photo glued in it, Jack devoured "A Sportsman's Sketches". He especially enjoyed the experience of visiting peasant taverns lit by flickering candle light, of Turgenev's hunter coming out of the cold into a the midst of a smokey, murderous, drunken rabble milling around a wooden bar.

3.

Jack went out late and took the Metro train downtown to a bar called the Art Klinik. The last leg to the club required him to walk through an old gutted-out building, past a head-high pile of construction debris, across a muddy pathway on boards until he reached a bar full of young women in flapper skirts and fishnets, all in a large cluster of dancers all moving in unison with the beat. Burly confused Russian men stood around clutching beers, trying to move with the music in a way that did not make them resemble a bouncy monkey.

Jack danced for hours in the crush. Then he came out alone, having looked deep into the eyes of several girls, trying to answer the question: "What would it take to win your heart?"

From the moment he stepped out of the crowd to ask a woman to dance, he knew he was performing an audition, and that by the end of it his worth will have been decided. Like any young man, he stabbed out randomly in search of excellence, trying to find some niche where he could excel and distinguish himself professionally enough to attract a woman and her life to his. He knew in the post-internet world of journalism, it remained a winner-take-all profession where only a tiny few can make a living. Lacking an Ivy-League degree or its connections, he knew his only chance was breaking a big story. Then, clawing his way into one of the few paying gigs left. Jack had come to Russia to fall in love and make his fortune. Both of those goals depended on him doing his job well.

A professor of Meteorology met Jack at the international airport,

Pulkovo-2, in St. Petersburg. Andrei Brezhukov recognized Jack by his height. They drove in from Pulkovo-2 airport after Jack cleared customs, even showing the agent a huge folding knife he had in his suitcase for protection. Andrei asked Jack what brought him to St. Petersburg.

"A job," Jack said. "On a newspaper."

Andrei drove using both lanes, so potholed where the roads. He glanced over frowning at Jack in a way that indicated he was impressed. "And also, I was hoping I could find some Russian woman who might want me as a boyfriend."

Andrei looked over from his driving, perplexed.

"And as a *husband* too," Jack said. "I'm hoping I can meet some women."

Andrei settled back in his seat and looked now at Jack with full understanding. Jack felt he had showed his cards, and if Andrei took offense at the waves of Russian women who were exiting the country he did not show it. His arms drooped from the steering wheel now, slack, showing that he was resigned to seeing women leave.

"I think you won't have any trouble finding a woman who wants you, Jack," Andrei said. "The trick will be finding the right one." Andrei drove Jack to his own apartment and introduced him to his wife Katya and his two sons.

Jack sent an email to his friend, Thor, alerting him of his safe arrival. Then, Andrei introduced Jack to the Russian couple who agreed to rent out their front room to him for two weeks. Jack had arrived in February on the 13th, which was *Old* New Years, or the still-celebrated date of the New Year's holiday before the calendar was shifted to the Western style.

4.

Jack walked outside in the snow-coated landscape. He applied for a job as a reporter on a newspaper funded by Western money and with a frat boy editor who had staffed the English-language St. Petersburg *Post* only with fellow Ivy League Greeks.

In his interview with Cartwright Jedistan, the editor of the *Post*, Jack told of his prior experience working as a reporter, columnist and editor. Cartwright asked Jack questions without taking any notes, with his feet on the corner of his desk. He tossed a football into the air as he quizzed Jack.

Looking around at the Editor's desk, covered with the blue and gold colors and logo of the Fighting Irish, Notre Dame, Jack began to expect "the question" a full minute before he got it.

"Where, ah, where'd you go to school Jack?" Cartwright asked.

"University of Iowa," Jack said. Cartwright caught the football and held on to it. He looked differently at Jack.

"You, ah, got any story ideas?" Cartwright said.

"Well, yes," Jack said. He held his coat draped over his knees. Light streamed into office on to Cartwright's face, smooth cheeked with little sign of a beard and a crimson flush to his cheeks, making him look like a blushing young lad.

Jack did not get the job. He went back to looking for jobs, hoping his savings would last.

Jack had grown up with his grandmother Mara, who lived on her Social Security. Both his parents were dead from a car going 60 miles per hour that slammed into them. Jack had called his grandmother right after he landed in Russia but she did not entirely understand that he was living in Russia and he stopped calling her.

Then one day he picked up a copy of another newspaper: "Nevski Novosti" which was bilingual Russian/English. Jack went there and called on the editor unannounced.

The editor, Alexander I. Krasnie, worked as a reporter for many years before he started "Nevski Novosti" with his own money.

"Do you need a job?" Krasnie asked Jack, minutes into their conversation, putting a smile on Jack's face. "We could use you."

Jack smiled and reached out to shake Krasnie's hand. The editor stood almost as tall as Jack and he wore a beard under his chin in the manner of the Amish, Jack thought.

"I would be honored," Jack said.

Alexander led Jack out of his glass-doored office across the hall from an open room. It was the paper's newsroom and four people tapped away on computers. Jack's eye shot to a blond-haired woman in a red top. She tapped away at her computer with excellent posture—unlike the other three—who all appeared clearly Russian, with facial features that one say in countless near variants as one walked the streets of St. Petersburg.

"This is Vasya our computer genius...Yelena, a reporter...Sarah—"

"*Hughes*," said the blond, standing up and shaking Jack's hand. "Sarah Hughes," she said. It took Jack a moment to place her accent but then he did and thought: *Scottish*.

"I am the Managing Editor of *Neva News*," Sarah said.

"*Nevski Novosti*," Alexander said, correcting her. "*Neva News* is the subtitle."

Sarah smiled and dimples appeared in her cheeks. Jack thought she was devastatingly beautiful and he held a smiling gaze with her slightly longer in a way that became a small flirtation merely because he held her gaze too long.

"Jack is going to be a reporter," Alexander said. Sarah's gaze flicked over to Jack and he could see her now assessing him for his probable talent or absence thereof in the area of supplying her with copy to fill the spaces above the ads. Jack also knew that *Neva News*, not *Nevski Novosti*, would be going on her resume when she returned to Scotland to take grad school at the University of Edinburgh.

Though he had plenty of Russian women to pursue, Jack got greedy and flirted with Sarah. They eventually went out together on a date. Jack made a pass at her. She accepted his peck on her lips and he let his hands too quickly roam over her chest after they had both finished three bottles each of Baltika-4 beer. Then it got icky and they stopped going out. From then on, there existed a sub-current from Sarah to Jack, a flow of the waters of irritation. Sarah colored all of her verbal interactions with Jack through a filter of distrust and questioning of his qualifications to do his job.

"Oh, we can't send you to cover that story," Sarah announced to Alexander Ivanovich, referring to Jack, who was taking assignment of a story when Sarah injected herself into the conversation. "They can't possibly have taught you the proper law of libel and slander at that farm college."

Jack stood in front of Alexander's desk, feeling awkward, pleading his case to be given a chance to spend more than two hours on a cover story.

"Go ahead, do whatever you want," Sarah said, her voice taking a mocking tone. "Nobody's stopping you, 'Kipling'," she said, making reference to a personal conversation he and Sarah had shared, laying in the sheets. Jack had told her he like to read about the life of Rudyard Kipling. After that, she mocked Jack at every turn, refusing from then on to refer to Jack as anything else but variations of the name of Kipling, or saying "our 'Kipling from Dirt U.'"

In fact, Jack liked Sarah very much. She was his first Russian crush even though she was not Russian.

5.

Jack had passed the previous few years failing miserably with one woman after another and he allowed himself to believe that he could find a Russian woman and marry her.

"I'd like to write about the kids—the dead ones from the sewer—you remember when I mentioned that?" Jack said. "I want to show they're not garbage."

"Yes," Alexander said before Sarah could criticize the idea. When Alexander continued: "Great story idea—do it," Sarah said nothing and gave a long exhale ending in a wheezy sigh.

"Thank you, Alexander," Jack said. "I won't let you down." Jack wrote in his reporter's notebook.

Jack looked up from his note taking. Sarah stared right at him with rage in her eyes. Jack could not prevent a slight smirk from slipping to the upturned corners of his mouth, also giving the smile to his eyes in a way that enraged Sarah.

Jack ignored her and dwelled on the image of the dead girl being dragged like a stiff grasshopper across the dirt to a pile. He tried to see her face in his mind before it rotted and turned into white tar. He knew everybody would agree with the sewer worker that a pile of dead homeless kids, parent-less, outcasts, had no place in Russia. If their parents did not want them, why should anyone else?

"'Orphans are garbage'," Jack heard the words of the sewer worker echoing in his thoughts. It made him angry. Being an orphan himself, he took it personally and felt a warm rage simmer inside him, a desire to fight back against the arrogant people who thought he was a worthless orphan. Jack wanted more than anything to find out what was happening to the 'worthless' orphans.

6.

Jack earned little from his reporting and was burning through his savings quickly. He knew he was in a race with time to either get the biggest story of his life and earn his way out of the certain doom that waited when his money ran out. When that happened, he had no choice to bail the country and return in shame to Iowa.

He had been a series of disastrous dates with Russian women who lived in disparate parts of St. Petersburg. He traveled to see each of them in their home regions and, invariably, they led him to local cafes and he burned his capital and found that each of them, without exception, cared about finding a man with wealth and power, with a single-minded dedication that made American women seem like amateurs.

By the time Jack stopped dating catalog women, his cash had been reduced to one fifth and he found himself totally dependent on the money he earned from the paper. That amount was controlled by Sarah.

7.

Walking home near his apartment, Jack was stopped by two twenty-something women. They tried to beg a cigarette from him.

"Don't smoke," Jack said in Russian and though he had studied Russian for three years and was pretty good, they detected his American accent. The thinner of the two girls was named Zhanna and she spoke most of the time. It was clear at least that she and her friend Natasha, who was not rail thin like Zhanna, traveled as a pair.

Working late at night in his apartment, trying to get Maternity doctors from around the city to talk on the record about "refusal births," Jack answered a knock on his door at 11:30pm. It was the pair Zhanna and Natasha.

The two girls came in and Zhanna popped a cassette in Jack's tape player and asked if he had any Pepsi-Cola.

Jack fetched three glasses and he spoke with Zhanna while he found himself drawn to Natasha, who smiled in a way that seemed intimate and even familiar. He found himself looking without restraint at Natasha and then, after Jack squired the two of them to the all-night cafe under he Nevski Melody disco, both girls got drunk and Natasha spoke Jack in her murky voice that came from deep in her throat. He led her drunk back to his apartment and just lay next to her, feeling in a buoyant ecstasy at having a woman with him. Natasha was only 19 and had never stepped foot outside of the neighborhood. She spoke with a dusky slur to her speech. She behaved one way around Natasha but when Jack accompanied her to visit her mother, he saw a side of her that was calm and respectful. He decided at that moment, as he sat with Natasha between himself and her mother on the couch, watching a Russian movie, that he could think of no happier outcome than marrying Natasha.

Chapter II

1.

VLADIMIR Szlotov glanced in his BMW's rear-view mirror and decided no one was following him. It felt good to drive in the country on the outskirts of St. Petersburg. Szlotov knew the way to Pushkin but it had been years since he had been there, thirty kilometers from St. Petersburg. The last time he went there by *elektrichka* train, because he did not own a car.

Szlotov drove on the snow-coated Shushary Highway. He was on his way to a meeting with his business partners. It was a partnership they created at the end of that craziness called the Soviet Union. Szlotov was meeting Zortaev, the head of the *organizatsiya*, a brutal man with a condition that made his face grow a thick rind. Everyone avoided looking at his face. This lack of eye contact made it easier for Zortaev to pursue his brutal nature.

Szlotov, 46, had served in the security services at the same time Zortaev had but they did not know one another. When the security service fell apart, like everything else in the Soviet Union, there came a point when men like Szlotov and Zortaev had to thrust themselves ahead. It required strong men to impose order on St. Petersburg.

Szlotov's father was a butcher, a man who his whole life worked hard for the state. He died a worn out man. His knuckles looked like joints of meat at the end of his life. Szlotov lapsed into a daydream about working with his father, cutting meat, seeing his father swing the heavy wood-handled cleaver on the table.

Vladimir Szlotov grew up the son of a butcher in the Soviet Union. There was always extra meat for the butcher to sneak out and so Szlotov the son grew up solid and muscular. Szlotov remembered sitting back in the blood-soaked butcher shop, white porcelain tiles floor to ceiling. Old, hacked-up wooden tables with puddles of blood around his father's feet. Over and over, like a ticking clock, Szlotov's father hacked and hacked his cleaver. At night, when his father came home and took off his shirt, his mother Masha Ilovna rubbed cooking oil on his shoulder and knuckles. Vladimir always stared at his father's knuckles, huge gnarled knots. Every movement of them brought daggers of pain. His father had no escape in the Soviet Union but his son did.

Szlotov saw what happened to his own father. It sent Vladimir Szlotov, the son, into the federal security services.

2.

Szlotov rounded a bend and saw the meeting house whose columns made it look like it had been built in the 18th Century. Parked in front of the white stone building were three identical black Mercedes. Next to that, Druzhnev's Maserati. Loitering near the three Mercs were Zortaev's bald *bullki* in black pinstripe suits but with scarred-up faces from childhoods of fighting and bullying others. That and their teeth could not be helped. Szlotov parked his BMW 7 and got out in his long black-leather coat. Zortaev's men tipped their heads dutifully to Szlotov but there was a tinge of rage in their faces. Szlotov felt offended by the facial expression Zortaev's men gave him, as if they were angry at him—for what he did not know. He returned their looks with his own menace although he had come alone without Sergei or Ivan—his own security detail. It occurred to him as he walked his usual smooth gait with neither haste nor languor, that the meeting seemed odd. The call said to "come alone". This was supposed to be a high-level meeting.

Szlotov stepped inside, shed his coat and gave it to *Sidon*, one of Zortaev's *bullki*. Sidon snatched the coat away and glared, his cheek muscles standing out beneath his slicked-down black hair. Sidon wadded Szlotov's coat into a ball. Szlotov dropped his gaze silently to Sidon's hands and then to his face. Szlotov felt the eyes of all the *bullki* held anger.

He felt naked. Without his crew, he was alone. He followed a hallway that ended at double mahogany doors. A pencil of light spilled underneath. Szlotov walked with his mouth shut and his mind tight. He stopped with his hands on the doorknob. He took a deep whistling breath and opened both doors together.

Light flooded into the hallway. A black leather couch with a row of brass nails along the edges stood between him and another leather chair on which sat Dmitri Zoltanovich Zortaev, first in command of the Tambov syndicate, the *organizatsiya* to which Szlotov belonged. Zortaev held a brandy snifter with a finger of cinnamon-colored liquid. He grinned at Szlotov so that creases formed in the rind of scars on his face.

"*Drasti*, Vladimir," Zortaev said, and smiled as he glanced to his left. Szlotov followed his gaze to where he saw Pavel Druzhnev, laying on a love seat like a 17-year-old boy, with an unshaven face, his legs splayed apart and undignified like a dog, his face pretty but ruined by his habit of reposing with his mouth gaping like a *doorak*, and breathing through his mouth like a fool with a sound audible across the room. That noise had annoyed Szlotov from the first

14

moment he met this man-boy Druzhnev—the man who controlled one-third of the Tambov's territory, the richest part, making it easy for him to cull huge sums from oil shipping.

"Good evening," Szlotov said to Zortaev. Then, as a wolf swung his head to gaze on a weak animal, Szlotov swung his head to address Druzhnev. "Pavel," Szlotov said to Druzhnev, and dipped his head slightly.

"What are you drinking, Vladimir?"

"Brandy," Szlotov said, though he usually took vodka. Zortaev got another snifter and filled it with amber liquid. Zortaev licked the top of the brandy bottle before he re-capped it.

Zortaev took a long gulp from his brandy and then some over spilled and dribbled down his chin. Zortaev took the stains in stride and showed no reaction to the wet patch on his tie, shirt and suit coat.

"Vladimir," Zortaev said, setting down his snifter. "This thing we have, it works only when you and I know our places. If we stay in our places, then I am happy, you—Vladimir—are happy *too*." Zortaev bobbed his head in affirmation with each of these statements, the width of his smile widening with every bob. Szlotov leaned forward on his knees. His suit bunched over his shoulders where the tailor had added padding to make Szlotov's shoulders look broader.

"But if I find, Vladimir, that my home has been invaded—well, no man can be happy with such a situation," Zortaev said, his eyebrows lifted dramatically and his cheeks puffed out. "Is everything clear so far?" Zortaev asked, looking into Szlotov's eyes.

"Yes, I understand," Szlotov lied, still not understanding what the meeting was about.

"And if, say, our friend and partner Pavel Ivanovich—" Zortaev nodded to Druzhnev "—has his own games, his own men and their friends, then it is without strain that one imagines, Vladimir, that such men each have grandmothers… Do you follow me, Vladimir?"

"I do," Szlotov said and glanced at Druzhnev, who sat splayed on the love seat in his insolent posture, displaying his eggs to the room. Druzhnev now had a toothy smile that showed the gaps in his upper teeth. His gums had a perpetual reddish glow.

"The Fontanka Canal," Zortaev said. "The Fontanka marks the *edge* of your territory—am I right?"

Zortaev stopped there and waited for Szlotov to agree, but still it was not apparent to Szlotov what the problem was. Szlotov allowed a long, toothless smile on his face.

"What?" Szlotov said and looked at Zortaev and then at Druzhnev over on the love seat with his eggs and that smirk for an answer. "The hell is going on?"

Zortaev reached for the brandy. He refilled his glass and licked the top of the bottle.

Druzhnev sighed and swung his feet down to the floor. Szlotov stared back at Druzhnev in a rage.

"A couple of hooligans," Druzhnev said, standing over Szlotov. "Ransacked their way through a neighborhood not far from Gostiny Dvor. These two *hooligans*—" and he said this word with special vigor "—dressed up as *Militsiya*, pounded on the doors of grandmothers, and told them some bullshit about wild animals in the wet wall." Druzhnev crouched down next to Szlotov's face. Zortaev also leaned in close, his face creased in a mixture of discomfort and expectation. "And now all these *facking* grandmothers made a huge stink over these two bastards. My boys say it has turned the neighborhood against them."

"What did the men look like?" Zortaev asked.

"One of them looked a rat. The other—that bald, fat bastard was—"

Zortaev held up his palm to stop Druzhnev.

"The two men were dressed like *Militsiya*," Zortaev said. "They convinced the *babushki* that wild animals were loose in the wet wall?" Zortaev stopped talking and laughed. He looked to Druzhnev who found no humor in the situation.

"It's really very dangerous, Vladimir," Zortaev said. "Killing *babushki* is a dirty thing. It creates big troubles and must not be done. There's such little money in grandmothers…"

"What gives you a reason—" Szlotov said, sitting, trying not to let the situation get out of hand, "—to believe these atrocities were done by *my* crew?"

Zortaev greeted Szlotov's defiance with silence and hardened his face. From the muscles standing in his cheeks, the grind of his teeth and a long exhale—it was clear he was angry. Zortaev stood and walked to the window, his hands behind his back, gripping each other. Zortaev spun around and walked toward Szlotov.

"What don't you understand, Vladimir? If you keep doing these raids, killing grandmothers for a few rubles, then even *I* cannot help you. Get it? I *too* need money. As a result of these raids, I now have to pay bribes to people I did not pay before and who I cannot bully. For these expenses I need only one thing—*babki*. So, as a penalty, for going across the Fontanka, the *babki* from you, Vladimir, must double."

Szlotov gritted his teeth and exhaled. He managed his anger without giving any sign of his rage. Szlotov knew precisely which two men carried out the raids because he recognized them from the descriptions: Fyodor and Vasily. They had been combing over Szlotov's region, using precisely the '*wild animal*

16

in the wet wall' ruse, which Szlotov himself invented as a foolproof way to gain entrance into the apartments of old *babushki* who never spent a ruble. Before this con, there never had been a way for Szlotov and his crew to get the *babushki* to open their steel doors. Szlotov himself invented these techniques. Internally, Szlotov found it laughable that he had been doing this same gag, the one Zortaev found so dangerous, for at least six months.

"Grandmothers were *killed?*" Szlotov asked carefully, to avoid suggesting that leaving a 63-year-old lady living penniless, alone in the apartment her deceased husband had left her, was not the same as slitting her throat and letting her bleed out over the bathtub.

"No more!" Druzhnev roared. "Stay on *your* side of the Fontanka Canal, and *go fuck yourselves.*"

"Indeed," Szlotov said.

3.

Szlotov drove home from Pushkin in the darkness. He saw the lights of St. Petersburg come up in the distance as he drove down the tree-lined Shushary highway to the city and then on to Prospekt Nevski and on to Mayakovskaya street. The entire drive back he stared ahead and felt anger simmering inside. Certainly he would speak with Fyodor and Vasily about keeping on *our* side of the Fontanka. Szlotov had agreed to the Fontanka Canal as the dividing line between their territories back in 1990 when he and Zortaev, both freshly unemployed from different parts of the Center—the KGB—made the Tambovs together. Zortaev viewed St. Petersburg as a lawless mess that needed a strong hand to guide it into the post-Soviet era. Zortaev invited Szlotov and gave him his childhood home as his territory, the poorest region of St. Petersburg. This arrangement appeared to give Szlotov a larger share of the city but in fact it enabled Zortaev to tax the oil supply of the city. "Perhaps it's time for that to end," Szlotov thought.

He turned left on Mayakovskaya and parked next to an old building, *his* building. He parked his BMW next to a row of others just like it. By habit he scanned the area before he entered the building. The hallway led to a door.

"You made it back," Sergei said, smiling. He was Szlotov's second and a childhood friend, one who had grudgingly played the subordinate to Szlotov and resented the fact. Szlotov poured himself four fingers of vodka in a glass.

Sergei stared at Szlotov wordlessly. Szlotov sensed, from Sergei's look of alarm on his creased forehead, that he felt threatened. Sergei was no more secure than his boss. Szlotov threw back his vodka and set the glass down for a

17

refill. He flipped over a second glass and splashed it full of vodka. He handed the splashing glass to Sergei and then Szlotov tapped the bottom of his glass against the rim of Sergei's glass.

"*Na zdarovia*," Sergei said, and drank it all.

"To your health," Szlotov replied. Szlotov broke a slice of bread in half and sniffed it. Sergei broke off a chunk of bread and ate it. They both stood silent a moment, recovering from the vodka,and then Sergei took another bite and said:

"What did they want?"

Szlotov looked away and tried to decide for himself what occurred at the meeting. He knew Druzhnev was a greater rival than ever, that Szlotov needed—somehow—to squeeze even more money from the region—on *this* side of the Fontanka.

"Zortaev raised our tribute—he *doubled* it—in fact."

"*Svoloch!*" Sergei barked. "The pig!" Standing still, Sergei physically shrunk in place, diminishing as he tried to imagine how they all would double the number of rubles they paid up to Zortaev and still earn enough to make it all worth it.

"What are we going to do?" Sergei said. "It's time for Zortaev…to go."

"Watch it," Szlotov said. "He's still my partner. If he really needs the money—"

"*My God*, Vladimir," Sergei said. "We already tap everything. Hitting even the *babushki*."

"*That* was the rub, Sergei," Szlotov said. "Fyodor and Vasily tapped some grandmothers near *Gostiny Dvor*"—referring to a shopping area on the far side of the Fontanka, clearly out of Szlotov's territory.

"Fools!" Sergei said, and took the vodka for himself, sloshing his own glass full. They both followed the ritual, draining glasses and sniffing bread, and found themselves in the same place as before—without any ideas.

"Let *me* talk to them—I do not want to kill their initiative."

The front door opened and in came Ivan, the new driver.

"Ah, sir," Ivan said. "We have more of them…the *kids*."

"In my room," Szlotov said.

4.

Szlotov emerged from the shower. He wrapped himself in a towel and left the bathroom. Standing there, surprised at seeing his boss in a towel, was Ivan. Beside him was one of the sewer kids.

"Bad time?" Ivan said, gripping the shoulder of the young boy with greasy hair and buck teeth. The boy stood passively under Ivan's grip, and stared gape-mouthed, his buck teeth gleaming—slimy under the bright lights in Szlotov's room. Szlotov went to his closet, dressed and emerged in a t-shirt he had last worn in Czechoslovakia, when he ran agents there for the KGB.

Szlotov knew how similar running a KGB foreign residency was to running a mafia crew. In Prague, Szlotov recruited nationals to become agents, his eyes and ears, his arms and legs in foreign cities. Szlotov himself had performed the dance that was finding talent and matching the man or woman to the task. Szlotov stared in the mirror at himself, while Ivan and the sewer kid waited. Though he did not intend to go out, he put on a crisp white shirt. He buttoned the top button and added a blue necktie tied in a half Windsor. The eyes of Ivan and of the boy watched the colorful tie, which was blue but resembled the scales on a steel-head salmon, that organic yet metallic look, the shine of dry oil.

Szlotov slid up his tie and faced them as if for the first time.

"Well?" Szlotov said.

Ivan yanked the buck-toothed kid forward. Szlotov gave the lad a cursory glance. Then, giving his professional appraisal, Szlotov lifted his eyebrow and sighed.

"Maybe the peder—" Szlotov began to say, but then stopped. Even *those* customers had minimums. "*N'yet*, not even...trash," Szlotov said and turned away. He walked to the kitchenette where he and Sergei kept a running game of *shakmati*. Szlotov studied the board a moment, and moved a bishop into a rook-protected position of attack on Sergei's Queen. He could picture the alarm on Sergei's face when he saw the move.

A gleam of joy flashed across Szlotov's face. Then he looked up and abruptly popped from his thoughts of chess. Ivan and the boy stood where they had been. Ivan frowned, then scrunched up his shoulders and presented his palms.

"Mr. Szlotov," Ivan said. "I...don't get it. What do you want me to do with him?"

Szlotov felt irritated. His breath sailed out his nose and his lips puckered in agitation.

It dawned on him that he could not afford to waste even this buck-toothed reject. *But what use is such an ugly boy*, Szlotov asked himself. *No good to the pornographer or the pederast.*

In his mind, Szlotov recalled his days in Prague, walking along the Vltava River lined with stone embankments and squat stone buildings like the ones in St. Petersburg. Along the river, Szlotov remembered a conversation he had there with Yakov Lezhnev, who later emigrated to Israel. Yakov now worked in Tel Aviv as a transplant surgeon. He described that business as a license to print money. "The greatest need is for the children, especially for those with rich parents," Yakov had said. "They will pay anything to save their children."

"No," Szlotov said. "Put him back down in the hole. I have an idea how he can help us."

Ivan smiled and his face turned cheerful. Ivan grabbed the boy by his collar and led him away. Szlotov stood alone in his room and put on a CD of Prokofiev's 3rd. He poured himself a short glass of cognac and stared out his window into the cool night, and Prokofiev's concerto wound up. His severe manner and the stiffness on his face was the mask he held up to the world and his men.

Szlotov drank and remembered standing in the butcher shop while his father worked. His father brought home slabs of meat that would have cost a pile of rubles except that Szlotov's father had *vlast*, power, pull—connections—and a smile that caused doors to open, secretaries to give way and problems to resolve themselves spontaneously. Szlotov thought how he differed from his father. Szlotov the son had none of the joy of his father, none of the sheer happiness at being alive. Friends who knew Szlotov's father, also called Vladimir, smiled at the memory of his old man, the meat cutter. Old friends invariably smiled and looked off over Szlotov's shoulder as they recalled his father. Then their smiles were replaced by grim frowns and looks of concern as they looked back at the younger Szlotov and the problem of how to handle him.

Szlotov earned as well as he could but he had no oil terminal on his side of the Fontanka. He had only tiny Mom-and-Pop businesses. He needed his *own* big business. He needed to convert the raw material of his region, homeless kids, into maximum *babki*.

Szlotov tossed back the last of his cognac and went to the elevator. It hummed loudly as the door slid aside and he got in. It descended two floors and Szlotov got out. Immediately he was confronted with the two men in the uniforms of the *Militsiya*. Seeing the two cops did not alarm Szlotov as he recognized them as his men Fyodor and Vasily.

"Vladimir Vladimirovich," Vasily said, lowering the eyelids of his deep-set eyes. His pointy face stretched the skin around his nose and chin.

"Good day, Vasya," Szlotov replied with a slight incline of his head.

Szlotov originally found Vasily after he had lost a fight in a club. In the fight, Vasily had taken on four men, all bigger than himself. Vasily was a nervous man with a pinched face and the feeling that his eyes were too closely placed together but he was a hard worker. It seemed to Szlotov that Vasya needed to be constantly reassured of his place in the organization. Since praise cost him nothing, it was an acceptable price.

While Szlotov spoke to Vasily, Fyodor looked at the floor and bit his fat lower lip. Szlotov saw that Fyodor heard through the ranks about the grief they had caused Szlotov when they strayed beyond the Fontanka.

"Everything is fine," Szlotov said. "Hit the free weights."

"*Spacibo*, Vladimir Vladimirovich," Vasily said, glad-eyed. "I will."

Szlotov walked around the facility, seeing who was going out to earn and who was sitting in the kitchen feeding. No one in the entire brigade was in the gym or on the exercise machines.

Lastly, Szlotov opened the basement door. He looked down into the blackness. He heard chatter coming from the livestock held in wooden pens. The humidity and smell hit Szlotov in the face as he walked down the wooden steps to the basement.

The chatter coming from the pens settled down as the stairs squeaked. Szlotov stepped into the basement in his blue tie and suit.

Wooden crates lined the basement—with homeless kids inside them. The Doctor, Mansoor Moosorovic, scurried out from his chair in the corner. The basement air felt wet. Szlotov disliked the smell of wet mildew that crawled into his awareness.

The Doctor came up and made a wet embrace of Szlotov, giving him a two-handed shake when one was sufficient.

Just looking at the Doctor's teeth made Szlotov grimace. His bloody gums and wobbly teeth looked painful as the Doctor stretched out his smile. Though Szlotov called him 'doctor,' none of his men trusted Mansoor. They knew, when the attending physician was Mansoor, death was near. Dr. Moosorovic lived in the basement, tending to the collected homeless children.

At first, the kids were a nuisance to Szlotov, until he thought up new ways to use them.

In the second floor of his building, Szlotov kept rooms for making films. The end product was of such poor quality that no money could be made from it. A better resource turned out to be prostitution, which earned a steady income but then the children and, especially the girls, required feeding and cleaning and occasional antibiotics and sulfa drugs.

Again, Szlotov felt himself caught in a bad business that made no money and required the girls to be baby sat. He needed a way to get everything from the kids at one go, and then dispose of them. Szlotov remembered his friend, the transplant surgeon: "The rich will pay the highest prices to help their own children. For their children—they will pay dearly. The rich will fly anywhere, do anything, or pay any sum to save their child."

Szlotov's eyes opened wider. A flush of ideas swirled in his head. The dirtiest, ugliest bucktoothed kid was clean on the inside.

Chapter III

GALINA lay naked in the tub. Cold water inched up her backside. Her grandmother Ludmilla scrubbed Galina's 8-year-old skin with a brisk hand and a bar of lye soap. "When I'm done, you'll be clean. But now you're filthy and I must scrub you, you filthy, wicked girl." The rhythmic travel of her grandmother's slack, pink flesh continued without cease. Galina shivered, laying up to her shoulders in the icy water, since her grandmother never added any *hot* water to Galina's bath, thinking hot baths would turn Galena into a loose woman, comfortable with her legs apart, ready to get pregnant from the first boy who pressed. Though hot water was free and could never run out, though she did not pay for hot water since her apartment had no water meter, she refused to give hot water to her granddaughter.

Galina shivered in the cold. Her *babushka* Ludmilla, whose son had died in the Afghanistan war, held her down in the water so her limbs could be properly scrubbed.

After Galina endured ten minutes of her grandmother's arbitrary scrubbing, forcing her pink old fingers into any hole or cavity in Galina's body without asking permission or considering the pain involved, the bath ceased.

When Ludmilla was finished, she abandoned the bathroom. Galina shivered in the water, laying alone for a minute before she used her toe to pull the cork and get out of the bath water. She rinsed the tub out and got it ready for her brothers, who would get hot baths.

Galina skipped up the concrete steps to her grandmother's apartment. In hand, she carried a brown *banderole* wrapped in brown paper and bound in brown twine. The twine was tied tightly at the knot, as if a pair of strong hands had pulled it tight. Galina shook the package and found it light. It felt empty as if the matter inside was important.

"Here is a package," Galina announced as she entered her grandmother's apartment. Her littlest brother Pavel ran in from the kitchen with her other brother Andrei right behind him.

From the kitchen came Ludmilla, wearing a blue pattern dress that fit her like a potato sack fits a pile of potatoes. Her body inched her forward at a steady rate, though her feet had barely enough time to hop forward from step to step, the stationary leg almost unable to bear the load.

Galina waited, still, without jittering or making smacking noises with her mouth—anything that might annoy her grandmother and make her slap Galina.

After she plopped in her chair and dust powdered the air, Ludmilla snatched away the package.

Her toothless upper and lower jaws chewed on nothing and slacked her cheeks to no effect as the well-used creases in her face expressed her exasperation at the tightness of the knot in the twine, and the difficulty of undoing it so the twine could be saved and reused. While Galina stood by, silently, without motion, her grandmother's agitation grew as the seconds ticked by and the knot remained.

"Scissors," Ludmilla said, shaking her fist so the jelly in her upper arms trembled.

Galina ran to the kitchen and brought back a scissors. She put it on the table next to her grandmother.

Ludmilla cut the twine near the knot. She spread open the package and found a personal letter inside, written in a rough man's hand. Galina caught a whiff of a bad smell, of fish and stale mildew. Under the letter was another inner package. Galina saw her grandmother's fingers enter the folds of the inner package and out spilled color. Color and paper and thick piles of squares that Galina saw and stared at and knew all at once was money. Galina looked up from the money to her grandmother, who looked different, altered, as if her entire face energized, as if all her woes were gone. Galina did not know what the money meant. She sensed from her grandmother's face that it was good news. Her grandmother closed her eyes, pressed the letter to her breast and lay back in her chair, as shiny trails appeared under her eyes.

"Thank *God*," Ludmilla said. Galina felt neither good nor bad. A quiet calm had overtaken her grandmother. That made Galina feel relieved.

Galina sat on the corner of the couch, out of the way of her grandmother.

"Galya," said her grandmother, surprising Galina by using her pet name. "This means, Galya," said her grandmother, fingering the stiff pile of rubles in her hand.

"I don't...understand," Galina said, thinking her grandmother was going to buy her that deep-blue scarf she had adored for weeks. Perhaps the extra money meant that they would take her brothers Andrei and Pavel out to buy their own shoes like they should have. All these ideas passed through Galina's mind. She considered every wild idea a girl who spent her life in a village called Chilkovo next to the town Chudovskoy, deep in Novgorod, could imagine.

Galina waited for her grandmother Luda to explain. Instead, Ludmilla stopped in mid-sentence—her mouth agape.

"Galya," said Ludmilla. Her grandmother's suddenly pitying tone of voice turned Galina's stomach into a turbulent roil of anxiety, punctuated by her pounding heart.

"What's happening?" Galina asked herself. She felt dizzy and lost, falling back into a gray tunnel in her mind but with one link open to her grandmother. Ludmilla, the only family Galina and her younger brothers had.

"I'm old, Galya. My son is dead and so is your mother. She's gone. You must accept that, Galya," said Ludmilla, sighing from the weight of the chore but continuing. Galina remembered her mother in the white stone Chudovskoy Station, leaving for Chechnya. She wished her grandmother was wrong. "You know I can't afford to feed all of you," Ludmilla swallowed.

"I will eat *less*," Galina said, flushed, cold and in a panic. "I don't need anything. Just let the boys—"

"—the boys can *stay*, Galina," Ludmilla said and then lost steam.

Galina looked down. She felt drained of energy, hopeless. She would not move her arms if thrown in a river; she would allow herself to drift underwater.

"Ladna," Galina said softly. "Okay. I'll go," she said. Tears rolled down her cheeks. She held her breath and said no more, wanting to vanish, to turn invisible, someone who bothered no one. On reflex, Galina now backed away from her grandmother. Her father's mother now repelled her.

"No, you *still* do not see," Ludmilla said. "Galina, this money," and she flourished the thickness of money, the bills wandering from the stack as she waved it. "A man sent me this money. A man from Tbilisi—Astrakhan is his name—he paid this money for *you*."

3.

Within a day, Galina stood dressed in her winter coat, such as it was, with her grandmother Ludmilla and brothers Andrei and Pavel, each of whom wore brand new mittens bought that morning from the bazaar.

In her mind, Galina fell from the point where she thought about having fun, of protecting her brothers, to numbness, to a feeling of amputation, of going away, of sacrificing so others can live. Galina knew only the instructions she got from her grandmother the night before.

Once again, as the train idled in the station giving off an electrical smell of burning and ozone, grandmother Ludmilla stood and barked out her last words to Galina.

"Astrakhan *bought* you," Ludmilla said. "You are now his. Forever. That's it. Oh, yes, *this*," Ludmilla said. She reached into her coat pocket and pulled out a long white scarf. The white scarf carried over its length a single red cross and then four smaller red crosses.

"Astrakhan said you should wear this: it's how he will know you." Galina draped the white scarf around her own neck and stepped up aboard the train, her small wooden suitcase with all her clothes in her right hand. Her grandmother waved goodbye. So did Andrei and Pavel. Galina stared back at them in a daze. She could not believe this was happening to her.

4.

Galina rode the train, sitting with her wooden suitcase on her knees, feeling the top of her head lifting from fear. She sat alone, staring at no one and at everyone, trying to see who was going to hurt her. She cried for the first hour after she left the Chudovskoy train station. She stared down at her worn canvas shoes. With her tongue she felt the chip in her lower front tooth. She did not know what it meant that Astrakhan or whatever-his-name-was had bought her. But she knew it meant she would never see her brothers or her grandmother again. She held her breath in to keep from crying. She listened to the steady "clop clop" "click click" as the train passed over the tracks. She watched the countryside going past. Next to the tracks stood trees, stripped of their leaves, waiting and watching the trains go by. Galina knew only that she was headed for Leningrad. Enough money had been spent on her that whoever Astrakhan was, he would want something for his money.

She asked a man with a stained shirt where the train was going. He said "Leningrad" but then another man in glasses, who had been reading a newspaper, corrected him. "St. Petersburg—*that's* where this train is going."

Forests of trees passed as she headed for a place she had never been, the city of millions up in the cold—St. Petersburg.

The darkness began to lift. Galina woke to see the train heading into a large city, one with wooden buildings along the tracks. Sometimes the train slowed. A sign read "Sankt Peterburg" in white letters over a green background. Around her neck she felt the white scarf with the red crosses on it. She pulled it out of her coat and made it lay on the outside. The train slowed as it entered the station with a tall tower in the middle. Galina grabbed her wooden suitcase, and headed for the door with the rest of the passengers. She saw women with head scarves carrying glass jars filled with mushrooms and other vegetables. They had come from their dachas. Galina knew this was normal for them to come into St. Petersburg, but for her it was new and terrifying. She knew no one there but she knew that her mother had a sister Anastasia who lived somewhere in St Petersburg on an island called Primorsky. Galina did not know her last name or where exactly she lived. Galina could not stop dwelling on the thought that someone named Astrakhan had bought her and she would be his property. Anxiety kept her from thinking of anything else.

The train finally stopped rolling. The lack of motion felt strange to Galina and made her heart sound like it was pumping too fast. She held her wooden suitcase and waited her turn behind the crowd. She was curious to see Astrakhan. She expected him to have black hair, the thick black hair all Georgians had, though she had never known an actual Georgian.

Galina stepped forward. The cold wind of St. Petersburg slapped her face. She saw all around her people meeting, men taking up the suitcases of women and walking off with them, the women always looping their arms around the arms of the men. Galina stood still and looked at the other trains all green and neat and exciting in the huge station. She looked at the face of every man who passed her. An old man with a week's stubble, a high forehead and deep wrinkles on his face, especially around and under his eyes, walked past her with a scowl. The white scarf around Galina's neck flicked in the wind as the other passengers thinned out and now everybody who passed noticed her.

Galina looked toward the terminal to see if anyone was standing there—a man or somebody, and she felt a panic of not knowing what to do. She did not have a return ticket to Chilkovo.

"What am I going to do, if nobody meets me, I'm all alone," she thought and felt the cold tears coursing down her face. A strong gust of cold Northern wind found inside her coat and chilled her to the core. Galina wailed out a sob.

"*Ah-cha-dee!*" shouted a gruff voice behind her. "Stop it!" A strong hand grabbed her from behind and pinched her shoulder. Galina spun around with huge eyes. She stared at the man who grabbed her.

It was the old man who had walked past her. "The yap you will close *now*," Astrakhan said, speaking Russian words Galina understood but in a way that sounded foreign. "Let that be the last time I give you that advice as," he said, starting to walk and dragging her along beside him. "The next comment I make on your tongue will be to slap that face."

Galina walked with some resistance, carrying her own suitcase. Astrakhan himself turned back to her and stared into her eyes.

That moment—when Galina looked deep into the black wells that were his eyes—scared her and made her know that she would be beaten; she would have no more days as a girl; now she would be his woman.

27

5.

Galina climbed in his car hugging her wooden suitcase on her knees. She stared ahead as he drove through the slushy streets of St. Petersburg and the high granite curbs on Prospekt Nevski. Then he turned down a side street a long way until Astrakhan's Opel had made so many turns that Galina was lost. With every stop she heard the high-pitched whine of the car's engine. The letters of the words on the dashboard were foreign and that added to her confusion with every unfamiliar word he said. He was angry and disappointed. She did something wrong. She listened to him mutter and argue with his car. She was startled when he punched the dashboard and followed that up with a stream of angry words directed at the engine. Galina grimaced with every one of his blunt actions. She stole a glance at him and saw the dark areas under his eyes and the thick pig bristles of his beard. They were stiff and thick and she found herself staring at him when he glanced over.

"What are you looking at," Astrakhan said and gave her the back of his hand.

"Nothing!" Galina said, opening her mouth for the first time.

"That's what you'll get if you don't do as I say," he said. She met his eyes. The look in them said that he looked on her as his property, one who he would kill if it pleased him. Galina felt the hairs on her neck creep up. The top of her head lifted, like it was electric. From the look in his eyes, the flex of his cheeks, the veins standing out from his neck and the sound of the steering wheel creaking under his fingers, Galina knew he was dangerous. She sat back in her seat and hung her head, feeling inside of her the urge to cry but willing herself to hold in her tears.

Astrakhan jerked suddenly to the left and drove behind a gray cinder block building with a stand of trees next to it. He parked the Opel and got out. Galina got out and walked behind him over the muddy path through an arched brick tunnel. At the end, concrete steps led down to a steel door in the building's basement. Astrakhan spit on the ground and jammed a large brass key into the basement door. He pulled the key toward himself and then used another key to unlock the inner door. Galina looked around the area, which was industrial. In all the surrounding buildings, the lights were off.

She did not see many cars parked except ones with thick layers of snow on them and around their tires.

"Come on, *sooka*," Astrakhan barked, using the Russian word for 'bitch'. He then added a stream of guttural reproaches in Georgian.

The door cracked open and cast light on a wet, low-ceilinged room without windows. Galina stopped in the doorway and tried not to breath in the acrid smell of sweat, back-flowing sewage and mold. Her eyes fell on the main room with a brown cloth couch and a single greasy sit spot which faced a television and was surrounded by piles of food trash, chicken bones, cored potato carcasses and beer bottles overflowing a garbage can. Astrakhan walked swiftly into his apartment and flicked on a fluorescent light in the kitchen. Roaches by the dozen scurried for cover under plates, dirty dishes and a sink filled with greasy, congealed water and that carried its own stink of decay and rot. A gray athletic sock floated in the sink as a dish rag. Stacked on the floor were dirty dishes, with foamy brown water. Astrakhan headed for his bedroom. He pulled on a single bulb over his bed, a single large mattress laying on the concrete floor, growing blue-green fuzz near the floor.

"What are you staring at!" Astrakhan yelled at her. "I'm a man. I work. I have a job—not like you. From time I *five years old* in Tbilisi, I earn money—not like you, *sooka*," he said. After a bit of hesitation, he came over and stood by her. He picked her off the ground and stood her feet on the couch, so he could look her in the eye. She looked at his brown teeth, smelled his horrible breath and felt his belly pressing against her legs. His tongue wiped his greasy lips and his dirty hands moved up and down her back; it made her feel dirty. Her heart raced from panic. She felt dizzy and sweaty and confused at the same time.

"I have work for you, princess," he said. His eyes opened wider, and he started to breathe quicker and pull her tighter against him, even as she tried to cross her arms in front of herself to keep him away.

He reacted to her resistance by hugging her tighter. Galina felt terrified. She could not breathe. She felt his hands go under her clothes. Tears flowed down her face as she thought "This is my life now. This is what my grandmother wanted for me. I am no good for anything else," and with these thoughts and her growing exhaustion from pressing him away, she suddenly went limp. Astrakhan pulled her tightly and then he seemed to emerge from a daze and let go of her. Galina tumbled back on the ground and hit her head on the corner of his table. Her head made a noise when it hit the table.

She rolled on the ground and held her head, wailing.

"I had it much worse in Tbilisi," Astrakhan said and stepped over her to get to his chair. He turned on the television to ORT Channel 1 news. He turned up the volume to drown out her noise. Astrakhan got up to get a beer and, when he returned, he stepped over Galina, still clutching her head. "Hey," he said, and nudged her with his boot. He took a drink of his Baltika-4. "Get busy on that kitchen—it's filthy. Clean it."

Galina rolled over and faced the kitchen. Filthy stacks of dishes. Piles of trash. But she thought that she would be happy to do it. She wanted to work—

29

anything her grandmother asked her to do. She set to work on the dishes.

Galina spent the next three hours cleaning Astrakhan's kitchen. After two hours, Astrakhan got his coat and hat and left the apartment. He locked the door from the outside. Galina waited until he was gone fifteen minutes before she dried her hands and walked up the stairs to listen at the door. She heard nothing. She tried the door. It would not move. No windows. She looked along the ceiling for a shaft or hole but she saw nothing. She looked at his desk and tried to understand what the papers there meant. But the writing was in Georgian. It looked to her like ink blots or the feces of cockroaches. She hated him already. Yet knew he hadn't given her a reason. Galina remembered her grandmother with pain. She lingered on her grandmother's decision to sell her. It slashed her heart to know her grandmother thought it okay to sell her. Yet, Galina loved her grandmother. Her anger was reserved for this man, Astrakhan.

After she finished cleaning every last bit of filth in Astrakhan's kitchen, she sat on the floor in a shadow and waited. She was asleep when she heard Astrakhan return. First, she heard him singing. She tried to understand the words but they were not in Russian. Then, the singing got louder. She heard keys and Astrakhan stood silhouetted in the doorway. He stumbled down the stairs. In a few seconds, Galina got a whiff of his alcohol breath—vodka. Galina hadn't smelled vodka for years since before her father went to Chechnya and got killed.

"Where are you, *sooka*," yelled Astrakhan, holding unsteadily to the bottom of the stairs. Galina saw him swaying and from that judged how drunk we was. She ran from the kitchen to her hiding place behind his desk.

"There you are!" Astrakhan said and pounced on her. In a moment, the drunk old Georgian captured her by faking one way and then doubling back. He grabbed her shirt and turned her toward him. "I'll not have my prize run! I paid and I plan to have you earn out that money. It won't come cheap." With each word, he added the punctuation of a vigorous shake until Galina trembled and wept silently, the prisoner of his grip. Astrakhan emerged from his alcoholic daze just enough to notice the streaks of wet on her cheeks. Astrakhan's brow pinched, he rubbed the flat of his palm over his stubbly face, and let her go. She ran and hid behind his desk. Astrakhan staggered back and waved his hand with a dramatic flourish, as if he were pleading his case in court, "Not *that*—" he said. "Astrakhan is friendly. Hard-working man. I paid. I sent money, you, little Russian *sooka*!"

Galina said nothing but hunkered behind the desk. She sneezed at a dust cloud she had stirred up. Astrakhan approached and tried to drag her out. Galina broke his grip and pulled away from him at his every lunge, the same way she would have behaved toward a dog with white foam dripping from its mouth.

Galina crouched behind the desk and peered up at him. The drunk

Georgian had not advanced. Galina wiped the damp from her face and only succeeded in smearing the dirt already there into a brow-line of mud.

The moment he saw this, Astrakhan clicked his tongue and shook his head.

"You're such a dirty, dirty girl," he said, shaking his head. "Don't you feel that filth on your face?" Astrakhan smiled big, showing his brown teeth and overlarge gums. Galina wiped the same hand across her forehead and made it more evenly dirty. Astrakhan replied with a wide, mocking grin that angered Galina and made her want to cry.

"I'm dirty because I cleaned *every*thing," she said, rising to a standing position. "All your shit."

Astrakhan smiled for real for the first time.

"It has a tongue," he said.

"My name is Galina Pyotrevna Yosheva," she said. "I can read. Write. I can do sums. I work hard."

Astrakhan smiled wider. "On that last point, we shall know soon enough."

Galina felt a chill go through her. She looked in his eyes and felt strange. He looked at her closely with his brow lowered. His smile evaporated like a puff of cigarette smoke next to a window. What remained scared her. She wanted to cry. She crossed her arms and pressed her back against the wall.

"Please..." she said in a soft, powerless voice. "Don't hurt me, please."

"Yes you *are* a girl," he said with a peculiar lilt in his voice that did nothing to lower Galina's anxiety. She pressed herself back against the wall next to his desk. The only way out was through him, up the concrete stairs and out a door that was always locked. She looked in the kitchen to the drawer where the knives were. She noticed them when she was washing everything. There were a dozen knives in the drawer. For an instant, she thought that maybe she could hide one somewhere and then hold the knife up to him like she had seen on TV but she was afraid. He would notice one of his knives missing and guess who must have done it. Her heart raced.

"A dirty girl," he said and took down a bottle of vodka. He took a swig and swallowed it down hard. His eyes were blurry and looked wet after he pulled the vodka. He slammed it down on the counter and took three wobbly steps toward Galina.

"Don't touch me!" she shrieked and tried to run past him but he grabbed her and pulled her towards him. She whimpered but he held her fast. He dragged the 8-year-old by her shirt to the bathroom. When she neared the room, Galina sobbed and worked in a frenzy to claw his hands away from her. He added a second hand to her arm and then started pulling off her clothes. She felt shame and wanted to go far away. In her mind, she went back to her bedroom in

Chilkovo, with her brothers Andrei and Pavel. She stared off silently as he ran water, took off her clothes and sat her in the hot water, as billows of steam filled the bathroom. She sat in the water and the temperature filled her body with alarm. She flinched and tried to climb out but Astrakhan's strong hand stopped her and held her in the hot water. Galina stared up at the ceiling and breathed quickly and shallowly as his beefy hand, his man hand with a lifetime of calluses from his work shuttling small quantities of goods back and forth from Turkey to Russia, held her down.

"I work, girl," he said. In her mind Galina was not there. She looked with an earnest intent into the dream taking place in her mind, the place where she was happy and safe and did not feel so alone. She felt his hands touch her in places that felt uncomfortable. His rough soapy hands touched everywhere. Galina felt shame and she came back from her dream.

"No, don't," she said, quietly. At these words, Astrakhan jerked his hand away. He exhaled through his nose and looked down.

Galina curled into a ball and pressed her legs together closely in the water. After a moment's peace, she lay quietly in the water, thinking Astrakhan and his probing hand had left her. She released from the ball and lay with her eyes closed in the water hot enough that she began to enjoy it. Then she felt a shiver run up her back. His heavy paw landed on her naked rump and started to smear back and forth with a dirty rag. Galina hiked in her breath. She felt she was going to die. His hand moved again. Galina stiffened her body and twisted her legs together like rope. She used every bit of strength to hug herself and stop the dirty feeling from this man who bought her, his hands moving all over her naked body, appearing in places to touch her that made her feel dirty. She reacted to each new finger by jerking away from his dirty olive-colored, scarred hand. To her, Astrakhan *was* his hands. He was the rude, intrusive hand that she could not bear to see near her, with its meaty, hairy knuckles and the yellow stain from cigarettes and the yellow cast to the whites of his eyes. Galina pulled back in disgust the first time she saw his fingers, seeming over-swollen at the knuckles and probing, always taking from her wetness and touching her in places that he had no right to. Galina felt besieged by his hands and his urgent need to touch her, to stroke her in places where she did not want to be touched. He pulled her out of the water and dried her shivering 8-year-old body with his muslin rag.

She knew, during the time when she cleaned out the kitchen that Astrakhan did not buy her for a live-in house keeper. She felt under siege. She looked at the white porcelain in his bathroom with a strange feeling, knowing this was her life: as the maid, property and wife of this horrible man.

Galina did not want him to touch her. She tried to know where he was at all times so she could stop him from touching her. Keeping an eye out for

Astrakhan meant she was forever on the run, darting back and forth from under his desk, to behind the refrigerator—which scared her with the hot tubes and electrical burning smell. But he could not reach her behind the fridge. The entire second day, Galina spent behind the fridge. After the first time he found her there, he tried to push the fridge back against the wall but the shape of the wall stopped it from going further and it remained her only place to hide.

Galina felt it was the only place where he could not touch her. She sat there in her spot—barely wide enough for her to sit and hug her knees with the concrete shelf above her and the cold concrete basement floor below. Though she felt cold and her bare feet never seemed to get warm, Galina felt like she could be happy hidden in her little spot.

It went dark. Galina heard the buzz of the fridge. Then, she heard the creak of his bedsprings and soon him snoring loudly. The fridge hummed for a while, giving off warmth through the pipes, but then it shut down, the tubes on the back of the fridge cooled and Galina began to shiver. She listened to the steady breathing of Astrakhan, the fearful sound of his inhale, and the gurgling outflow over his foul encrusted tongue. The apartment was dark except for a green light next to the TV. Astrakhan kept a blanket on his chair. Slowly she stepped out into the darkness of his room. She followed the green light and, as she crept, listened to the sound of Astrakhan's breathing. A single footstep away. She moved past him and registered no change in the speed or smoothness of his breathing. She saw the tail of his blanket dangling from his chair. She grabbed it and reeled it in as quietly as possible. Then, standing in the dark, right as she rolled the last of the blanket into a ball, she heard a loud crack as something plastic bounced on the floor. Astrakhan sniffed awake. Galina rushed for the fridge. His arm stretched out in time to grab Galina's thin shirt. She squealed and pulled, straining against his one hand.

Neither Astrakhan nor Galina uttered a sound, save the grunting and yelping of Galina, as she struggled in the dark to detach his fingers from the back of her shirt. He kept his grip tight. Galina at last slipped her shirt over her head and ran to safety behind the fridge, wrapped in the blanket.

6.

She woke up behind the fridge, her back sore from the cramped space. The apartment looked dark. She crept out and felt cold from not wearing her shirt. He breathed and a whistle ended each exhale. The regularity of his breathing guided her as she crawled out. She felt hungry. The light from the TV glowed over Astrakhan's silhouette in bed. On the floor under his hand she saw her own shirt. She walked there and reclaimed it. He didn't react. She looked up the basement steps to the front door and saw a padlock. She went to the fridge and carefully forced it open. Light spilled out and cast its glare across the dirty concrete floor. Astrakhan reacted, still asleep, by repositioning himself on his bed. Galina stood motionless with the fridge door open. A long sausage cut in the middle lay next to an bottle of *kefir*, which she unscrewed and drank right down. The cold *kefir* tasted slightly bitter and rich. It filled her mouth and gave her its milky taste; she felt okay and comfortable. She put the *kefir* back on the shelf and saw that he had tomatoes on a lower shelf along with an apple, which she grabbed, and a dirty beet, which she did not. Galina looked over the top of the fridge door and saw Astrakhan was still asleep, but having turned over so his nose faced her. Galina ducked down below the opened fridge door and gnawed on the end of the sausage. It was stiff and meaty and had round white blobs of fat that tasted greasy. Galina bit off a chunk and chewed it. Before she emptied out her cheek, she took another, bottle-emptying drink from the *kefir* and after she was done, focused her eyes at something blurry.

It was Astrakhan, standing there with bleary eyes, frowning at her.

"What the hell are you doing!" he yelled. Galina grabbed the sausage and tried to run back behind the fridge but Astrakhan got one of his meaty paws around each of her ankles and hauled her out. She squirmed and cried and kicked and clawed at everything in reach but then Astrakhan bear-hugged her and brought her underneath him.

Galina stared up at him and his salty t-shirt draped over her face as he held her down. She gagged and could not breathe. She felt him on top of her, crushing her. She breathed rapidly, taking as many shallow breaths as the space between her and the Georgian would allow. She felt his weight hurting her, and she started to claw in front of her like a street cat in Chilkovo. She felt her fingernails rake against his stomach and he sprung off her suddenly and cried out *"Yope Tvoy Mat!"* (Fuck your mother!) Galina sprang off the bed and ran up the basement stairs. She rattled the lock as hard as she could, trying to shake it, turn it, move it some how so that it would open, and then she felt a knob, shaped like a large pill, and she rotated it, and the lock clicked.

"Hey!" Astrakhan roared, laying on his back, feeling the pain from the deep fingernail rakes on his stomach. "I'm not done with you! Stay there! I *paid* for you... You're mine!"

Galina could not stop his words from entering her head. She heard them and knew it was true. Her grandmother and her brothers were alive because of his money. What other life did she deserve. She felt the heat of his logic. She felt ashamed; she scratched him. She knew how painful that was. Her fingers found as fast as possible how to get out. She saw in slow motion his feet get underneath him; she heard his feet, scratching along the concrete as he scrambled behind her. The basement door popped open. The cool air of freedom reached her face and she ran into the night, heading for the concrete archway.

"Stop!" she heard him yell, crisp and near. The words echoed off the concrete tunnel. Galina ran through the tunnel and then toward the best lit area. She saw Astrakhan had covered half the distance between them. He ran holding a club. Galina felt her blood go cold. She ran in the wind on the snow and the sound of her footsteps crunched underfoot. She lay on the speed and ran as fast as she could. She reached a small cluster of tin kiosks like the ones they had in Chilkovo. It was like the place where she spent her girlhood. She looked back and saw down the street that Astrakhan had stopped running a good way back. He stood hunched over with his hands on his knees, panting. Galina smiled and ran on past the kiosks, until she found herself on the far side, where she could see Astrakhan if he rounded the corner. Though she forgot to grab her coat, she had kept his blanket, which she wrapped around herself as she stood in the cold, peering from behind the corrugated tin kiosk that sold vodka and cigarettes. She waited.

Galina looked for any sign of Astrakhan. She looked at all the kiosks: for meat, for lottery tickets, another for tobacco and vodka. She noticed the people who came and went, the *babushki* who were dressed with scarves around their heads, walking with dignity like all grandmothers did, with their packets of things: potatoes, beets, powder for clothes washing. Each of these women walked away and only one lady looked over at Galina and took notice of her.

Galina looked down in shame, thinking that her grandmother Ludmilla would be angry at her for having run away. She looked up from her memory and saw that the lady had not moved and continued to stare at her. Then, the woman dropped her gaze and went on her way without a second look.

A young dirty-faced boy with black hair made his way around the group of kiosks, looking in trash cans, and looking at people's pockets. He worked his way around the kiosks and it occurred to Galina that he would eventually come her way. She saw him come closer, meandering, walking with his head down. He looked about 16. She didn't like him. In his nose, she could see black hairs coming out of it like a pair of rat whiskers. He came her way following a jagged path, with starts that moved a few paces nearer followed by a scurry somewhere else.

Then it seemed he must have stood too close to some old lady waiting for the *tramvai* train. The old lady shouted at him and tried to grab the back of his coat. The boy squealed "Let go!" In a high voice, he repeated "Let go!" as he tried to pry the woman's fingers from the back of his dirty coat collar. Finally, he bit her fingers and broke free. He ran across the square right next to where Galina stood. He hid behind the kiosk right next to her. He saw Galina. She backed toward the open where she could see the woman. The boy looked at the ground, not in Galina's eyes.

"Is she still there?" the boy said suddenly.

"Who?" Galina answered, in a voice lower than his.

"That hag."

"Oh," Galina said.

"I'm going to get her," he said, picking up a rock. Galina now felt scared of him.

Suddenly, just across the square, she saw Astrakhan. As she saw him, he broke into a full run. Galina shrieked. She ran and cried, knowing he was right behind her. She whimpered as she ran and then, as she glanced back, she saw the boy running behind Astrakhan. Then she heard them pile up. She turned back and saw the boy had tripped Astrakhan. She ran a long time and then hunkered down on the side of the road, where she could see a long way back. She waited for an hour and saw no sign of Astrakhan. The sun neared the roof tops and the wind cut through her blanket but still Galina waited exactly there and did not budge. Then, in the blue light of near darkness, she saw the boy coming down the street. Hunched over and moving in fits, first to one side of the street to check trashcans there, and then crossing back. Always coming closer. As he drew nearer, she smiled. In her freezing-cold place, she was happy to see a friendly face. When the boy reached her, she startled him by stepping out of her hiding place.

"Hey," she said. "Thanks for the help."

The boy smiled at her. His left eye was bruised. He had scuff marks on his cheeks and chin. A cut that ran along the bridge of his nose and was still bloody.

Despite his wounds, the boy smiled cheerfully.

"Murat," he said, offering Galina his hand like a dog offers its paw. "Koof," he added "is my family."

Galina smiled and by habit curtsied as her mother taught her. Murat Koof returned the smile. His eyebrows stood out swollen from his face as did the bristles coming down from his nostrils.

"I know just the spot for you, kitten," Murat said. He led Galina down an alley to an open green space with two soccer nets at either end. Murat headed for a dome-shaped sewer grating. He lifted off the heavy lid and climbed down in the sewer. He stopped with just his head above the top and yelled to Galina: "Come on, what are you doing? It's warm down here."

Galina flew to the opening. Just as she was chest high in the hole, she scanned the area. She did not see Astrakhan. She took a slow, careful look around, already feeling the warmth on her legs. She looked at a concrete apartment building that abutted the soccer field. On a balcony she saw a man standing there. She felt a flush of panic as she realized he was watching her. He was tall, broad shouldered and held a short glass. Galina stared back at him and decided she was safe. Then the man on the balcony smiled at her and waved. Galina waved back and she felt okay, seeing the whites of his teeth.

She went underground and saw the floor was dirty and the air hot. Steam pipes half a meter wide ran along the floor. A candle burned. In that light she saw the glistening eyes of a dozen little kids, all sitting and some laughing, others laying on their sides with clear plastic bags clutched in one hand and a line of drool puddling under their open mouths. There were other girls too—and other kids—all with faces streaked brown with dirt, tangled hair, wearing greasy adult-sized clothes. Galina found a spot and then saw that Murat was the only one still moving. He went around the room and seemed to have close contact with a whole set of little kids, sitting silent and alone, with dirty faces in the dim light frowning . Koof made his way back to Galina: "I need you to stay here tonight—" Murat said. He looked her in the eyes. "I need to know your name, too." Galina didn't want to tell him her name but she did, and then he left her alone. Murat went back up the ladder and Galina stayed in the sewer, she watched the ladder and expecting at any moment to see the legs of Astrakhan.

Chapter IV

1.

JACK Land sat on the edge of his balcony and played with fire. He looked out over his neighborhood along Metallistov Prospekt, and had his arm around blond 19-year-old Olga, while he pointed out the various landmarks.

"This is Metallistov Prospekt, to the left," Jack explained in his half-inebriated state to Olga, who had lived on that street her entire life.

"We say '*Prospekt Metallistov,*'" Olga said, correcting Jack.

"That's what I *said*," Jack said.

"No," Olga said and then waved it off.

From behind, Jack felt his arm lift off of Olga's shoulder and Natasha said:

"Olga, you can ask me if you want to know where to go."

Olga took offense and Jack hid behind Natasha as she escorted Olga to the door of Jack's apartment. The trash taken out, Natasha came back with her glowing angel smile and she slipped her arms around his neck. Though having her in his life was an unnatural benefit, an exploitation, he actually wanted to get married and start a family and be able to rejoin the course of normal life he had always paralleled but never joined. Jack knew he was insanely lucky but he hoped to build a homestead in somebody's heart.

Jack knew it was a longshot, but—being a Russian-speaking American in St. Petersburg who met new beautiful women every day, he was an optimist. He lived a daily miracle of understanding Russian. Not bad for six semesters of studying Russian. Of all things, learning Russian well enough to live and work in St. Petersburg had earned Jack the respect of his friend Thor. Commodities Trader Thor had always been the rock star and now it was Jack's turn to sparkle.

Natasha stepped on the balcony and rubbed her hand on his forearm.

"Why are you standing out here," Natasha asked. In her eyes was the look of wetness, of heat, of the knowledge that *she* was Jack's girlfriend. Of all the Russian girls he had met in St. Petersburg, she had the best chance of accompanying him back to America when that inevitable day came.

Jack knew Natasha wanted to claim him, but he was not yet sure who he would choose. It might be Natasha with the sleepy eyes and the lethargic voice, or Olga, the blond with the killer figure. Olga had first appeared at Jack's door at about 11 pm., accompanying the eternal pair, Zhanna and Natasha. They were two 19-year-old girls from the Bolshoi Okhta region who had completed the Russian high school system and had no plans thereafter and no future other than a life working in a corrugated-tin kiosk in the cold, selling cigarettes, beer and vodka to their high school classmates, also with no lives.

Every night since he had moved to his apartment, he found these "girls from the region" at his door. He met Zhanna and Natasha in the parking lot of a nearby grocery store. Jack—a man in his thirties, 6'4" with the confident walk of an American—had just been walking by when Zhanna asked him if he had a cigarette.

Jack told her in Russian that he did not smoke.

The sound of his American-accented Russian, his smile, the ease of his engagement and the duration of his eye contact which he shared equally between them both, told Zhanna that this was no ordinary man. Jack explained he was an American who lived in St. Petersburg, worked as a reporter for a Russian/English newspaper and also taught English on the side.

Of course, Jack first had tried to actually date the women he met in St. Petersburg but they were too swank and ran when they heard he was a reporter and not a business owner with a jet. Jack understood he would never be able to keep a woman like that when, inevitably, they emigrated from Russia back to America with him. Just as telescope manufacturers must anticipate sag in the design of giant lenses, just as a rifle's aim must be compensated for wind and gravity, whichever girl Jack chose must be one who would be happy to live back in America with him. So far, Natasha, with her drab mother and fatherless life and shared rituals with her mother, seemed the nominee.

Jack liked it when he heard that Natasha and her mother watched TV serials together, such as *Brigada*. Jack liked that because it reminded him of one of the few things he and his grandmother Mara had done together. Jack had raised himself and he liked how Natasha doted on her mother.

Always in the back of his mind, too, was the knowledge that he would be taking Natasha away from her mother and taking her daughter away to a better life. Jack smiled with the guilty knowledge that he would benefit.

In reality, both Natasha and Zhanna were young and beautiful. Jack thought that Zhanna, who resembled Michelle Pfeiffer, was the prettier of the two. She also was a bit too thin. Zhanna was 'Paris' thin while Natasha was 'Chicago' thin, which Jack preferred. Jack's pal Thor, resident of Chicago, preferred Paris-thin all the way. Thor had made some money and he no longer trusted women. Once time Jack had been entertaining Natasha and Zhanna when Thor called from the states. Jack put Natasha on the phone and she said: "Hello—pleased to meet you" in her usual slurred voice.

"Jesus, Land-Man," Thor said to Jack. "I think that girl is already drunk enough, even to sleep with you. Cut off her vodka supply, dude."

Jack explained that Natasha spoke with a kind of a slur, which wasn't especially noticeable in Russian except when she spoke slowly and then it made her seem drunk.

"I sure hope she's worth it," Thor said. "Well, I gotta get back to work—you okay there, you Communist?"

"Yeah," Jack said. "I'm good." Jack looked at Natasha and smiled. Jack liked Natasha but he had to consider too how well Natasha might cope with living in the states, especially in the Midwest. Having grown up in a big beautiful city like St. Petersburg, Jack figured Natasha might be underwhelmed by Des Moines.

Jack had met Natasha's mother, sat at her kitchen table and eaten from a plate that Natasha's mother piled with jellied sweet pickles, sours, gherkins, cream sauces and the ever-filled cup of tea with its tin frame holding the glass. Jack had endured Natasha's mother, who watched ORT Channel 1 in the same room with Jack and Natasha, not once smiling or showing any pleasure as Jack sat there, his arm around her daughter, as the light flickered in black-and-white on their faces.

After that night, Natasha started to stay behind and spend the night after Zhanna and the other girls left. Jack loved this daily bit of good fortune until he felt tempted by another slice of good fortune, Olga.

The first time Olga came over with Zhanna, she sat on the couch and said nothing. She drank some of the soda Jack bought and bobbed her foot to the music coming out of the small speaker in Jack's reporter's tape recorder, their only source of music, which played Jack's only tape, by Tatiana Bulanova. A week later, when Jack took all of them to a disco, he watched Olga's sexy dance. Then he looked over at Natasha: wounded by his attentions to Olga. He watched the gorgeous group of girls he had run into and he remembered himself as a teenager. Russian girls treated him like a rock star, an *American* rock star.

Each of them who knew the situation facing Russia and knew what it meant to go home with Jack. Natasha was the current queen and she did not cope well with the need to constantly confront challengers. She started to get drunk and stopped trying to worry about every new woman who met Jack.

2.

Natasha stood next to Jack on the balcony. She stroked Jack's arm with the palm of her hand. She looked up at him with a glow in her eyes and a breeze moved her hair. "She's remembering last night," Jack thought and smiled at the memory. The tape player inside restarted. Andrei Brezhukov came out with his eternal grin. He enjoyed the chance to hang out with 19-year-old girls and drink beer and absorb some of Jack's American-in-St.-Petersburg rock-star ambiance.

"I'm ready to make that trade," Andrei said in English, which Natasha did not understand. Andrei sipped his Baltika beer and leaned forward, as if he expected a response. Natasha scowled at Andrei. Whenever he and Jack spoke English, she thought they were discussing her.

"Speak Russian, Andrei," she said.

Jack stood on the balcony, enjoying the soft feel of Natasha's hand. He was almost able to block out Andrei and totally focus on the skin of her hand, passing gently over the hairs on his arm—when a small truck drove on to the soccer field that the balcony overlooked. Jack took another long sip from his beer. The truck crossed the field and stopped next to a raised sewer grating. Jack knew homeless kids lived in that sewer. He winced and felt the same anxiety he himself had always felt, a sense that there were no parents who were going to appear and save these kids. These kids were on their own. Jack got a chill inside as he remembered how he felt when, at 18, he faced living alone.

The truck parked and rolled back on its brakes. A man in a dirty t-shirt stepped out of the driver's side and slammed the door with his fingers. The driver walked to the back of the truck. His eyes scanned the area without moving his head. The passenger door popped open. Out walked a shorter man, wearing a sky blue warm-up jacket and matching terry-cloth slacks. The driver opened the back of the truck. He took off the sewer grating and dropped the heavy metal lid aside with a clang.

Jack's heart thumped. Andrei saw Jack's mouth hanging open and followed Jack's gaze to the open sewer.

Jack had first realized there were kids living in there one morning when he woke at 5am and stared out his window without turning on the lights in his apartment. Overnight, it had snowed hard. The whole of the soccer field looked like one continuous blanket of snow untouched by a footstep. Then, in the midst of the blue light emerging from the darkness, Jack had seen movement around the domed sewer grating. There were dozens of tracks in the fresh snow, all heading toward the sewer grating. The journalistic hairs on the back of his neck rose. It smelled like a story. Jack's newspaper ran its pieces in both English and Russian—if the piece was worthy. Jack depended on those double payments to pay his rent. So he was on the lookout for anything unusual. He knew his grandmother Mara had saved him from a similar fate when his folks died. Who helps a homeless kid? Nobody. They were easy to ignore. The homeless kids lived in the jungle, the streets, cold and sewers. In the jungle the homeless kids lived in a world without rules. Nobody looked out for what happened to little kids in the sewers late at night. Kids could scream all they wanted for help but nobody was coming.

"What the hell is he—" Andrei said, and he was interrupted by a shriek, and then a high-pitched wail from the sewer. The head of the man in the dirty t-shirt emerged slowly from the sewer. His face showed he was straining to lift something heavy that was thrashing as he hauled it up the ladder. Then he breached daylight with his right hand bleeding, gripping a shock of black hair on the head of a ten-year-old girl, screaming and thrashing, tears flowing, her fingernails raking the tops of his hands. After her legs cleared the top, the man dropped her forcefully on the ground and the other man grabbed her around her chest, pinning her arms to her sides, and tying her hands behind her back with white slip ties.

Jack felt enraged. "How could you!" he wanted to yell down at the man but he lived in Russia where the *Militsiya* would not help.

The dirty-shirted man kissed the backs of his fists and dropped back down in the tunnel.

Jack, Andrei, and Natasha stood mute on the porch as the two men dragged another shrieking girl from the sewer by her hair.

"What is this—shouldn't we call the police?" Jack said. He looked at Andrei who replied by lifting his brow. The gesture meant the same thing it meant the first time Andrei had to explain some exasperating aspect of Russian life, like not needing to pay the electric bill.

"*No*," Andrei whispered. He mouthed the word '*mafiya.*'

Outside, a young, red-haired girl—the one Jack recognized—shrieked as she was being dragged out. She came out kicking and swinging from her hair, which the man gripped.

"No!" Jack said out loud. Andrei hissed and raised his palm at Jack to stay silent. "We have to *do* something," Jack whispered. Jack felt frustrated at the certain doom of these kids. They were going to die. Nobody came forward to save them, not the *Militsiya*, not their parents. They were each alone as these *Mafiya* men came and cleaned them out.

"Are you nuts?" Andrei said. Natasha stood next to Jack and looped her arm under his, holding her other hand over her mouth in the face of the cruelty they all witnessed, crying silently and whimpering. Natasha whimpered and clung to Jack's arm. The two mafia men worked to as a team to wrestle the red-haired girl into the back of the truck. As they did, another homeless girl emerged by herself and ran away to freedom. It was the girl who Jack had waved to.

"Why are they doing this?" Natasha said and cried. Jack wrapped his arm around her.

"*God* knows why!" Andrei said, angry, ignoring his own pleas for quiet.

The man in the dirty shirt went back down in the sewer. He poked his head above ground, empty handed. He brushed off his clothes and got in the truck on the passenger side. The truck started to roll off the soccer field, but its wheels spun in the mud, burdened by a much heavier load in back. The truck worked its way toward to street and escape.

Jack abruptly walked off the balcony to the telephone. Andrei followed him.

"What are you doing?" Andrei said.

"Calling the *Militsiya*—don't you think we should?"

"No," Andrei said and lay his thumb on the button to kill the call. "Not in Russia. The police don't work for *you* here. You don't pay them one *kopek*: why should they help *you*? There is tremendous danger here." Andrei spoke the best English of anyone Jack had met in St. Petersburg. He made sense. Jack felt a need to stand for something he believed in. In the same spirit that made Jack rescue feral cats, he felt drawn to this class of forgotten kids who somehow got thrust on the mercy of the ice and hunger.

"I see," Jack said. He realized only the rich could expect protection from the bandits and hoodlums who were the daily street rabble of St. Petersburg. If the police would do nothing, then there was only one force on the side of the just—good people who fought back when evil occurred in front of their eyes. "Aren't you the least bit curious, Andrei, where that truck is headed?"

"No," Andrei said, dropping his black eyebrows over his eyes, the perfect moral cover for his indifference. "I do find it regrettable," Andrei said. "Surely that these children—that such things could happen to....But what is it to me? Am I their father? No, I have my *own* children."

"Hah!" Jack said with his American smile of smug arrogance. "If this were happening in *America*, I'd be in my car following that truck, just to see...." Jack stared at the truck, still working its way through the mud to the curb, its wheels sinking with the load in back. When he turned Jack saw his mention of *America*, of how things were done *there*, had the predicted effect on Andrei, an associate professor of meteorology, a man who enjoyed the American Jack Daniels whiskey he got from visiting Japanese colleagues. Andrei, the owner of a white, mud-spattered Lada four-door, idolized the American Ford Mustang. He had a photo of a Mach 1 pinned up on his dashboard.

Andrei's eyelids hung down, shrouding his eyes as he took a bitter puff on a cardboard Belamor Kanal cigarette. Andrei raised his chin and his mouth was set. He met eyes with Jack.

"Let's go," Andrei said and ran for the apartment door. Jack followed and yelled back to Natasha, "Don't drink all the beer!"

They both jumped down flights of clammy concrete stairs. Andrei hit the landing and bounced the wooden front door away. He got in his unlocked Lada and got it running just as Jack opened the passenger side. Andrei threw it in reverse and the white Lada trundled down the muddy path between two apartment buildings in time to see the black truck reach the road on the opposite side of the soccer field. Andrei drove around the mud and made up time on his springy Russian shocks to keep the black truck in sight. Andrei flew on to Prospekt Metallistov going South and kept his distance from the black truck. For once, Jack found himself happy to ride in a rickety Lada. Its commonness made them invisible.

"What would *you* do with a bunch of kids?" Jack said.

"I can think of a lot of things," Andrei said. "*All* of them bad."

They reached Yakornaya Street and traffic slowed. Jack saw, reflected in the truck's side mirror, the face of the man in the dirty shirt. The man's face was blank, unsmiling, staring ahead, a man at work, doing his job.

"Prostitution?" Jack asked.

"Maybe," Andrei said and turned on Yakornaya. The truck drove on Yakornaya across the Bolshoi Okhta river and then across the wide Neva River. It turned on Suvorovskaya and following that to Prospekt Nevski. They drove through the streets of low stone buildings that retained the ambiance of the 18th Century and made one feel it would not be unusual to see Pushkin or Tolstoy walking. The truck stopped for the traffic at the T-intersection with Prospekt Nevski.

"Look, the back door," Jack said. Inside the truck someone kicked at the back door. They were homeless, *bezprezorni* kids who had been abandoned by their parents because of how much starvation the parents themselves experienced. The parents think the kids will be able to earn more as beggars.

"Damn! This is insane! how could they just herd them up, like *cattle.*"

"They're alive, at least," Andrei said and followed the black truck past Dvortsovaya Square and its tall pillar. Andrei drove in such a way that a second car was always between his Lada and the truck, which turned on Mayakovskaya Street and then into an alley. Andrei slowly rolled into the alley. In the slowness of his dirty Lada's travel, the tremble in his hands was evident in the effect it had on his car. Jack felt butterflies in his stomach—adrenalin. Back in high school in Ames, he felt this same way when he was a pole vaulter trying his third attempt at 12 feet 6 inches, which would have gotten him into state for the Little Cyclones.

Jack and Andrei crept into the darkened alley. Behind the buildings was an enclosed brick courtyard made by the backs of all the buildings that fronted to Nevski Prospekt or Zhukovskovo Street. The entire area was one asphalt, brick cage with only one way in.

"This is no good, Jack."

Jack said nothing. He kept alert for movement. He felt on alert for motion around him, a sensation he remembered from sparring in Tae Kwon-Do against his friend Thor.

Andrei drove into the middle of the asphalt. By chance Jack saw the truck on the right. Just a sliver of it could be seen, parked. In furious silence,

Jack urged Andrei to quickly pull ahead to hide them behind a brick warehouse with ragged plywood covering every window.

Wordlessly, Andrei stopped the car. Jack got out, and walked around the back of the building. He peeked around the corner. The truck was parked next to a rusty gray boxcar, illuminated by a mercury light. A steel door stood at the top of concrete steps. Wooden slats covered and barred the ground-level windows, but there was light coming through the gaps. Standing next to the basement windows was a tall red Russian fire hydrant—which always reminded Jack of the water pumps on his grandmother's farm back in Iowa. Jack looked at the basement windows but they were all heavily barred and then covered with rough wooden slats that allowed slivers of light through.

Jack walked heel-to-toe on the asphalt, trying not to make the gravel scrape. Two more cars entered the enclosed courtyard. They drove toward the building. Jack's heart raced. Andrei had already ducked down and the two cars drove past his Lada without changing their speed. The two cars—both long BMWs—parked on the far side of the black truck. Out of them came five men, all dressed in tailored black suits with neat haircuts, pencil ties and cuff links reflecting the mercury light. The men hiked up the concrete steps and went inside. Jack wanted to run. He felt sure he had stumbled onto a mafia lair, and would be shot if they caught him. The building had two more storeys and a peaked roof. These men were Russian mafia. It was the Russian mafia collecting the kids. This was where they ran their operation.

Behind him, a black Mercedes drove in, its lights passing over Jack, standing there, crouched over, peering at the Mafia's home base. The Merc's headlights swung past Jack and then they drove toward Andrei's car. Illuminated by the headlights, Andrei's Lada shot off like a rocket, and disappeared around the corner in a second with only the dust left standing. The Merc parked. Jack was already running in the opposite direction. Fear rose in his chest. "I need to get out of here!" He realized what a fool he was for thinking he, a reporter, could do a damn thing to save these kids. He ran and jumped over a short fence, whimpering as he ran. He didn't want this mistake to cost him his life. He turned left on Liteny Prospekt and headed toward Nevski Prospekt. He made it to Nevski and at the corner, he waited and looked back. Two men burst into the street, running. Jack yelped. He ran for the subway as fast as he could. He ran under the archway, blasted through the glass doors and swiped his *Yedinaya* card. He ran down the left side of the long escalator to the bottom, offending a few ladies on the way. At the bottom of the long escalator, Jack walked out into the middle of the crowd and waited for the next train. He waited and the crowd milled. Then he heard faint screaming from the escalator. A train rumbled in the tunnel. Jack moved to the end of the platform, far away from the escalator.

The blue Metro train arrived and screeched to a stop. The crowds exited and entered the train. Jack saw two men fight their way to the bottom of the escalator. Jack was trapped. There was only one way out. Jack jumped on the train. But, owing to Jack's height, one of the men saw him. The two ran towards Jack. The train was four cars long. As the men passed the second car, the male voice on the subway intercom said in Russian: "Be careful, the doors are closing." The two men made it into the far end of the car nearest to him before the doors closed. Jack felt his heart pump as the train pulled away. Trapped again. He looked over to the window between cars and saw the two men who had followed him.

The shorter man squinted from eyes that seemed deeply sunken in his eye sockets, as if the evil those eyes had seen caused them to sink back. This man looked at Jack with a crazed and cross-eyed stare, as if his inability to grab Jack drove him insane with anger. The other and scarier one, stood a head taller than his partner and easily saw over him. This man, Jack saw, wanted to know why Jack was standing out there in the dark, staring at their building. The taller man worried Jack. He had his hair closely cropped, almost like a soldier, and he looked powerful and able to kill.

The train entered the next station, Ladozhskaya. The doors opened. The two men watched Jack, who moved to the far end of his car, away from the two bandits. He stood by the door and, as it opened, Jack stepped off of the train. The short squinty man and the big one joined Jack on the platform next to their train car. The train intercom repeated "Be careful, the doors are closing." Standing twenty feet from the men on the platform, Jack stepped back on the train. After an instant of hesitation, the two men both stepped back on the train. The doors began to close and right before they did, Jack stepped off the train. The shorter man went wild inside the train, trying to pry the doors open and then raining a volley of punches on the door.

The train carried the two men inches from Jack's face. The short man roared but the other smiled.

Chapter V

1.

VLADIMIR Szlotov turned a corner on Prospekt Metallistov and entered the neighborhood where he had grown up. His mother Masha Ilovna Szlotova still lived in the same apartment. Most of the other apartments were rented out but Szlotov's mother refused to move because that was where she had lived all her life with her husband Vladimir Sr, the butcher. Every time Szlotov went to see her, he felt like he stepped back into his childhood.

He turned a corner and encountered two young girls, in fur-collared blue coats standing in the dirt path.

"Good Morning," Szlotov said. The girls stood still—petrified. The shorter one stared at him wide-eyed, her mouth hanging open. Szlotov stepped toward them. The two girls suddenly screamed. They dashed away as fast as they could run. Szlotov stood there, feeling annoyed that now even children feared him. He had been courteous. They should fear only when he gave them a reason to fear.

Szlotov walked with the easy gait of a man who has nothing to fear. When he encountered people who recognized him, they gasped and halted in their tracks. As he walked through them, everyone stopped what they were doing and followed him with their eyes. Even as a teenager, Szlotov had been a tyrant. Now as a man Vladimir Vladimirovich Szlotov made men quake in his presence. All traces of smile dropped from their faces. Their hands and legs quivered. They each held their breath and waited for him to pass by and leave them unharmed.

Szlotov saw a man with gray sideburns and big floppy ears, and remembered taking his pocket money. Szlotov remembered the kid having those same big floppy ears. His name was Pieter. Now fully grown, Pieter Anatolevich looked prematurely old, his arms pulled up against his chest and his hands held like claws. He seemed to remember the last time they two had crossed paths. Szlotov had demanded protection money and the man had refused to pay it. His parents objected.

"They said I should just punch you—butcher's son," Pieter had told Szlotov, then in his teens.

Now, Szlotov stopped and locked eyes with this older man who was Pieter Anatolevich, much older, shaken. He apparently remembered how Szlotov had paid Pieter and his parents back, by catching their old cat Grus ha and shoving a firecracker down its throat.

Szlotov smiled at the memory and shifted his gaze from the image of the old cat exploding in their faces to the eyes of the man—Pieter—now, walking past, his face wet with sweat and anxiety.

Szlotov rounded the corner and entered the dirt lane between the apartment buildings. The cat killing had served its purpose at the time, Szlotov reminded himself. He looked carefully along the length of the alley formed by the two apartment buildings, a habit he formed during the childhood he spent in this same spot.

"Consider it a warning," Szlotov said to himself, smiling, remembering what he had told Pieter. Szlotov had taken some money from Pieter but eventually he compromised and allowed Pieter to stop paying. Such compromises disgusted Szlotov. He thought of his father's profession: a butcher does not compromise with the steer. The long, sharp knife pulled across the throat, the blade tugged on the skin and sliced through the cow's muscles, arteries and viscera. Blood gushed on the concrete and the steer went down.

When Szlotov decided a person needed to die, he preferred to do it as quickly as possible like a butcher, before the target could get scared, start to beg and behave rashly. The target only glimpsed Szlotov for one instant before metal flashed and his blade—feeling red hot—plunged into their body in a wet rage. When he did so he imagined he was his father quartering a pig. Szlotov grew up watching his father at work on the meat. And whenever he killed *wet*, with a knife, he fell into a rhythm of cut and slice, cut and slice whether the carcass was cow or man. Szlotov thought of his father, of the gnarled hooks that were his hands, and then one day, the state stopped paying and made his father leave.

Szlotov reached the end of the alley. He headed toward building 3 where his mother lived in apartment #86 on the ground floor. Across the hall, in another apartment that Szlotov owned, lived three of his own men. Their job was to make sure his mother was not troubled. Because of that, all of the neighborhood had the joy of living with a group of up-and-coming hoodlums, thugs who slapped old men and chased children. Punks who forced teenage girls down into the basement. These men wanted to perfect the 'attitude' they would affect when they became famous gangsters like Szlotov, a man who terrorized a whole city.

As was the rule in the Russian mafia, Szlotov had neither wife nor children. Family represented a weakness, a vulnerability. His only living connection was his mother. She was guarded. She was a weakness he tolerated. As he told the other men in his brigade not to see their mothers, not to have children, he always saw a glint in their eyes as they thought of the men who guarded Szlotov's mother. It was a job for lazy men.

Szlotov opened the wooden front door to the building and looked inside. His mother's door was on the left but there was no sentry in the hall, as he expected. The door opposite his mother's was open a crack. Szlotov knocked loudly on his mother's door. Seconds later, he heard a commotion and the door opposite his mother burst's open.

"Stop!"

Szlotov spun around and faced the young man, his jaw muscles stood tight. The young punk frowned in a way that revealed his gold canine teeth and then he gasped.

"*Mr. Szlotov!* For*give* me."

"It's nothing," Szlotov said. "You were right to challenge me."

From behind her closed door, Szlotov heard his mother ask who was there.

"A murderer," Szlotov replied through the door.

"Okay, I'm opening up," said his mother, Masha Ilovna Szlotova.

Smiling, Szlotov waited for the inner and outer steel doors to open.

"*Oy*, Vladchik!" his mother said. She threw her arms around him.

"*Mamochka*," he said. "Don't you listen to who is outside your door?"

"Oh, of course not. I can barely hear a thing," she said and handed him his pair of *tapochkees* as he stepped out of his shoes. After he put on the worn *tapochkees*, she led him to the kitchen table. He glanced up at the corner of the kitchen at the gilded icon of him, the Lord Jesus. Szlotov himself had stopped believing in God about the same time the butcher market—the place where his father had hacked away at meat for 39 years—stopped paying his father. Szlotov raged internally at a God who would allow such evils.

His mother went to the fridge, got *kvass* and poured him a glass of the Russian beer.

"How are you feeling, *Mamochka*?" he asked, drinking her homemade *kvass*. As he lifted his glass, he stared up in the corner at the shrine to his father, his leather apron, a cleaver and a large black and white photo of the man, with the customary grim facial expression like all Russian portraits. His father, a man who died unappreciated, who hacked his own body to pieces from the constant splitting of gristle and bone. Szlotov was not about to live—or die—like his father.

"Fine, under the circumstances," his mother said, avoiding his eyes when she answered, which told him all he needed to know.

"Do you need anything?" he asked her, reaching for his wallet. He handed her a wad of rubles.

"*N'yet*," she said, pushing back his handful of 100 ruble notes. "I need none of *your* money," she said. The word 'your' offended Szlotov. She meant the money he acquired from criminal enterprises.

"Well then, if you don't need me—we're through," Szlotov said. He rose from his mother's kitchen table. As he stood to go out, his father's frowning face looked down on him from the shrine. "Papilla's," Szlotov said, addressing the photo in the shrine, "see if you can get her to understand. This is my business. I need to make a living somehow and I cut meat like you did." Szlotov's voice echoed in her apartment. He saw it made his mother feel uncomfortable when he spoke to the photo. She washed the counter top with a dishrag and straightened the jars.

"No, Vladchik," his mother said, crying. She wrapped her fingers around his and clung to him. "Forgive me, Vladchik. Stay, please, Vladchik. I'm praying for you. You're my son. I'm praying for your soul. I light tapers for you."

Szlotov no longer looked in her eyes. His jaw set. He didn't believe any of that. The muscles on the top of his closely-shaved head bulged. His mother disapproved of him. She always hated the mafia. His eyes teemed with ways to grow the *organizatsiya*. Always he thought of the *organizatsiya* as his *real* family. They were the real saviors of Russia, the people cunning enough to make business in this land of thieves. Szlotov looked down at his mother, whose cheeks shone streaks of wetness as she stood with him at the door.

"Mama, don't be afraid," Szlotov said and opened the door. He kissed her forehead. In her anxiety she gripped his arm and would not let go. Her eyes filled with wetness and she whispered his pet name.

Szlotov broke her grasp on his arm, put on his shoes, pushed her hands back across the threshold of the door and shut the outer door. He shook his head. Then, he spun on his heels and pushed open the door of the apartment across the hall.

"What's going on here?" Szlotov said.

"I was just coming out—"

Szlotov waved his hand for silence. "What is your name," Szlotov asked.

"Dmitri."

Szlotov shut the apartment door with a crisp slam and followed Dmitri deeper into the apartment. Without another word, he entered the bedroom. One of his men slept in bed while a second sat with his back to Szlotov, playing a crude Tetris game on a computer. Szlotov fired a shot at the computer's monitor, shattering it. The man playing the game fell on the floor amidst the glass. The man in bed rolled over and became entangled in the sheets, giving Szlotov time to walk over and point the gun at his face. The man in bed struggled to free his arms from the sheets but he was helpless.

Szlotov sighed and holstered his Glock. He rubbed his finger against the trigger.

"What kind of crew is this?" Szlotov said. "Do you realize who lives across the hall here? If anything happens to her, I will cut off your heads and burn your mothers into ashes. That goes for all of you. Is that clear?" he said, louder and with more anger. "From now on, every day and every night, one of you will be seated in a chair—" Szlotov spotted a wooden one with a stiff back and no padding on the seat. "This chair, in the hall, watching my mother's door. Is that clear? The man who sits there must do one-thousand pushups a day, also. Is that clear?"

"It's clear," Dmitri mumbled. The other two echoed him.

"All right," Szlotov said. "If not, I will kill all of you and your mothers." The three of them gulped and stared at the floor. Szlotov turned to leave. He waited in the hall until he heard the wooden chair scrape along the bare floor and drop on the wood. As he stepped outside he punched his fist into his palm and growled. He thought: "How can I succeed with men like these? With little baby men like these." As he left the Bolshoi Okhta neighborhood, he knew he could think for his men but he could not physically be everywhere. It was not the boss who implemented the plan but his men. Walking, Szlotov passed a trash can and heard a slurping sound. Sitting inside of the trash was a little boy, licking the inside of a tin can. Szlotov stared at him. "A little rat," Szlotov said. "Expects to find his dinner in the trash. Useless, lazy children." He went back and kicked over the trashcan and scattered the trash and the boy. Startled, the boy looked with big eyes at Szlotov and then ran away crying. Szlotov went on, wondering how to use such useless children. Then, he stopped walking. He stood in silence as snow flakes fell from the sky.

2.

Vladimir Szlotov drove his BMW 740i on Prospekt Nevski in St. Petersburg, past the building that contained the largest bookstore Dom Knigi. As he glanced reflexively at the store's window, caring to see what they had, he instead saw the face of a homeless boy, standing in front of the window, in a dirty man-sized coat. Szlotov screeched to a stop and the boy barely reacted. The boy, bundled in a greasy nylon coat with sleeves longer than his fingers, had brown scuff marks around his mouth, like he had eaten excrement. A drop of saliva dropped from the boy's lip.

"What good are you, boy?" Szlotov asked himself. Behind him a car honked its weak horn. This boy was like the new members of his crew. They dressed in black and loved their pistols and saw their job as performance art, not business. They posed and acted tough but they had no ideas. They waited for Szlotov to give orders.

He turned up the volume on his car's stereo and drove forward on

Nevski.

Szlotov was determined to collect every ruble, even those squeezed between the fingers of beggars. Even the beggars had to pay protection. He followed the wide street and thought again how much it reminded him of his post in Prague during his years as a station chief. Then he turned down a side street and entered an industrial area. He drove up to a large concrete, steel-roofed building called Chus Meats. Smoke rose from a chimney. Brown grime from old blood covered every surface. At one end of the factory were corrals where doomed cattle entered. On the other side lay concrete and heavily worn asphalt drives where endless Mercedes trucks moved out the raw meat that was the product of the factory.

It lay on the edge of Szlotov's territory and was, therefore, fair game. Szlotov circled the factory and noted the exits and then he parked in the rutted lot next to the factory. The lot was mostly empty but for several Ladas, a Datsun and one solitary Volga. Szlotov walked past the Volga and dragged his finger across its hood. The Volga, while not expensive by German standards, was the priciest Russian make.

Szlotov pushed his way through the doors and entered the factory. In front of him, a man in bloody white coveralls pushed a cart carrying a bloody steer. All around him rang out the high pitched whine of the band saws as they spun free and then a lower tone as they bit into meat. The saws fell into a low groan when they sliced through bone. Szlotov stood in the middle of the shop floor and looked around at the workers. Among the many butchers cutting meat, or feeding scraps of meat into a floor-to-ceiling grinder, one of them took notice of Szlotov. The man switched off his band saw and turned to face Szlotov.

"Visitors are not permitted here," the man said.

Szlotov stood in the factory and faced the man who had spoken up. The man looked to be in his thirties, a man with a girlfriend who carried his seed and so he thinks he is the rule giver.

"My business here is with the owner, not with a laborer," Szlotov said.

"I am Pokcha," said the young butcher, stabbing the air with his finger. "I have cut meat here for thirty-six months."

Szlotov wiped away any trace of mirth on his face. Around them, the band saws rose in their pitch as every pair of eyes stopped pushing meat into the blade and stared at Szlotov and Pokcha.

From the railing overlooking the shop floor, alerted by the whine of 40 untended band saws, out came the owner of the factory, Anton Chus, who had worked there his whole life and bought it after the privatization.

"What's going on—" shouted Chus from the railing but then he followed the eyes of his employees to where Pokcha stood nose to nose with a well-dressed man unfamiliar to Chus.

All the band saws were shut down and a crowd of workers surrounded the two of them. Szlotov faced Pokcha calmly. The young butcher squinted and clenched his cheeks. Pokcha stood and faced Szlotov, feeling afraid of this man while his pride held him in place, stopping him from running away.

Then Anton F. Chus stood at the front of the circle.

"What do you want? This is a private factory."

"This factory is not safe," Szlotov said. "It is wooden. Fires are dangerous."

Chus did not blink but he stood deflated, knowing he was in trouble.

"These are things, Anton Fyodorovich," Szlotov said, now addressing only the factory owner Chus. "We should discuss in your office."

"I have no secrets," Chus said, suddenly yelling.

"Very *well*, then," Szlotov said. "Starting today, you will give me 30% of your gross receipts."

"Go to hell!" Pokcha said, breaking the silence. "What gives you the right to just come in here and invade—like Hitler!"

Szlotov turned from the real man to the boy. Pokcha stood with his hand in the air. He lifted his eyebrows in regret and fear the instant Szlotov wheeled on him.

"We'll see who gets there first," Szlotov said as he ran up on the young butcher. Pokcha yelped when Szlotov's hands landed on him. The young man did not struggle and let Szlotov grab him by the hair.

"Let go of me!" Pokcha shouted. Szlotov controlled his own breathing and made sure to block Pokcha's windpipe. Pulling Pokcha by the hair, Szlotov flipped on a band saw and dragged Pokcha's head into the blade, splattering his blood until the limp, half-headed body of Pokcha flopped on the ground and Szlotov was left holding the hair attached to the top of Pokcha's skull. They could not call the *Militsiya* because so many of the police worked for the *organizatsiya*.

Szlotov opened his hands and allowed Pokcha's scalp to drop. Then a chorus of tears rose and only with force could some of the factory's workers stop others who did not realize that a man like Szlotov might come alone but that did not mean he worked alone.

"For what!" shouted a heavyset woman with dyed black hair wearing a pink smock.

Szlotov felt the tension and the eyes of hatred on him. These angry stares did not touch him. This was business. If not Szlotov and his crew, there would quickly be another crew and maybe one even worse than Vladimir Szlotov and his brigade, who at least avoided hitting people without money—something that could not be said about Zortaev's men, who inflicted beatings and killed for no reason at all. "If they think I am bad," he thought, "they should meet Zortaev." He felt spatters of blood drying tight on his face and he used his handkerchief to wipe the blood spray.

Suddenly, from the crowd of workers, all whispering and stepping away from Szlotov, emerged Chus himself, pulling at the lapels of his coat. The look of craven fear on Chus's face relaxed Szlotov. Having verified that Chus would comply, Szlotov looked around the room at all the petrified meat cutters, dull and submissive like the steers they hacked apart. In the back of them he saw a lanky young man move toward the door.

"Stand there!" Szlotov barked. The man stopped and returned. Szlotov turned back to Chus.

"It's *thirty* percent, then?" Chus asked.

"Thirty-*four*," Szlotov said. "Then, we see whatever *goodies* we can find in your books."

When Chus heard a predator like Szlotov discuss his own, hard-earned "goodies" with such relish, the expression on Chus' face contracted and darkened, as he lowered his horizons, knowing he would not be buying his wife a *shooba*, not a mink, chinchilla or even rabbit. Now, by paying Szlotov, he would be buying his own life and the lives of his wife and children.

"Good," Szlotov said. "So now we are partners. This factory will make us rich—both of us—or it will burn to the ground, leave you dead and all of these people without a factory to work in."

Chus kept silent and ballooned his lips.

A pool of red spread around the topped head of Pokcha.

"I will send a man to dispose of this troublemaker," Szlotov said. "You will give this man I send one-thousand American *bucksov* for cleaning your mess here. You killed him yourself. If you had cooperated, this man would be standing now." Szlotov broke off from speaking with Chus and walked away from the coppery smell of blood. He opened his phone and called Sergei.

"Old friend, sorry to bother you…I'm at the factory. I have a *wet* problem," Szlotov said. He folded his phone and returned to Chus, who stood in place, his chin cradled in his hand, in silence.

3.

Szlotov returned to the factory a week after the incident with Pokcha. He parked in his spot by the door. Szlotov was now, effectively, the owner of Chus Meats. Getting out of his car, Szlotov stepped on the broken concrete pathway that led to the old and weathered front door to the factory.

As Szlotov crossed the threshold, a wave of "*Tikah* Quiet," rippled through the plant like a shock wave. Chus, tucking in the tail of his shirt, rushed downstairs to greet Szlotov.

"Good Morning, Vladimir Vladimirovich," Chus said.

For Szlotov, there never had been any question about keeping Chus. Szlotov had threatened to kill Chus's entire family, his wife, children, parents and siblings because he needed Chus to behave. "Unless you sign this document," Szlotov had explained. "I will wipe your family from this earth." But he needed Chus to run the place. For now.

Chus eventually signed documents making Szlotov sole owner of the meatpacking plant. He had no option except being a prisoner in the factory that had been stolen from him, no choice but to slave for Szlotov and his gang.

Without answering the salutation from Chus—who Szlotov liked to torture and planned to kill eventually—Szlotov looked at the workers around him, who had frozen still and silent when he appeared. Everyone remembered what happened to Pokcha.

He had not answered the 'Good Morning' from Chus because already Szlotov was angry. He had read the factory's books. He knew what a mess it was.

"Why are you all standing around?" Szlotov shouted. Suddenly, everyone got busy. A millisecond passed and the factory was in pandemonium. Everyone scrambled to find something to occupy themselves, from the men who ran *sosiski*-stuffing machines to those stacking boxes or even Chus himself, who picked up a box that had fallen from a stack.

Chus crouched down and held three large boxes. Szlotov grew irritated by the spectacle of his top man in this factory, Anton Chus, with nothing better to do with his time than hold cardboard boxes.

"Anton Fyodorovich," Szlotov said. "What the *hell* are you doing?"

Chus bolted up to his full height. After a second of hanging in his two hands, the three boxes he had been holding popped out of his grasp and landed on the floor.

"Nothing," Chus said, shaking, his face flushed, as Vladimir Szlotov approached him. Szlotov was not a tall man. His presence did not come from his size or height. Chus put the tips of his thumbs in his mouth and grimaced as Szlotov approached him with his arrogant gait, swinging his arms like a teenager.

"Take it easy," Szlotov said. He exercised the fierceness of look that paralyzed people like Chus with fear. Szlotov smelled the fear and used it like a prod to make others do what he wanted.

Chus scurried back to his office and sat at his desk with his hands on his knees. Szlotov locked the door. In Chus he saw the unshaven, weather-beaten face of an old butcher he'd once robbed. Szlotov looked into his captive's eyes, searching for any hidden fire that might cause Chus or one of his daughters to come after Szlotov someday. As a businessman, Szlotov considered himself also a victim a thousand times a day, when the rubles collected by his crew were pocketed. This anger boiled behind every decision Szlotov made and it percolated in the background every time he decided the time had come for violence.

"How's business?" Szlotov asked Chus, who did not want his daughter to be cut into tiny strips and be presented to his wife Yulia in the Metro station by little homeless children, who would then run away. Szlotov thought that Chus himself would be killed by the cruelest methods.

Chus stood next to the glass looking out with his arms limp at his sides.

"Business is okay," Chus said without enthusiasm.

Szlotov heard this tepid endorsement from the head of his factory. Then, an abrupt feeling of dread washed over Szlotov. He realized he was, again, carrying dead weight. In this case, the entire factory. Most of his profits, the right of a businessman like Szlotov to buy for cheap and sell for dear, were wasted on inefficiencies. Szlotov grabbed Chus by the wrists and stared at his hands. Chus had normal knuckles. His hands did not carry the dozens of scars that had crisscrossed the hands of Szlotov's father.

"These are not a butcher's hands," Szlotov said. "These are the hands of a lazy man. My father's hands were like knotted wood."

"Your father was a butcher?" Chus asked.

"Yes, my father swung a cleaver every day of his life," Szlotov said, angry. "He ruined his hands for the Soviet Union. It repaid him with nothing, with insolence." Szlotov advanced on Chus and shouted in his face. "He was not a lazy boss like you who sits up in his office while the business goes to hell."

Chus stood mute, his mouth open, his face a living embodiment of Edvard Munch's "The Scream."

"Why aren't we making any money?" Szlotov asked, while Chus—the man who knew the factory—stood in limbo. Szlotov already knew why. The factory relied on neighborhood butcher shops but all of them were behind in their payments and Chus hadn't the courage to make them pay.

"Because of the rotten *meyasa*," Chus said, using the Russian word for meat. Szlotov thought of chewing a chunk of steak, fire cooked and still sizzling from the coals, and having warm fatty juice roll down his chin. "*Good* meat is expensive," Chus continued. "The meat we *can* afford is rotten. Surely I can find meat—but I don't have the money to buy it and nobody could afford it…it's just *too expensive*." Chus said his conclusion with a triumphant tone that irritated Szlotov.

Szlotov thought about meat and where to get it. Ukraine had cattle, he thought. Then, gradually, a smile appeared on the side of his face, starting with his right eyebrow.

"Listen," Szlotov said. "*Listen*—leave it to me. I'll supply the meat."

"What?" Chus said. "What are you talking about?"

"I have an idea," Szlotov said, and smiled.

Szlotov had more questions but for now he felt irritated by the sight of Chus. Having pored over the factory's books, Szlotov got used to seeing Chus' fat handwriting, and smelling faint potato soup dripped on the pages. Szlotov knew about all the butcher shops that owed money to Chus. All these unpaid accounts irritated him. It was another example of weak people who avoided confrontation and, thereby, left their work undone. Chus let his soft heart strangle his business.

Szlotov went out to the parking lot. Leaning against their BMWs, Sergei and Ivan approached him.

"Problems?" Sergei asked.

"No," Szlotov said. "Except for his incompetence." Sergei enjoyed hearing that and he put on his sunglasses and got in his car, as did Ivan.

They drove back to the office in their identical bulletproof BMW 740i's, one driven by Sergei in front and another by Ivan, the new driver, in back. Sergei and Ivan each carried a Kalashnikov in their cars and they had earned their places as Szlotov's bodyguards. The wave of grandmother invasions had made Szlotov some enemies, Chechen veterans who came home to find their grandmothers had been invaded. Even Sergei had argued against hitting the grandmothers until Szlotov stared Sergei into silence.

Szlotov decided to travel in convoy, to be more careful, after the close call with Pokcha.

They reached their building and Szlotov stopped at the entrance while Sergei drove around the building. Behind Szlotov, Ivan pulled alongside and sat idling. His Seven was too close for Szlotov's comfort—but he let it go. He felt he had gotten too harsh. It was dangerous. Persecuted people discover courage. Szlotov knew he needed to control his temper. What happened with Pokcha was terrible. "'*To subdue ones enemy without fighting is the highest excellence*'," he heard in his own mind and shook his head in disgust at himself. Szlotov remembered seeing his father down a steer with a machete. Until it settled down and died, a 1000-kg steer could still do plenty of damage.

Szlotov stared in his rear-view mirror and allowed Ivan's mistake to go unmentioned. Sergei drove up and waved "all clear." Szlotov pulled in and parked, stepping inside from the chilly night air. Szlotov went straight to his floor and threw his shirt on the floor. He stood and stared at it a second, then he left the shirt on the floor. He sat in his green velvet armchair and stared across the room without letting his eyes focus land on any one thing.

He got himself a bottle of *kefir* yogurt. He took down his copy of Sun

Tzu and re-read about the value of a speedy victory. He had thought this was the advice from Sun Tzu but instead he decided he should have tried to win without fighting.

There was a sharp rap on his door. Then, one more loud knock.

"Szlotov," Sergei said, lingering in the doorway. Though it was late, Sergei still wore his gray shirt buttoned to the collar and a dark blue tie tight around his neck.

"Yes," Szlotov said.

"Another batch from the Georgians."

"Yes," Szlotov said, tired. He went to the adjoining room and slumped in a leather chair with padded armrests. A doctor-style examination table stood in the middle of the wood-planked floor. A muslin blanket hung on the table. The outer door swung open and Sergei led in a nine-year-old street girl with big, kitten-like ears. Sergei lifted her up on the examination table. She sat in a dirty t-shirt, jeans and bare feet. Szlotov assessed her from his seat. About eleven years old, he guessed. Not too disgusting. Could be cleaned up.

"*Baton-chik*," Szlotov said. Sergei led away the befuddled girl who didn't understand what had happened, that she had just been sentenced to death as a prostitute. At the last moment before Sergei left, Szlotov started into his eyes and saw how deeply he disapproved.

Just outside of Szlotov's office, Sergei handed the girl off to Ivan and, without pause, he grabbed a short dark haired boy. The short-haired boy thrashed against Sergei's grip. The boy thrashed more frantically the closer he got to Szlotov. Sergei had to carry the boy, who was 12, by holding the boy's jaw in one hand and the hair on the crown of his head, to get the boy to look Szlotov in the eye, the way Szlotov preferred it.

"Name," Szlotov asked the boy.

"Verzheny," the boy answered with clear diction. He was obviously intelligent. Szlotov felt a twinge as he pictured himself in this boy's place.

An instant in the ribbon of eternity hung undecided. In the slowdown of time Szlotov hung, and let his mind drift for a moment on the future of this young homeless boy Verzheny who might have been a Pushkin or a Rasputin, but whose talent would now be wasted.

Szlotov felt uncomfortable choosing death-by-prostitution for this boy. He lingered another tick of the second hand before he said: "Useless, Trash."

Sergei grabbed the boy's arm and led him away. A frown passed over Sergei's eyes.

"Vladimir," Sergei said. "Why are we doing this? Zortaev will never be satisfied. It's time."

"We *need* the money, Sergei," Szlotov said.

4.

Three identical BMWs drove down Prospekt Nevski on a creamy winter night. Unlike the last time the Tambovs met in Pushkin, Szlotov came with both Sergei and Ivan. As Szlotov drove his Seven, he followed the tail lights of Sergei in front of him. Ivan's headlights bounced behind him. Szlotov liked traveling in convoy. Behind him, Ivan slowed down to look at the Moika Canal that ran parallel to the road they drove. A gap opened up behind Szlotov.

Sergei reached Prospekt Nevski and stopped at the corner. Szlotov looked for any sign in Sergei's taillights. Sergei was Szlotov's only remaining friend from his days back in the neighborhood of Prospekt Metallistov. By custom, Sergei would only use his blinkers if he saw something. A left turn signal meant cars on the left. A right meant on the right. Left then right meant *Militsiya*. Sergei turned right without signaling. Sergei seemed angry lately.

Szlotov took the right and turned on to wide Prospekt Nevski, on their way to the Nevski Palace Hotel and its restaurant on the second floor with a buffet and a rare feeling of opulence. They slowed for a red light. Szlotov looked outside at some Gypsy women who stood on the sidewalks with their dusty allure and dark streaks of immorality shading their shiny faces.

At the light, Szlotov observed Ivan driving up, tightening his tie. The light changed and Sergei led them all to the Nevski Palace hotel. Sergei headed into the garage and Szlotov followed him. Ivan blocked the street entrance with is own car.

Szlotov and Sergei continued up the winding concrete channel to the top floor, the one place where Szlotov—conscious at all times that some daughter of a silenced enemy could come after him anytime—felt safe.

Once, right after Szlotov had been made third-in-command of the Tambovs, he had been climbing out of his car in front of the Nevski Melody disco. A girl with a bouquet of carnations walked toward him. Szlotov reacted like his KGB training had taught him to react: he took out his Glock and put a round in her forehead. The girl folded at the knees and flopped on her face in a pool of red. Szlotov hopped back in his car and drove off, fifteen minutes before the *Militsiya* showed up and arrested a man going through her pockets. The episode had been a huge mistake but it left Szlotov wary of his surroundings at all times.

Sergei parked on the top floor and headed for the stairs while Szlotov waited. He called Ivan.

"I'm listening," Ivan answered.

"We're here," Szlotov said. Ivan then arrived. Sergei called from the stairs.

"It's clean," Sergei said. "Enjoy."

"Good," Szlotov said to Sergei and then to Ivan: "Watch the cars." Sergei turned his back and walked back to his car. Ivan nodded and threw a stick of gum in his mouth and started to chew.

Szlotov felt insulted. Insolence. Ivan was nothing like the man he replaced. Mikhail Burzhensky, a trusted man, a chess player, a sunflower farmer, who was gunned down at age 36. There was no comparison between Mikhail and Ivan, who at 24 years old, was so green and unsure of himself he did not recognize the dangerous game he was playing.

Szlotov entered the stairwell alone. He walked silently down the concrete steps so the faint tapping of his shoe leather echoed the length of the stairwell. He reached the floor and met Sergei: alert, his dark eyes that would not hesitate to kill always scanning, looking back and forth for motion, risk or danger. Szlotov knew about the myth circulating that said he couldn't be killed. In reality, nobody ever broke through the protective vigil by Sergei.

They walked through the ornate, polished hallways with a tint of gold metalwork at waist level and covering the doorways. Without ceremony, Szlotov strode into the foyer of the Nevski Palace Hotel restaurant. Left of the entrance stood a small desk and a woman, smiling in a most calm, accepting way to Szlotov and Sergei as if each were kind businessmen, who stopped by the store after work to pick up butter for their wives.

With help from Sergei, Szlotov doffed his long coat. In so doing, he pulled back his Brooks Brothers suit. The eyes of the hostess spotted the black triangle next to his kidney that contained his Glock. Sergei started to take off his own coat but Szlotov stopped him.

"I'm going alone," Szlotov said. "Just principles were invited." Sergei glared. His face flushed red in anger.

"I'm a principle too," Sergei said and left.

Szlotov entered the long dining room. The room was built in tiers, with a step taking him down to a long table by the floor-to-ceiling windows. There sat Szlotov's boss. Zortaev, who forbade anyone from using his real name *Dmitri* or especially his patronymic *Zoltanovich*. Doing so was enough to get the person who said it stabbed and disemboweled, as had happened to more than one deceased idiot.

Zortaev sat alone in the main dining room with a dirty plate under his chin. It was covered with the broken shells of lobster claws, crab shells and trout bones, all foods that were not on the menu but that were nonetheless on his plate. Zortaev had an ownership stake in the restaurant. The formerly white napkin that hung like a greasy mechanic's rag around his throat made a shiny outline to the lower half of his face, which was shiny already from the oil in the food he had gorged on. The rind on his face was shiny too, from the butter he that had gotten smeared there. A mostly-empty bottle of vodka stood next to his full water glass.

"Thought the meeting was at eight but instead of leaving I ate," Zortaev said, as he wiped his greasy hand on his lap napkin and extended it greasy to Szlotov, who shook it. Szlotov sat down and relaxed. Szlotov always found it grating how a bumbling Khrushchev of a man like Zortaev earned and spent vastly greater sums of money than Szlotov and his brigade. When Zortaev and Szlotov got together to form the Tambovs in Leningrad, Zortaev was his usual self, an asshole, the same riled-up behavior that got him kicked out of the security service. Zortaev claimed one part of what became St. Petersburg and gave the other part to Szlotov. They had been walking along the Fontanka canal and Zortaev announced he would take the half of the city on his left and that Szlotov could have the rest on the right. Years later, that choice gave Zortaev easy money and forced Szlotov to be a criminal genius just to survive.

Zortaev cracked open another lobster claw and munched the rubbery meat. Zortaev smiled with his mouth full and it raised creases on the rind of his face.

Number one in the Tambovs, Zortaev feared no one. Though he felt some irritation at the Maleshevski band who had invaded their territories. When Szlotov and Zortaev had first met, Zortaev appeared to be a simpleton. In fact, Zortaev was a brutal man. When confronted by a traitor to the *organizatsiya*, Zortaev was unwilling just to kill the traitor. He made it known that the traitor's wife, children, brothers and parents would also be killed. The traitor's family would be wiped off the face of the earth.

This practice, first implemented by Zortaev himself, started after he received a wound in Afghanistan. Zortaev had been shot in the head. He survived but his compassion did not. His lack of concern and rigid adherence to his practice was such that any bullet-to-the-temple killing was branded a "Zortaev killing". For permeating St. Petersburg with fear and keeping out the Maleshevski band, Szlotov felt beholden to his boss, despite the higher payments he expected. Now Szlotov was thinking it was time to cancel his service.

Szlotov got water and a linen napkin from the waiter. Zortaev made a sign to the waiter and then he pointed at Szlotov's place and then he flashed a peace sign. The waiter nodded and closed his eyes as he walked off.

"There are worse places, to be early, than Nevski Palace," Zortaev said, with a grin. His teeth were thick and too big for his mouth so his cheeks flared out, making the rind on his face more prominent.

Before Szlotov settled in, the waiter arrived with two lobster claws steaming from a plate which he set in front of Szlotov, who smiled and stuffed the corner of his white napkin in his shirt collar without loosening his tie.

Close on the heels of the first waiter came another with a plate balanced on the tips of his fingers. Perched there was a white platter of steak. Contrails of steam followed the plate as it followed a looping path to the table, to the right of Szlotov, beside the lobsters.

The eyes of both men fell on the meat and then rose up to look at each other, smiling, eye to eye.

"*Life*," Zortaev said and steak juice overflowed his chin. "He *sometimes* is good."

Szlotov laughed. This 'sometimes' was directed, he expected, at the recent good fortune Zortaev's crew had experienced, with money streaming into Zortaev's *organizatsiya* from the oil sector by the docks.

"Business is good," Szlotov lied. He didn't know how he was going to keep up his earnings. There were no more grandmothers to fleece. Every business with two kopecks to rub together was already paying tribute based on gross revenue, not net. The beggars paid every ruble they had to avoid a beating. Putting the bums to work was an exercise program for his *baklany*. Part of the initiation for a punk involved beating a homeless person to death using only their fists.

"Bus-i-ness," Zortaev said, holding the word in his overcrowded mouth and caressing it as if it were a mistress who had given him many nights of delight and pleasure. "She is *great*." He poured his water glass half full of vodka and emptied it.

Szlotov said nothing and examined his steak knife for sharpness. While Zortaev's jaw continued to grind a chunk of steak, his wet eyes tracked Szlotov, as if he did not trust him. Szlotov pointed his knife at the light so the spectrum danced on the blade. He shifted the focus from his knife to the face of Zortaev, still grinding on the t-bone steak. Szlotov thought he could just ram the knife home in Zortaev's heart, then hold him down while his blood squirted out in a stream on the white tablecloth. "I'm sure the waiter and staff would thank me," he thought.

Szlotov ran his thumb over the sharp blade of the his steak knife. He stabbed the steak, which he preferred over lobster though he grew up in St. Petersburg, an Atlantic Ocean port. He dragged the knife across the meat, splitting it down the middle and it looked the same as a man's thigh did when cut by a bowie knife. Running his thumb against the blade, Szlotov remembered the spurt of blood, the shriek and the terror of being carved open alive. Holding a knife comforted Szlotov, as he—like Zortaev—could never look away when another man held a knife in his vicinity. Szlotov carved off two strips of steak and dragged them through the gravy while Zortaev watched the knife and

64

chewed.

"*Devushka!*" Zortaev bellowed at the waitress. "Get over here!"

Szlotov closed his eyes and exhaled slowly. Zortaev yelled again after the waitress already stood at hand. He came from the Kupchino area of Leningrad. On the streets around the Kupchino metro station, Zortaev learned to throw a knife and cut anybody who looked at the rind on his face. Zortaev knew no boundaries. He licked his butter knife before he returned it to the common bowl.

"Another lobster," Zortaev said. The waitress nodded and darted for the kitchen.

"Stop!" Zortaev said, braking her. "Come back," he said. She returned bewildered and afraid.

"Yes?"

"I want a *live* lobster."

"I don't know if—" she began to say but, instead, ran to the kitchen.

In a slurry of fluids moving inside him, rumbling and squeezing, Zortaev burped and added in a long, loud fart to complete the relief. The restaurant froze for a moment. All were silent. A beat passed and the head waiter bent to whisper to Zortaev.

"Sir," said the head waiter in his softest voice. "Sadly, I must report that, while we have lobsters, we have none that are alive. As it stands, sir, we cannot satisfy your order." Behind the head waiter, upset and distracted, stood the *devushka.* She held her tray flat as a shield in case shell casings started bouncing off the floor.

Szlotov now watched Zortaev, hoping to gauge his boss's mood. After the head waiter left, a subtle change occurred in Zortaev's face. His light complexion looked pale. Thin white lines stretched over the muscles in his cheeks, and stood out. For the first time, Szlotov noticed Zortaev was sweating. Zortaev had his fist around a crystal goblet of ice water, leaning on it like a crutch. The head waiter stood back out of Zortaev's view with the *devushka,* waiting to see what Zortaev would do. A drop of sweat gathered speed on the long white expanse of forehead on Zortaev's head and it rolled down his cheek, following a vertical scar.

"I want a *lobster!*" Zortaev roared. "I want a live one, right here!" The head waiter scurried up next to Zortaev. He stood at attention. The black hairs on his mustache flared.

"Of course, sir," said the head waiter, before he rushed back to the kitchen for his hat and coat.

Zortaev at last drank his water. As soon as his goblet hit the tablecloth empty, he cried out "*Devushka,*" as one might call a local barmaid.

"*Yes,* Mr. Zortaev," she said, shaking.

"I want water, now," he said.

"*Immediately!*" She ran to the kitchen. After she left, he poured his water glass full of vodka and drank it down. Szlotov had sat with Zortaev for thirty minutes. They had not, however, discussed the reason for the meeting, which was the business difficulties Druzhnev was having. Pavel Druzhnev was 38 years old, second in command of the Tambovs, a former member of the Russian army, but he was still a child. Szlotov saw him as a mouth-breathing pretty boy whose unkempt hair stood out in odd directions. Druzhnev was second in command only because Zortaev favored him, because of some agreement that Zortaev announced, that he and Szlotov were going to stake Druzhnev by giving him a portion of their regions.

"I have already sat here for two hours," Zortaev said, smiling to Druzhnev when he at last walked in.

"Sorry to keep *you* waiting, Herr Szlotov," Druzhnev said. The German reference offended Szlotov because it referred to the nickname he had during his KGB days in Prague. It renewed Szlotov's conviction that he would, one day, silence the mouth breather. Both of them.

"And I've been here for an hour," Szlotov said, and he thought: *Druzhnev—bastard! Second? Never.*

"It is not important," Zortaev said and silenced the both of them. He played with an empty lobster claw and moved it under his nose to smell it.

Druzhnev yelled "*Devushka!*" and ordered a steak bloody rare and a Baltika-4.

"Yes, it is stupid."

"We three are the heart of the *organizatsiya*," Zortaev said, putting his arm around Druzhnev and placing his palm on Szlotov's shoulder. "We're all on the same team."

Zortaev, a man good at nothing but stealing, leaned back in his chair. He relaxed and let his lips peel apart. "We *help* one another."

Szlotov chuckled to himself and Zortaev turned on him.

"No? Why not? What's so funny?"

"Nothing, the same team—yes—we're on it," Szlotov agreed. "But some of us play harder positions than others. Some regions have oil depots and others have blocks of homeless."

"Such hooey he talks about me," Druzhnev said, and stood in a clench. Szlotov did not do anything but vent his rage through his eyes, thinking: *I will kill you, Pavel.*

"We'll get to that *shortly*," Zortaev said. "But—"

"Yes, I am," Szlotov said. "It's ridiculous. My team earns and they do so with a shit region. Everybody is poor. Now you want still *more babki?* What happened to the money I already gave?"

Zortaev sat back and fingered his neck rind, his mouth stretched in a frown. Below the surface boiled the dismay that was filling Zortaev until it exploded in rage.

Druzhnev narrowed his eyes in bottled rage at Szlotov for showing defiance.

"Times are tough for my brigade too, Szlotov," Druzhnev said—a liar, telling Szlotov that he was actually doing okay. "Well, we haven't tapped our *grandmothers* yet," Druzhnev said, "so we're not *that* desperate." Zortaev laughed along with Druzhnev but Szlotov did not.

"Instead," Szlotov broke in. "Your crews sit on their asses and play video games, earning easy money from the oil depot while my teams work hard in the weight room."

"Your punks beat up homeless people," Druzhnev said. "For *tiny* money."

Zortaev himself enjoyed the conflict. He leaned back and rested one hand on his enormous belly and shoved away the lobster shells, and then looked for any pieces he missed.

"Even in Afghanistan, soldiers didn't kill old people," Druzhnev said. "You robbed the *babushki*. After that, Vladimir, you hit the beggars. That is bad business. It invites much trouble and yields so little money."

"So, what *else* then?" Szlotov asked Zortaev directly. "What choice is there? Dmitri Zoltanovich, do you want easy speeches or a wallet full of *babki*?" Szlotov stopped himself before he went too far.

In the lingering silence that followed this exchange, neither Druzhnev nor Zortaev ventured any reply. Then the head waiter returned sweaty in his long coat carrying a wet canvas bag. He stopped at the kitchen and held up the bag which contained a thrashing lobster.

Druzhnev waved his empty beer bottle and the head waiter nodded.

"*Babki* of course," Zortaev said. He was startled when a domed stainless steel dish rolled up on a cart beside his table. The grateful *devushka* came ahead of the cart to scrape the old shells into a bucket.

"Mr. Zortaev," said the head waiter with his hand poised on the lid. "You ordered lobster, *live*." The waiter pulled away the domed lid and Zortaev moved his face near the dish to sniff it. When he focused on the dish he saw moving lobster claws. Raising itself up on the platter, the lobster reached out with its claw and clamped on to Zortaev's thick waterfall-like lower lip. Zortaev batted with his arm and knocked his goblet of water on the floor. In the time it took for the goblet to reach the floor and shatter, Zortaev gasped and roared out in pain. Knocking back his chair, he stood and shook his head like a dog drying off after a bath, shrieking and trickling blood on his green tie.

Szlotov stood back but then he saw the lobster's grip was good. He tried to catch the lobster's tail. Once, he caught it and held on but Zortaev screamed twice as loudly and so Szlotov let go.

Druzhnev flew to his feet and pulled out his pistol. The *devushka* and the head waiter ran into the kitchen, only to peek out a moment later.

"That's not necessary, Pavel..." Szlotov said.

Druzhnev fired and hit the lobster in the tail. After the shot, the restaurant was in pandemonium. The lobster released its grip on Zortaev's lip and dropped to the floor. Zortaev took the Glock away from Druzhnev and shot the lobster twice through the thorax, causing it at last to drop its dukes. Then he handed the gun back to Druzhnev. He picked up the dead lobster and threw it on his plate. Though his lip gushed blood he broke open the claw covered with his own blood and ate the raw meat. Oblivious to the pain in his lip, he jammed the raw flesh into his mouth. From the corners of his mouth, red wet foam slid down his chin.

Druzhnev and Szlotov remained standing, neither saying a word. Druzhnev still held his gun as the smoke from the shot dissipated. Szlotov kept his eye on the gun.

Bleeding so his plate had a lake of blood, Zortaev peeled the scales away from what remained of the tail.

"Bastard, you shot off half my tail," Zortaev said, his voice sounding drunk. "Bastard."

Druzhnev and Szlotov exchanged a glance. That glance by Szlotov consisted of an incline of his head toward Zortaev, which they both knew meant: "We both need Zortaev dead." Druzhnev, in his blue silk collar and well-coiffed head of hair, replied by nodding with his tongue pressed into his cheek.

After Zortaev finished the claws, tail and was crushing his way through the legs, Druzhnev put his hand on Zortaev's shoulder.

"We need to go see a doctor right away," Druzhnev said. Zortaev was dazed and lost. The most powerful boss in the St. Petersburg Tambov syndicate had been turned into an incoherent slob with a swollen, bleeding and gashed lip. Druzhnev helped Zortaev out of the restaurant. The cloth napkin under his chin was soaked with blood. Szlotov implored Druzhnev—that now was the time to solve their common problem. But Szlotov suddenly relented and decided he must do them separately.

In the garage, Sergei and the other drivers drew their guns, expecting a shooter.

"What happened?" Sergei asked Szlotov, holding up his gun, ready to die.

"An accident," Szlotov said. "Get my car at once." Sergei threw his gun on the ground in exasperation.

"No," Druzhnev said. "We'll take my car. It will be faster."

His eyebrows lifted in anger, Sergei looked at Szlotov for answers. "Vladimir, this has got to stop. We're working for a madman!"

In reply, Szlotov told Sergei with his look: *Later. We will talk about this later. I've been thinking the same thing.*

Just outside the doorway, blocking other cars from leaving the garage, sat a cobalt blue Maserati Quattroporte. Szlotov had never seen a real Maserati, but he recognized the Maserati logo of the trident. Druzhnev opened the passenger door and Szlotov transferred control of Zortaev to him. Behaving like a drunk, Zortaev fought against them. Zortaev got into the bucket seat and it gripped him like a leather suction cup. Druzhnev got in the driver's seat of his own car with his usual smile. Szlotov closed the car door without getting in. Druzhnev leaned over and talked to him through Zortaev's window, which he had lowered.

"Get in—you have to hold him," Druzhnev said.

"I have a car here. I will follow you to the Doctor."

"No," Druzhnev said, pushing open the back door of the Maserati. "I need you to *control* him. This is a *Quattroporte*—it requires my attention."

Szlotov met eyes with Sergei and said: "Please follow in *my* car." Sergei shook his head and headed for his own car.

"Vladimir, this has got to stop. I need to—" Sergei said, one foot in his car. Szlotov slashed the air with his hand and Sergei stopped talking. Szlotov got in the Maserati and his hands came to rest on the camel-colored leather upholstery. He glanced at Zortaev, bleeding all over the leather.

Riding in back, Szlotov felt quiet disgust at Druzhnev: he made enough to pay full price for this flashy Maserati fifty times over while Szlotov worked every angle, emptied every pocket, plundered every secret stash of treasure in every run down apartment in his district. In the end the problem started with the poverty of his territory. The place where he was born did not have much treasure to harvest. Vermin like Druzhnev could—with no hint of creativity—generate millions of dollars in *babki*. He had cash hidden all over St. Petersburg in safe deposit boxes, closets, and under mattresses, yet Druzhnev couldn't even be bothered to attempt to appear like a legitimate businessman and buy his car from a dealer, instead paying $30,000 bucks for the Maserati, stolen from Dusseldorf, rather than the list price of $160,000. With his fancy clothes, Druzhnev seemed to not understand that the principals in the Tambovs were not supposed to call attention to themselves. Idiot.

The engine came alive and it growled with a high whine like a jet engine chained to the tarmac. Gesticulating wildly, Druzhnev walked the shifter through the gear pattern and ended with it in first. Then he drummed his feet on the clutch and gas so the car rocketed forward and held Zortaev tight to the seat. The Maserati threaded itself at high speed out of the parking garage. Its nose appeared on Prospekt Nevski. With only a brief glance at the traffic, Druzhnev let out the clutch and the Maserati shot forward as if fired from a cannon. Szlotov was pinned against the seat while Druzhnev ran the car up to 140kph, a speed that made the other cars appear all but stationary. He steered like a madman, the tires screeching as he veered around slower cars. Twice Druzhnev hopped the curb to avoid a deep pothole. Szlotov did not enjoy riding in a car he himself was not driving.

Leaving Prospekt Nevski, they arrived at Szlotov's building. The pitch of the Maserati's engine lowered as Druzhnev entered the parking lot.

"What? What? What?" Zortaev cried out, waking up and lurching from his seat against the windshield. "Where are we going!"

"Calm down," Druzhnev said. He took his hand off the shifter and pushed back the still-bleeding Zortaev who was so drunk he didn't understand his lip was severed. Druzhnev got out of the Maserati and stretched his legs, then leaned against the car and lit a cigarette. Szlotov emerged from the back seat and hauled out Zortaev. Zortaev's face was smeared with bloody ribbons of saliva. His muscular jaw hung slack. His tongue extended and dragged itself across his bloody lip. Druzhnev threw away his butt and grabbed the other arm of their boss. Together, the second and third in command of the Tambov Syndicate shouldered number one, the toes of his Italian shoes dragging behind him on the asphalt. They went up the concrete steps into Szlotov's building and then directly toward the basement stairs.

Szlotov and Druzhnev met rat-faced Vasya, eating sunflower seeds. He dropped the bag when he saw Zortaev's face.

"What happened?" Vasya asked. Szlotov and Druzhnev carried Zortaev down the concrete stairway to the basement without answering.

Hearing the commotion, the Doctor ran out in a panic from his corner. Wooden cages lined the sides of the basement. Inside each, one or more homeless children sat, their faces up against the slats, watching as Szlotov and Druzhnev carried their boss to a table. "Wow!" they yelled. The tablecloth was stained brown, red and black in blotches. Druzhnev wiped the table bare, smashing a row of bottles on the floor. After they lay him on the table, Druzhnev got a look at the basement. Dozens of kids sat inside wooden cages, staring intently at the man lying on the table, bleeding. With an expression like he did not care for the smell, he met eyes with Szlotov and said, "I don't even want to know."

"Mansoor—this man heads the *organizatsiya*," Szlotov said. "Can you fix him?" Druzhnev and Szlotov took a step back, to clear the way for the Doctor. Dr. Mansoor Moosorovic, Lebanese, a jack-of-all-trades medical man, was Szlotov's house physician.

"Gunshot?" asked the Doctor, gritting his teeth.

"No, *lobster*," Szlotov answered. *"Can you fix him?"*

Druzhnev looked around at the rest of the basement: dark, wet and filled with the sweet smell of fresh meat. On the tables were strips of tough cord as tie-down points. The cement floor was wet from a recent mopping. The water in the buckets was ruddy. One bucket had something white and waxy, tissue like the membranes on chicken, sticking up out of the water, with its ragged cut edge shiny in the light from a single bulb in the ceiling of the room.

"I'm..." the Doctor said. "I'm..."

Across the room stood a row of high, narrow tables, upon which a body lay under a blanket. The Doctor bit down and his cheeks bowed. His teeth wobbled as he bit down, especially the incisor, second from the left. Mansoor looked down and bit hard on his teeth.

"Vladimir," Druzhnev said, with an abrupt sound that got even the attention of the Doctor as he examined the lip wound. He stared closely and pursed his lips. He pulled apart the jagged edges of the pale, rind-covered skin that formerly was the lower lip of Dmitri Zortaev, 45 years old, ex-KGB. Szlotov whispered into the Doctor's ear that Zortaev was a disabled Afghan war veteran who had sustained a head wound and was capable of lashing out.

Tightening the skin around his eyes as he explored the wound, the Doctor began to breathe faster and fling around his instruments, which were tools from the hardware store that he had adapted. The Doctor's lips quivered. Looking through his thick glasses, his eyes appeared enormous. His eyes showed fear.

"Vladimir," Druzhnev said, backing away. "I can't watch this. I'm going."

"N'yet. Stay," Szlotov said out, holding down Zortaev as the Doctor stretched apart the cut lip to see where the cut stopped. The Doctor worked and his lips vibrated.

"What?" Szlotov said to the Doctor. "Why aren't you starting?"

"I'm afraid," said the Doctor. "It's out of my league. I can't do this. I'm scared." Several of the caged kids laughed at the Doctor. He yelled at them and rattled the mop handle across their cages.

Szlotov released a deep sigh. He saw the Doctor's trembling eyes milky-white behind his thick glasses.

"It does not need to be perfect," Szlotov said. "Come on—you can."

"No, it's impossible," the Doctor said. "The cut is too jagged, I can't— "

Szlotov grabbed the Doctor by his upper arm. His glasses fell off his head, and revealed his left eye, cloudy white. The Doctor held up his fingers to protect himself. He drooled on himself.

"Please, I don't want to die," he said to Szlotov in a whimper.

"What are you talking about? Stitch his lip, the quicker the better—that's all."

The Doctor bent over simpering. His hair hung in waxy locks as he leaned over. He hung his head and when he raised it his wet cheeks looked out of place on his hyper cheerful face.

"I can't," he said.

"Szlotov," Druzhnev said, while their boss sat bleeding on his shirt and the Doctor trembled in place next to him. "Who is this quack? Let's take him to a polyclinic."

"Why *can't* you fix him?" Szlotov asked the Doctor.

"Because," said the Doctor, now wanting to be silent and not go on with what he was about to say. "I cannot...sew."

"We're going," Druzhnev blurted. He raised Zortaev and put one of his arms under his own. As he began to sober up, Zortaev started to feel the pain. He growled out loud. Mansoor hopped in the air following the growl.

"Come back," Szlotov ordered.

Mansoor turned his profile toward Szlotov, showing the moss-like hair that covered his cheeks.

Szlotov looked at the mossy sideburns. After several seconds of silent rage, standing next to the Doctor, Szlotov said: "How is it possible that a *doctor* did not learn to sew?"

The Doctor hunched over, removed his glasses, and showed his milky white eye to Szlotov.

"You still must try," Szlotov said.

Mansoor slumped. The skin on his face sagged under his glasses. He shuffled to the far end of the room and cracked open a dusty trunk. He took out some clothes and set them on another table. Out came a cardboard box and from that an even smaller cloth sack. He held up an old needle and muslin thread.

Druzhnev, now paying attention, looked at the dirty needle. He pointed it out to Szlotov.

"What is going on, Szlotov? What *the fuck* is going on? Why don't we take him to a polyclinic?"

"Because no clinic in St. Petersburg will take him," Szlotov said. "He made the doctors pay protection. They are scared of him. He hates doctors—" Szlotov said.

"—his face," Druzhnev replied.

Listening to Szlotov's conversation, the Doctor started to breathe faster. He held the needle so light was visible through the eye. He grabbed the free end of the roll of thread. The Doctor struggled to grip the thread and by then he had lost the needle. He held up the thread and licked the end to get it through the hole. Druzhnev growled and said "This is ridiculous." Then the Doctor held up the needle and jammed the frayed thread at the hole.

"Give me that," Szlotov said. He took the needle and thread from the Doctor, cut the end neat and threaded the needle. He pulled it through, knotted the end and set the threaded needle on the pillow next to Zortaev. Zortaev's eyes focused on the needle laying next to him, as if the sight of the metal he was about to meet sobered him up better than anything else could have.

Szlotov and Druzhnev looked on in silence. Zortaev lay on the bed with his knees bent, hanging down. The Doctor took the needle in hand and approached his patient's face. Looking at the various white lines around Zortaev's face, it became apparent to the Doctor that Zortaev had already undergone extensive re-constructive surgery on his face. The Doctor moved closer until he looked straight into the up-looking eyes of Zortaev. From his lack of focus it was clear to the Doctor that Zortaev—muscular, stocky, quick—was almost unconscious. The Doctor moved the needle and thread along the surface of Zortaev's chest. His movements were jerky as his poor eyesight prevented him from judging depth well. While he guided the needle, the Doctor stopped to scratch with his free hand and then the Doctor slipped and rammed the needle into Zortaev's upper lip. Zortaev exploded in pain and clawed at the Doctor. The round things his hands wrapped around and squeezed were the Doctor's testicles. The Doctor wilted and fell to the ground, grimacing like a slaughtered lizard.

His balls having been turned to applesauce, the Doctor lay on the ground for five minutes until at the urging of Szlotov he got up sweaty and exhausted. He moved to the head end of Zortaev, who was now awake with his eyes open.

Szlotov held on to Zortaev's right wrist. Druzhnev too came up and grabbed Zortaev's left arm. The Doctor got down on the floor and found the needle and thread. Wiping it on his shirt, he returned to Zortaev's lip, which had ceased gushing blood and now reduced to a steady trickle. From above, the Doctor bent down near to Zortaev's upside-down face. His jaw looked like an enormous moving plate, his teeth grinding. The brought the sharp point of the needle to the edge of the cut lip. Then he pressed it into the healthy skin right next to the wound.

"Aahhh," Zortaev screamed in a rage and he tried to grab the Doctor but Szlotov and Druzhnev held him down. So, his anger found expression in his legs, which kicked up and caught Druzhnev on the back of his head. Still holding on, Druzhnev sought to shake off the kick.

"You enjoying this?" Druzhnev said, looking at Szlotov. After he had Szlotov's attention, Druzhnev expanded his implication to mean 'working for Zortaev.' Szlotov shook his head "no." Szlotov wanted to buy what Druzhnev was selling but he also did not want to play sucker to a scam.

"We will have to talk," Druzhnev said. The Doctor stabbed his lip again.

"Bastard!" Zortaev shouted. Now irritated, Druzhnev changed his posture so that his inner leg's knee rode on Zortaev's thigh. Once he saw, Szlotov adopted the same pose, though it was harder to do since Szlotov was shorter than Druzhnev. Instead of resting his weight on Zortaev, Szlotov hung by his inner leg and his other toe just reached the floor. When he was set, Szlotov nodded to Druzhnev.

"Let's do it," Szlotov said. The Doctor, weary already, returned with the needle pinched between his fingers. The lobster's claw had severed the lip for two centimeters. The fleshy raw edges of the skin turned up in a ruffle like kale. The Doctor reached out with his bony fingers. A line of grit outlined his thick fingernails as he grabbed the edge of Zortaev's lip between his thumb and forefinger.

"Ah! *Fuck your mother!*" Zortaev shouted and then ended with a deep growl as he tried to free his arms. Szlotov and Druzhnev rode Zortaev's arms and kept him down. After both nodded that their grip was good, the Doctor held his breath and stabbed next to his finger with the needle.

"*AAAAHY!*" roared Zortaev as the Doctor pushed the needle deep into the edge of Zortaev's lip. After the needle broke free from the lip and dragged the thread, Zortaev lifted Szlotov into the air. The second stab came into the adjoining section of lip and it hurt no less than the first. After the needle passed through the other part of the lip, the Doctor balked.

"What…are you waiting for?" Druzhnev asked.

"I don't—"

"Tie the two ends together—tightly," Szlotov said, "but not so tightly that you tear it." The Doctor did as he was told and Zortaev gave a fresh but depleted roar from the burning pain. The Doctor tied the second stitch and did a third one. He was going for a fourth stitch when Szlotov stopped him. Smiling and surprised at himself, the Doctor dropped the needle and grinned in a way that showcased the picket fence that was his smile.

"That'll do," Szlotov said. Druzhnev and Szlotov helped their boss to a sitting position. His lower lip was joined by the three crude stitches, whose ends stuck out in a "v" shape. He was disoriented but they helped him to his feet and got ready to leave. Szlotov himself tied the last knot and cut the tails short.

"Thank you, doctor," Zortaev said at the door.

"No inconvenience," said the Doctor, beaming.

The three gangsters headed out of the basement, Zortaev walking first up the wooden stairs. Once they got upstairs, all of Szlotov's crew stared in silence at the infamous Zortaev.

Druzhnev turned to Szlotov. "What the hell kind of a doctor doesn't know how to put in stitches?"

Szlotov did not answer. Szlotov helped Druzhnev get Zortaev belted in the front seat of the Maserati and then, without ceremony, Szlotov stood by Sergei. They both watched Druzhnev's Maserati disappear around the corner.

"For *this* guy we're cleaning out the *Babushki*?" Sergei said, not having moved an inch since the Maserati rumbled around the corner. "You think these fucks are worth all this trouble?"

Szlotov stood with his eyes lowered, trying not to expose his lack of curiosity for Sergei's concerns because he himself was full of his own problems. "Yes, I agree," Szlotov said. "But for now we still pay."

"You're crazy, Vladimir," Sergei said.

Szlotov felt his entire body clench.

"If you continue to allow this," Sergei said, continuing his angry bout of insubordination. "You're an even bigger fool than your 'master,' Zortaev. Even I cannot protect you then, Vladimir. The men don't like this business—it's dirty."

Chapter VI

1.

G ALINA woke up and saw that most of the other kids had already left the sewer tunnel. She climbed up the ladder into the sunlight and walked to the cluster of kiosks. A cold wind blew and she saw Murat Koof crouched on the ground giving instructions to a girl Galina had seen in the tunnel. She had bright red hair and she did not look as dirty as Koof did. The girl was named Raisa and she seemed about ten. Galina stood off behind the kiosk cluster, watching Koof say his last words to her. Then Raisa walked into the kiosk cluster. After a few moments, Koof himself walked into the center of cluster. Galina ran up to the place where they had been standing. She saw Koof walking over to the vodka and Marlboro's kiosk and very publicly stand in front of it. Galina watched Murat Koof and she smiled, knowing he was up to something. The owner of the kiosk also had taken notice of Koof, his dirty man-sized coast, his dirty face and long black nostril hairs. The owner was ready.

Then Galina noticed Raisa standing nearby, out of view. Koof reached over the counter and yelled "Give me vodka" and he knocked over several bottles on the counter. Galina winced as the kiosk owner slugged Murat in the head. As everybody watched Murat get hit, Raisa grabbed two handfuls of Snicker bars. Raisa was gone before the other kiosk owner noticed a thing. Galina felt scared and so she ran back to the tunnel ahead of anybody else. She climbed down and lay still like she was asleep. Murat returned with a beaming Raisa, her mouth filled with an entire chocolate bar, happy smears of chocolate surrounding her mouth.

"A present," Murat announced. "A nice man gave them to us." He came over to the kids by Galina and gave each one a finger-sized chunk of candy. Galina waited and Murat came over to her and repeated "A present". Galina gasped at the sight of a huge, bloody welt above his left eye. Murat smiled as he gave her the candy. His teeth were bloody.

Galina took her piece and thanked him. Murat smiled in a way that made Galina feel embarrassed for having thought his nostril hairs were too big or that his face was dirty. She thanked him again as her mouth filled with the taste of chocolate. She repeated the strange name to herself: "Sneakers."

2.

The next morning, Galina woke in the sewer and she felt warm and for the first time not scared. She looked over the sewer full of sleeping homeless children, like herself. The bright sunlight streamed down into the tunnel through the open top and she saw Raisa sleeping curled up in a ball with her hand tucked close to her knees, like a kitten. Thinking that made Galina smile and reminded her of the people who lived in the next door flat in Chilkovo. They had a cat named Katuna. It was a white cat with a brown mustache or comb under its nose. Galina had been allowed to pet Katuna as long as she was gentle. Her grandmother did not want a cat but she did not mind when Galina talked about how soft the kitten's fur felt.

Galina tried to remember how that cat felt and she rolled over on her back and looked over at Koof. He had slept against the wall, in a sitting position. Around his mouth was fresh brown, from whatever brown thing he was eating. Galina stared at Murat and then he spoke to her.

"Rested up, I suppose," Murat said. He rubbed his dirty hand under his dirty nose.

"Yes," Galina said. "I really slept."

When Murat stared at Galina, his gaze landed just low and to the left. Galina felt uncomfortable when he did not look into her face and stared at something to her left that she could not see. He helped her and she tried not to ask him questions, ever since her grandmother Ludmilla snapped at her for being too full of questions.

"Want something to eat?" Koof asked.

"Yes!"

"Come, then," he said and spun on his boot. Koof led her out of the tunnel and right for the trade cluster. On top, Galina kept a look out for Astrakhan. Every step in daylight she expected Astrakhan to pounce on her and drag her back to his apartment. They reached the edge of the kiosks and Koof turned on her.

"See the blue kiosk?"

"Yes."

"Go there and wait for me. I will go over to the vodka kiosk—"

"—wait," Galina said, feeling her legs shake. "I don't have any money for food."

"Neither do I," Koof said. "I will make trouble and then you take two handfuls of candy bars over there and then run."

78

"I can't," she said. "I'm scared."

"It's easy," Murat said. "No problem." Galina took a deep breath but then she lost her nerve and just sighed. Murat gave her a shove and then Galina marched with her arms hanging limp at her sides next to the blue kiosk, that sold candy and chips. Galina stood five feet from the kiosk, staring at the candy bars, her mouth closed tightly in a frown.

Loose, casual, with a step that would have worked if his mouth were not smeared with shit and his coat muddy in front. Koof walked over with a loose waving of his hands from the wrists to the vodka kiosk. He stood there but the owner did not wait and came right out of the kiosk and grabbed Murat by the arms.

"You thieving little bastard!" shouted the kiosk man. Though the eyes of the blue kiosk owner were on her now, Galina dashed up on cue and grabbed four Snickers with one hand and three in her other.

Barely able to hang on to the stolen candy, Galina made it ten feet before a man grabbed her. The vodka kiosk owner punched Murat in the face several times. Then he tried to hold on to Murat and Galina, still being held herself, saw Murat crouch down and bite the hand of the vodka kiosk owner. The man roared in pain and then punched Murat on the side of his head. Murat went flying but he got up and stumbled away.

The other kiosk owner put Galina in a headlock, avoiding her teeth, though she never tried to bite. The woman kiosk owner came out, grabbed back the stolen candy bars and stopped to stare into Galina's eyes. Galina stood in custody and cried as the eyes of everybody stared at her. She felt ashamed and thought of her grandmother Ludmilla and she felt humiliated. In a quarter of an hour, the *Militsiya* came and it was an older, pale-faced officer. He had too many teeth in his mouth and a large pea-sized mole on his neck under his chin. Galina stared at his black mole while he questioned her.

"*Devushka*," the *Militsiya* man said. "What did you steal?"

She thought hard before she admitted "Candy." The officer wrote that down and she thought his feeling toward her changed when he learned it was candy she took. After she began to cry quietly, the cop closed his mouth, closed his notebook and leaned back.

Though she felt terrified already, when he took out a pair of handcuffs and put them on her hands, Galina began to feel dizzy. The *Militsiya* man led her to his white car with the blue stripe. Everyone stared at Galina as he led her in handcuffs. She cried openly and held her arms in front of her. He put her in the back seat and drove them away. She rode in back, holding her arms out in front of her.

"Will this be your first time in jail?" the cop asked her as he drove.

Galina cried out loud but through her sobs she said, "I've never been in jail!"

"Oh, well, I'm sure you will like it very much," the cop said, picking at his teeth with a toothpick as he drove. "You do like *kasha*?"

Galina nodded enthusiastically in the backseat, trying not to look at the handcuffs as her short legs stood out straight in front of her. "I like it with cinnamon," she said and changed her mind about it and wished she had kept quiet.

"Won't get a lot of cinnamon in jail," said the cop with an offhand tone, as if he were stating a fact. Galina said nothing and felt her eyes overflowing with sad tears. She let them drop on to the handcuffs and felt a cold wind move through herself. She thought of her grandmother Ludmilla and how angry she would be at Galina. Already a criminal at 8 years old. A runaway and a thief who deserved what she got.

The cop stopped talking and drove over several smaller roads with low green trees and then they parked in a shady spot in front of a large wooden house. Galina's heart beat rapidly and she looked around. The wooden house seemed like a hospital but all the windows had crosswise bars and the ground around it was dirt and the grass was worn away except around the edges.

A tall fence surrounded the house and the cop got out of his car. He opened the back door and motioned for Galina to get out. Her posture was dominated by the heavy hinged pair of handcuffs she wore. She walked behind him inside the fence with a strand of barbed wire on top and wood that looked weather beaten. The cop stood in front of the door with Galina standing behind him, a step down, bearing the weight of the black cuffs tight around her wrists. The cop rapped three times with his knuckle.

"Vera," he called out in a sing-song voice. "My sunshine, I have a surprise for you." He rapped again another three times and after a long wait they heard a pair of heels clicking near the door and then the lock slid. Standing behind the door was a woman with high cheekbones, her hair in a tight bun, her mouth closed tightly and her hands gripped together, palm to palm.

"Vera, I have a present for you." With that the cop stepped aside and Galina saw a tall, stern, red-haired woman standing behind the wire grating. The door opened and Galina entered the place. Inside, the warmth, humidity and smell of urine hit her. The cop led her into the examination room tiled in white bricks floor to ceiling. Galina set on a worn wooden bench. The cop and Vera stepped into another room and left Galina alone with her handcuffs and her sadness.

Galina stood and waited, her face distorted by her tears, sadness and regret for her crime. Then, the police officer returned with Vera. The cop stood to the side while Vera bent over and put her face in front of Galina, so her red hair glowed like red-hot metal.

"Officer Kyatin told me of your crimes," she said to Galina and sealed up her lips after she did so. "You are a vicious girl and first shall be punished for your viciousness," Vera said.

Galina opened up her mouth wide and tried to explain how Murat Koof made her do it and that it wasn't her idea but she felt frightened. She started to say something but she did not know whether to talk about Astrakhan or her grandmother back in Chilkovo and what happened to her mother and that her mother had a sister Anastasia who lived somewhere in St. Petersburg, but then she didn't say anything.

Vera stood and turned to the cop. "Oleg, most likely," she said. The cop made an exaggerated frown and thanked her again before he took off the handcuffs and set Galina free. The cop walked to the door and Galina tried to walk out behind him.

"No," said the cop. "You stay here with Vera." Galina stomped and punched the air.

"No," Galina shrieked. "Let me go. I don't want to stay."

Out in the hallway came a pale-skinned, dark-haired man with deep creases along the sides of his cheeks. In the face of the cop and in Vera, Galina saw the eyes of people who went home and were nice to somebody. The cop, even as he brought her to the orphanage, betrayed a smile in the corners of his eyes, as if he knew Galina was in trouble but that she would be in no worse trouble after. But now in front of her stood a man without a smile, a man who looked like he did not care if she cried.

"Process her, Ivan," Vera said.

Vera and the cop left. Galina stood with her arms to her sides, in front of this man Ivan. Galina saw his eyes working over her, as his thick tongue slopped around in his mouth, organizing, arranging, pondering his thoughts as he jabbed his tongue first in one corner, then in another, brooding. Galina shivered and sucked her thumb tips in her mouth. They stood alone in the examination room. A large window streamed daylight into the room.

"Take off everything," Ivan said. "Now."

Galina rubbed her wrists and did as she was told. She stood naked in front of Ivan. Without smiling or changing the waxy expression on his face, Ivan connected a red hose to the faucet and turned on the cold water. He let the water run out of the hose a minute to let it get cold. Ivan ran his fingers through the stream of water and clenched his teeth, pulling in his cheeks at the creases. Then he turned and sprayed Galina in the face. After letting the full force run in her face, he tracked her mouth with the water as she hunched over coughing, to keep the force in her mouth.

After he had finished hosing her off, Galina stood and shivered. Then he threw her a raggedy t-shirt and sweatpants. He left the examination room and led Galina to the main day room. The walls were scraped down to the plaster around the corners. Sitting in a line by a small, glassed-in room sat several dozing kids, dressed in rags similar to hers but with extra scraps wrapped around them for warmth. The entire room felt freezing cold. The workers sat inside the glassed-in room. They talked and laughed and looked warm. Then as Galina found herself a spot on the floor to sit, she saw the director Vera put on a shawl and come out of the office.

A plump boy with a funny-shaped head squatted in the middle of the floor. He stuck out his left finger and then tried to pull off his own fingertip with his right hand. Repeating this motion, the boy cast a long fiber of drool from the corner of his mouth to the floor. Galina wanted to clean him up but she was afraid of touching anything. The boy repeated the word "*gorka*" over and over, which did not make sense because people only were supposed to say the word "bitter" when somebody had just gotten married. They were supposed to sweeten the bitterness with a kiss but nobody was around who was going to get kissed. The boy rocked back and forth on his bare feet as he pulled his own finger, "gorka". As director Vera walked by she said:

"Varik—be quiet," and she added a swift lash from a small whip that Galina had not noticed before. From then on, Galina kept track of Vera's whip. Varik rocked back and moaned from the lash, clutching his head. A lake of yellow came from the floor and Galina felt nauseous. The entire room and every inch of the orphanage smelled of pee. She saw that all the other kids in the room were disabled somehow. This made her feel terrible and abandoned as if her own Grandmother Ludmilla had just thrown her away because she was a wicked girl who deserved nothing better than dying in the gutter.

Galina started to cry and then she looked up and saw an older boy staring at her. His teeth hung over his lower lip. His greasy hair stood up in spikes. He stopped and stared at Galina in a way that made her nervous. She got up and walked down the hallway to the rooms there. The wood looked old, worn and rounded. She reached the last room on the right. It was full of kids laying in cribs, with no color or noise or light, just a thin gray blanket wrapped around contorted limbs that were pulled into painful-looking bent positions. In the next room four cribs were jammed in tightly. She could not see the legs or bodies of these kids because they lay in canvas sacks that were cinched up to their throats. These kids looked at her but made no attempt to roll over or react physically, other than rolling their eyes to look at her. Galina entered the room and walked up to one of the cribs where a little blond-haired girl with bulging eyes and a look of anxiety.

"Hello—my name is Galina."

The blond-haired girl moved her limbs inside the bag. The delay and sudden jerking movements of the girl reminded Galina of the way a lizard moved. The girl was trapped in the sack and inside her own body. It felt heartbreaking. It seemed to her the sack was too tight around the necks of the children. She reached into the crib through the bars and tried to untie the knot.

"*Nellz-yah*," barked a low voice behind her. It was the Russian word that said "No no". It was the favorite word of every grandmother. Galina looked and saw it was the buck-toothed boy with the greasy spiked hair. He was closer and she saw a thick coat of green on his teeth, a white layer of rot on his tongue. "If you untie the bag, Ivan will beat you," said the boy, his lips curiously immobile as he talked out of what seemed like a second inside mouth.

"I think she's choking," Galina said. "Shouldn't we get somebody?"

The boy grinned wider at the novelty of that. Galina looked away from his teeth. "You shouldn't be in the sack room," he said. "Didn't you know that?"

Galina felt concerned. The boy's expression changed into a pinched-brow expression of anger. His scummy grin was replaced by wild-animal anger. Galina felt trapped. To leave, she had to go past him. She stepped slowly out of the room and as she passed him, she felt a hot sting on her rump. He pinched her and squeezed hard as she passed him.

"Oww!" Galina cried and ran back to the day room. He followed her and his smile returned with his scummy teeth.

"That's is a warning," he said.

Galina ran to the other side of the day room, near Varik, who continued to yell "*Gorka*" but just to himself under his breath. Galina stayed away from the pinching boy, who was called Victor.

She tried to stay out of the way, not taking up a chair or provoking anybody into bothering her. But then every time she looked up she saw that Victor was staring at her with one of his hands down his pants, kneading something. He stopped when Ivan came out and handed him a bowl of cold kasha. On the side of her bowl she saw dried traces of a differently-colored soup. She angled the contents of her bowl away from the stain. She did not have a spoon. Everybody else took a metal spoon from their pockets but Galina didn't have one. So she drank her kasha, which made the cold grainy food go down easier as it tasted like workbook paper.

3.

Galina woke in the dark in her new bed. She pulled the thin blanket close under her chin. She looked into the blackness and saw nothing. The room had no windows at all and only a single *fortochka* window above the door. A pencil of light came under the door. She stared into the blackness and listened to

83

the blackness. Then, faintly, she heard someone in her room breathing. The sound was faint, like a dog slowly breathing with its mouth making an occasional whistle. She opened her eyes wide and opened her mind to hear every sound. Then she heard the floor creak from the other side of the room. Galina's heart beat and she was afraid; whoever stood there would know she was terrified.

Galina lay still with her hand on top of the bed sheet. She waited as long as she could and then she flung the bed covers off and ran for the door. Light streamed in from the space between the door and the frame. She moved her face near the opening, which was just wide enough. Then she saw something behind her coming forward. She screamed and hauled the heavy door open. A hairy arm blasted forward and slammed the door shut. Before the light went out, Galina saw the angry face of Victor. He stood next to her and his hands where on her.

"Don't touch me!" she yelled but nobody came. Victor pulled her down on the cold floor. She clawed to get away and felt his wet mouth on hers, touching her, wetting her skin and making it feel cold.

"Oh how horrible," Galina screamed. "Stop it. Let go of me—I want my mommy!" Victor laughed and she felt him root around with his wet scummy teeth all over her neck and ears. She tried to push him away but she was not strong enough. Galina screamed as loud as she could. "Help! Help me somebody, please." Nobody came. Then she yelled "Fire!" over and over until her door opened. Light flooded in around the form of Ivan, the head orderly. In the glare of the full light, Victor no longer smiled. He rolled back off of Galina, whose shirt was torn at the neck. Ivan stood in the doorway and exhaled loudly through his nose. The creases in his cheeks pulled in deeper in expression of his anger.

"*Sooka*," Ivan said. "Bitch."

Galina said nothing and she held the torn edges of her shirt together. Clicking footsteps came down the hall. Vera stood in her nightshirt, bleary eyed, her red hair up in a knot, carrying her hand whip. She saw Galina and Victor, cowering in the corner, and the first word Vera said was "Slut". She came in the room and moved near Galina, who pressed herself up against the corner. Then, suddenly, Vera raised her whip and lashed it back and forth against Galina dozens of times. Galina was cornered. The whip stung her skin and each lash left her with another strip of skin that stung.

"We take you in this house and you bring your slutting ways from the sewers here—*well*," Vera said and gave Galina a good, stinging shot with her whip. "We won't have any of that corruption here. Not while I am the rector." She walked past Galina and addressed Victor head on. "Go to your room," she said and Victor scurried away. Vera propped her hands on her hips. She looked

84

down at Galina, scowling.

"Get a sack," Vera ordered Ivan and he went instantly for it. He came back with a mildewy canvas drawstring sack.

Galina squealed and tried to run out of the room but Vera casually grabbed her hair and stopped her. Ivan lifted up Galina's feet and fed them into the open mouth of the sack.

"No!" Galina wailed, half from getting her hair pulled and half from terror at being put in a sack. But in an instant Galina became a prisoner and Ivan tightened the drawstring around Galina's throat so tight Galina felt she could not breathe. Vera smiled. She and Ivan lifted Galina back on her bed in the sack and tied her to a bedpost.

After Galina was securely tied down to her bed in the canvas sack, Vera sat down on the corner of Galina's bed and looked down on Galina, who felt scared and helpless. Vera looked down on Galina with disgust. Without warning, Vera slapped Galina's cheek hard.

Galina gasped in surprise and then wailed in pain. Vera silenced those tears with another slap to the face. Astonished, Galina flew into a rage in the sack but she could not escape. She felt in back it did contain a hole but it was strong and she could not tear the whole open. Every time Galina tussled against the sack, Vera administered another slap to Galina's battered face.

"Calm down!" Vera commanded.

"Let me out!" Galina shouted.

Ivan appeared in the doorway with a round basin and it scared Galina and she gasped right before the basin tilted and poured liters of cold water on Galina. She settled down immediately. Ivan smiled. He and Vera left the room. The lights went off. Galina lay in the wet sack, shivering, staring up at the ceiling in the dark. She rolled up into a ball in the sack and dragged it out of the puddle on her bed. She lay awake feeling like nobody in the world liked her, that she would spend the rest of her life in that sack, staring at the ceiling.

Then she heard a clicking sound nearby and she jumped away in the sack. She struggled anew to squeeze open the neck of the sack. Behind the noise of her own struggles, light streamed in the room as someone slipped in her room and shut the door.

"Let me go!" Galina shouted into the darkness. She settled down and directed all her attention to listening. Silence. Darkness. Then a squeak underfoot as some person standing in the darkness transferred their weight from one foot to another. Then, as her heart pounded, she smelled the breath of the person standing in complete darkness next to her bed. Then she felt a heavy hand, the hand of a man, arrive on her body. The hand felt its way around Galina's body through the sack.

"Stop!" Galina shouted. "Help! Help!"

In response, the hand went around the back of the sack and came in the whole. Galina screamed in the dark and kicked her legs but the hand had her and it roamed anywhere it pleased and she was not strong enough to push it way.

Galina endured this until the hand suddenly withdrew, and she heard footsteps in the hall. Then the door popped open and outlined in the light was Vera, in her night clothes, robe and cap, her eyes smarting from the bright light. Right behind her appeared Ivan instantly and not looking tired at all.

"What is all this screaming?" Vera said, now awake enough to be irritated.

"He was attacking me!" Galina said through her tears.

"You were dreaming, child," Vera said.

"No I wasn't," Galina said, pointing at Ivan from inside the sack. "That man, standing there, put his hand inside this bag—"

"Liar!" Vera said and slapped Galina's face. After the sting wore off, Galina saw a crowd gathered at her door, including Victor and Varik.

"You are nothing but trouble, young lady," Vera said.

Vera and Ivan closed in to Galina's bed. Ivan reached back and shut the door. Vera leaned over the bed. "No little street slut," Vera said in a voice that rose just over the line of being audible, "is going, while I am here, to pollute the minds and bodies of these boys. Now," she said with a vicious hiss in her voice as she leaned over to Galina, "get out."

"Now," Ivan said, leaning equally close. Ivan untied the sack from the bedpost and opened it so Galina could get out.

Overwhelmed, Galina held her breath and tried to press as close to the wall as possible. The both of them stood there with harsh frowns and crossed arms. Galina put on her shoes and walked slowly to the door. When she reached the hall, she saw every child in the orphanage awake at their doorway, watching Galina getting shown the door. Galina continued in her walk of shame to the door. Ivan accompanied her. The cold air slapped Galina's face and as she passed out of the orphanage back to the streets. She heard the creak of the closing door and the voice of Ivan, just before it slammed, saying "*Sooka.*"

4.

Galina walked back toward the area where she had first been caught helping Koof steal the candy bar. She stared down and avoided the eyes of people she met. She felt sad and unwanted and worthless and the feeling of sadness was so overwhelming she could not hold up the corners of her mouth. She found a stump and sat on it, thinking of stepping in front of an auto bus. She still felt terrified of being trapped in the sack.

After fifteen minutes of sitting and getting colder, she got up and headed back for the sewer where she had stayed. She found it and lifted the metal lid. As she descended the ladder, Galina was shocked to see bloody hand prints at several places along the ladder. She thought it looked like blood, brownish, like a blood drop on the floor when her brother Pavel got a nosebleed. Galina reached the bottom and it was empty. The same piles of clothing, papers but all the other kids were gone. Galina looked around and she saw no sign of the others but it was warm and she felt safe for the first time since she went with Koof to steal the candy bars.

Galina lay down and slept for awhile and she woke suddenly to the scraping sound of somebody removing the metal sewer lid. She lay quietly and covered herself with the pieces of clothing.

She heard voices talking as they came down the ladder and quickly she recognized the voice of Murat Koof with several other young children

"This place is warm and safe," Koof said. "Take any space you like, it's yours."

"Thank you, Mur-chik," said the voice of a young child. They reached the bottom and Galina saw from her corner it *was* Murat Koof and another homeless girl. She and Koof talked for a second and then the girl stopped talking and wheeled her gaze over to Galina, who thought she was hidden. Koof followed the girl's gaze and looked

"What the hell!" Koof said. "What are you doing here?"

Seeing that she was visible, Galina spoke. "They put me in a children's house, "Galina said. "It was horrible and..." Galina stopped as the vision of Victor and Ivan and Vera flashed through her mind.

"I never expected to see you again, Kitten," Koof said. "Never."

Galina had nothing to say.

Koof returned to the ladder and left.

Chapter VII

1.

JACK had never seen a human being angrier than Sarah.

"You *bloody* idiot," Sarah said, in her angriest Scottish brogue. "You've killed us. You have bloody *murdered* this newspaper."

As the newspaper's Managing Editor, it was Sarah's job to approve every story before it went in the paper, even though Alexander Ivanovich was the Editor. She had gone on holiday. Upon her return Sarah discovered that Jack Land, her Yank reporter, trained in a lackadaisical American J-school, had not run the pages she pasted up in advance. Instead, he swapped in a story of his own about bloody homeless children found dead in the sewers.

"You had a good thing going," Sarah said. "and you just threw it away." She looked moist eyed at Jack. Her face was puffy and hot. Jack made no motion because he knew she was remembering the few weeks when they dated.

Sarah stood by the editorial desk and rapped her knuckles on the top of her desk until they grew red and swollen. Her jaw hung slack, and her bruised hand trembled as it held the newspaper that had been printed with her name on the masthead. "It's a *disaster,*" she said. "And why *for fuck's sake* did you have to blame the Mafia for it?" She wanted to hit something and instead she slapped the wooden desk with her open palm and scattered papers in the air. Lena, the Culture Editor, ducked under the copy desk. "You bloody *bastard.* The *Militsiya* have not even blamed the mafia—who in hell made you the judge and jury?" She stalked around the newsroom, growling as she crumpled the newspaper in her fist.

"This *isn't* a joke. You can't slander the Russian Mafia," she said, shaking her hands next to her head. "This isn't St. Petersburg, Florida—it's St. Petersburg, *Russia.*" She went to the doorway and looked back. "I trusted you." She slammed the door. The glass window with the words NEVSKI NOVOSTI on it rattled near its shatter point. Jack sat at his desk, mute, staring at his paper, his pen held in the air over his notepad. The top of his head felt like it might pop off and explode. Her reaction made him angry and embarrassed by his own story which, now that he looked at it through her eyes, *was* poorly sourced.

Jack needed a feature story idea and the cash that came with it. He needed to make his rent and was desperate for story ideas. The Russian reporters knew the local gossip and always had lots of story ideas but Jack was on his own. An American living in St. Petersburg, desperate to hide that he was broke.

His monthly *Yedinaya* card was good for two more weeks. After that he was on foot in Russia in February. Still, no one—not even Sarah—would pity him. Every Russian assumed all but the most stupid Americans were wealthy. Jack knew his friend Thor could help. Thor would say: "I'll send you a plane ticket, Land-Man. Come home now. We'll set up up with a stripper I know who works on the South Side. Doesn't have a lot of teeth but she never lets that cramp her style."

Jack wasn't interested in going home. He started a new life in Russia. It gave him a chance to do-over a part of his life and fix it. He knew as well as any journalist that newspapers were evaporating. His only chance to stay in the field was some big stories that he could use to land his next job.

2.

When he moved to St. Petersburg, Jack had wangled himself a job at a Russian newspaper *Nevsky Novosti* by offering to do a story on abandoned babies. The idea came from a talkative woman he sat next to on the Air-Austria flight that flew him to Russia. She said life in Russia had become difficult—especially for pregnant women. After they delivered, many got out of bed and walked off without claiming their babies. They called them "refusal births."

Jack pledged to check out the story and Alexander I. Krasnie, son of a famous Soviet-era journalist, agreed. Jack took his interview kit including his tiny digital recorder and went down the wooden stairs. He took the Metro to the nearest maternity hospital on Lomonovskovo.

There he tried to interview a Kazak surgeon with a belly that stretched the button holes on the front of his white coat. The surgeon flatly denied that such a thing as a "refusal birth" occurred in Russia. His flat refusal prevented Jack from pursuing the story or finding the mothers. He decided that prostitution was the most plausible explanation of how sewer kids survived.

Using off-the-record interviews, Jack assembled a newspaper piece on the phenomenon of abandoned children who lived in the sewers. The story focused not only on the existence of the sewer children but also that the mafia used the children for prostitution, pornography and rape. Jack remembered the red-haired girl pulled from the sewer.

The newspaper was now under siege because of Jack's article. Thugs harassed Konstantin, the newspaper's tall delivery man with a bushy white mustache and a resemblance to Nikita Khrushchev. Sarah swore two young men followed her home.

"They were skinheads," she said. "They wore warm-up outfits—that's the Mafia uniform."

The article alleged that the Russian mob, or the "Thieves-in-Law" snatched up the homeless children as prostitutes or in porn.

Jack sat quietly in the newsroom, bracing himself to get fired, to be hungry and alone and unlikely to inspire anyone's charity. His leg pumped under his desk. Vasya Timofeyevich, the computer wizard with the handlebar mustache and the cheap *Belamor Kanal* cigarettes, muttered the word "*Kuz-yole.* Asshole" when Jack came in the newsroom in the morning.

Yelena, the reporter with long straight hair who hated to show her feelings, cried silently at her desk. A death threat hung over the head of their dear Editor, the irascible Alexander Ivanovich Krasnie, who insisted that his patronymic always be used. Each repetition of his father's name reminded him of his father Ivan Sergeivich Krasnie, a reporter famous during Soviet times. His father's memory drove Alexander Ivanovich to run the story on the sewer kids. Krasnie said the sources on the piece were iffy. Jack had turned it into a medium-length piece that alleged St. Petersburg's Tambov Syndicate had tapped into the resource embodied in the children who lived in the sewers. The only lead Jack had came from an off-the-cuff comment from a *Militsiya* officer who said he had noticed the Tambovs periodically rounded up the street children who lived in the sewer pipes around the Pioneerskaya Metro station.

3.

Natasha didn't like it when Sveta was there and she got angry and stormed off.

"She's helping me!" Jack said in hurried Russian. He had studied Russian for about three years. Russians always told him his accent was good but his Iowa sense of distrust made him also think the Russians were goofing on him, making his Russian an inside joke. In any case, Natasha herself had introduced Sveta to Jack. Now, Sveta slept on his couch.

Jack found out more about the orphans from Sveta, a teenager from the neighborhood who was an orphan. He never asked her whether or not her parents were dead. Sveta, 16, had slept on his couch a few nights. She formed the core of the "two" anonymous sources he quoted in his piece. Sveta said: "Everybody knows it's the mafia!" The main problem was the unsubstantiated allegation that the mafia did it.

Sveta said she had lived in the steam tunnels under St. Petersburg.

"It *easy*," was all she would say about the tunnels, exhausting her English vocabulary with those two words. After a few more days of prodding her to take him there, of declining to let her raid his fridge until she helped him get some interviews, he coaxed Sveta into agreeing to take Jack where the homeless lived. When she realized Jack would follow through, she stopped in mid sentence. With Jack standing between her and his fridge full of *sosiski*, Sveta pulled out a ragged scrap of paper and flattened it on the kitchen table. Using a nub of pencil from the same pocket, she dabbed it to her lips and began to scratch out a map.

"No no no," Jack said and stopped her. "You need to take me there *yourself.*" All traces of joy drained from Sveta's face and she said "*Ladna.* Okay" in her customary monotone way. She reached for the folded butcher paper bundle on the counter with 3 ½ links of *sosiski*, Russian hot dogs. Eating Russian hot dogs was always an adventure due to their lumpy texture and faint bouquet of rotting meat along with the still-good cartilage, lips and snout. That, wrapped in the most succulent intestine, comprised the *sosiski*. He gave her all he had on the promise that she agree to take Jack the next morning to the Pioneerskaya Metro station, where they would find a series of concrete cone-shaped manholes.

The next morning, Jack got up before Sveta. She lay in the dark on the couch under the smaller blue blanket that had come with the apartment when Jack rented it. From the way she lay, curled up in a ball with the blanket tucked in, Jack saw she was cold. It reminded him of his first few nights here in January checking on the Stalin-era radiator which, despite the appearance of warmth, could be the coldest thing in the room, a chunk of cold iron. Other times, the radiator would glow hot as a blast of steam rose from the steam pipe and prepped the room to fire pottery. The next day, Jack looked up the word for blanket, "*Odeyala*", in the dictionary. He spent 147 rubles on a blanket—about $32. Jack threw his own blanket off and walked past Sveta, sleeping with her head pulled in tight like a kitten straining to close its eyes harder in the daylight. Sveta was still waking up when Jack was at the door.

"Time to get up, Sveta." Playing the part of the kitten, Sveta rubbed her rounded fists into her eyes, spooling herself up to wakefulness.

"Good Morning," Jack said, translating his American customs into Russian. So, he said "Good Morning" to everybody. Russians hated being accosted with "Good Morning!", but Sveta knew she was still operating under the good graces afforded a welcome guest. She tolerated Jack's annoying American curtsey and countered with "What's for breakfast?"

"*After*," Jack said, pointing his finger at her coat and shoes. "Pioneerskaya Metro."

"Oy, *Bozha moi*," Sveta said, covering her eyes. "My God."

Sveta shrugged. She fished a butt out of her coat and held a lighter up to the cigarette. Jack stepped over and pushed Sveta's cigarette away from the burning flame.

"Downstairs." Sveta shrugged and said "Okay."

They hit the street together. Jack led her past an old woman wearing a scarf she rocked from side to side as she walked. The woman looked with alarm at Jack and then Sveta, imagining the worst, that Jack was a pederast. Such opinions were the greatest danger Jack faced in Russia. They could raise a stink that made some punk stab him. Then, nearer the entrance to the *Produkti* store, Jack and Sveta blended into the crowd.

They took the #10 tramway train to the Novocherkasskaya Metro station about ten minutes away. Payment was on the honor system with random agents who roamed the system to do spot checks and see if passengers had tickets with the tramway train's unique stamp. Blue sparks rained down as the tramway car rumbled down the track.

Jack led Sveta on and off the subway. They got off at Pioneerskaya Metro Station. On the street, cold winds blew across Prospekt Ispytateley. Across the street lay vast Udelny Park: filled with trees, shrubberies and homeless.

Sveta walked into the park without hesitation along a break in the foliage. They walked ten meters in. She led Jack in among a throng of dirty-faced kids. Several of them knew her. She continued deeper in the park over a grassy ridge. Sveta shouted to three young boys walking up the other side of the ravine.

"Boys, come here" she shouted, and squinted at them as she lit up another cigarette.

"What for?" shouted back a blond-haired boy, medium height in a muddy coat so big his hands disappeared.

"My friend here's a reporter. He will give you food if you let him ask you some questions," she said. "He's an *Amerikanets.*"

The taller boy spun around with vehemence and lifted the arm of his big coat to give Jack the finger.

"Fuck off, *Amerikanets*!"

After he told Jack Land where to go, the boy ran toward a line of trees and disappeared into the forest. Jack followed Sveta to the crest of a grassy rise. He looked down into the valley. A blanket of mist lay on the floor of the woods that stretched on without end to the horizon. As he followed Sveta into the forested area, the ground became green and uneven with a carpet of living green plants salted with brown, orange and yellow stalks of dry foliage. Sveta followed a slight trail in the dense undergrowth between tall white-barked birch trees, each ringed with black gashes. Jack listened to the hiss of the wind in the tops of the birches and then he heard a thumping noise coming from the Northwest. They walked on without speaking with Sveta leading him down an incline until they saw off to the right the shimmer of a lake. Jack stopped to look at the line of trees on the far side of the lake. There, he saw people walking along the shore. Sveta led him to the bottom of a wash. The two of them walked in the channel of a dry stream. After they had walked in the channel for two hundred yards, Sveta climbed up on the bank and there was a cement building buried in the ground. To Jack it looked like a World War II pillbox. Boys stood around the outside of it. They scattered when Sveta approached. One of the boys, smaller with dirty tangled hair, ran into the pillbox. Seconds later an older boy came out and smiled at Sveta.

"Svetka," the older boy said. His face was smudged with dark dirt stains. His hair was tangled into two main clumps that swung on either side of his head. Sveta walked toward him but the older boy didn't move.

"Who's *he*?" asked the boy.

"A friend," Sveta replied.

"What does he *want*," the boy asked.

"To get you some help," Jack piped up in Russian and the boy took a step back in reaction to the deepness of Jack's voice. "Why do you live here?"

The boy swung his gaze to Sveta. In reply, she lifted her eyebrows and wrapped her lower lip over her upper lip, telling him to stay calm. A second passed and a scowl washed over the boy's face.

"Fuck *off*," he said and turned away. Sveta glanced at Jack and then followed the boy. "*Fedya*." She lowered her voice so low that only Fedya could hear her.

"Fedyusha, I'm begging you. He's letting me stay there and he feeds me."

"And *bangs* you—"

"*N'yet*," she said. "He does *not*. No way."

"—or he *wants* to give you the meat," Fedya said and all the boys within earshot laughed in a motley collection of sounds that reflected the sorry state of the teeth exposed by the laughter. "Or maybe *we*'ll give the meat to you ourselves," Fedya said. The tone of the laughter changed and rose in menace.

"*Ladna.* Okay. Let's go," Sveta said to Jack. She walked back the way they came.

"Stop," Fedya said to their backs. "Why *should* I help you?"

Now, Sveta and Jack turned back.

"I'll feed you," Jack said, forgetting that he had used the Russian verb that meant feeding an animal. It was the equivalent of saying, in English, "Shall I tie on your feed bag?" Fedya and the others were hungry enough to fall on a feedbag of oats. Sveta gritted her teeth and looked Jack in the eyes.

"Aren't you forgetting me?" she said.

"No, you won't go hungry," Jack said and smiled.

94

"What have you got to eat?" Fedya said, after he shed the pose of an aggressive skeptic for that of famished kitten about to drop tongue into a bowl of fresh cream.

Jack smiled again at the quick results of his bribe.

"Bread, cheese."

A spontaneous groan of hunger rose from the boys who gathered around the pill box in the gloom of twilight. All tasted the saliva of deep hunger. They yearned to taste a crust of that bread and cheese as it crumbled on their tongues.

"Potatoes," Jack said.

A round of "*Oy*" shot around the group of hungry children. Jack looked at their faces and he saw they had each gone off to their thoughts, and their moving jaws showed they remembered the taste of a hot potato, flaking into chunks inside their mouths and under their tongues.

"Meat," Jack added after a long pause. If only Fedya would agree to answer the American's questions.

The shrill sound of the moaning boys distracted Fedya. "Quiet!" Fedya was upset at the chorus of voices that somehow implied that the feed was going to any other mouth but his.

"Okay then, "Fedya said. He threw away the rock he had been holding. "But not here. Come with me. There are too many ears here."

Neither Jack nor Sveta knew what Fedya meant but they followed him downhill. Trouping behind them were eleven additional boys, hoping to get a taste.

"And we don't need any company," Fedya said. One by one the followers turned back. Fedya led Jack and Sveta deep into the woods to a pond where the bushes were thick and there was only a single path in. They followed a path formed by tying back branches with pieces of twine. They turned a corner and encountered a cave made in the middle of a bramble by tying back every branch. The space was airy, full of light and safe. In the pocket of space lay a group of dirty-faced boys, huddling in one large shivering mass. The severity of the shivering of the boys alarmed Jack. It was way beyond the effect of cold. Jack cocked his left eyebrow and looked to Sveta with an expression that said "Does this seem weird to you?" Sveta turned to Jack and, smiling, she brought up her hand like she held a megaphone. Sveta sucked the air and rolled her eyes back. "They're glue sniffers," she said and wiped her brow from the heat.

Fedya talked to another boy who was the leader in this group. The other boys looked at Jack with ferocity on their faces like wild animals.

"Where are the adults?" Jack asked.

"We don't let them in," Fedya said. "There are enough places for them. Kids can't go there. We have to go to a *Detski Dom*." All the boys grimaced at the mention of an orphanage, which Jack knew was worse than living on the street. All of them were tense around Jack.

As Jack and Sveta waited, Fedya argued with the boy, whose name was Kural, which meant King. The arguing in Russian was too quick for Jack to follow. Sveta allowed the bickering to continue for a minute. Then she tapped Fedya on the shoulder and said "He has enough money to feed everybody, so cool it." At this intervention, Kural seemed to calm down but he retained a residual frown that showed his anger. Jack worried that he didn't have enough money to feed all of them.

"What's wrong with them?" Jack said, pointing out the boys who seemed to be shivering although it wasn't that cold.

"It's not your thing," Kural said, slashing the air with his finger. "You have not been here months caring for them." Kural side stepped the question of why they shivered. None of them would admit their shivering was caused by industrial glue that was similar to sniffing toluene or gasoline. The glue sniffer put a dollop of the clear aromatic glue in a plastic bag and inhaled the contents. It solved a variety of problems in street life such as the need to eat. The glue destroyed the part of the brain that told the boy to feel hungry. Sniffing glue relieved them from feeling cold, pain or sadness.

"Why is glue the answer?" Jack said and pulled out a pad of paper, to jot down the reply.

"Tell me why I don't stab you right now," Kural said. His smile revealed two brown rows of teeth and every other tooth gone. Seeing how Kural smiled, another smaller boy with a tight mouth smiled too. The boy's head was large and the lower half of his head was small.

"Tell me why not I kill you now?" Kural said, "No big people here!"

Sveta stayed at Jack's side with her palms up. As the argument erupted, Fedya took a step back in silent horror as his feast slipped away.

"Because I will feed you," Jack said. The persistent critic Kural said nothing for a moment.

"Hah, I'm not hungry," Kural said.

"We're all hungry," Fedya shouted. His anger erupted and he stuck his finger in Kural's face. Kural swung and punched Fedya next to his eye. Fedya's legs buckled and he dropped. A torrent of blood gushed out of his nose on to the front of his shirt as his head drifted back and smacked the ground. After the bounce, Fedya's body fell limp. Fedya made no movement except for the glimmering river of blood flowing out of his nose. It soaked a red delta on his dirty shirt. The life flowed out of him and cooled on his chest, which no longer rose or fell but just hung dead and still. The boys tweaking with the glue lifted out of their glue comas. They saw Fedya's stiff gray face. He was dead and would have to be moved.

"Are you a complete idiot?" Sveta shouted. She slapped Kural. He fell down and held up his hands to block her punches. Sveta did not relent and instead lay a series of flat punches against his blocking hands until Kural tried to alternate which of his hands was on top and, in the switch up, Sveta slipped in past and landed a thud against Kural's cheek which knocked him down unconscious.

It all happened so quickly that Jack had no time to react to the original blow against Fedya's temple or to the sudden gush of blood and the angry counter-attack from Sveta. She continued to beat on Kural until he fell and Sveta stood up, her hands foamy and bloody up to her knuckles. She stepped over the unconscious body of Kural to Fedya, her old friend *Fedyusha*. She caressed his cheek and closed his eyes. She sat on the ground and cried. Jack sat and so did all the other boys who still shivered. Jack thought "What a horrible situation these children live in." He noticed that the boys, though dirty, had spots of wetness on their arms and legs, where sores or a thorn snagged and punctured their skin.

Sitting next to Sveta, next to the head of Kural, whose face grew ashen, was a smaller boy with a tight little mouth and a head shaped like a light bulb. The boy lay on the ground, his hands palms up, in front of him. Sveta turned to the boy next to her. His little forehead wrinkled between the top of his head— where his hairline ended—and his eyes, which were located midway down the arc.

"Do you speak?" Sveta asked the boy.

"Yes," he said.

"How are you called?"

"Oksana," said the child, giving a girl's name.

Jack looked anew at the 'boy' and realized that the boy had the cheekbones and mouth of a girl.

"Where are you from, Oksana?" Sveta asked, and glanced at Jack with a pointed look at his reporter's tape recorder, which he started recording.

"Petersburg," said Oksana, getting her lips to make the Russian word that was the name of their city.

"How old are you?"

"*Nuh' zzz-nye*" the little girl struggled out, which she intended to mean 'I don't know' but instead she said something like 'duh nuh' which is unintelligible even to a native speaker. Russian, the language of Tolstoy, Dostoevsky and Pushkin, a language which was free for the taking, had been denied Oksana because she lived alone in the world on the street, hungry, cold with no one to talk to.

Jack felt a tightness in his chest at seeing her. Oksana had already missed so much development she would be, even if she were rescued right then and not allowed to decline farther, more of a talking monkey than an active member of the human race. Knowing that many people sat in restaurants eating steak and lobster while these kids lived in the cold in the forest with no protection from the worst nature and humanity had to offer. Jack's sense of outrage was fueled by his thought about what would have befallen him if he had been parent-less in St. Petersburg.

"Where is your mama?" Sveta asked, with a melody in her voice that said she had already decided to be angry at the mama and papa of Oksana. They had shared a night of sweaty pumping and grunting fueled by the vodka. Oksana's mother consumed more vodka before, during and after Oksana's pregnancy, giving her head its characteristic shape.

Oksana did not answer but her five-year-old hands rubbed each other like she held a bar of imaginary soap while in fact from the dark layer of dirt on her hands, the black jagged lines under her fingernails and the many red dark scratches, soap had not touched Oksana's hands in a long time.

Sveta repeated her question. She got down on one knee so her face was closer. Oksana did not move. She looked to the ground with a shiny bead of wetness welling in her lower eyelid, the only clean spot on her face.

Jack stood back and held his breath. He felt awful for inspiring this session of brutality by Sveta.

"Sveta," he said. "That's enough."

"Quiet," she said.

The pain evident in Oksana's face tore at Jack's heart. But he had no way to intervene. He froze in silence waiting for Oksana to answer. She had lived so long alone by herself with these others in the forest with nothing.

"Mama," blurted out the little voice, as tears rolled down from her eyes across her dirty cheeks.

Sveta, Jack and all the children who had lived around Oksana for so long held their breath, wishing the little girl would tell her secret.

"Mama held my hand," said Oksana, panting. "Then she let go and I was by myself and I stood, and I'm still here."

Jack had not written down a word. He thought of his own mother who worked so hard to make his life happy. This girl had only the other homeless children to help her.

"How have you lived?" Sveta asked, putting her hand on the shoulder of the girl. "How did you survive?"

Oksana's shoulders started to jerk up and down and she started to cry.

"I try," said Oksana, in her trembling voice, "but at night I'm so scared. I hear barking *sobaki* and I'm afraid." By now, Oksana cried and Sveta pulled her misshapen head close to her.

"Forgive me, Oksana," Sveta said and stroked the head of the tired, dirty little girl who had slept every night with her hands palm together under her head, as she lay on the dirt in the cold, looking up at the stars and hearing the crickets and howling dogs in the distance.

Jack cried. Through his blurry vision he saw the little hand of Oksana rising up to touch Sveta's arm. Widening his focus, Jack looked around and saw buried inside their dirty faces were the wet glistening eyes of the other lost ones.

"Why don't you all live in the city, in the sewers where it's warmer?" Jack asked. Hearing the depth of his voice as he spoke, a couple boys ran off in a crouch. From their exposed butts, Jack was surprised to see the ones that ran were naked, clothed in a thick layer of dirt and scab.

After a silent moment passed, voices shouted out from the crowd of boys gathered around *"N'yet,"* mixed in with a loud voice that blurted out "It's dangerous. Men come."

"Ah," Sveta said. "If you are scared of danger then why stay in the *forest*?" Sveta crossed her arms while she waited for an answer from the parliament of dirty faces, some with bulging eyes, bulbous foreheads or other obvious problems. These kids had been rejected by even the other homeless kids.

Jack hoped one of them could explain but he feared the articulate one lay alive but unconscious on the ground after the beating Sveta had inflicted.

"Well?" Sveta said, using the short tart Russian word that meant: *"Get on with it already."*

No murmur or answer.

"Are you wooden?" Sveta asked.

"I'm afraid to live in the city," Oksana said at last. "In the city, punks do bad, bad things to us."

"Like what?" Sveta barked. "What? What? What?" She spoke in the common Russian way of repeating a word three times in a row to stress the speaker's complete exasperation.

Oksana shied away like a beaten puppy, unable to face Sveta's rage.

"Bad things," Oksana said, at last. "Blood."

4.

Jack walked against the strong wind up to the card table where in the middle of a pile of flaked off dirt, were potatoes piled. The man's mutton chop cheek whiskers trembled in the breeze. His face was tanned from standing in the cold, snowy landscape every day and a wound on his cheek was just scabbing over.

"How many kilos of potatoes do you have?" Jack asked the man in Russian. the vendor stood still and Jack knew he was trying to place Jack's accented Russian in one of the Baltic states or perhaps Estonia.

Widening his eyebrows in consternation, the potato vendor glanced at his sack of potatoes, ones he himself planed and then dug out of the ground, dusted off and schlepped them to this market. The vendor lifted his gaze and he weighted his decision because these potatoes came from his own dacha and its plot of land around it that he cultivated to the limit.

"Thirty kilos," said the vendor. Jack looked over the pile and frowned out his own decision to spend his hard-earned money.

"How much for all of them?" Jack said.

The vendor did not react at first but then a smile inside spread and he took out a pad and a nib of pencil. Touching the nib to his tongue, he carved out some numerals. Elated, the vendor scratched an underline under a price. Jack got out his wallet and handed over the rubles. To the surprise of the vendor, Jack shouldered the potato sack and walked off before the vendor could protest.

As he walked down Metallistov Prospekt, Jack caught a lot of stares from his Russian neighbors who no doubt thought Jack had quit the newspaper business and gone into the potato selling racket.

He lugged the potatoes up the stairs and then he got out his long key like a metal fish spine. He thrust it in the lock, rotated and pulled back the key, engaging the gears that opened the outer steel door. The inner door opened up on its own.

Standing inside Jack's apartment, wearing an apron, was Sveta Kleptova, Jack's 19-year-old roommate. Sveta's eyelids drooped and she sighed hard.

"Thanks God you're home," she said. "I'm fucking exhausted."

Behind Sveta ran a small blond-haired girl whose eyes bulged out and whose teeth looked like sticks were piled in her mouth.

"*Priv'yet* Anya," Jack said and the girl darted back into his apartment.

"Why oh why did you have to promise to feed all these kids?" Sveta said.

"There was no other way," Jack said. He carried the potato sack to the kitchen and dropped it on the floor.

"This cannot continue," Sveta said, on the second day of feeding them. "That kid Ova? Remember him? Shit in the bathtub again. None of the kids will be able to take a bath until you get the tub usable again."

Jack wrinkled his lip in disgust.

"Vova!" Jack called out in his small apartment/soup kitchen.

A small eight-year-old boy stepped forward in shame, his eyebrows and mouth down turned. It was a small apartment and nine children had followed

Sveta back to Jack's apartment to get fed, as he promised.

"Vova—what happened?" Jack asked the boy. Vova said nothing. His facial expression just grew more tormented and agonized.

"Shouldn't you be cleaning up the tub?" Jack asked the boy.

Now, with steams of tears sliding in shiny lines down his cheeks, Vova shook his head side to side in the international symbol of defeat.

"No," Vova said.

"Then get busy," Jack said and rose from his crouch. He had not even gotten his coat off and hanging on its hook by the door before he had to start mediating squabbles. "And after the tub why don't you help me clean some potatoes?" Morose and glum, Vova nodded that he would do it.

"*Dobray vecher*, Captain Land," said Vika, the seven-year-old girl who came in with all the other kids from Udelny Park, for a feast. That was yesterday and Jack had not taken Natasha seriously when she said the kids would come eat and then stay for the three hots and a cot. Jack thought he could thread that camel through the eye of a needle and achieve the impossible, helping them without having it take over his life. Of course, Jack was wrong and Natasha was right. It reminded Jack of living in college around campus. Every small attic room or basement nook became a defacto hostel. Friends used to living on the margin between good manners and outrage found during college years they could sponge off their friends for about a month each.

Jack faced the issue himself with a potentially endless train of homeless kids. Vika always smiled and acted cheerful. Jack observed Vika, always smiling, looking like she expected to get a present. Even the gift of a potato or a slice of thick rye bread was the greatest thing in the world to her. Vika slept hidden under the desk.

"Good evening, Vika," Jack said, not knowing why she called him 'captain'. Maybe it was related to the Russian soldier's cap Jack had found buried in a closet. The cap probably came from a soldier who had visited the prostitute who lived in the apartment before Jack.

After they consumed two huge meals of potatoes, rye bread and link *sosiski*, most of the kids left but not Vika, Ksenia, Sashaka and of course Oksana.

Five year old Ksenia, who was mute, and who Jack and Sveta had only estimated to be five-years-old, had a knot on her forehead that looked to be well healed over. She was small and covered with black soot from having lived in old tires. Ksenia ate as much as the other kids from the soup kitchen he and Sveta carried out, to fulfill the rash promise Jack had made, to feed them all.

While he was handing out steaming hot potatoes and slabs of rye bread, Jack saw in the mirror attached to this armoire a pair of legs scrambling to climb under the couch. Jack was mildly surprised at the crude deceptions of a kid and also concerned about the complications he was inviting into his life. Ksenia inhabited the dusty space beneath the couch.

Sasha, a Kazak girl with a flat expression, straight black hair, silent and discrete in every movement, even as she resorted to sucking her thumb. Sashka did not hide. She sat on the floor holding her knees and Jack wrapped her in one of his coats.

The entire time Oksana was awake, she had her face buried in the crust of a brown slab of bread, crumbs sticking to her cheeks.

Sveta led the kids to Jack' apartment and when they arrived, Jack had in the Russian fashion removed the inside door and turned it into a long buffet table on two seat backs. Steaming pans of cooked potatoes, huge amounts of smoking, natural casing *sosiski*, bread and the *coup de grâce*, cheese.

5.

Jack and Sveta considered their soup kitchen a success. Eventually, each of the kids ate as much as they wanted, took a bath, washed their clothes and left.

Udelny forest left Jack in a foul mood. As if the lives of the homeless kids were not bad enough, there were always other, stronger people willing to exploit them, like what he and everybody saw from his balcony. The mafia.

That building on 56 Zhukovskovo Street lay like a sliver under his skin. He wanted to know what was happening inside that building. Jack looked at the street side of the building and it looked like a hotel but there was no sign or identification other than the address.

Jack called up Andrei at work. He reached Andrei through the department secretary since Andrei was only a Pro-Rector, not a full Rector and so he did not have his own phone.

"Andrei. I've been thinking about 56 Zhukovskovo," Jack said.

"Still? Jack—do you have a death wish or what?"

"I'm wondering what became of those kids," Jack said. "What are they doing with them?"

"Take my advice, Jack. Grab one of our Russian girls and go back to your Midwest where it's safe. Get out while you can. It's not safe here, even for a Russian. Go!"

"Not my style," Jack said. "I'm staying."

"I don't see why any of this is your problem," Andrei said. "Your problem is finding Russian pussy."

"No, it *is* my problem," Jack said, showing his rage. "The moment I had to stare at a dead kid's face, it became my problem. The first time I saw kids being kidnapped right in front of me, it became my problem."

Finally, Jack said, "Where can I find the building plans for 56 Zhukovskovo Street, Andrei? I'm going to get inside that building and get those damned kids out."

Andrei exhaled deeply through his nose. "At the Admiralty. Department of Buildings for the Oblast," Andrei said. "But they won't make it easy."

6.

Jack got off the Metro downtown. He still had a long way to go to the Admiralty, where the records were. He got off on Gostiny Dvor and walked the rest of the way there on the wide sidewalks as the Russian-chattering people on the sidewalk kept him aware of tiny fragments of their lives. At the end of his walk, the Admiralty stood on his left, its white columns and orange color bright against the snow. To his right, stood the Hermitage Winter Palace and in front of that, in the midst of a vast courtyard, the Alexander Column, a tall monument to the Tzar who defeated Napoleon. Jack wound around the Admiralty until he found the way in. He walked down the long corridors, ending in a single window and then a grid, cryptically describing the locations of the various departments. Jack stood in the hall and absorbed the signs before he ventured farther. Irritated clerks told him to go somewhere else.

"Where, exactly, can I get a building plan?" Jack said.

"God knows," an old lady clerk said, slapping the air with her hand. "Who are you to make such questions?"

Jack held up his press pass with his face and the word "Journalist" along with the palm-sized tape recorder he carried with him at all times.

"I'm not giving interviews," the clerk said, agitated.

"So you won't tell me where this information can be got—or is Russia too *primitive*" (a word offensive to all Russians) "to keep records of the buildings that fill its second city?" The clerk glared at Jack and took out a square of brown wrapping paper. She smoothed it and wrote down leg-by-leg directions to get to the office.

"*Spacibo*," Jack said and took the brown note.

"Go to—" she said and Jack was in motion, following her directions to a building on the other side of the Admiralty. He had to step back outside to get there. Then he found himself at a glass door at the end of a hallway. The swinging doors parted and Jack stood at the counter covered with stacks and stacks of paper. He began to speak but a man with a thin mustache, baggy clothes and stringy greased back hair pointed him to a side desk with forms laying in a pile. Jack put down the address of the building. The building was wide and so he feared he would not get the rear of the building where the mafia were.

He finished the form and handed it to the man, who in turn handed it back with an irritated triple-tap on a question: "Reason for ask."

"Gazeta," Jack said and the man nodded, frowning.

In twenty minutes, the man returned with a long cardboard tube. He showed Jack inside and himself spread out the meter-wide architectural drawings for a hotel built decades earlier. Facing Zhukovskovo Street stood a hotel, which had been called the "Rus". It had a large number of suites between the street and the back courtyard but the back was devoted to a huge kitchen and the basement below that had been built as a wine cellar with wooden shelves like stacks in a library.

Most curiously, running through every floor from the kitchen on the first floor to the basement, all the way to the roof where a small Russian-onion-dome like cupola stood as the pulley for a dumbwaiter. As soon as he saw the dumbwaiter, Jack thought he could use it. He looked over his shoulder and saw the librarian had gone off to other business. Jack stood and put on his coat.

"Thank you," Jack said.

7.

Jack answered the knock on his door in the traditional way and then without actually hearing the answer, he opened the door, expecting it to be either Natasha with her sleepy eyes or she and Zhanna, the better looking one who Jack had never even got to first base with.

Instead, it was Andrei Brezhukov with his professorially black-rimmed glasses.

"Come on in," Jack said. "For the record, I'm all out of Jack Daniels."

Andrei did not smile as he walked in. He took off his coat in Jack's living room, the one with his laptop sitting on his desk with papers and interview notes scattered around that.

Andrei held up a copy of Jack's newspaper, *Nevski Novosti*.

"What in the hell," Andrei said and his voice trailed off but an angry frown stayed.

Jack looked away in shame and anger at himself.

"I know, it was fucking shallow," Jack said. "I just was on deadline."

"Sewer prostitutes?" Andrei said, quoting the headline that Jack himself had chosen. "*Bleen*, Jack," Andrei said, using the most potent equivalent for 'fuck'.

"What I wrote was true—it was just…superficial." Jack said, and instantly wished he hadn't said so.

"So, that's how they sell newspapers in America," Andrei said, inciting his first smile since he had arrived. Andrei took out one of his Belamors and lit it up in Jack's room, not feeling obliged to go out on the balcony which was cold. He considered Jack's standing so reduced by the lack of reporting on the piece.

"I just can't waltz into their headquarters, knock on their door and say I want to interview the big boss about what they are doing to the homeless kids."

Andrei attended himself to the task of extracting as much harsh unfiltered tobacco smoke from the cheap pinch of tobacco in the Belamor. He did not feel any more need to humiliate Jack and was evidently savoring the effects of his words.

"They're like cockroaches," Andrei said, spitting a thread of tobacco. "They hide in the daytime and come out in the dark. There's no way to drive them out."

Jack agreed. Every crack, every corner offered a hiding place. Jack had been lucky seeing the mafia at work from his own window.

"We need to spray some roach killer in their lair," Jack said.

8.

Ninety minutes later, Jack and Andrei entered the same parking lot they had last seen when Jack ran for his life to the subway. They saw no other cars and so they continued forward until they reached the gap between the two buildings that allowed them to see the back of the mafia lair at 56 Zhukovskovo Street. They saw lights on in the second floor of the building and there, just as Andrei had remembered it and as it appeared in the plans, the cupola on top of the roof.

Risking everything, they drove past the raised concrete stairs and the truck trailer parked next to it.

As they passed the front Jack said:

"There—see? A fire hydrant and it points parallel to the building.

"I don't know, Jack. Seems pretty dangerous for a professor of Meteorology to pull off."

"We do it late," Jack said.

"I don't know," Andrei said. "It sounds like a stupid idea." Andrei gunned it and they circled around and left the back parking lot without having been seen.

9.

At 4:45 the next morning, Andrei and Jack reappeared in the same parking lot but with their lights turned off. Both were dressed in black. Andrei drove but he kept glancing over at Jack in irritation.

"Oh, Jack," Andrei said, unhappy with the charcoal that Jack had gotten from the walls of his oven and smeared on his face. Andrei immediately complained that Jack's makeup was unnecessarily theatrical and that with it he was only succeeding in getting dirty charcoal all over Andrei's fabric upholstery.

"I'll pay to get it cleaned," Jack said, knowing full well he would not follow through. The parking lot behind the mafia office was full of cars, all parked. There were no lights on in the windows above the cars.

"Katya would kill me if she knew what I was doing," Andrei said.

"You're helping to expose a travesty," Jack said. "Remember: one long flash is 'go'. Two short flashes 'no go'," Jack said.

"I must be crazy," Andrei said. Jack looked at him a second longer and then he got out of the car and ducked along the building. Andrei drove away and Jack climbed on top of the truck trailer parked next to the building, using a ladder he and Andrei had both seen. Silently, so that none of his footsteps caused a clanging noise, Jack climbed up the height of a one-story building by getting on top of the trailer. Jack lay flat on the roof of the trailer and stayed near the edge as it bowed in the middle from his weight. He stared at the vicinity and saw the distant lights of a street lamp.

Along the near edge of the trailer, Jack walked until he came even with the drain pipe. He placed the tip of his sneaker on a bracket holding the drain pipe and then climbed up the pipe. The moment his entire weight hung from the drain, it groaned and lowered a half inch. Jack held still and then when he was certain it was not going anywhere, he continued bracket by bracket up the side of the second floor until he was able to grip the gutter and then flat handed his way over the edge. The gutter held his weight. Jack lay flat on the asphalt roof. His heart pounded. He saw the cupola at the top. From his vantage point, he saw the other adjoining rooftops. The tops of the buildings were like a long adjoining surface. Jack walked hand to knee like an alligator until he was at the top, level with the cupola. It perched at the very top of the v-shaped roof, about three

106

yards wide.

Andrei said every cupola had a door so the roof could be accessed. Jack worked his way around the cupola until he found the door. It opened freely. Inside the cupola he found it thickly coated with paint, dust and pigeon droppings. Laying off to the side was a broken dumbwaiter pulley, laying off to the side with its shaft bent and covered in layers of dust and cobwebs.

A new pulley wheel hung in place and a dusty brown thumb-sized rope disappeared down the shaft. Jack now understood he was committed. He pulled out his flashlight and went back outside. He flashed it long on Andrei's car. Andrei quickly got out of his car.

Jack reeled up the dumbwaiter and pulled the dusty rope until he was able to pull the dumbwaiter out of the shaft. He looked down and saw the shaft went down the entire height of the building.

Jack now waited until he heard water splashing from a high-pressure spray. Andrei had come through—his job was to open the fire hydrant then run away with the coupling, making it impossible to turn off, as water flooded the mafia's building, and flowed in between the wooden slats into the basement. Jack hung just inside the cupola but looking outside he saw water streamed out. A lake of water began to fill the parking lot. The, the streetlights flickered, sparks flew from a transformer on a utility pole and the whole area went into a black out. Somewhere inside the building, an alarm sounded. Jack climbed silently step-by-step down the dumbwaiter shaft. As he passed the second floor, he heard muffled voices and footsteps on the other side of the wall. He continued down to the basement he noticed that all the floor-openings had been sealed off. His heart beat like a jack hammer.

Jack moved down into the basement, not with his camera and reporter's notebook but with a crowbar and his own knowledge and ability to control his body that he had learned back in Iowa, living and working on a farm, with its corn cribs and the explosive danger of a 2,000-pound steer on the rampage because it didn't want to go down the chute. Jack knew from those summers on the farm and from his ability to make his own way in a Russian city where everybody but him was a native, that he could do this. Jack also grew up with his grandmother in a way that involved lots of time to himself. Jack did not join the National Guard because of his asthma but he did run the 200yard dash and pole vaulted. Then, he studied Tae Kwon Do for years.

As Jack moved, hand by dusty hand, slicing through cobwebs in the darkness, he listened to the occupants of the building he was invading wake up and yell as the water from the fire hydrant began to fill the basement. From the sound of the water Jack knew he was just a dozen feet above the basement floor. He heard screams, and realized it was the kids. Though everything was pitch black, the sounds of the screams and the water below drew him down. At the bottom, he saw light reflecting off the waves of the water accumulating in the basement.

Jack stopped at the floor of the dumbwaiter and he had to jump up and land with his knees locked before the boards shattered and he plummeted into water with a huge splash. Floating on the surface were wooden crates, each topped with live, trapped children, bobbing like otters with only their wet heads above the water.

The trapped children screamed: "Let us go!" Jack grabbed the nearest floating crate, pulled the door off its hinges and fished out the kid. A wet, shivering boy with mud on his face looked up at Jack as his friendly hand took the boy out. The boy's look of gratitude emboldened Jack. He fed the boy's reaching arms up to the dumbwaiter chute.

"Climb to the top but wait for me at the top," Jack said, not having any plan at all what to do once he got them to climb out. Jack grabbed a second corner-floating crate and cracked it open. He pulled out the exhausted girl from inside, all of about 10 years old. Then Jack looked above him and he lurched back in horror. A man with wet hairy cheeks cowered above the water level but he did not react to Jack cracking open every cage and feeding every single kid up the chute. Then, he himself went back up. As he moved upwards, he saw the tangle of climbing children above him and all the kids seemed to know that being quiet was now important.

Jack reached the top and once the girl right above him slipped but she landed neatly on his shoulders and Jack just kept on going up. At the top, he glimpsed a circle of faces in the dark cupola. Then, the last light went out and the entire block plunged into darkness.

Jack watched the tail lights of two cars drive away. He looked at the parking lot and thought it was clear enough for him to lead the kids on the roof and let them jump to the top of the trailer. When two of the six he released were across, the first found the ladder and those two were gone.

"Hey!" came a voice from below him. A head stuck out the window and stared up at Jack. It was the rat-faced man from the subway.

He recognized Jack instantly and ducked back in the building. Jack jumped down to the now-dented trailer top and then we went down two rungs of the ladder on the back of the trailer before he jumped. As he ran, he glanced around and saw not a single kid—they all ran away. Jack ran and again felt scared, wanting to kick himself for the audacity and stupidity of the whole thing. It was another invitation to die. How dare he risk his life.

In an eerie replay of the situation he had been in before, Jack ran from the lair of the mafia toward the Nevski Prospekt Metro station. It was full of people and all he could do was get in line at the top of the escalator. The rat-faced man arrived, winded, one hand hidden in his coat—obviously carrying a gun. Jack looked the man in the eyes, which sat in deep circles of darker color, like the skin around an anus, and the rat-faced man squinted. Jack's heart pounded. He thought whether to run or stand and if he was about to get shot in the face.

Jack stared at the mafia man in his gold warm-up jacket with blue piping along the shoulders. His face told Jack the man was comfortable killing people.

The rat-faced man smiled and scratched the inside of his nose.

Jack felt winded and his temple pounded. Then, suddenly, he reached into his trouser pocket and pulled out his reporter's tape recorder. He turned it on so the red light shone.

Jack held the palm-sized tape recorder to his mouth and said, in Russian:

"He's in the station. Come and grab him!"

The smile dropped from the eyes of the rat-faced man. All that remained were the dark circles. The man looked over his shoulder and then back at Jack. Then he ran away. Jack breathed again. After he caught his breath, he knew he would have a great email to send his friend Thor in Chicago.

Chapter VIII

1.

CARRYING a flashlight in the dark room, Szlotov paced back and forth in the kitchen at the front of their building. In the kitchen, along the walls, stood his entire crew. The only man sitting, his long hair wet and his eyes big like a dog that has shit on the carpet, was Dr. Mansoor Moosorovic, hunched over and hugging himself.

"And you did nothing, yourself, to stop this man from stealing the product that our men worked so hard to gather from every shit sewer this side of the Fontanka?"

The basement remained full of water. Szlotov knew it would take at least a day for the Master to come and pump it out.

"Damn plumbers!"

The electrical system had been completely shorted. The fire hydrant was obviously a malicious act but the question was by whom? His first thought was to blame Druzhnev but the story the Doctor told, of some tall non-Russian man who appeared in the basement and opened the cages, was disturbing in the extreme. It could mean an FSB agent or worse—American FBI.

"The water," the Doctor said, reaching up to Szlotov with his palms upturned. "Swim I cannot."

"Vasya," Szlotov said. "Fyodor mentioned that you saw somebody too—FSB?"

"I…Vladimir Vladimirovich…did not see the man that closely. I agree he did not look Russian. But I got only a glimpse of him," Vasya said. Everyone stared at Vasya, as no one was used to him talking so much.

The front door opened and Sergei entered, carrying a small newspaper.

"We have bigger problems," Sergei said.

Chapter IX

1.

GALINA Yosheva opened her eyes. Her cheek pressed against the concrete. The ground felt as wet and cold as the deep earth. She lay on a slab of concrete three meters underground. Meter-wide pipes carried hot water from the central heating plant for this district in the Pioneerskaya Metro region. Galina pushed her knees away from her chest. Her body felt numb where it had touched the cold ground. She cringed, clutching her stomach. A Russian superstition damned any woman who allowed her womb to touch the ground to being barren, childless and having the seed of life extracted from her. Because Galina always lay on her side and never allowed herself to even roll over her womb, she hoped that one day she might have her own child who she could protect and keep warm forever.

She stretched her sore back, and looked at the pipe next to her. A boy named Vadim with black hair and big ears lay still on his back on the pipe. His body had the slackness of one who slept well and forgot for an hour that he lived in a steam sewer and ate out of garbage cans.

"*Kuz-yole*," she said. The spot on the warm pipe next to Vadim had been empty all night. The night before, Vadim ordered her not to take the spot as he expected Ivan to return. Certainly Ivan—who went around the city collecting glass bottles for half of a ruble (not enough for a normal Russian person to bend over and pick up in the mud) deserved the spot.

"Asshole," she said at Vadim. She went to the ladder. She should have slept on the warm pipe. The tunnel stank from boys who pooped on the sides of the steam pipe instead of going outside. When a boy died in the tunnels, the air stank so bad that they could not return to the tunnel for months until the sewer workers discovered the body and carried it away. If that didn't happen, then eventually the rats ate the body down to bones and bones don't smell so bad. It took a few months for the death smell to fade.

She had tried to feed little Georgi before he died. She tried to get him a potato. Georgi was a timid boy who never left the steam sewer to look for food. Instead, he clutched a small yellow bucket for no reason other than it gave him something to hold on to for security as he re-lived the scenes of cruelty and violence his little eyes had endured. Galina found an apple core to feed Georgi, the four-year-old boy with dark straight hair, thin lips and a concerned look in his eyes. Georgi's eyes expected brutality and so he didn't move to pee or poop or eat. That was before he died. Galina abandoned his body, still clutching his yellow bucket. After that, they all found new sewers to live in and the group of kids she knew vanished and new ones came.

Now, she lived in a tunnel inhabited by mean boys who tried to pull her pants down.

She went up the metal ladder to the surface. She poked her head up in the manhole, in the middle of an untouched green, flat soccer field. Air flooded her nostrils. She felt alive and starving. She needed to eat but it was important not to be caught going right for the trash. She did not want to be beaten by the officers of the *Militsiya* for eating trash. She could not decide which was worse: the *Militsiya* or the older street boys.

Last time, the older boys let her go. They already had Larisa. That time, Galina had pulled up her pants and scrambled away. A pack of boys gathered around Larisa and dragged her down. Boys from all around the alley rushed in to get a little while they held her down. The distraction allowed Galina to scramble backwards and run away from her friend Larisa, lost under the jabbing and pulling of so many street creatures. The men from all around ran to the spot where fourteen-year-old Larisa lay at the bottom of it all. Galina ran. She abandoned her friend to the mercy of homeless glue sniffers and sewer urchins.

Galina ran behind the building; there, she met several other men tearing at the clothes of another street girl, exposing her breasts, as she lay unconscious on the ground, her head to the side, her arms flopping.

Galina's foot snagged a rock as she tiptoed past. The men looked up. Galina tore off at top speed. A man ran after her. She shrieked and whimpered as she ran. Several boys pounded the earth behind her. She ran for the corner and hoped to bank right before they caught her. Galina felt tears wet on her cheeks. The sounds of multiple footfalls slammed the earth behind her. The sound made a roar. At her earliest moment, Galina banked hard to the right and deflected herself to the side as two boys jumped. They missed her, and at the corner, rolled into a heap of dust and denim. All but one of the boys landed in the pile. The lone boy who dodged it sped around the corner and chased Galina with redoubled rage.

She pumped her arms and breathed in a confused pant, running out of control, just letting her legs propel her away from her lone pursuer. She reached the public market and began to slow down. The boy followed her a little way into the public area and then muttered "*Piz-dets* cunt" and turned back.

She jogged until no more footsteps were behind her. She slowed to a trot and then stopped, hunched over, panting in the center of the outdoor bazaar. She scanned the buildings on the horizon. Galina looked for movement, for a sign that the boys waited at the edge of the market or behind the subway station. Nothing caught her attention but she still jogged on another few minutes until she was far away from Pioneerskaya Metro station.

A row of kiosks stood beside a busy intersection. She smelled the aroma of lamb's meat. A cylinder of lamb and goat rotated on a pike dripping juice over flames hovering at the base of the coals. She smelled the meat and was lifted into the air. The owner of the kiosk took a 5-ruble note from a fat woman with a yellow scarf in her hair and handed her the *shaverma*, a lamb-filled flat bread wrapped in paper. Since it was nothing more than a juicy pile of shaved lamb's meat, piled inside a thin paper wrapper. a *shaverma* was in danger of splitting in the middle where the meat was piled and spilling on the ground.

Galina watched the lady, a fat woman with saddlebags, brown hair pulled back in a bun and wrapped in her yellow scarf. As the woman moved from the kiosk engrossed in her *shaverma*, the woman moved forward with clumsy, distracted footsteps. Galina darted behind her and jammed her thumb up the woman's butt.

The woman, white yogurt and cucumber sauce running down her chin, jerked into a spread-eagle position. Her arms jerked upwards and the *shaverma* rose straight up in the air and, as it fell, air spread the stack of meat. The *shaverma* in its white wrapper hung in the air with a slight rotation. Then it fell and Galina got under it and cupped her hands below the meat pile. She caught the majority of it as she ran by. She jammed it in her mouth and dashed across the market, jamming the meat in her mouth. She heard behind her the loud screaming of the woman, followed by the low, ethnic shouts of the kiosk owners.

Scarfing down the meat, Galina felt a pile land in her stomach. She ran and felt overfull from the meat. She went behind a brick building and lay down to sleep behind some boxes of trash.

Chapter X

1.

AFTER Jack escaped from 56 Zhukovskovo Street and from the mafia killer only by his wits, he collapsed on the subway platform in horror at the risk he had taken. He felt lucky—foolishly lucky—and glad to be alive. His foolhardy entrance into the mafia's building only freed the kids to go back and be homeless.

Jack felt disgusted at himself in all regards. The only article he published on the topic was sourced only by a sewer worker. He had accepted the jack-ass opinion of the sewer man, who told him the dead children were mafia prostitutes. A ridiculous explanation. It explained nothing. It didn't explain why the kids were killed. Why would anybody want to kill homeless kids? Who could do that to kids who lived in the sewers?

Remorse over his 'sewer prostitute' article kept him up at night. He had blown his chance. Street lamps outside his window shone through the green drapes and bathed the apartment in a green glow. The cold apartment made Jack check every window by moving his nose along the seam, waiting to feel a stream of cold air. He ate three *sosiskis* and some white pill-shaped bread called a *baton*. He finished a bottle of Baltika *4* beer. Everything argued for sleep but Jack felt welling in him a sadness deep enough to cloud his vision.

He thought over the path he followed to reach this point. Learning Russian back in Iowa, saving money for the trip, getting his apartment in St. Petersburg, freelancing for two papers, hustling through the cold Russian wind to get interviews whose nuances might take repeated listenings to glean. Then his luck in getting hired by *Neva News*. He had written a shit piece about homeless kids being forced to become sewer prostitutes, when there was a real, great story behind the schlock. Jack had added only one other source, the official source, who said: "It was not the fault of the Acting Director of Public Health," that so many children had been found in the trash gang-raped and stabbed to death.

As Jack watched the aftermath of the scandal, he couldn't escape the conclusion that Sarah was using his mistake to keep him under control. Sarah kept mentioning the "Sewer Hookers" story as the sort of American tabloid tripe the paper would never again publish.

"Not on my watch," she said, lit from below by her computer screen.

Jack kept researching in the hope he could do a crack investigative piece on it but Sarah Hughes kept watch on him by the second. She knew Jack wanted to soften up the chief to ease the old Soviet from the Gulag to the

117

modern world. For that, Jack needed to get some terrific interviews, some bloodthirsty Q&As where he broke his source down to tears, weeping over the scab of a bad memory he had ripped off. Jack knew he needed to shake up these kids so they came forward with strong emotions that would help him tell their stories. The key to his plan was Sveta but she had been avoiding him after what happened in Udelny forest.

"Are you happy living in the sewers?" Jack tried to ask a teenage girl digging in a trash can. She hesitated a moment and then burst into tears. She rattled off shrieks of phrase that contained snippets of horrifying memories of beatings and rapes she had endured. Then the girl ran off crying, before Jack could give her some money for food.

He tried to go interview the kids alone but they ran.

Back in the office, Jack worked with the material he had and tried to fashion a great piece. Every time he looked up he met Sarah's eyes. For the second day in a row, Jack found an excuse to borrow Krasnie's big dictionary. When he brought the book back, he said, "By the way," to Alexander I. Krasnie, but then Sarah came racing down the hall and slid to a stop outside Krasnie's office.

"Yes, Sarah?" Krasnie asked, expecting something. Sarah put her hands in her pockets and kicked the floor without speaking. "The *dictionary*—but I will wait."

"Nonsense," said Krasnie, a gentleman of the old school. "First comes woman." Jack stepped aside and Sarah stepped in to use the dictionary on Krasnie's desk and Krasnie watched her.

Sarah asked for paper and a pencil. She thumbed through the pages and stopped on a word. After she had copied the word on to the paper, Krasnie called out: "Shil*l*elagh Stick? Why are we putting word *shillelagh* in our newspaper? To please the Irish tourists?"

Jack enjoyed the pained tone in Sarah's voice as she stumbled to explain why she needed to use just that word.

"Fine then," Sarah said. "I'll leave it out." She exited Krasnie's office, flashed a glare at Jack and headed across the hall to the newsroom.

As Krasnie chuckled, Jack dropped in the wooden chair along the window. Whenever anyone sat there, positioned to look out at the sunset, it caused a shift in Krasnie's outlook. He became more of the late middle-aged man with a son working on TV in Moscow who liked to down a few Baltika 4 beers in his office after everyone had gone home. He became less the gruff editor and more of the journalist who pulled his way along during Soviet times as a reporter, one who had loved to fight against power. If he pitched the story as the weak against power, he could make Krasnie run a hard-hitting story on the whole deal.

But, every time Jack took a seat in the wooden chair and looked out using his story voice, all hushed and lyrical, Sarah scrambled into the room and monitored the conversation with her arms crossed, shaking her head: "No more 'Sewer Prostitutes.'"

2.

It was dark when Jack left the paper. He wandered home in the gloomy St. Petersburg night. The temperature dropped. His and other footsteps quickened like those lost on a cold Northern night.

Jack headed for the stairway down to the Metro station, with the stream of home-going folk, but by chance his eye rolled over the word "Pioneerskaya". He changed course and decided not to go home. Instead, he walked against the flow of traffic. He felt like he walked at the behest of a thousand tiny strands of impulse, pulling him forward to the stairs that led to Line 2, the Blue Line, where he didn't know anybody, didn't have any friends and would be going into hostile territory. Instead of going to the Yellow Line where he knew people, Jack went to the Blue.

On the Blue Line he waited for the train and got on. On the far side of the crowd stood a striking young woman. He had never seen her before. She was pretty. Her curves had a strange effect on him, making all the skin on his body tingle. Jack looked at her. He wanted to talk to her. He did not want to go foraging for homeless children to annoy by asking a lot of questions. Riding the rocking Metro train on the Blue 2nd Line, he found himself staring at the girl, who looked in her early twenties. Her arm hung from the chrome bar overhead. Paralyzed by temptation, Jack held his breath. He contemplated the outcome of following her as she left the train at *Chernaya Rechka*, the next stop. He thought of following her up the stairs and then going past her on the escalator and dropping his glove at the moment when he got in front of her, giving him an excuse to turn and look into her beautiful eyes. At that instant, she would fall in love with him. Or not.

The alternative was staying on the train and watching her leave at Chernaya Rechka, seeing the doors shut, riding past her and feeling an entire line of destiny slipping away, his life with an unknown girl. The train slowed and she unlooped her arm and stood by the door. Then she exited the train. Jack Land felt a deep sigh vent that destiny from him.

At the next stop, which was Pioneerskaya, Jack wandered off the train. The cold air iced his cheeks as he stepped outside into the weather and a gray expanse of concrete, the zig-zagged roof made in the Soviet 1960s. To the left were a line of corrugated tin kiosks with crowds milling around. To the right of the kiosks Jack stopped at the top of a five-step stairs. He kept his head still and tracked the foot traffic, looking for anybody not moving. Near the bottom of the steps, an old woman abandoned one garbage can and trudged toward another. She moved her legs with stiffness at the knees—as if both her legs were logs and that she walked point to point with tiny steps.

A young woman bounded up the steps to the station with strong thighs under her rose-pattern skirt. Jack looked for any kids and he saw none except ones walking with their parents. Jack walked through the look-a-like Russian concrete apartment buildings, created always in groups of three, like stacked cracker boxes. Jack looked for any clump of trees. Behind the third building he saw one of the concrete cones, topped by a steel manhole cover. They led down twelve feet and workmen used the tunnels to service the hot water and steam lines that ran between buildings. Jack stood ready to lift the lid. He hesitated and felt ludicrous. Instead of giving up, he thought about the lovely girl on the train who got off at *Chernaya Rechka*. Leaving her had to mean something. He didn't notice anyone watching him. He poked his finger in the hole and pulled up on the lid, not knowing if some kid was waiting on the other side with a razor, ready to slice off the finger. Jack raised the heavy metal cover, cast with the logo of the *Izhorskiy Zavod*, the great steel-making factory. He peered down into the gloom. He dropped the cover on side and looked down at the bits of straw that wheeled down with the dust in the slanted rays of sunlight. No movement.

"I'm listening" he shouted. He moved his foot to the steel tube that was the top rung. Dried mud coated the ladder rungs. He picked his way down to avoid gumming up his hands because it could also be dried poop. The stench of human feces was potent and overpowering but he kept on going down into the sewer. He knew steam pipes ran through these tunnels, so any smell of sewage must have come from people, not pipes. A halo of light streamed down on him in the cold concrete cave. He stood on the wet floor in a layer of mustiness. Across the room ran steam pipes between the apartment buildings and the local heating plant. Alongside the pipes sat sacks of plastic junk, tied up but since abandoned. Jack flicked on his lighter. Shadows flickered. As he moved his lighter flame along the pipe, he saw that sections had been wiped clean by children sleeping there. At his feet lay scattered the bones and feathers of a crow. The flame led him in a cone of light that exposed artifact after artifact from children who lived here long enough to leave some rag or other shiny trinket. He stumbled forward, hunched over and his shoe struck a rock and sent it bouncing off the wall. The sound echoed and then the long sewer tunnel was silent again. Every detail of the sewer fit his expectations until his foot crumpled a crisp 1-ruble bill. Was a ruble worthless to even a homeless child?

Jack felt queasy, the farther he moved from the circle of light cast from the opening. After he'd finished his exploration, he climbed out of the hole into the light and cool fresh air. As he emerged, he noticed a woman standing rock still, staring at him with a wrinkle in her brow. She scowled. Then the woman broke off her stare and hurried down the street. Jack lifted the steel cover and set it back in place. It clanked into the slot and he began to wonder how hard it would be for a kid to lift. He sat and leaned against the concrete cone to make some notes in his reporter's notebook. Since he had zero interviews, he kept looking for some kid who knew about what the mafia was doing. At the far end of the field was a another concrete cone. Jack went to it, pulled off the lid. He called down the hole. Nothing. He climbed to the muddy floor that smelled of fermented human excrement. Clothes lay in bundles on the sides of the pipes. Sections of the grimy pipes were wiped clean. Some small body had lined up on that warm pipe. But the clean spots had gained a new patina of dust. Many days had passed since the last child slept here. It seemed that this entire neighborhood had been cleaned out.

His lighter flickered to half its length and then extinguished. In the dark he walked towards the light. He put his lighter in his pocket where it burned his thigh through the pocket linen.

"Ow! Fuck!" he shouted. He heard a scratch from the opposite end of the tunnel.

3.

Back in the dark recesses, he heard another scratch. The sound placed the image in his mind of an arm clawing on concrete. Jack turned back to face the darkness. Over his shoulder, light streamed in from the opening. It reached half way to where the sound came from. He walked deeper into the darkness along the pipe. In the dark his feet bumped into something. Jack got out his lighter. It sputtered and the scene flickered into view. On the ground he saw a grade-school-aged girl, lying on her side. Her upper shoulder was bent forward, hiding her face in the crotch of her elbow. It was a girl, sleeping in her winter clothes on the concrete floor. The girl had not yet woken up. He crouched down and touched the little girl's shoulder. The girl felt stiff and he rolled her over. She was dead. Her eye sockets were dried out and sunken. Her lips were purple and leathery like dried chicken breasts. Her hair was long, blond and fell in obscene locks across her sunken dead face. Jack stood up and cracked his head against the ceiling, making himself fall into the mud.

He climbed out of the lifeless steam sewer tunnel and realized how fragile and defenseless he was. His back was muddy. Wet mud flopped off the back of his coat at random intervals as he walked back to the kiosks. His eye alighted on a *shaverma* kiosk made of the usual corrugated tin outer skin but with a Turkish oven inside it. On a vertical metal pike turning over the spit was a cylinder of lamb and goat's meat. Jack headed straight for the shaverma stand and bought a greasy, dribbling roll-up for 7.5 rubles or about $1.25. The Georgian took the 10 ruble note and passed back a few ruble notes change. The Georgian's eye twitched as he tried to settle on a nationality for Jack. Taking the meat sandwich from the Georgian in its butcher paper wrapper, Jack tried not to think about the body and the sunken eyes and the leathery tongue. Jack thought about the story he would do for the paper and the horrible state of a country that permitted its children to die in a sewer. He took a bite of the lamb. Juice spilled over the corners of his mouth and on the front of his shirt. He used his shirt sleeve to pat his chin. As he performed this embarrassing clean-up job, he looked at the people around him. He scanned the area and, off the edge of the last kiosk, saw the hunched-over figure of a dirty-faced young child in a dirty coat and over-sized trousers with tears in the front. Jack stopped eating his delicious *shaverma* and carried it to a cylindrical garbage basket that was overflowing and right in full view of the dirty-coated child 20 feet away. Jack placed the full steaming shaverma on the top of the trash heap, so it would stand upright and be visible to Dirty Coat. Then Jack walked across the road until he could see the boy, Dirty Coat, and the food offering.

Within two minutes Dirty Coat went to the trash can and collected his greasy prize. Jack followed Dirty Coat as he ran to a line of trees. The boy gnawed on the *shaverma* as he ran and choked down large chunks of it unchewed. In the woods, he forked left and vanished into a copse of birch trees. Jack waited too long and Dirty Coat ran far ahead of Jack into the birch forest and Jack thought he had lost the little bastard and sacrificed his *shaverma* for nothing. Then he saw far ahead, the child broke free of the forest and sped across a green meadow toward a concrete volcano. Jack crouched down in the forest when it became a question of being seen. The child straddled the hole and lifted the lid up and to the side. The child slipped in the crescent entrance made by moving the cover. After the child disappeared down the hole, Jack stood and approached the concrete sewer entrance.

He stood next to the cover and did nothing. He knew if he dragged off the lid and clambered in the hole, he would scare the hell out of the child. Jack pulled away with pain as he put himself in the mindset of the child who was so bad off he lived in the sewer. The boy he had been chasing was the first one Jack found on his own. He remembered the first Russian family he met when he first moved to St. Petersburg, Valery and Irina. They were the sweetest couple: he a former theater director, she an actress. They let Jack sleep in their middle room for two weeks and then found a friend, Octavia, who had an extra apartment for

Jack to rent. Irina and Octavia were dignified ladies who never turned away from their noble impulses. That was what made them Russian.

Jack returned to the line of kiosks and bought two German chocolate candy bars.

The sewer lid was so heavy he questioned how any homeless kid could lift it. The five-year-olds would probably get trapped down there until a bigger kid came back. And if something happened to the older child, lonely death for the trapped one? Jack moved the lid to the side and it slid down the edge of the cone. He stared in the dark hole and accustomed his eyes to the dark floor. Then he dropped a German chocolate bar on the concrete twelve feet below. The candy's yellow and black wrapper was visible in the light streaming down. The chocolate bar lay flat on the concrete. It seemed like eons to Jack as he sat there, staring down at the chocolate bar, keeping motionless except for the thin strands of forehead hair that pulled one way or another with the breezes. After three minutes, Jack heard the echo of rock clapping on concrete. Then, from the shadows rose a figure. A pale arm reached from the shadows and snatched away the candy bar. The darkness around the circle of daylight was again uniform. The stealthiness of the snatch made Jack smile as he swung his leg over the entrance and started to climb down the ladder. Jack hung back and felt a twinge of guilt he hadn't felt on the previous two times he entered the sewers. This time he felt ashamed for invading this child's home. He went down anyway and looked in the direction of the snatch.

Jack sat on the floor and leaned back against the ladder. He shielded the light with his hand and looked at the dark and waited for his eyes to adjust. Along the floor, three abreast, ran pipes at least three feet in diameter. Following the light, he knew the size and layout of the room. He saw a few probable shadows where the child could hide.

Jack got comfortable, sitting with his elbows on his knees. In the gloom appeared a wet gleam of eyes moving, blinking and seeing.

"Tasty?" Jack asked in Russian. He received the reply on his forehead—the wadded-up wrapper.

Jack disregarded the insult. From his pocket, he took out the second chocolate bar in the same saliva-inducing colors of yellow and black. Jack displayed the candy bar for the general benefit of the homeless child, whoever it was. Jack was getting a chill and he decided he hated the idea of living in a damp, muddy sewer. Then, he tore open the wrapper of the chocolate bar. He let a show of ecstasy spread over his face, as if he were chewing the chocolate.

Before he threw the candy bar, he heard a guttural moan emanate from the darkness. Even now he could not see anything beyond black liquid pools of greater and lesser darkness that suggested myriad images but confirmed none. Though he could not see who, he knew a kid hung back in the darkness. It was a kid smart enough to still be alive, still able to resist the candy's allure. This show of restraint led Jack to conclude that he had—back in the shadows—cornered a rational person, not a deranged wild animal who might flare up in a frenzy. Jack knew he was dealing with a person who knew the candy was bait.

After Jack realized the situation—that the child held back in the darkness, barely breathing, waiting uncomfortably, still and silent, hoping Jack would just go away—it made it much harder to walk away without talking to the child. A stupid child would have grabbed the candy but not this one. Whoever lurked back in the shadows, it was a kid for whom nothing else mattered but fighting for a crust, for a half-chewed carrot end or a ragged clump of bad meat hanging from a bone.

"Chocolate?" Jack asked in Russian to the darkness, gesturing with the chocolate bar. The word produced no reaction. "Well, if you're not hungry—" he said, tore the wrapper and bit.

"*N'yet*," said someone. A dirty-faced girl flew at Jack, screaming. She attacked him with her fingernails and scratched the hell out of him. Jack fell on his side and blocked her with his feet.

"Stop, I'm a reporter," Jack said. He threw the candy bar and the girl followed it. Squatting with a gritty, smudged face, the girl gobbled the candy and stared at Jack with her lower lip sticking out.

"I have some questions," Jack said, wincing from the scratches on his forearms. The girl's face seemed to calm. The eyes that had gaped at him in fear now retreated behind slits.

"*Kuz-yole*. Asshole," the girl shouted at him in clear Russian. Her parents had cared enough to teach her to speak at least, even if that meant swearing in proper Russian.

"How are you called?" Jack asked. The girl slid back in the darkness where he could not see even the shine of her eyes in the dark. Then, she moved. She knocked over a metallic object that clanged and hummed a moment.

"How—"

"*Yope Tvoy Mat*. Fuck your mother!" barked back the girl.

"*N'yet*," Jack said, feeling flustered and upset at himself. He had screwed up his first good chance to contact a real homeless person. She was a source with *bona fide* credibility, a source with both feet in the story, not just her tongue. He felt ashamed for having upset her but he had rent to pay. The girl started to breathe faster and pace in the dark. He had her cornered. She rushed toward Jack and then back into blackness, and then back again shaking her fists in petulance.

"What—what—what do you want from me?"

"How called?" Jack asked, using the Russian style of clipped speech that consisted of verbs conjugated to convey the entire message. The girl stopped pacing and stared at him with her mouth open.

"Galina," she said, and she made a few more trips back and forth to the shadows. She blurted out, "Well?" with a nasal tone which showed she was irritated. "I don't give you my family name," she said.

"Very Pleased, Galina," he said. "Now, first question…why do you live here?"

"Fuck you," she said. "You don't care."

"I may be the only one in St. Petersburg to make just the right amount of stink to make a difference," he said—or imagined he said to her in his limited Russian. His attention was distracted by thoughts on what he could accomplish that reporters from the regular Russian press could not.

"*Yah ne prostitutka—fuck you*," she said.

"Why do you live here?" he asked again, and looked at the candy bar wrapper in her hands.

"Where *else*?" she asked him, irritated.

"With your parents?"

At that suggestion, Galina snorted and shook her dirty face "no" in disagreement.

"Mama is dead. I lived in Chilkovo with my grandmother, Luda," Galina said. "My grandmother put me on a train for St. Petersburg. She sold me to a Georgian."

Galina wiped her hand under her nose. Her dirty gray coat was too big. The sleeves were wide enough for a man. Jack felt a lump in his throat. He looked at her hair, at the scuffs on her face and grease stains on her coat. She sat on the floor like any child.

"What happened with the Georgian?" Jack asked.

Galina scowled and looked at the ground. She kicked at a rock and didn't answer. Jack wanted to ask again.

Without looking up, Galina answered in a matter-of-fact tone. "He looked for me. I went the other way. Simple."

Jack thought about her answer for a moment with a blank expression on his face. Then he threw his last candy bar to her.

Without ceremony, Galina snatched the candy bar and ate all of it. While he listened to Galina eat, he drifted into a daydream and reviewed the course of his own life. Growing up in Iowa under the hot prairie sun, with grandparents who were too tired to raise their son's boy.

Jack rubbed his eyes and made his face black with grease before he could catch himself. Thick valve grease smeared over his eyebrows. Looking at Jack's forehead, Galina smiled for the first time and, as she laughed, he saw she had good white teeth and was pretty.

"How long have you been here?" Jack asked.

"Questions, questions," the young girl shouted in an irritated womanish voice that surprised him with its vehemence. "I hate them."

"*Tikah,*" Jack said, in front of the ladder. Galina resumed pacing back and forth on the pathway between the pipes.

"Where are the others?" Jack asked.

"Gone. All gone, but me," she replied. "They didn't get me yet. They almost did once but I ran. But there's blood everywhere."

"What?"

"Men came. They got everybody but me."

"Who? Who came?"

"Men—big men—short hair and big muscles," Galina said, and breathed rapidly.

"What men?" Jack asked again, exasperated. "*Blood* everywhere?" he said, using the evocative Russian word "*krov*" for blood. It was the first Russian word Jack learned. From that moment in his life whenever he saw the red leak out of his body or another's, the word that came to mind was "*krov.*" The replacement of the English version of this word replicated his experience with a variety of other English words that had been displaced in his mind by their Russian counterparts.

"Georgians," Galina said.

"Mafia?" he said, hearing himself say internally "*Leading the Witness!*"

Galina looked back at him with a gentle look of confusion, as if she did not know what he was talking about.

"Who?" she said.

"They used a knife—stabbed you?" he asked.

"*N'yet.*"

He waited for her to elaborate but she did not, and it occurred to him that Galina was a girl with a head full of her own ideas and opinions.

"What was the reason?" he asked.

"*Pizdah.* Cunt," she said. Jacked looked at her as if she had just aged twenty years. "Take you away by your hair."

"Terrible," Jack said.

In response, Galina stepped back in the shadows.

"But you got away," Jack asked her.

"Yes. Happy New Year," she said.

"*Who* did this?" Jack asked, one last time. "*Mafiya?*"

"Bless God," Galina said, using the Russian idiom for praising someone who has just grasped the obvious.

It dawned on Jack that his first article had been right after all. Jack drifted above the moment, underground with Galina, and everything fell into place. The mafia exploited homeless kids. Only God knew what for. Galina emerged by chance as the only living witness to a crime that was the perfect revenue stream.

"Listen to me," Jack said to her, falling from his reverie. "Will you come with me? You can live in my apartment."

Galina stopped her pacing and looked at him.

"I not *prostitutka*," Galina said.

Now it was Jack's turn to smile but he was not pretty like Galina and he looked a tad crazy.

The light from overhead moved across the cement in the direction of Galina. The extra light convinced him she had calmed down, and he guessed he was just about to find himself with a lodger. Galina followed him up the ladder, and keeping her distance she rode the Metro with him back to his apartment.

There, after he had fed her and sent her by herself to take a bath, he got started on the sequel to his first article, but with the sharp teeth of facts. Jack was planning to report—if he could even get the article to run—that children were starving to death in the sewers. The majority of the city of St. Petersburg and perhaps the Leningradsky Region contained 60-thousand homeless children. The mafia harvested from this population. As these words marched across the page in his typewriter, Jack Land added his byline to the top in pen. He felt a tense gathering of fibers at the back of his neck. "Be careful," he told himself.

He left Galina alone in his apartment, sleeping on his couch. He got on the Metro and headed for the newspaper.

4.

Jack stepped in the newsroom in the middle of a hot story. A warehouse by the docks had caught fire and the smoke billowed up into the sky.

"Sarah, who's on that fire?" Jack asked her as he went to his desk, which was covered with several days of accumulated messages.

"Nice of you to grace us," she said. "You still work here?"

"Not unless Alexander Ivanovich has changed his mind," Jack replied. "Besides, I have a great story."

Sarah followed him to his desk and stood while he booted his computer.

"Another one of *your* big stories, *just* what we need," she said. "In case you haven't heard, we're still in a shit storm over your last piece about sewer hookers."

"This one is better; I've got interviews with the kids."

"*Fuck* me. Another buggering homeless story," she said, sounding

Cockney. "Bloody fucking awful."

Jack thumbed his folders until he found the photos. He flipped through those as Sarah looked on. He showed her face after face of young, dirty-faced homeless kids, with varying degrees of alarm present on their expressions. Then, he showed her a black-and-white photo of a young girl wearing a head scarf, barefoot, lying in an alley, her muslin dress torn open, splaying her breasts to the air as her head fell to one side. Another black-and-white photo showed a four-year-old girl with greasy blond hair tumbling on her shoulders, as she stood in the cold in a nightshirt clutching a rag with a look of alarm and panic, about ready to die because there was no parent who would come to her aid as she freezes or starves to death. When she saw the young girl, starving in the photo, Sarah's belligerent tone softened. She grabbed the photo.

"Where did you get this?" she asked.

"Pioneerskaya Metro."

"Here? You took it yourself?"

"Yes," Jack said.

"Where is this girl?" Sarah asked.

"Around Pioneerskaya—two days ago," he said. "I want to run a story about it."

"Out of the question," Sarah said, and slapped the desk with a ferocity that surprised him. "We're already in a heap of poo. All because the Russian goombas got their knickers full of *pelmeni* over what you wrote."

Jack waited a decent interval:

"It isn't your decision, you know." As Jack said these words, he imagined how he would narrate this triumph to Thor, who was used to thumping people on commodity trades. Jack would say how he had been toying with Sarah the whole time, knowing that ultimately it was up to Krasnie, the man with a beard and a swinging pair. Jack smiled as he imagined that conversation and then he shifted his focus to Sarah, staring at him.

"Bastard," she said.

Chapter XI

SERGEI handed the newspaper to Szlotov, who was puzzled.

"What's this?" Szlotov said. Everybody in the kitchen, including the Doctor and Vasya, fell silent.

"Just look at it," Sergei said.

Szlotov unfolded the small tabloid newspaper and stared down at the main story below the fold. "Mafia Sweeps Up Homeless kids." Szlotov's cheek muscles moved as if he were gnawing on a speck of carrot. Szlotov read the article and then flipped to the next page to read the rest.

"—'found near the Alexander Nevski Monastery'—Arkady," Szlotov said. He slapped the paper on the kitchen table and stood back. He closed his eyes while he exhaled through his nose with a hissing sound. "Why didn't you *tell* me what Arkady was doing?" Szlotov said to Sergei, who opened his mouth but uttered no words.

"You told me he had a solution for the bodies," Szlotov said. His faced flushed and the veins stood out on his forehead.

"That's what he told *me*," Sergei said.

"And to you, 'taking care' of the bodies meant throwing them in the Monastery canal?" Szlotov said, spitting with rage as he said the last word, "next to Alexander Nevski?"

"He didn't tell *me*," Sergei said. Szlotov shook his head in disbelief. Several threads of possibility became entwined in his mind. The homeless children, the *bezprezorni*, were worthless or else their parents or relations would have claimed them. They must *deserve* to be on the street, he reasoned. That alone absolved him of any guilt. Szlotov had a surgeon friend Yakov Lezhnev, who he met in Prague. Szlotov had learned from Yakov that certain doctors were willing to travel to places like Estonia or Kazakhstan to make use of these kids. Before the newspaper story, the problem of the leftover bodies was Arkady's problem. Bad news.

"Where is Arkady?" Szlotov said. "This minute."

"I'll drive," Sergei said.

2.

They drove over to the area around the Ladozhskaya Metro and arrived just the two of them in Sergei's car. Sergei parked in front of a modest four-storey apartment building. They walked to the third floor. Szlotov knocked on the door that Sergei fingered as the home of his junior recruit, Arkady, who was an excellent shot with a pistol but who was sloppy in everything else.

"Who's there?" asked a high-pitched voice.

"A Thief," Szlotov said. "Money or your life."

"*Who?*"

"A friend of Arkady's."

The bolt slid aside and a scared and elderly *babushka* stood behind the open door.

"Good evening, Madame," said Szlotov. "Can we speak with Arkady?"

"I'll get him—"

"—no, that's fine, we will," Szlotov said. He and Sergei entered the apartment and walked through a narrow hallway to the kitchen. They walked softly and stiffly. In the kitchen, the found Arkady, his back to them, watching a black-and-white TV on the fridge showing the children's show *Eralash.*

Arkady sat with a bowl of soup under his chin and a spoonful of *borscht* on its way to his lips. When Szlotov and Sergei entered his kitchen, Arkady froze in place with his lower lip extended.

"Is it yummy?" Szlotov said, over smiling.

"What happened? What did I do?" Arkady said. The look of gleeful quiet on Szlotov's face masked the bubbling rage he felt and also his wish to take out his rage on someone. The carved-up bodies needed to disappear. Szlotov wondered if he was the only one who followed through, who finished things, pushed in the shiv, grabbed the man with a vice grip and held him there, by the nose, until Sergei came up and got the man's arms.

"Seriyozha," Arkady said to Sergei, using the endearing form of his name to escape the doom about to fall on him.

"I'm the one," Szlotov said, "who should be asking 'what happened.'"

A frown tugged down the corners of Arkady's mouth as he understood the terrible mess he was in.

Szlotov sat opposite Arkady. He threw his leather gloves on the linoleum-topped kitchen table covered with ceramic bowls of jellied cucumber and pureed turnips.

"Sergei, show him," Szlotov said and waved his hand at Arkady. From inside his coat, Sergei produced the newspaper, which he slapped down on the

131

table in front of Arkady.

Moving his finger down the lines of Russian words, Arkady read the first page of the article. He had little to say. When he was done with the first column, he pushed the newspaper back and knocked over his tea, which soaked the newspaper. Sergei took it away and used a dish towel to dry it off. Watching from the doorway to the kitchen, Arkady's mother held her head and gnashed her teeth in silence as Sergei used her best towel to dry off the newspaper, leaving black streaks on it. After the newspaper was dry, he handed back the towel.

"Well?" Szlotov asked. "The bodies?"

Realizing his peril, Arkady slumped in the chair and covered his face with his palms, exhaling like a corpse.

"I dumped them," Arkady said, stuttering. "I dumped the bodies in the river."

"Why didn't you *bury* them?" Sergei asked, as if it was only common decency; after you've gutted and de-meated a dozen homeless kids, the least you could do is put them in the ground.

"I just dumped them in the canal," Arkady said, letting his eyes fall cross-eyed. Sergei growled and punched his fist into his palm, without breaking his stare at Arkady.

"And now," Szlotov said, holding up his hand to calm Sergei. "You are going to *fix* this." Szlotov stabbed the article with his finger. "Start here— eliminate the reporter. I've got a better plan for the bodies." Szlotov stood and put on his gloves. Arkady hesitated but then he rose and put on his coat, like he was going to a firing squad.

The three of them left with Arkady's mother's staring red-eyed. She begged them: "Please, gentlemen," she said, the word filling her mouth. "Don't hurt my Arkasha, he's all I've got." The three returned to Sergei's BMW. Szlotov got in back and had Arkady ride in front of him, an arrangement that seemed to cause some discomfort for Arkady, though he still got in front. Sergei drove them to the address where the newspaper was located.

"And how will I know him?" Arkady said, as they looked up to the second floor and saw some lights on in a few rooms.

"*Ask* for him," Szlotov said. "When he comes—*pop*. Blow his fucking brains on the wall." Szlotov smiled to comfort Arkady.

"I...This is my first time," Arkady said, turning around. Szlotov glared at him.

"I will go with you, Arkady—but *you* will do it."

The two of them walked across the street that paralleled the Little Neva River.

In the cool of the morning, the scent of the ocean was strong and they heard the rumble of diesel traffic as they walked to the entrance. The doorway led up a wide, rickety wooden staircase. Szlotov thought Sun Tzu would not have approved this uphill battle field. Szlotov let Arkady go up first. In front, Arkady took a few loud, tramping steps up the middle of the wooden stairs. Szlotov reached out and stopped him. Leading with his finger, he tugged Arkady to the side of the stairs and showed him how to walk, with control over how fast he allowed his weight to be transferred to the stairs, all with the goal of silence. So trained, Arkady walked silently up, making scarcely a sound. They reached the second floor and looked down the hall, completely dark for most of its length. Half-way down, light streamed through a pane of frosted glass and the cracks around the door. Arkady got a few steps from the lit office. He read the newspaper's name on the frosted-glass window and pointed it out to Szlotov. Arkady shook like he had a fever. He pulled out his gun. Szlotov grimaced at the strange weapon. He put his palm on Arkady's shoulder and pulled him away before he could knock.

Szlotov motioned with his finger "Show me your gun." Arkady handed him a home-made zip gun, made from a short length of iron pipe that had many turns of wire wrapped around it, a block of wood for a stock, and rubber bands. It was as thick as a bratwurst. "What is this?" Szlotov asked in a hissing voice. "Think this is a fucking joke?"

"No, a gun such as this has no ballistics," Arkady said, in effect recounting the schoolboy myths he had heard to his boss, a man who was infamous for blowing up a cat when a debt was not paid.

"Take this," Szlotov said. He handed his own Glock to the boy, who grinned upon feeling the weight of a real pistol in his hand.

Arkady tapped the barrel of the Glock against the frosted glass of the office with Невски Новости (Nevski Novosti) on the door.

In reply, Arkady and Szlotov heard the wooden back of a chair groan. The wooden floor squeaked. Then there was a scraping sound as the wooden feet of a chair were dragged back and then left empty. Long footsteps crossed the room, casually. The door opened and in mid-sentence a man spoke "and for the Primorsky district, I think we'll need to—" and the man stopped speaking. He was a tall, Slavic-looking man with glasses and chinchilla-brown hair below his jaw line.

"May I help you?" the man asked Arkady.

"*N'yet*," Arkady said.

Expecting a smart-Alec response, the bearded man turned away:

"Right now we're closed. Come back—" and after that word 'back' had left the man's mouth, a *crack* sounded. The copper-coated shell pierced the man's suit coat and then his skin. The bullet pierced his descending aorta. He gasped; he looked beyond the man holding the gun at a photo on the wall. The editor, Alexander I. Krasnie slumped to the floor in a wide lake of red.

Arkady breathed faster as smoke rose in a thin line from the barrel of the Glock. He opened his hand and the gun tumbled forward. It landed on the floor with a clatter. Arkady started to run away but Szlotov caught him by the arm.

"Another in the head, to make sure," Szlotov said. Arkady went back, wet-faced, and picked up the gun. He fired it a second time into the man's head, though his aorta had already bled out by the time Szlotov caught Arkady's arm and walked him back.

Szlotov saw a notebook on the dead man's desk: "Addresses". He grabbed it. They ran out of the building and encountered no one. Sergei asked no questions. He understood the meaning of two shots and the meaning of the delay between them. Sweating, Szlotov took off his gloves and said, "You didn't ask his name."

Arkady was exhausted and mute. It was his first killing.

Chapter XII

GALINA awoke to a ferocious pounding on the door of the apartment. She bent at the waist to sit up but instead she banged her head on the couch she was sleeping under. Her back was sore but she was not cold and had a blanket around her legs that felt comfortable. She was still scared of the American but he was clean and fed her.

"Bastard," shouted someone on the other side of the door. "Open the door, you bloody murderous bastard." Galina did not understand what was happening but she could hear and feel the anger. The pounding was joined by kicks. The person kicking the door was angry.

Over in his narrow bed, Jack groaned and threw off his covers. His naked feet walked on the cold floor. In his boxer underwear, Jack shuffled without *tapochkees* with the eyes of a newborn kitten to the door.

"Who's there?" Jack asked in Russian from behind the double-locked door.

"Open the door!" screamed the voice. "Sarah. You know, Sarah your boss from the paper *Nevski Novosti*, the one *you* killed."

"What?" Jack said and unlocked the door. Galina pulled in her legs and coiled into a ball below the wicker couch. She kept silent and tracked the legs of a woman as she entered the room with her street shoes on and Galina imagined how her grandmother Ludmilla would have reacted back in Chilkovo, a time that seemed now so long ago. The woman who entered the apartment—Sarah—turned on her heel.

"They killed him," she said.

"What? Who?" Jack said.

"Krasnie."

"*What?*" Jack said, and he started to breathe like had just run across the room. He paced the floor. "How did it happen?"

"Yelena found him this morning. They shot him in the face and the stomach. He was ice cold when she found him in a puddle of blood," Sarah said. "His son thinks it was mafia—because of your two fucking articles."

Jack collapsed in a chair, holding his head. Galina did not understand but the face of the American told her it was horrible.

"No," he said.

"Yes, you arrogant American," Sarah said. "You think you're exempt from the rules? You think you can just play with the lives and hearts of other people without consequence?"

"This would never happen in the States," Jack said.

"This is Russia. I warned you. I told you that you did not understand these people, that you would not be able to until you lived here for years…and *now*…" Sarah started to cry. She sat on the corner of Jack's bed. "The paper is toast. Where am I going to work? Bloody hell, I'm going to miss Alexander Ivanovich. And you…*you* are in danger, you know. You should turn yourself into the *Militsiya*."

After she said those words, Sarah spied the pair of eyes staring back at her from under the couch.

"What the…*fuck* is going on here," Sarah cried out. She grabbed Galina's wrist and dragged her out. "What's going *on* here?" Sarah repeated but with an implicit judgment in the melody of her tone, as if she had decided no good or licit reason could justify Jack Land, a single American man, mid-thirties, having an eight-year-old girl sleeping under his couch.

Galina wrapped herself in the blanket that had been covering her and wished they would stop shouting. She had not uttered a sound except the high-pitched squeak "*N'yet*" and then Sarah pulled away the blanket. Galina cried and clawed the angry woman's hands with long red nails. She said nothing.

"You're sick," she said. "You're sick and dangerous. You have cost Alexander Ivanovich his *life*, me my livelihood and now you're setting your sick, pederastic sights on the flower of Russia's youth."

Galina did not like this lady. Without her blanket she felt cold, and angry herself at the blond lady with the sharp fingernails. Galina decided she would scratch back the next time.

"This is Galina, the girl from the *story*," Jack said. Sarah halted with her mouth puckered in the shape necessary to make the sound of a letter "P", for the word "puh-zhal-oo-ista" but she was speechless. Then, she turned and gave the blanket back to Galina.

"What is your name?" Sarah asked in Russian, quickly.

"Galina."

"Nice to meet you," Sarah said in Russian, with a friendly tone. "Galina, tell me—did he try to get in bed with you?"

Galina stayed quiet and answered after a pause.

"*N'yet*. I was here. He was there."

"Galina, this is important. Did he *touch* you?" Sarah asked in Russian.

"Sarah," Jack said. "This is unnecessary."

Galina bit her lip and shook her head "no". Sarah wheeled on Jack.

"Why is she here? What are your plans for her?"

"I'm helping her to stay alive."

"Helping corrupt her, is more like it," Sarah said.

"That's a god-damned lie. She just said I didn't touch her and you're

137

trying to turn that into a future crime."

"No the crime was what you did to Alexander Ivanovich!"

Galina did not understand the language they were speaking but she got the sense that it was not good for her and she retreated under the couch and wrapped the blanket tighter around herself. She slipped back in memory of living with her grandmother in Chilkovo and sleeping in a bed made of straw in warmth and comfort. She remembered the darkness and photos on the book shelves, black and white photos of the mother and father of Ludmilla, who she had not seen or heard from since she got on the train in Chilkovo for the meeting with the Georgian Astrakhan who bought Galina through the classified ad Ludmilla had placed in a St. Petersburg newspaper, offering a young, pure bride to a man with the fee and the fare.

Galina came out of her memory and Sarah crouched down a foot from Galina's face.

"You cannot live here," Sarah said. Galina understood and was frightened. Galina started to cry.

"Look," Jack said and pushed Sarah to the door. "I'll figure something out—but you need to go right now."

"Why?" Sarah said.

Galina hid under the couch and put her thumb in her mouth.

"I *interviewed* her," Jack said. "I felt like a shit. I took her story and gave nothing in return. So I bought her supper. Then, seeing how hungry she was, I couldn't just kick her back to the sewers."

"You felt like a shit," Sarah said. "Now we're getting somewhere."

"Fuck off," Jack said, and looked her in the eye. "What would *you* have done?"

"I would have taken her to an *orphanage*."

"A *what*?" Jack said with his voice screeching out the pitch of his indignation. "Have you *seen* those places? The kids tied to the beds, laying in their own piss and shit? Is *that* your suggestion?"

He reached out and put his hand on her shoulder, and she jerked it away.

"Don't," she said. "You're not my type."

The American left the room and went to the kitchen. Sarah got down and walked on her hands and knees to the couch. Sarah rolled to her side and lay on the wood floor in front of the couch. She looked eye-to-eye at Galina, who on instinct moved as far back as she could under the couch.

"What do *you* want, little girl?" Sarah asked in Russian.

Galina understood the question and she fell into thought and no longer saw what she was looking at. Thus distracted, she went back to Chilkovo and she looked up at the person who held her hand as they walked together in the snow with her breath foggy. The big woman holding Galina's hand was her mother Sonya Kirilovna, the woman whose smiling face was one of the few moments of early life Galina still remembered.

"Babi Luda, I want Mamma," Galina said. Jack heard her.

"What did she say?" Jack asked Sarah.

"*Balooda*," Sarah reported, with certainty. "It's…a kind of boots worn by children in Novgorod. She wants a pair of those boots. You should get her those, you *profiteering*, Communism-slumming American shit."

"Can't afford to," Jack said.

Jack repeated the word "*balooda*" he had just gotten from Sarah, not the word Galina had just said. So, Galina thought it was a new word and she spent a lot of energy trying to understand or remember what the word *balooda* meant. Jack play-acted like he was putting on boots, then he tapped his shoes. She did not understand what he meant, so she asked "Shoes?"

Himself now confused, he decided to ask a question. Then, his question was misidentified as an answer by Galina. The whole confusing mess was stressful for Jack and so he escaped from the tangle by declaring: "I'll just get her a pair of those '*baloodi*' and be done with it," he said, changing the number of the fictitious word '*balooda*' from singular to plural.

"Fine then. So long," Sarah said. "Well, I guess then, I'm off."

Jack accompanied her to the door. Jack sighed and said in clear Russian: "Do you want some new boots?" Galina came aglow at the surprise and she nodded vigorously. Galina put on her torn-up sneakers and they went downstairs. Six blocks away, near the Neva River, was a big sign on a building. Galina smiled because she knew they were going there. When she overcame the awe of the many shoes, and understood that she was getting shoes, she rushed up to a pretty white pair with an ankle strap and a tall white heel. Jack followed her around for a while without commentary except for his smile. Galina, at last, settled on a pair of white ankle boots and the clerk gave Jack a ticket that he took to the cashier and paid. Then Galina was allowed to try them on.

As they walked out of the shoe store, Galina smiled and looked happy. That made Jack feel great.

Galina followed Jack down into a tunnel. They followed steps underground. She had never been down the steps before. The noise got loud. They encountered other people who frowned at Galina. They followed her with their eyes as she went through the turnstile and Jack put in another brass token for himself. Not knowing where he was taking her, Galina stepped on to a stairs moving down. The escalator was long and stretched farther down than she could see. People stood at regular intervals on the moving steps going down and up, and tall cylinders of light stood in the middle as they passed. At the bottom, the stairs turned flat and they walked off the rumbling escalator. They entered a large flat platform with cliffs on either side. Then, trains rumbled in the station. Galina followed Jack inside, for the first subway ride of her life.

Chapter XIII

WITH a feeling of butterflies in his stomach, Jack stepped outside with Galina in tow. He held his breath for a moment, the first time they reached free air. Jack waited and tried not to let her notice that he was watching her.

Galina looked up and shielded her eyes from the light with her hand.

"Where are we going?" she asked.

Jack had no idea. Were he in America, there would be an embarrassment of options for a homeless kid. But in Russia none of that applied. Orphanage? Jack knew he could not call the cops for help because the Russian *Militsiya* were all crooks or at best they would deliver a kid like Galina to an orphanage. There was nothing worse than a Russian orphanage—Jack knew that.

They started toward the subway and after they left the narrow channel between Jack's building and the one next to it, the cold wind reached them. Jack instantly felt that he and Galina were both under dressed. Steam rose in billows from the sewer gratings and the mist settled on everything into a coat of white hairs. They continued until they came to the *tramvai* stop. Galina stopped walking when Jack stopped but the perplexed look on her face showed her patience was eroding.

Jack thought of going down to Dostoevsky and visiting some ex pats there. Then he thought of the best of all ideas, going to see Sarah Hughes. Sarah had already lived several years in St. Petersburg when Jack arrived. Sarah knew the Administrative buildings, the numbers within the *Militsiya* precinct stations that didn't ring off the hook unanswered. Jack remembered at the paper, seeing Sarah on the phone with some *Militsiya* guy and, from the smile and the preening she did, Jack knew she was using her sexual wiles to gain a source in a manner frowned upon in J-school. After seeing her coo and giggle into the phone, Jack wanted to throw her a towel and send her to the showers.

Jack knew that Sarah was not too proud to take special measures to curry favor with a source. It occurred to him that his best shot for how to save Galina might come from a cut-throat reporter like Sarah Hughes.

Jack led Galina across the street and they waited for the *tramvai*. The lumbering train appeared at the end of the block. He pointed out the red *tramvai* train to her.

"*Da*," Galina said. "I rode it once with my Mama."

Jack knew at once that must be a painful subject. He stood mute next to her and waited for the train. Standing at the stop with Galina, Jack looked across the street and saw Zhanna staring grim-faced at Jack. Zhanna looked sad and her hands hung limp like paws. Zhanna stood, horrified. The tramway train car arrived and stopped between Jack and Galina and Zhanna across the street. The doors to the tramway car folded back. Galina stepped forward but Jack did not move. The driver of the train stared at Jack and raised his eyebrows and shoulders.

The driver pulled the doors shut and drove off. After the train cleared, Zhanna again stood facing Jack and Galina. Jack led them across the street and when they were face to face with Zhanna, she said, "Long time, since 'Tash and I came over," Zhanna said, ending with her eyes on Galina. "Natasha wants you to call her, Jack."

"You think so?"

"I know so," Zhanna said.

Jack stepped back from her and glanced at Galina to imagine how it might work. Without any plan, Jack led Galina around the corner to a plum-colored building. They walked up three flights and Jack knocked on the door of the apartment of Natasha's mother. Natasha herself answered the door when Jack knocked and it took her a fraction of a second to notice Galina, this eight-year-old girl standing next to him, and Natasha's head lopped to one side.

"What's going on?" Natasha said, not allowing the door to open.

Jack looked at the way she stood, the look of attraction in her eyes while her mouth expressed a frown of distrust and wound.

"Natasha," Jack said. "I just wanted to tell you that you were completely right." Jack glanced at Galina. "It turned out pretty much the way you said."

Natasha stood up straighter and let go of the door to cross her arms. Natasha lifted her brow to acknowledge her victory but also to express her disdain for Jack. Since Natasha no longer held on to the door, it wandered open and—standing behind Natasha, striking a similar crossed-arm pose, stood Natasha's mother.

"What does that *man* want?" said Natasha's mother, closing her robe up to her neckline.

"He came to show us his pet rat," Natasha said, hissing out the last word. Natasha's mother came up and scowled at Galina.

"What is with this child?" barked Natasha's mother. "You're not some sort of pederast?"

"Heavens, no!" Jack said. "I'm trying to help her get off the streets. She is eight years old."

Natasha's mother stood menacingly with pale white skin and blue veins on her forehead and a band of gray hair since her last dye job, topped by an angry face.

"Why are you homeless?" she asked Galina, harshly. "Where are your parents? You take narcotics? You a prostitute?"

"No!" Galina said and started to cry.

"Thanks," Jack said and started to lead Galina away back down the stairs.

"Jack," Natasha said, wet-cheeked. "I'm sorry."

"It's nothing," he said and walked with Galina downstairs back to the tramway stop.

Jack and Galina waited together in silence and then Jack looked down and saw that Galina was crying.

Galina said: "I'm sorry I'm so much trouble."

"You're no trouble at all. You want to be happy and I want to help you be happy."

Another red and white *tramvai* train appeared at the end of the street, rocking side-to-side as it rumbled over the Stalin-era tracks, arcing the wire overhead.

They got in the tramway and sat side by side. Galina still acted uncomfortable on the tram. She startled every time the overhead wire sparked and sent glowing embers of red hot metal on the ground. The bright flashes appeared without warning. They got off at the square that was Novocherkasskaya Metro station and took the stairs underground. They passed all of the shops built into the walls and went right to the subway. At the turnstile, Jack put in a jeton for Galina and then he got his own monthly Yedinaya card. They rode the long escalator to the bottom and took the next train until they reached the Chernaya Rechka Metro station, where they got off the subway.

2.

As they exited the subway at Chernaya Rechka, Jack felt Galina's hand in his own and he knew he had opened a can of worms. They exited the station through howling winds and flurries of snowflakes that appeared out of the sky. They walked together toward the market of kiosks made of corrugated sheet metal slapped and fastened together into small shacks. Various shopkeepers stood in hooded coats with padding under their torsos and furry *shapka* ear-flap caps on top of their heads. They sold bottles of *piva*, beer, and vodka and Marlboro cigarettes—the *crème de la crème* down to the cheapest *Belamor Kanal* cardboard smokes. Jack led her through the main alley of the kiosks and then at the transition where metal sheds gave way to cloth tents, he saw a copy of the newspaper, the St. Petersburg *Komsomolets* with the headline "Editor Killed". Jack stopped next to the stall that sold newspapers. His heart pounded. He could not move. Galina bumped into him, as she had been looking at the kiosk that sold meat. Over their heads flooded the sound of the newest Soyuz compilation, which had begun to flood the airwaves. Jack scanned the headlines. In the worker's newspaper *Trud* he saw a story below the fold about the Mafia-style killing of Alexander I. Krasnie, a journalist with a long career in local newspaper circles.

Jack bought both of the papers with headlines and walked on with both of his hands holding the newspaper with the longer story. He found out things he had never known about Krasnie, such as his years as an investigative reporter in Moscow. Krasnie's years wearing a bad suit over a sweater and tie and punching a typewriter. Jack never knew that Krasnie offended so many powerful people in Moscow that he took a lump of cash, left Moscow and took his stake to St. Petersburg, where he opened his own newspaper, the one where Jack worked. As he read the life of his former boss, a wave of admiration swept over Jack. Alexander Krasnie, here was the epitome of the crusading journalist, but in a communist country.

Galina walked along him although she could have run away had she been so inclined. A photo on the second page of a young Alexander Krasnie was tragic and depressing. In the photo he looked up smiling with his modest beard hovering around his chin. Jack recalled all plans for the future Alexander Ivanovich had described on late nights re-doing pages three and four times to make them better. All the ideas he had for growing the paper were all for naught.

Hearing him say "Good article"—was the equivalent of winning the gold medal. When he read the second story about the abandoned children, he returned it to Jack with those exact words, "Good Article," which was his highest compliment.

Having now folded up the newspapers and placed them under his arm, Jack and Galina walked across the street. Now, in this section of St. Petersburg, even Jack felt nervous and uncomfortable. He didn't recognize any landmarks.

For the few weeks he and Sarah dated, they rarely went to Sarah's apartment. Instead, they met at Sennaya Ploshad. They went shopping for fresh tomatoes, dusty just-from-the-dirt potatoes and tried to find turnips for Sarah, though Jack had always feigned dismay when their search for turnips was fruitless. For the few weeks they were dating, Sarah had wanted to keep her relationship with Jack secret, so they always headed to his apartment. She insisted they leave work separately and then take different trains to Sedovaya Metro station. She was happy coming to Jack's apartment to have sex but never in her own apartment. Sarah was willing to depart in surprising ways from her apparent Edinburgh orthodoxy. In short, Sarah had a bad girl streak; she liked being spanked. She liked having Jack shout out a wad of guttural obscenities, punctuated by a sharp slap on her rump.

3.

By memory, from the single time he visited Sarah's apartment, Jack looked up at her balcony and counted the floors. Then he took the narrow elevator to her floor and knocked. Galina stood at Jack's side. She was so nervous in these unfamiliar surroundings, she was happy to stay right next to Jack.

After a delay, the inner door unlocked and Sarah asked: "Who's there?" Jack answered and she opened the door.

"Hi Jack, what's the—" she started to say and then looked down to Galina. "I *see*. You're selling homeless children door to door. I knew it would come to this the first time I heard you were running an orphanage."

"Sarah. You know how sorry I am about Krasnie," Jack said. "What more can I do or say."

"To start with," Sarah said. "You could find me a new bloody job!"

Jack hung his head and had no reply. His actions—writing the story about the Russian mafia—led to the death of his editor and the destruction of his newspaper and both of their jobs.

The three of them stood together with Sarah's door between them. Then Sarah said dropped her arm from her door and hung her head, sighing:

"*Where* are my manners. My mother would be disgraced." She opened her door wide and ushered Jack and Galina into her kitchen. They sat around Sarah's square kitchen table, the right size to hold one chessboard. Sarah put on the kettle and foraged in her cupboard, while mumbling about "half-way decent biscuits". Jack noted the presence of a tea cozy, with a pair of red tassels hanging down from where it knotted around the handle. In short order, Sarah produced a pair of tea cups and she set them down in front of both Jack and Galina. To these she added small saucers, chipped china. She had a pill-shaped loaf of white bread that she sliced up and then topped with a dollop of honey. Galina's eyes rounded with joy and she addressed herself directly at mopping up the honey. Both Jack and Sarah quietly watched her cope with its sticky goodness feeling good and happy. Jack snuck a look at Sarah, standing by the sink, and he caught her smiling. Her smile vindicated Jack's approach, of trying to tell the story of one person, of trying to help Galina.

Jack caught her eye and pleaded with Sarah. "What should I do?"

Jack had not asked that question out loud. Instead, he looked at her with the pleading eyes of a dog.

"Ah," Sarah growled. "You damned *choob*! Now is not the time to ask—and I told you before what I thought and what did you do? You ignored me."

Jack stood mute, unable to contradict her.

"Now," Sarah growled. "Of *all* times, you decide to express your doubts?"

Jack sat frowning, staring at the light reflecting off his tea, feeling guilty as charged.

"Now, *my bonny lad*, is not the time. You're stuck! She's here unless you can achieve some kind of a miracle."

Her tone changed and Jack saw that his fate had changed. Sarah had lost her faith in him.

Sarah snatched away Jack's cup. Tea splashed on the table. She threw the china cup roughly at the sink and it shattered. Jack and Galina both startled at the crisp sound. Galina started to whimper. Sarah turned around, angry. She stared at Jack and said: "There's only one answer for you, Jack: *Detski Dom*!"

Sarah used the phrase for the dreaded 'orphanage.'

Galina shrieked "No!" She flew out of her seat and slipped around Sarah . Galina was at the front door, tugging and pounding on it, twisting the knob, trying to escape.

"Calm down," Jack told her, hoping that she might still be a kid.

Galina turned her back on Sarah's door and dashed for the living room window, trying to get it open. Jack came right after her. Glancing behind her at Jack, she grabbed a book off the shelf and swung it back to smash the window. Jack caught the book, a picture book on the Orthodox Cathedrals of St. Petersburg, on the back swing. Galina let go of the book and as quickly Jack dropped it and grabbed Galina's wrists. Like a monkey, Galina walked up the side of Jack's body, hanging from the wrists he held, until Galina could pummel his head or thereabouts with her feet. Having been subjected to this treatment at an earlier time, Jack waited until Galina's feet were shoulder high, meaning she was upside down, to release his grip on her wrists, thereby allowing her to fall. He caught her around her waist and carried her off like a cat out of the room.

"I will *not* take you to an orphanage. You will *not* end up a statistic." Jack tried to say to say in Russian, but because his Russian was so imperfect she responded by wrestling free and sprinting for the front door. Jack relaxed and waited for her to reach the locked door, but when she got there, the door swung open and Galina bolted out, down the stairs and vanished into the city.

4.

Jack was dumbstruck when she disappeared. An instant later, Sarah held up Galina's dirty coat, which had been left behind.

"How did she get out?" Jack yelled, and stomped on the floor. "I *swear* that door was locked."

"Well, it's all for the best," Sarah said. "You can bring a wild Russian street kid indoors but it isn't going to work." Sarah spoke with casual detachment. She opened a drawer and pulled out a glass candy jar, out of which she pulled a mint that she popped in her mouth.

"That door was *locked*. She tried it before and it was locked," Jack repeated, as if reaffirming his testimony to the karma judiciary. Jack wanted to slug her for being so flippant. Getting Galina killed would be the last piece of bad news he could bear. Jack wanted to help these people. He learned Russian, moved to St. Petersburg and started building a new Russian life. He loved the Russians and he wanted to help make things better for them.

"You did the right thing, letting her go," Sarah said and sat down in her wicker chair, with a sigh.

"You're right, I *am* just letting her go," Jack said, and then, in the flick of an eyelash, he grabbed Galina's coat and ran out the door, down the concrete stairs to the street. Jack stopped on Savushkina street and the traffic was lite. He ran for it. To his right he saw the iron railing with the paper clip-like design along the river Chernaya Rechka, which meant Black River. He looked down the left at the row of four-story buildings that lined Chernaya Rechka. The river itself was tranquil and it was at that moment that Jack knew he had lost Galina forever.

Jack walked in sadness along the river. He took out a pad of paper and started writing: "Dear Thor, today I fucked up majorly and hurt the one person I had decided to help. It's breaking my heart…"

Chapter XIV

1.

S ZLOTOV decided to build a new team, keep it secret from his crew and even from Sergei, who was present at the recruitment meetings that Szlotov conducted in the basements of apartment buildings around the region. Szlotov decided he could feel out all his future rivals and get them on his payroll. For this, he had Sergei go down to the *Komsomolets* newspaper to place an ad that said: "Looking for 19-year-old men to work in a private security service—no experience required." This last point was not a sign of flexibility—he only wanted absolutely fresh men. He wanted amateurs.

All this became clear to Sergei, when he followed Szlotov around town auditioning thugs for the spots in the Private Security Service—that being an amateur was not optional. Although he never posed the question to Szlotov, Sergei—his old pal—knew what he was up to. Sergei saw Szlotov picked the meanest, most relentless applicants. Of course, the decisions were not accompanied by explanations: just a simple "That's one" or "Next."

Any boys who Szlotov chose were given a numbered invitation to a second gathering in an hour where they would be introduced to the plan. As the young men with invitations left in jubilation and the others left in anger, Sergei faced Szlotov.

"What are you planning?"

"I'll handle it," Szlotov said.

To the invited boys, Szlotov announced the plan was a private security service where the members were not part of some government but were private employees free to take out any one who even posed a threat.

After he arrived at the martial-arts gymnasium, Szlotov saw seven men. Szlotov told the group of seven out of 24 who received the invites what he had in mind, a group of security forces not afraid to work outside of the law. At that moment, Szlotov stopped to scan the faces. Another moment later, Szlotov looked at each of the faces of the boys. He dismissed the number-one boy Dmitri, who looked confused after Szlotov said: "Your life is about to change." To Ivan, the fourth boy, Szlotov barked: "Get the hell out of here." Ivan obliged and left the gym.

Completing his first cut of the boys, Szlotov saw that number six, Pyotr, was quaking in his boots and trying to hide it. Szlotov stood up next to the boy, who couldn't be 19 and who shook even more as Szlotov approached.

Szlotov stood with his killer's mouth near the trembling ear of Pyotr. "Why are you here?" Szlotov said. "Have you ever hurt anything? Ever killed a dog?"

"No," Pyotr said, wetting his dry throat. "I could never do that."

Szlotov stood back and let those words stand as the verdict on Pyotr. Szlotov moved away and Pyotr slipped out of line and left. Standing like a picket fence were four boys. Number two, Viktor, stood firm and resolute in light of the assignment. Szlotov instantly liked Viktor and decided that Vik was the find of the exercise. He would lead the remainder of the boys in a mission that Szlotov had in mind. Left over with Vik was Timofey, who looked like a toss-back until Szlotov saw Timofey and Viktor pair as leader and deputy. That left two more. Ilia was a young giant guaranteed to be selected unless he was dumb as a tree stump. Pavel, on the other hand, was small by comparison. His expression and his heavy-lidded eyes were calm. Pavel, a small young man who hunched over as he stood, presented no menace, no threat but still he remained.

"I once killed a squirrel," Pavel volunteered. Szlotov noticed how little Pavel moved his lips when he spoke. The lack of change in his facial features comforted Szlotov because it made him realize that Pavel would be free of remorse, a skill and talent Szlotov prized. He led the four of them out of the gym to a Volga truck with a soft cover over the back. Looking in the rear view mirror, Szlotov saw the four of them in back, on benches along the sides, facing each other, having no idea what they would be expected to do. While he drove the Volga truck, and shifted between the gears, Szlotov slid open the sliding window that separated the cab from the cargo area.

"Fellows," he said. They all stared at him, alert. "Tonight you are on stage. This is your audition. This evening we will determine what kind of men you are. Szlotov drove to Udelny Park and parked along the shoulder. He got out of the truck and scanned the trees along the horizon of the deep park. After a moment passed and he heard no sound from the back of the truck, he slapped on the side and yelled "Let's go, Let's go," and the four boys jumped out the back. Viktor, Timofey, Pavel and finally big Ilia emerged and looked around. Szlotov led them into the park. The boys trouped after him in the same order. After they had ventured 100 meters into the forest of Udelny Park, he saw a small homeless boy dart from the open behind a bush. Szlotov stopped and pointed.

"Do you see that?" he said. None of the boys said anything. Szlotov thought none of them had seen the movement. After the silence settled in, Szlotov dropped his arm and exhaled hard out his nose.

"Nobody saw that?" he repeated.

"I saw it," Pavel said, stepping forward of the other boys.

"You saw?" Szlotov said. "What did you see?"

"I saw... a *mongrel*," Pavel said.

"Correct," Szlotov said. "You saw a mongrel. And what do you *do* to a mongrel?"

"Throw it in the trash," said big Ilia, the giant in comparison to the others.

"*N'yet*," Szlotov said. "That's a waste. What are mongrel dogs good for?"

"Killing cats," Timofey said, and smiled.

"They're fun to kill," Pavel said with no change in his expression.

Szlotov nodded to these two uses but without enthusiasm.

"Sex," Ilia said. "All types of sex" he said and no one said anything. This caused Szlotov to arch one of his eyebrows.

"It happens," Szlotov said. He led all of them to the left into the dense undergrowth. Coming over a crest, they flushed the same little boy they startled before. Szlotov pointed to the hunched-over homeless boy and said "There's a dog. Kill it before it kills you." The four boys held back a moment. The dirty-faced young boy with tangled, sandy-brown hair hid under a bush. None of the boys struck and then Pavel, the boy with the firm expressionless face, flew forward and rained his fists down on the head and chest of the boy, who shrieked in pain. Hard fists accelerated on to his head and then Pavel landed some blows that sounded hollow on the head of the boy as if he were hitting a watermelon. The boy who lay on the muddy forest floor now made no more sounds except for the hollow thumps on his body that caused it to bounce up after the punches landed. Breathing hard, his fists wet and the inside of his thighs wet from losing his bladder, Pavel staggered off the dead body of the boy and stood, gape mouthed, facing Szlotov with the contorted and lifeless body of the boy behind him.

"Good job," Szlotov said. "The rest of you will carry the body to the back of the truck. One of you will go first—Vik—to make sure no one—not in the windows or anywhere down either end of the street—is watching. If someone can see—then you wait until it is clear. Understood?" he asked.

"Understood," the three said, shocked by the whole event. Szlotov stood back in the underbrush as Ilia and Timofey carried the lifeless body. Vik went ahead, looking left then right. Then, Szlotov was pleased to see Vik scan the upper floors of the opposing streets to make sure no one there could see.

"A good choice," he said out loud, in regard to his own choice of Vik as the leader. He looked over and smiled at Pavel, who now carried the sweet smell of urine. The boys dumped the body of the smaller boy in the back of the truck. They returned and none of them smiled.

"Welcome to the game," Szlotov said. "Leave now or stay forever." None moved. The mafia master, third in command of the Tambov Syndicate in St. Petersburg, turned and led his troupe deeper into the bowels of Udelny Park. They first approached the lake but veered off to the left and walked back a few yards from the shore. Szlotov noticed, up on the brow of the hill, an old concrete structure. The outer edge of the concrete slab revealed it was a pillbox from the Great Patriotic War against Hitler. The thick concrete walls remained formidable but the outer skin was pockmarked from the pebbles that had once been stuck in the concrete.

Looking down inside of the pillbox, Szlotov noted movement. Lacking the eyes of a predator, the boys looked all around and did not notice the old concrete structure. Thinking in silence, with his tongue pressed to the roof of his mouth, Szlotov thought about the best way to organize the boys. Then, in silence, he brought Vik's ear close to his mouth. He whispered directions that included pointing at the open end of the pillbox and pointing out a hole in the back of the pillbox where plants grew and revealed an extra entrance.

Vik nodded and mouthed the word "I understand". He went right up to Timofey and gave his own abbreviated instructions and pointed out what the plan was. When both Vik and Timofey faced the concrete pillbox, Szlotov leaned over and spoke to Pavel, who was shrouded in a humid cloud of his own acrid piss.

"See that white building?" Szlotov asked.

Pavel nodded.

"There are dogs in there," he said. Pavel ran up the hill to the pillbox. Timofey and Vik tore after him but in the last few meters Vik angled off to the back end of the concrete structure and leaped on the top. Szlotov jogged up the hill. When he reached the place, a tiny girl with blond hair ran out shrieking from the place. Timofey leaped after her and climbed on her back and rode the small child into the ground. Timofey raised his fist to strike the frightened girl but Szlotov shouted "Stop" and Timofey did, fist hanging in the air.

Surprised, Vik and Ilia stopped punching the many small children who had been laying there asleep. The ground continued to moan and squirm. A variety of small bodies lay there in a wet, bruised bunch. Still crying, the small child had a big head and small face, like the shape of a light bulb. Szlotov held up the small child and said: "What is your name?"

The child shivered with fear, and did not respond to any but physical movements, which caused her to moan and flinch.

"Oksana," she said, and resumed crying. Timofey raised his fist again and the little girl on the ground wailed as she looked up and saw the fist of Timofey, fall toward her little blond head. Before it reached her face, Szlotov kicked the fist aside and it landed on the concrete.

"Ooooh," Timofey yelled and rolled on the ground, his knuckles bleeding.

Oksana opened her eyes and looked up, the corners of her mouth pulled down, surprised she was alive.

"Knock it off," Szlotov said, and picked her up. He handed Oksana to

Ilia to carry. "And don't touch." Tightening his jaw, Ilia threw Oksana on his back. The girl wrapped her arms around his thick neck and parked her dirty bare feet between his pants and his belt.

"And now," Szlotov said with his voice raised as if he were making an announcement. "Carry these bodies to the truck."

"For what reason?" Timofey blurted. Szlotov answered by boxing him on the ear.

"Because," Szlotov said. "These bodies are trash. Trash like these makes Russia weak. And no work is done until the trash is collected."

"And what kind of work is this," Timofey said, rubbing his sore hand and his ear, alternately.

"When you get my age," Szlotov said, ignoring the insubordination implicit in Timofey's question. "You can decide what you work on. Until then leave the thinking to me." Without further argument, the boys resumed their former activity. Each carried a body out of the pillbox, down the hill back to the truck with Vik again at the front as a lookout. Other than Vik, each carried out the body of a small child, who might require remedial beating on the spot to finish them off. With Oksana clinging to his shoulders, Ilia picked up another girl from the concrete floor who was half unconscious, blood leaking from her nose and eyes. Ilia picked up the girl by the hair and then he punched her face.

The limbs hanging from his left hand fell limp. He threw the body under his arm and headed up the hill to the truck. Vik stood by the truck and motioned up Pavel, Timofey and Ilia with the bodies. When they had all taken the last one out of the pillbox, Szlotov followed Timofey to the truck, which was stacked with the corpses of small boys and girls. Timofey carried the last body over his shoulder, holding the little boy's ankles and letting the head and arms flop side-to-side behind him. As Szlotov assembled the group behind the truck and Pavel closed the tailgate and then tied the cover down, Szlotov allowed his eyes to drift and focus on the sidewalk behind the truck, where he was startled to see a woman standing, frozen in place with her eyes open, her tongue protruding and her throat showing signs of peristaltic action, like she was ready to vomit.

"Relax," Szlotov said and walked toward the woman. She wore a black scarf around her head, covering wisps of white hair and peculiar red blotches on her cheeks.

Although Szlotov had spoken to her, the woman stood motionless and petrified. Szlotov approached her and put his arm around her shoulders. His other hand holding her wrist, Szlotov walked the woman to the back of the truck. The boys leaped back in horror at seeing the woman, who could have been any of their grandmothers.

"*N'yet,*" the woman said as she saw the four blood-spattered boys standing there. Tears rolled down her cheeks and she struggled with Szlotov.

She tried to free her arm. Szlotov took his hands off her shoulders. He put them over her neck and, with technical accuracy learned in the KGB, pressed the flat edges of his fingers on her carotid artery and collapsed it, thereby causing her to faint. For good measure, he jerked her chin to the right until he heard the satisfying crunch like mashing a pile of crackers.

The boys winced at the sound but Szlotov angled his head while he held her body for the boys to get in back. The boys climbed in the truck and helped Szlotov load her into the back of the truck. With one final look around, Szlotov tied down the back and got in to drive. Before Szlotov took off, he stared in back to check on the condition of his cargo.

Right up next to the window, their faces pressed as close as possible to the window and the fresh air coming through it, were Vik, Pavel, Ilia and Timofey. Behind them, Szlotov was surprised at how tall and steeply piled were the bodies of the boys.

Szlotov drove off and was surprised at how much weight the Volga had gained. Cycling through the gears, Szlotov headed for Prospekt Nevski, and he smiled when he imagined the expression of Dr. Mansoor when they pulled up. As he drove along, the light changed from green to yellow and, contrary to his custom, Szlotov decided to stop. The big, heavy truck nosed down as the truck tires dug in and stopped them. The boys in back slammed with a scream against the window.

A millisecond after the boys hit, a wave of juice splashed red up on the window, followed by the thump and wet slap as the tower of bodies tumbled forward and buried the boys against the window. Under the pile of bodies, the face of Ilia remained in view, pressed against the window next to a red smear.

"That's enough," Szlotov yelled, irritated. "Make it orderly." With that command, the four boys in back strained together and were able to roll off the clump of cold bodies. Working through the gears, Szlotov drove the truck to his building on 56 Zhukovskovo Street with a steel door that led straight into the basement. Backing up, Szlotov backed the truck up next to the basement door. After he parked and turned off the engine, he jumped out of the truck and went smiling to knock on the steel basement door.

He rapped hard on the door and of course there was no reply. Considering the truck's cargo, Szlotov decided against using his Glock to get the Doctor's attention. He instead opted for the subtle approach, which meant fire. He took out a Zippo and grabbed a strip of newsprint on the ground. He rolled the newsprint into a tube and slipped it under the Doctor's door. He pushed the tube down and lit the end so the smoke funneled inside. After at least twenty seconds, Szlotov heard the sound of feet rumbling across the concrete floor, exclaiming "Oh my God," and the door swung open. Standing there was Doctor himself, his glasses perched on the tip of his nose and his left eye as cloudy and milk colored as ever.

"Shhh," Szlotov said to the Doctor, who stood in place with wrinkles of concern knitting his brow. The Doctor's tongue nervously explored his diseased gums as he opened the door. Szlotov looked for someplace to put the bodies. He saw the wood-slatted cages in the far end of the basement. Szlotov clicked his tongue as the Doctor waited.

"Fellows," Szlotov called back to the truck. "I want Vik first." The Doctor turned his head sideways and looked at the cloth flap of the truck where the head of Vik, as if on cue, peered out of the hole, looking around before he allowed his bloody torso to become exposed as he climbed down, and made a strong case for remaining the leader, as he made an elaborate show of checking out the area. It was enough to make even Szlotov smile at the show, knowing the region was one of the worst in St. Petersburg. Then, without prompting from Szlotov, Vik untied the flaps and motioned to the boys inside to start feeding out the bodies. As the head of the first gray-skinned boy emerged in the hands of Timofey up in the truck, the Doctor came unglued.

"*N'yet,*" he screamed and ran at the truck to stop the corpse from coming any farther. "What the hell is this?" As the Doctor ran forward, Szlotov came after him and stopped his progress with a palm on the shoulder.

"It's nothing," Szlotov said, and gave a rare smile. Still unwavering in his objection, the Doctor moved his jaw side to side so his bottom tooth hooked between the two above it. The pain and bleeding around his gums and the throbbing pain distracted him.

"Where to?" Vik asked Szlotov.

"Next to the wooden cages," Szlotov said.

"Impossible," the Doctor said. "Unbelievable...I'm not running a morgue."

"Listen to me," Szlotov said, looking the Doctor in the eyes from a distance of twenty centimeters. "I tell you what kind of business you run and for tonight, you are running a slaughterhouse. I will bring you some punks with sharp knifes to help."

To this short address, Dr. Mansoor had no retort. His reaction was evident in his hyperventilation. Without intervention from Szlotov, the boys transferred the pile of gray-red bodies into the basement, next to the cages. In the cage next to the pile sat a few young kids, wide eyed. They froze in place as the gray clay-like bodies, piled up next to them.

Finally at the edge of the truck bed, stood the girl Oksana. She emerged wide-eyed from the truck and stood there. Turning, Szlotov noticed the *devochka* (little girl) and said:

"Oh, I forgot." As Ilia hiked in his breath and twitched in Oksana's direction, Szlotov grabbed Oksana by the upper arm and plucked her from the truck and through the air, plopping her down at the feet of the Doctor. "Here you go, a present."

Looking gape-mouthed at the floor, the Doctor asked, "For what do I need this?"

"Everybody needs a pet," Szlotov said. "Give it a knife and teach it to butcher. We need all this meat de-boned." And with that, he scanned the room and made sure that everything was orderly.

"Well, that's it," Szlotov announced, slapping his hands together. "Boys, the Doctor will give you a hose and a mop. Clean the truck and yourselves." Oksana stood under the grip of the Doctor. She looked up in awe at Szlotov. He paid no attention to the other people in the room, he was so consumed by his thoughts. Not waiting to be prompted, Vik stepped forward and tapped the Doctor on the arm.

"Doc," Vik said, staring up with his boy eyes into the old man eyes of the Doctor. "Doctor," Vik repeated and shook the Doctor's free arm enough to break the doc out of his scowling reverie. The Doctor glared at Szlotov, who was making his life miserable and always tossing new problems into his quiet basement where he wanted to be left alone.

When the Doctor did not respond to the gentle tug, Vik jerked his arm and got a "quit bothering me."

"Give me a hose and mop," Vik said.

"Get it yourself," growled the Doctor, pointing his thick dirty thumbnail at a corner. Vik went there and found the hose, which he opened and sprayed around the room.

"Watch out—" shouted the Doctor. He shielded his radio from the water spray. "This is a sensitive instrument." He emitted a mucus-filled growl.

Vik laughed at the Doctor's reaction. He dragged the hose and directed the water spray inside the truck.

"Ilia," Vik said. Ilia stood frozen looking at the puddle of blood. Then, he snapped awake and leaped up in the truck and took the mop.

Vik resisted the urge to spray Ilia as they cleaned all the blood stains from the truck. Then Ilia yelled for Vik to spray the front of the truck. Without missing a beat, Vik angled the spray at the back of Ilia's head and drenched him. Ilia threw down the mop and leaped out of the truck. He meant to run downstairs but instead he hit the door sill with his forehead. The impact knocked Ilia off his feet and he landed head-first on the steps.

Dropping the gushing hose, Vik ran over with Timofey, Pavel and Szlotov himself.

The four of them watched a red scrape well into a bubble of blood on Ilia's forehead. Szlotov pressed on the scrape to see if the bone was broken.

"*Blyat!*" Ilia roared, returning to full consciousness.

157

Hearing this, Szlotov smiled and leaned back against the cold concrete wall. The Doctor stood apart from the injured boy. He led Oksana into the wood-slatted box on the right. They had to walk around the stinking, leaky pile of bodies. The Doctor opened the box, swung the wooden door shut and threw a lock on it. Putting her hands on the wood slats with her small fingers white from gripping the pine, Oksana peered to her right and saw three dirty children, alive, in the adjacent cage. Oksana was assaulted by the stench coming from the feces piled under the other box.

"I don't have time for this garbage," the Doctor said, wringing his hands.

"Put him in the truck," Szlotov said. After everything was clear, Szlotov loaded up his crew and closed up the back of the truck. The job was done. He drove back to the original place where he drafted them. As he drove to the basement of the apartment building where he found these four boys, he asked each of them for a telephone number, which he wrote with a short pencil into a black book. He was about to send them away. He took out his wallet, peeled off four hundred-dollar bills and gave one to each of them. The boys took the money and walked, grinning, into the morning fog.

Driving the truck back to the sausage plant, Szlotov got on his cell phone and called up Sergei, telling him to come and pick him up.

"Where have you been?" Sergei said, with much urgency in his cell phone. "What is all this about?"

"Relax and be comfortable," Szlotov said, smiling. "Just come to the parking lot of Chus Meats."

"Right on it," Sergei said.

"And one more thing," Szlotov added. "I have a new assignment for the three punks in number 87."

"Eighty-seven?"

"Prospekt Metallistov," Szlotov said. The location was clear. Sergei and Szlotov had both grown up in the same building. "I want them to go visit the Doctor."

"The Doctor?" Sergei repeated with his eyebrows raised.

"The *good* Doctor."

"Ah," Sergei said and nodded. "For what reason?"

"The Doctor will explain. Tell them, though, to bring dirty clothes to change into and lots of opaque plastic bags. Tough ones."

"Understood," Sergei replied. Szlotov got ready to hang up.

"Any questions?" Szlotov said.

"Yes," Sergei said. "What is going on? Why are you doing this?"

"It's nothing," Szlotov said. "Don't think about it. More revenue."

"I will send the men right to the Doctor," Sergei said, summarizing his assignment and eager to do something.

"And after you send them, send *Ivan* to take their place in apartment #87, Got that?"

Sergei made no reply for a moment. "Clear," Sergei said. He always lingered at the end of conversations.

"Well, that's it then," Szlotov said and hung up his phone. "*Quite a day's work*," he told himself.

2.

Two hours later, Szlotov slapped Sergei on the shoulder and smiled his cold, powerful grin. They sat together in Café Galla, which Szlotov effectively owned.

"Let's go to the Nevski Melody," Szlotov said, which was located in the ground floor of a hotel in the *Bolshoi Okhta* region near where they both grew up. When Szlotov named the place, Sergei flinched. Nevski Melody was the disco where, years before, a girl had approached Szlotov next to the entrance. He shot her in the forehead at point-blank range. Sergei stopped in mid sentence with his lips pressed together as if he wanted to speak. He waited ten seconds without saying a word.

"Vladimir," Sergei said to Szlotov. One of his rights as a long-standing companion was using Szlotov's first name. "Vlad, do you think we really should return there, after the…" and there Sergei trailed off. Even though he was brave enough to use Szlotov's first name, he lacked the courage to mention the girl who Szlotov had shot and who almost got him put in jail. "…After *her*."

"Nonsense," Szlotov said and smiled more for effect than true joy. Szlotov no longer cared. A man of his power and stature lived by another code: getting things done. Szlotov no longer waited for others to take action; he needed to be in charge of his world like Stalin. "We will go *exactly* there," Szlotov said with no hint of hesitation in his voice. Sergei, having been in Szlotov's service long enough, knew better than to say another word on the topic.

"Understood," Sergei said, lowering his eyelashes in deference.

"And we will get some girls," Szlotov said.

"Girls?" Sergei asked with his eyebrow raised. "Who?" Szlotov smiled. He knew that Sergei had no woman which he attributed to his job but in fact stemmed more from his quiet, shy disposition than lack of opportunity. In fact, even when they were teenagers, women went straight to Szlotov. It was Szlotov, with his short dark hair, his solid black eyebrows that dominated his face with the double arch over his fierce eyes, who seemed to catch the eye of whoever he laid eyes on. In a way, Szlotov had been like Sergei's father over their lives. It made him trust Szlotov's judgment.

"For me," Sergei said, with a rare bloom of assertion. "There will be no girl."

"Nonsense, why not invite that *devushka* from the tobacco kiosk on Yakornaya Street."

"What?" Sergei said. He turned his palms upward as if he had never heard of Yakornaya Street or the kiosk or the girl who worked there. Szlotov knew better. It was two blocks from Prospekt Metallistov—Sergei had grown up in #85 while Szlotov and his mother lived across the hall in #86, the same place where Szlotov's mother still lived.

Szlotov smiled, having fun after his hard work in Udelny park.

"Okay," said Szlotov. "I will pick her for you."

"When?"

"Right now," Szlotov said. He picked up his cashmere jacket and left Café Galla without concerning himself with the bill for the runny *Kefir*, the black bread as tough as linoleum and a tiny glass of French cognac. Szlotov headed for his BMW while Sergei headed for his.

"Ride with me," Szlotov said. "I'll show you how it's done." The two childhood friends drove through St. Petersburg. They turned on to Prospekt Nevski and continued past the Paris-like buildings and the big green Moskovsky Vokzal across the drawbridge named for Alexander Nevski, turning left in Ploshad Zanevski on to Novocherkasskaya street, which fed on to Zakornaya to the right. Sergei became anxious as it became clear to him that Vladimir Szlotov had noticed the kiosk where the girl he liked worked. And, when Szlotov drove to that kiosk, Sergei grew nervous.

"This isn't the right one," Sergei lied.

"Yes it is," Szlotov said. He parked the car in front of the kiosk, three meters away from the window. "Get going. She might not even be working." This possibility emboldened Sergei. He marched with resolution across the pavement until it became clear from his slowed gait that the girl, Yana, was indeed working and that Sergei was petrified. After a moment, Sergei returned to the car with a bottle of Baltika-*4* beer, smiling.

"Is she coming?" Szlotov asked.

"I did not ask her," Sergei replied.

"Again," said Szlotov and he ordered Sergei back to the kiosk. This time Sergei stayed longer. He stood at the window on one leg and then on the other, talking, and letting other customers continue to come up to the window. After about three minutes at the window, Sergei returned, walking but with his head held high, blushing across his cheeks from the lowest edges of his jowls to under his eyes.

"Coming?" Szlotov asked. Sergei smiled and mused at his thoughts. "Is she coming?" Szlotov repeated.

"Oh, no," Sergei said, still beaming. "She has to work," and then he tilted his head in the direction of the kiosk, as if that would alleviate his lack of communication.

"Back," Szlotov ordered. "The answer must be 'yes'."

"She has to *work*."

"Here," Szlotov said. "We have other work for her." He reached for his wallet. He took out his wad of money, including both Russian rubles in the tan color with the highlights of red, and American hundred-dollar bills. He folded away the rubles and thumbed off four Ben Franklins. "Take this," he said and handed Sergei the money. "Try again," Szlotov said and waved his hand in the direction of the kiosk. Sergei held the money between his fingers without moving, seeming submerged in thought. Then, after the delay, he opened the car door and went back to the kiosk. This time he blocked the window with his shoulders and did not move to allow other customers to pass. After he backed up his BMW about a meter, Szlotov could see the face of the girl, who had sandy brown hair. The conversation continued until, at one point, Szlotov saw Sergei's elbow move into the kiosk to hand over the money. Szlotov felt amused as he watched the scene unfold. He wished he could know how Sergei had offered the money—as a price for her sexual favors or as promised replacement for the receipts she would lose that night. Szlotov saw the metal doors going up inside and then the girl, Yana, came out and put on the shutters. Sergei helped her. Then she came out, stone-faced, a plain blond, in her coat. She came over and then bent over to peer in the car where Szlotov's eyes waited for her, unsmiling. Despite her fear, she got in back with Sergei. Sergei said nothing.

"Where are we going?" Yana asked. Her voice was high and reedy.

"To Nevski Melody," Szlotov said.

Yana relaxed after she understood they were headed to the famous Nevski Melody disco. The disco was located along the mighty Neva River. Szlotov parked in front of the disco. Sergei opened his door and helped Yana get out, but he kept his eye on Szlotov and the Sverdlovskaya Lane North and South that bordered the Neva River. Sergei put his hand on his pistol inside his coat. Time seemed to slow down. Szlotov and Sergei exchanged looks that indicated where and how Szlotov wanted to enter the new situation. Sergei did not mask his sense of irritation at Vladimir for having brought them once again to the one place in all of Petersburg where Szlotov was not welcome. Yana stood near Sergei, her brow tensely wrinkled, her eyes wide, and her face taut.

After one-and-a-half seconds of vigilance, Sergei moved to the door and Yana followed alongside as the captive of his hand. He scooped her by her upper arm and brought her to the door of Nevski Melody disco where she entered the small antechamber first, followed by Sergei.

"We want tickets, two men," Sergei said, thereby implying that Yana would be considered a prostitute who was exempt from charge. Sergei himself was unfamiliar with the act of asking for and buying tickets since no mafia member paid anywhere but in the case of this particular establishment he decided to bypass the usual process and just buy for them out of his own supply of rubles that he kept folded up in an inner pocket of his wallet.

"Hundred-lemon," said the woman behind the counter, charging Sergei the full rate. That cleaned him out and triggered a rumble of Russian profanity that he spilled out along with the money. The woman gave Sergei the tickets. An instant later Szlotov came through the door, slapping one of his brown cashmere gloves on top of another. The clerk who sold Sergei the tickets dropped her jaw as Szlotov passed and went downstairs to the disco. Szlotov smiled, feeling that his anger might be abated by a good night in the bar with a dozen-or-so floozies. Then Szlotov entered the disco and appraised the room. He noted an entrance on the far side of the room led to another room. He would watch that entrance. Along the mahogany bar on the left sat a bald-headed man with a blond walrus mustache thick as a banana. To the beat of Russian disco, four sweet young things worked it out on the chessboard dance floor under roving colored lights. One girl was wearing a white leather micro skirt that didn't come much below her hipbone. She was hinged at the waist and rocked back and forth with her forearms parallel. Szlotov watched her dance. The other three on the dance floor were journeymen hookers. They probably went to high school during the week. Then, every Friday and Saturday night, they came here for free to dance and maybe take a Ben Franklin from some rich man. Surrounding the dance floor were black leather booths. Sergei sat Yana at a table. As she took off her coat and exposed the reasons for Sergei's fascination, all across the disco arms folded among the girls who came to this club week-after-week and who thought: "Now who is this bitch with two guys?"

As Szlotov took off his coat and revealed his suit and blue tie beneath, the tail of his coat pulled back his suit and exposed his gun holster.

The two waitresses saw the gun. They stood frozen for a few seconds until Szlotov smiled with his perfect teeth at them and said "Don't be afraid". The brown-haired girl in front who looked about 19-years old wavered in her frozen footsteps. Then she darted back into the kitchen. The second waitress, about 27, fat and with a line of dark hairs over her lip, lingered a moment longer to get a good look at Szlotov. He saw her stare at him and knew. She must have been there the day he shot the waitress in the forehead for startling him.

"*Devushka!*" Szlotov shouted at her. The waitress came over. "Brandy for the gentlemen and wine for the lady." She stared in his eyes and Szlotov nodded, in his mind saying "Yes, I *will* kill you if I must."

At this table in the darkness of Nevski Melody, Szlotov loosened his tie and unbuttoned the top button of his blue Oxford shirt. The air in the disco pounded with the hump and bump of the bass-driven beat. On the dance floor several muscular girls humped the air. As if by a gravitational force, Szlotov found his eyes drawn back to the young things. He noticed Sergei and Yana did not talk. She sat next to Szlotov and Sergei on her other side. Szlotov chewed on a drink stirrer he found laying on the table in front of him. Sergei swaggered up to prominence as he regaled Yana in his idiosyncratic way of the life of a bodyguard. Szlotov didn't listen. He watched a young blond woman in blue hot pants dance well on the candy-colored floor. Szlotov had begun to feel in command of his world. As his constant passion was money, he was always different from the other boys; he was willing to take chances when the other boys were not.

"Some good strawberries," Sergei said, nodding his head at the laboring hind ends hawking their wares on the dance floor. A *strawberry* was the term he and Szlotov had used since childhood to describe vivacious girls like these.

"I sent out a new crew today," Szlotov said. Szlotov was, of course, referring to the crew of punks that he gathered in full view of Sergei without ever committing to a purpose for them. After the announcement settled in, Sergei's brow furrowed and his whole attitude sobered up as he understood what Szlotov was talking about.

"Sent out?" Sergei said. "To do what? Damn it, Vladimir, why am I working for you, as your bodyguard, if you won't take me with you? You think this is the life I want? I should start my own crew. I was with you and Zortaev in the beginning and I am now your bodyguard? This is *unacceptable*, Vladimir."

Sergei had spoken a little too loudly and Szlotov was forced to utter a terse "*Quiet*," which said everything.

"It was an *experiment*, Sergei. I promise you, very soon you will know the outcome of my experiment," Szlotov said, using the special Russian word that meant *anything goes*. "We collected street kids."

"More?" Sergei said, after hesitation. "So *that's* where you were. Why did you keep this a secret from *me*?"

"For many reasons," Szlotov said, none of which he explained. He wanted a new crew who were hungry. Sitting next to Sergei, Yana stood and announced she was going to the toilet.

"Be quick about it then," Sergei said.

With Yana gone, and the two of them sat together in Nevski Melody and Sergei repeated his previous question but with an air of exasperation.

"The pretty kids," Szlotov said, taking a drink, "are useful for their orifices—working on their backs. The glue sniffers, the sick ones, are good only for their meat. Now, I have a use for every one of them. Especially the healthy ones, Seriyozha," Szlotov answered, using his childhood nickname for Sergei. "They get to meet the Doctor. He cuts up the pie and we will sell the slices to my friend Yakov." This was so important that Szlotov himself wanted to lead the first harvest, along with the crew of punks that he had cast for the raid, punks young enough to take a hit and keep on fighting.

"And for those pieces of the pie, kidneys, eyes, hearts," Szlotov said. "It means *big* money." Sergei sat back in his chair and hung his arms in surprise at the scope of Szlotov's plan.

"When were you going to tell me, Vladimir?" Sergei asked.

"I just did."

"Shhh," Sergei said, having snapped out of his shock enough to know that such matters must at all costs be kept secret. "Let's not talk about it, not here," Sergei said.

Yana came out of the hallway where the bathrooms were. Szlotov watched, across the checkerboard dance floor, the far hallway he had kept an eye on all night. Yana walked out from the right and made her turn to walk back to them. Along the left wall ran the mahogany bar, dark and oily, with several stools unoccupied. Seated at the mahogany bar was a young blond with blue hot pants, working a swizzle stick between her tight 17-year-old teeth. When Yana walked by her, the blond girl pounced on Yana and started speaking face-to-face, with Yana holding both of the blond girl's wrists.

Breathing out of his nose, Szlotov rose from the table and walked up to the blond girl, whose back was presented to him in the turned-up manner of a baboon and so, with his left hand, he reached up with his hand upside down, to pinch her as if he was getting a dash of turmeric out of a spice jar. Szlotov executed this move on the blond girl and she leaped up two feet in place and on the way down she rotated and swung her fist at him. He caught her fist and held on as he rotated her falling body counter-clockwise so she landed on her face on the hard floor. The girl lay there and the entire house stopped in place to watch. It all happened so fast that the people who saw the original fall were outnumbered by the ones who saw Szlotov reach across the girl on the floor to take Yana's hand. Szlotov led Yana back to their table while murmurs and disquiet overtook the disco. Sergei came behind them but Szlotov led her to a chair and sat her down. Sergei sat down next to her.

"What happened?" Sergei asked. She whimpered: "That whore said 'this isn't your territory'. And I told her 'I don't *have* a territory' and that's when she punched me in the…"

"Little Kitten," Sergei said. He rubbed Yana's shoulder.

"Sergei," Szlotov said. "Go get our… our girl water from the bar."

Feeling stripped away from her, Sergei gritted his teeth and went to the bar. He returned with an iced glass of water for Yana and a shot of rum for himself. Szlotov was not thirsty. He kept his attention focused on the blond girl—who still nursed her arm from her hard landing—in case she decided to throw a shot glass or worse. Sergei threw back the rum neat and burped. After he burped, Szlotov exchanged a look with Yana, in which he lifted his eyebrows as if to ask her 'Are you okay?' Yana lifted her head.

"I want a drink," she said.

Sergei returned from the bar with another two shots. He set them down on the table, one in front of himself, the other in front of Szlotov, who folded out his lower lip and said "Don't need it." Without a word of acknowledgment, Sergei took his own shot and then followed that with the other. Yana sat back in her chair with her arms crossed under her bosom and her chin resting on her chest.

"I'm tired," Yana said and then yawned in a visual corroboration.

"So what?" Sergei said, looking down at the bottom of his shot glass for any last droplets of rum. He dabbed his finger into the bottom well of his shot glass and transferred the oily rum sediment to his meaty tongue and ignored her.

"Be quiet," Szlotov said and tapped the table with his left hand's fingernails, each with an even arc of white for the uniform distance he cut his nails. He craved perfection in all areas.

Sergei sat back in his chair in silence. Szlotov leaned forward on his elbows and Yana leaned toward Szlotov and rested her forehead on his upper arm.

"Why the hell did we come here?" Sergei yelled.

"*Because*," Szlotov said and pivoted on his chair to face Sergei. For a second of tense silence, the two of them stared into each other's eyes and scowled. Finally, being the beta wolf, Sergei looked away and smiled into a full episode of laughter.

"You win, yes—always—Vlad is the leader," Sergei said with an exaggeration in the rhythm of his speech, as if giving a sing-song imitation of a child's voice. "'Let's go ask Vladdy Szlotov'," Sergei said. Szlotov felt mortified to see the kind of sour mood Sergei had fallen into.

"Calm yourself," Szlotov said, after a moment of consideration.

"Well, you don't *always* get your way," Sergei said, and laughed. Sergei sat, his arms crossed, with a residual smile that indicated he was keeping a secret.

Szlotov took a deep breath and tried to allow the remark to fade into the vapors without picking it up off the vapors and remarking on it.

"Like, for example?" Szlotov said. Yana herself waited to see the outcome.

Sergei gave a broad grin as his reply. Twenty seconds ticked by with Sergei leaning back in his chair, smiling, knitting his fingers together behind his neck, still without giving an answer to the question.

"Well?" Szlotov said using the nasal Russian word that signified vast irritation. Szlotov lifted his eyebrows in unison to signify it was an ultimatum.

"Very well, then," Sergei said, huddling next to the table. "I will tell you a little something. That reporter you yourself helped kill? Remember?"

Szlotov's face snapped into the shape of an exclamation point, his eyebrows pressing forward from his scalp, his upper lip pinching together in the shape of a volcano and its caldera and within him boiled the fires of anger that did not appear on the surface.

"I remember," Szlotov said with the cold monotone of one who does not yet know if the memory is sound.

"Well," Sergei said with a cutesy insubordinate bounce in his. "The man *you* killed was the *editor*, not the reporter. You—Comrade Szlotov—were made the fool."

Other than the swelling of his cheeks from his gritted teeth, Szlotov gave no outward evidence of the rage brewing inside him.

"This is the truth?" Szlotov asked.

Pulling his lower lip back covering his lower teeth, Sergei nodded.

"Okay," Szlotov said. "It's time to leave. Girl," he said, turning to Yana, "we'll take you home now."

Bewildered by the entire evening, Yana threw on her coat and followed Szlotov out of the disco, followed by Sergei. They returned to the car and drove to Yana's part of town, near the Zvoznaya Metro station. There was no conversation beyond directions and when they reached her stop, Sergei got out of the backseat first, irritated that he wasn't driving. Before she exited the front seat, she turned back to Szlotov and smiled, saying "Pleased to meet you" and then she left. Sergei acted sullen and he refused to meet eyes with Szlotov.

As they drove away, Szlotov looked at the streets signs for the intersection, and he tucked the information into his memory.

3.

They drove away from Yana's apartment.

"Okay," Szlotov said. "You still have the newspaper about the waif children?"

"Yes, in my car," Sergei said. They drove there and Sergei found the

166

newspaper for the *Nevski Novosti* which carried the story.

"Here," Sergei said, handing Szlotov the browned newspaper.

"Don't care about the story," Szlotov said. "I want the masthead."

Sitting in Sergei's front seat with one Italian shoe in fine tan leather on the wet ground, Szlotov held his arms up and read the paper's roster of employees.

NEVSKI NOVOSTI
Publisher: Vadim Blodski
Editor in Chief: Alexander I. Krasnie
Managing Editor: Sarah Hughes
Culture Editor: Yelena Smartova
English Editor: Jack Land
Computers: Vasya Khodney

Szlotov spoke the names of the staff and his mouth got stuck trying to pronounce the name "Jack."

"What kind of name is this 'Jack'," Szlotov asked.

"Like President Kennedy?" Sergei said, looking to Szlotov for a nod. "You know, the American who Fidel Castro shot?" Szlotov shook his head: he didn't recognize the man. Sergei laughed, delighted to know something Szlotov did not. "*Jack* Kennedy?" Sergei said.

Szlotov shook his head.

"You know," Sergei said. "He *fucked* Marilyn Monroe."

"Ah," Szlotov said. "Now I remember him... Sickly. Second son."

"Yes," Sergei said, beaming from the entire encounter.

Sergei then pointed at the Editor: "*This* is the man you killed." Then he shifted his finger to the name 'Jack Land.' "And this is your man—the *Amerikanets* who walks the streets of St. Petersburg and breathes the same air as you and I."

"Okay," Szlotov said. He took out his cell phone and made a call. "Sasha, Szlotov speaking."

Szlotov listened to the other party on the phone.

"Thank you Sasha, I'll be there," Szlotov said, smiling. "By the way, I have a little something for you—a name in that killing—you know—the one where the children were all cut up and pitched in the landfill. Yes." Szlotov

167

listened for a moment. "Jack Land—an American. Reporter."

Szlotov smiled as he stared down at the ground and listened to his cell phone with his leather shoe pressed on the ground outside the car. He laughed and said: "You would love Sochi. Yes." Szlotov listened and then said: "Sasha, there's another thing. Some old friends from school. I know names but need a few addresses." Szlotov gave the *Militsiya* officer who was his friend the names Sarah Hughes, Yelena Smartova and Vasya Khodney.

"*Spacibo* Sasha," Szlotov said and pulled out a notebook and pen. He wrote for a moment and said "Together? How easy. And Hughes, Sarah. British...thank you." He wrote down the information. "Have fun in Sochi, bye-bye." Sergei sat in the passenger seat and smiled. Szlotov dialed a second number.

"Valery," he said. He waited a moment and then he smiled and said: "My friend. No, everything is great. I'm calling with a tip. I've become aware that there's an American working in St. Petersburg. His visa has expired. Reporter. Jack Land. The *Militsiya* are looking for him in connection to those bodies of kids that turned up all chopped up in the dump. Yeah, pretty terrible American, the pigs."

Szlotov listened for a few moments and hung up the phone, smiling. He turned to Sergei.

"We've done some reporting on our reporter, and if they can't find him, we will." Szlotov sat thinking. Then he said, "Seriyozha, please lend me *your* phone for a moment."

"For what reason?" Sergei said. He was reluctant to hand it over.

"I want to call someone anonymously," Szlotov said. Rolling his eyes, Sergei handed over his phone. Szlotov pressed a few buttons and then stared long at a number. He handed the phone back to Sergei and entered a number into his own phone.

"Who do you want to call?" Sergei said, after a period of silence.

"Call? Oh, I changed my mind. I will call Boris," Szlotov said and proceeded to do so.

"Leontev?" Sergei asked.

"Yes, Boris Leontev," Szlotov said. He waited for the phone to ring. Just hearing the name Boris Leontev, Sergei knew it was something big. Szlotov would not bother Boris—the most famous assassin in their *Brotherhood-of-Seven Thieves*—for any trivial reason. Boris had been 'off-duty' for the past few months because of a gunshot wound. The wound was in his left shoulder. The word around the ranks was that Boris had lost his nerve.

The call went through to Boris. He and Szlotov exchanged some small talk.

"Listen," Szlotov said. "I have a job for you."

"I'm not working yet. I'm still recovering," Boris said, with an impatient sigh.

"An American," Szlotov said, knowing that Boris hated Americans and would do anything to kill one.

"Got it," Boris said, and then sighed with great force. "Okay, where do I go?"

"Come to the office," Szlotov said.

"Okay," Boris said, mobilized. "In an hour?"

"An hour," Szlotov said. "I'll be seeing you." Szlotov lifted his Italian-leather shoe off the wet concrete, closed his door. They drove back toward Prospekt Nevski, crossing the Palace bridge over the wide rippling waters of the Neva, the outflow of a continent. His car was running warm and he alternated glances at the temperature gauge with his attention to the road, silently infuriated at the recurrence of a supposedly-resolved problem with the thermostat.

Szlotov remembered the last conversation he had with Boris before the shooting. Boris had controlled the daily collections from his territory. He had a nightclub owner near Prospekt Ligovsky who wasn't paying proper tribute. Boris had confronted the owner of the Candy Man disco with the obvious signs of his prosperity, the long lines of sweet young things waiting to get in every night, the crowded dance floor. The owner said they were all hookers and they danced without buying any drinks and could not be charged a cover. Boris had gone to the owner's apartment. When the man left in the morning, Boris had planned to get him. Instead, Boris was surprised to find the owner armed with a pistol with his finger on the trigger. Not being a professional killer, the disco owner had aimed for the heart, not the nostril, and so his bullet had pierced Boris next to his left arm. Boris was right handed and so he fired a round up each of the owner's nostrils. As the former owner of the Candy Man disco dropped to his knees, Boris had put another pair of rounds into the top of the man's head before he felt overcome by pain. Boris worked alone and he was able to get into his own car and drive a few blocks away from the murder scene. When Szlotov received the call from his friend Boris, they were a few minutes apart but Szlotov had heard Boris drop his phone. Szlotov imagined Boris slumped over in his car, dead. As he raced to the scene, Szlotov would not concede that Boris was gone. He called the Emergency Clinic and told them to prepare for a man shot by thieves trying to steal his car.

"We'll send the *Skorry* right out," said the clerk at the Emergency Clinic. "Where is his car located? Have you informed the *Militsiya*?"

The 'Skorry' was the joke of an ambulance service, which made a mockery of its name 'Quick Help' when in reality that help could arrive, in a typical life-or-death situation, 8 hours later.

"Don't bother. I'll bring him in myself," Szlotov had said. With that, Szlotov ended the call and stepped on the gas. He had seen Boris's car as the brake lights gleamed bright and steady on the side of the road, not stopped parallel but at an angle as if the car had just veered off the road.

Szlotov remembered the way he had found his friend: slumped forward on the steering wheel, gray faced, silent, his own syrupy blood pooling at his feet. Szlotov had dragged Boris out of his car and into his own car's back seat. He shut Boris's car door, got in his own and flew to the hospital, where Boris was operated on. Szlotov gave the doctor twenty hundred-dollar bills to keep silent about the gunshot wound.

All these memories flashed through his mind as he went to the basement where the Doctor performed his essential and cheaper services for the *organizatsiya*. Already there, sitting in his car with the lights off, was Boris. As usual, Boris was the first person to arrive for any meeting. Boris came early, prepared. Szlotov saw the dark two sides of hair astride his round, shiny bald head. Matching the two sides of hair were two dark black sides of his mustache, both above Boris's unsmiling mouth. Szlotov shut off his own lights and car. He got out and walked half the way to Boris's car. Boris got out of the car. His left arm swung with out any sign of interference or pain from a scar. As Boris came over his right arm swung with purpose. Boris came up to Szlotov and neither of them smiled. The two men stared into each other's eyes as they gripped and shook their two clutched hands.

Szlotov looked into Boris' eyes, with their gray pale membrane of color around the iris. Recalling back to the first time they met eight years earlier, Szlotov measured against the original to see how Boris was holding up. After an interval, Szlotov had to admit to himself that there were no signs of weakness or distress.

"Everything all right?" Szlotov asked.

"It's nothing," Boris said, and broke the handshake. Wanting to ask more, Szlotov turned toward the basement door. To his surprise, Szlotov found the basement door moved when he placed his hand on it. In the next moment, Szlotov shoved open the basement door. The floodlights shone on the Doctor, soaked in blood up to his neck, holding open a heavily-laden plastic bag, filled with rubbery chicken-breast-like slabs of meat. Standing frozen in the light, a dumb stare on his face, the Doctor held a handful of long strips of rubbery meat. The meat slipped through his blood-stained hands like flopping fish into the bag.

Boris Leontev followed Szlotov and closed the door. Boris, a man who had killed dozens of men, girls and even an infant by his signature method of a hat pin in the ear, was shocked. The sight of bags of meat being filled by the Doctor shocked him. Next to the Doctor were three other crew members—similarly bloody. Three young men did not speak and went silently about the task of slicing strips of flesh off the bones.

"Oh my God," Boris said. He covered his mouth with his hand as he looked downward and caught his first glimpse of the young girl's long blond hair hanging from the head of the otherwise de-meated child carcass. Szlotov smiled as he tallied the tall bags of meat lying against the wall. Four. The one they were filling made a fifth.

"Vladimir," Boris said, his brow drawn together. "For *this* you needed my help?"

"No," Szlotov said. "Patience." Szlotov launched into a spot inspection. He marched to the sacks of meat. "Dear Doctor—"

"Yes."

"Come here, Dear Doctor. Fine work. Very good. Next," Szlotov now made eye contact. "Everything okay?"

"Yes."

Szlotov stared into the dark, quivering eyes of the Doctor.

Turning away, Szlotov stepped in front of a pile of ruddy tissue: flat fleshy cables connected by a filmy web of rubbery tissue.

"What's this?" Szlotov asked. Dmitri, who was covered with a fine black power like coffee grounds and who stunk of feces, opened his mouth and throat like he was about to puke.

"Offal," Dmitri said, still choking down his vomit.

"Pick it up and put it in the bag," Szlotov said. "Right now, Dmitri, do it." Frozen in mid gag, Dmitri bent over and scooped his two hands into the rings of flat intestine, some with stool tumbling out under his hands. Dmitri dropped the innards in the open sack. He finished getting the entire mess from the floor into the sack and then scraped his hands off on the inside of the bag.

"Good job," Szlotov said. "Anything you miss will still need to be disposed of. Well, now" Szlotov slapped his hands together. He went to a small alcove next to the wooden stairway up to ground level. Under the stairs sat a ragged overstuffed chair with tears on the arms with the fill puffing out above the skin of the slipcover. Szlotov flopped in the chair and invited Boris with his hand to take the short wooden bench. Boris kept his jaw shut and stared with expectation at Szlotov, braced for whatever the *hit* was going to entail. Szlotov decided he needed to ask a few questions about the newspaper where that reporter worked.

"I want you to help me, in case the journalists are not giving interviews," Szlotov said. The tension in Boris' face melted away and he hugged the post. "We use the homeless kids for meat. Soon it will be organ transplants. The American is on to us."

"Let's get going," Boris said, rising from the bench. "And you tricked me, you *pig*. I thought you wanted my help *here*." Szlotov smiled with delight, and headed for the door with Boris behind him.

"Brother Szlotov," said Dmitri, the youngest of the three loading meat into the sacks. "What should we do with the sacks?"

"Ask the Doctor. He's done this many times," said Szlotov. Turning to Boris, he said: "Ride with me." Boris disliked riding in a car someone else was driving. He grimaced and grit his teeth in silence. Boris climbed in the front seat of Szlotov's BMW. As they raced up to speed, Szlotov glanced over at Boris, who had his Makarov pistol on his lap with the barrel facing Szlotov.

"Point that away from me," Szlotov said.

"What?" Boris said.

"Point your fucking gun the other way," Szlotov said. Shaking his bald head, Boris flipped over his pistol and resumed polishing the sides with his handkerchief, which was brown tinted from the oil that rubbed off. Szlotov pulled from his inner suit pocket a sheet of paper folded the long way. He handed the sheet to Boris.

"Read me the first address," Szlotov said. Boris flattened out the sheet and adjusted his arms to focus on the words.

"'Vasya Khodney' and his address is… not far from Metro Station Technologicheski Institute," Boris said.

With a nod, Szlotov turned in the direction of the Palace Bridge, which led off the island. They drove in silence all the way to Prospekt Nevski before Boris had the nerve to start asking some questions.

"How do you want this to go?" Boris asked. "What are we looking for?"

"Information," Szlotov said. "About an American—living in St. Petersburg. You *saw* where the *organizatsiya* is going. You know the American gangster, John Dillinger?"

Boris nodded, slouching in his seat as Szlotov drove them past the open air market of Sennaya Ploshad and the smell of fish rose in the car from the street side fishermen standing with just-caught fish hanging for sale on a string.

"Dillinger said," Szlotov continued, glancing away from the road to see if Boris followed him, "that he robbed banks 'because that was where the money was'." Szlotov smiled, showing his bright white teeth.

"Was that Dillinger?" Boris said. "No, it wasn't. It was that *American*, Willie Sutton."

"For us, Boris, there *is* no money in the banks. There *is* no money. The money is in the land and the people—even those kids are better off being made into natural-casing *sosiski* than they are steeped in the filth and sniffing glue."

Without a trace of levity, Boris returned a basic nod without a trace of enthusiasm, as if he were afraid even to breathe.

"You All right, Boris?"

"Yes," Boris said. "Our Mr. Khodney lives two buildings down, in *korpus* 2, apartment 29."

Szlotov parked on the sidewalk right next to the street, and popped his trunk. With his trunk open, Szlotov pulled out a crowbar. Boris looked in the trunk and decided to bring a rock hammer with one end a flat club and the other a long narrowed point. The two of them found *korpus* 2 and then within that building they found where apartment #29 would be. The front door was an old swinging wooden type with a glass *fortochka* window on the top. One door was open and the two of them entered the apartment building. The first stone step was bowl shaped from the decades-long tread of feet. Szlotov and Boris mounted the steps. On the plaster walls of the building were countless bits of crude Russian graffiti. Szlotov came around a corner with his meter-and-a-half hexagonal iron bar with one end sharpened into a flat blade forked into two smaller points. They rounded one last corner and saw, on the left, a green wooden door with the number 29. Boris made a few two-handed test swings of the rock hammer. As the two of them stood in front of the door, Szlotov listened. He heard nothing and placed his palm on the door. He pressed inward and the door was locked.

Looking back at Boris—who smiled back—Szlotov rapped hard four times with the tip of his crowbar. They heard footsteps scramble inside the apartment, stopping on the other side of the inner door and the outer one than Szlotov had rapped on.

"*Militsiya,*" Szlotov yelled. "Open the door." A few seconds passed in silence on either side of the locked door.

"Who?" asked the voice on the inside.

"*Militsiya*—open the door quickly." Szlotov said and smiled at Boris. They heard the locks inside being opened, and the door opened a crack. Standing behind the door was a small man with a Fu-Manchu mustache.

"What?" asked the man, when he saw that Szlotov was not wearing a uniform.

"Vasya Khodney?" asked Szlotov.

"Yes, and who are you?" asked the man, holding the door from opening any farther.

"That's enough questions from you," said Szlotov, raising the crowbar up and crashing it into the forearm of Vasya Khodney, the former computer wizard at the newspaper *Nevski Novosti*, which had ceased to be a viable source of work after its editor/publisher Alexander Krasnie was gunned down in the company's offices. Vasya fell back on the floor. A woman with shoulder-length brown hair screamed. Szlotov stood, crowbar in hand, standing over Vasya Khodney. Vasya looked at the forearm he now clutched, having had his arm broken from the blow. Boris came in. He closed and locked the front doors. The apartment had birch-wood shelves along the halls. On these were stacked dusty hardbacks volumes of Soviet literature, and vinyl records stacked at waist level.

"What do you need?" Vasya asked.

"Quiet," Szlotov said, and began to pace the floor with his crowbar. The woman fell back on the couch in hysterics. Vasya turned around and said: "Leyna, be calm."

"Yelena?" Boris said, pulling out a sheet of paper from his breast pocket. "There it is." Boris said to Szlotov. "She's the next one."

"How convenient," Szlotov said and walked up to Leyna. With a tortured expression, she stared back at him, in a lull of her hysterical crying.

"We have no money," Leyna said from a face splashed with tears, fluid overflowing her nostrils, and her two arms held up and her hands flopping at the wrists. "Leave us alone."

Szlotov laughed and exchanged an amused glance with Boris.

"We *know* you have no money," Szlotov said. "We want information."

"What do you know about an American reporter named Jack Land?" Szlotov said. Before Vasya answered, he looked over his shoulder at Leyna, who said nothing but put her hand over her mouth.

"Him," Vasya repeated. With his good arm, he reached into his shirt pocket. Szlotov tensed involuntarily as Vasya withdrew a cigarette, the cheap *Belamor Kanal* type. Seeing the *Belamor*, Szlotov smiled and relaxed a notch. Szlotov watched calmly as Vasya stuck the cigarette between his lips, picked up a cheap disposable lighter off the coffee table, and lit up, taking a deep drag of the acrid, unfiltered tobacco leaf.

"He walked in the office last January," Vasya said. "Spoke Russian—not fluently, like he said, though. When you spoke to him, he acted like he understood but he did not." Vasya took another drag from his smoke and winced from the pain in his arm. "He wanted to take *my* fucking job but I told him shit. He could not figure out my computer." Vasya smiled at the recollection. Then, the expression on his face changed. He no longer smiled.

"Then he did that fucking *article* on the sewer prostitutes," Vasya said. Behind him, Leyna burst into tears. Her tears overflowed her fingers. Boris took out his own white linen handkerchief with the oil stains and gave it to her. "And then Alexander Ivanovich was shot..." Vasya said and stopped speaking. Szlotov and Boris waited for half a minute while Vasya was silent.

"And where is, now, the *Amerikanets*," Szlotov asked.

"How should I know?" Vasya said, and fumbled through several empty packs of Belamor Kanal on the end of table before Szlotov kicked the table away.

"Now you need to know," Szlotov replied. "Where does he *live*, for example."

Leyna spoke up: "Prospekt Metallistov, I think."

"What?"

"On Prospekt Metallistov in the Bolshoi Okhta region," Leyna said.

"That's impossible," Szlotov said on reflex. Szlotov did not believe her because he himself grew up on the same street Prospekt Metallistov. His mother's apartment was still located in the same apartment on Prospekt Metallistov. That was the neighborhood where he himself had lived and where his mother still lived.

"What is his address?" Boris added.

"I don't know," Leyna said. "Look at the office—the records are there."

"We don't know anything about where that asshole is," Vasya said. "We hate him as much as you do."

"You should go ask that British *peez-dah,*" Leyna said.

Boris checked his list. "Sarah Hughes?"

Leyna smiled and sat back against the wall, pulling her upper lip down to cover up her one big tooth in front. "That's her." Leyna's long hair lay across her shoulders and she smiled so her one big incisor was prominent.

"Okay," Boris said and stuffed the list in his pocket. He looked to Szlotov and angled his head toward the door. "Ready?"

Szlotov stood in the living room of the apartment, his crowbar hanging from his left hand. He wanted to use the crowbar. He wanted to squash these two maggots—employees of the newspaper. They profited from his labor. They spread damaging information about the *organizatsiya*. Szlotov saw himself in his mind's eye swinging the crowbar into the girl's face and knocking that tooth into the next *oblast*. Szlotov shifted his gaze like a tiger to Vasya, whose Fu-Manchu mustache alone was torture enough for the woman. Szlotov wanted to leave but even more he wanted to give these two something to remember him by. It occurred to Szlotov that the only reason he got involved with the homeless and Chus was to pay Zortaev. Szlotov felt himself and his outlook darkened by simply the weight of his payments to Zortaev. It brought this bad attention. Now it was too late to keep the secret.

"Let's get going," Szlotov said. He and Boris retreated to the hallway. As they walked away from the apartment, Szlotov felt strange, as though he wasn't following his instincts. At the stairs, Szlotov heard the door slam shut behind them.

"That was a mistake, leaving them like that," Szlotov said to Boris as they cleared the first floor and exited the stairs.

"I know," Boris said, not slowing his pace as he walked out to the street. Szlotov popped his trunk and dropped the crowbar inside. Boris did the same with the rock hammer.

Inside the car, Szlotov consulted the Rolodex he stole from the editor's desk. The card for "Sarah Hughes" gave a small biography for her in addition to her address, which was near Chernaya Rechka Metro Station. Szlotov roared up to higher speed.

When they reached the area, Szlotov parked in front of the building. This time he dispensed with any extra weapon. She was female and a Brit at that. Harmless. The card even noted that she lived alone.

The threshold of the apartment building was a wide room. A narrow elevator with mahogany-grained contact paper stood opposite the door. To the left stood a green door that led to the stairway. The two of them walked the two flights up to the apartment of Sarah Hughes. Standing outside of her apartment, Szlotov put his ear to the door. No sounds. Boris was about to knock when Szlotov raised his palm and mouthed 'No'. He led the two of them away from the door. Szlotov counted the doors to the end of the hall. They went outside and looked at the balconies of the apartments. It was possible to climb up the outside, he decided. He went to his car, popped the trunk and plucked out a small drawstring leather bag which he shoved in his pants. Then, using the drain pipe and its wall connectors, Szlotov climbed up the outside of the building until he was at the level of the second floor balconies.

"Impossible," Boris said as he watched the 46-year-old Szlotov move horizontally by jumping from one balcony to the next. Boris kept up with him and moved sideways on the ground. After Szlotov landed on one balcony and scampered across it, an old man with gray-streaked hair, in an unbelted lime green bathrobe and carrying a newspaper, ran out and bellowed at him, Szlotov unholstered his Glock and held it at eye level. The man holding the newspaper raised his eyebrows and went back inside. On the ground, Boris laughed. Szlotov landed on the fourth balcony and he looked around. On the balcony floor, wrinkled, lay a large red-and-blue beach towel emblazoned with the Union Jack. The apartment was dark. Szlotov moved his eyes far to the left and inspected the courtyard between the four buildings, and the grassless expanse of dry foot paths. Holding his eyes still and allowing his focus to widen a bit, Szlotov got a wide view of the courtyard. Allowing his vision to become thus distorted, Szlotov monitored the courtyard for another few moments before he was satisfied it was empty. From inside his pants, he took out the leather bag and spread the neck. He pulled out an instrument like a screwdriver except that the end of the blade was flat and flexible like a putty knife. He palmed this item and drew tight the drawstring. Then, working in silence, he worked on the lock for the French door to the balcony. He slipped open the lock and it clicked. Inside the apartment, the person moved in bed.

Happy, Szlotov thrust open the balcony door. He presented his silhouette back-lighted by the moon behind the open door. A gust of cold wind

176

woke the figure in the bed; she screamed a piercing, high note that told Szlotov, better than a test for two X chromosomes, that he had woken a woman.

"What the hell are you doing!" shouted the woman with a British accent. Her legs thrashed under the covers as she scrambled against the wall in the corner, far away from him.

"Sarah Hughes?" he said. The woman gasped.

"Who are you, you bastard fuck," she shouted. "Who are you? She threw her Baby Ben alarm clock at Szlotov but he ducked. "What the hell…in my fucking apartment," When the last word left her mouth she turned on her bedside light and saw the face of Vladimir Szlotov. Sarah did not know who she faced but it was clear enough that he was not a 16-year-old cat burglar she could tell to go bugger off. Szlotov had not come to rape her. He was a professional. He came to pump her for information. Instead, Szlotov ignored her and looked around the room, admiring the sense it gave him of her personality. The photograph captioned Birmingham 1995. A map of the Leningradsky Oblast with its mass of green for the great forested lands that surrounded the city and its surrounding small towns such as Pushkin and the famous Kolpino, a tiny town that even Szlotov had visited in his teenage years when he found himself having a crush at age 14 on a young Kolpino girl by the name of Alexandra. Szlotov looked smiling away from the wall map to Sarah's face. He saw her face was framed with a shock of thick blond hair down to her shoulders.

"Don't be 'fraid," Szlotov said in English.

"Bloody Hell," Sarah shouted. "I bloody *will* be scared as bloody hell. What *the fuck are you doing in my room*, you Russian git!"

"I need to ask some questions—"

"Then make a bloody appointment!" Sarah shouted, pulling the covers up to her breastbone. "Come to the paper and make a statement on the record. I'm sure I could get *Sevodnya* to do a piece—"

"—about another newspaper you worked at there was an American reporter named—"

"Oh fuck-the-Christ to hell," Sarah said and groaned. She held her manicured fingers over her eyes. "That cow-fucking swine."

"Cow? Sounds like he's motivated," Szlotov said, feeling now as if he were just enjoying the company of this girl in a coffee shop with a plate of *pirogi* and a mug of hot green *chai*.

"What do you want to know?" Sarah said, curling into a ball under the covers.

"Who he worked with, his sources, his address, where he spends time," Szlotov said.

Sarah looked down at the floor a moment with her mouth closed and all loss of exuberance that she had only instants before.

177

"He worked alone," she said. "And he wandered all over the city for his interviews. He was—is—quite gifted in his interviews."

Szlotov waited, two of his questions waiting on answers.

"He doesn't go out much," she said. "He doesn't drink hard liquor unless he's reading Hemingway but he does like to go dancing—to the Nevski Melody, I think." Sarah smiled as she looked at the floor and replayed some memory in her mind's eye. "He tried to invite me to Nevski Melody but I told him they wouldn't let me in because the hookers would riot."

"You were right," Szlotov said, surprised at her, which disappointed him because he knew what must come next.

Sarah smiled with her under eyelids brimming with a bead of tear.

"His address?" Szlotov said.

Sarah started to cry and her shoulders heaved up and down, shaking as she let forth a torrent of sobs. After Szlotov listened to these tears for a moment he decided it was a delaying tactic. He moved toward the bed. Sarah shrieked and flew out of the bed, leaving the blanket behind. She ran for the door of her apartment in her purple panties and purple tank top. Szlotov laughed as he saw her slide up to the door and start to unlock it. He leaned against the wall behind her. She got the inside door open and then opened the outside door, only to meet Boris. He held up a sharp hatpin. The point would plunge deep into her if she came a step closer. She shrieked at the trap, as if she felt that her life was over if the door again closed. Szlotov grabbed her around the waist and Boris took control of her wrists. Szlotov put his free hand over her mouth as they dragged her back in her apartment and fell on top of her. She cried as they lay their weight on her.

"Let me go," she said in Russian, as if that would have any effect other than freeing her murderers of the trouble of understanding her pleas in English.

"She won't talk yet," Szlotov said in Russian to Boris.

"*Pravda*? That true?" Boris asked and followed up his question by plunging his hat pin into her butt a centimeter.

"Ah! *Fuck You*, you bastard. Ohh," Sarah responded with a fresh round of struggle against the weight of the two men. "I'm going to kill you two bastards!"

"Be Quiet," Boris said.

"His address," Szlotov shouted. "Or Boris will tickle you again."

"Land's a swine of a man," she said. "But I don't want him dead," she said.

Szlotov turned to Boris: "Do it." Boris plunged the hat pin into her right breast up to the depth of two centimeters, which made her scream and cry all mixed together. She shrugged their weight with the strength of a mother bear.

"Stop it," she said. "Leave me alone."

178

"Where is he?" Szlotov repeated and Boris held her head against the floor and pricked the tip of the hat-pin on the inside of her nose. Tears flooded out of her eyes.

"Prospekt Metallistov. Right after Shosse Revolutsiya." she said and then wept. "He's really a decent chap. It's such a tragedy to kill him."

"We just want to speak with him," Boris said. "Maybe I'll tickle him too for you." Boris smiled.

"Wait…what? *Where* on Metallistov?" Szlotov asked. His mind began to picture the street.

"Take the Number 10 tramway, it's the third building to the left of the *Produkti* store," she said. "Will you get off me now?" They obliged.

"Put on some clothes," Szlotov said. "You're going to *show* us. *Then* we will let you go." Sarah looked back at Szlotov hard to gauge his sincerity. She would of course be glad to get off so easy.

Szlotov sat down and relaxed. She pondered her options and then rose to her feet, her purple panties soaked. Szlotov spanked her purple rump as she walked by him to her closet. Szlotov decided, after she showed him where to find the American, he might give her a ride. Sarah went to her closet and emerged carrying jeans and a sweater. She went into her back room and kept the two Mafioso's waiting while she got another pair of underwear. As they left her apartment, Sarah walked in front of them. Szlotov got the feeling from the way she looked back at them that she was thinking of running away. They walked down the stairs and then Szlotov whispered to Boris that he should get in front of her before they reached the outside. As Boris attempted to cross in front of her, she placed her left hand over her breast where the pin had entered and then out of reflex, she swung her right hand and her fist landed squarely on Boris's ear. He stumbled from the blow and fell down the last few steps to the first floor landing. Picking himself up, with a scrape on his cheek and holding his chest where his gunshot wound was still healing, Boris marched up the stairs and raised his open flat hand to slap her face. The slap was so sharp, it echoed up the stairs. When Sarah raised her head, she had a large palm-shaped bruise on her cheek. Sarah got on her two feet and was near to springing, claws extended.

"That's enough" Szlotov said and got in-between them. The three of them got in Szlotov's car. Sarah and Boris got in back together. Boris sat in the middle of the back, crowding her behind Szlotov. She tried to keep her leg from touching Boris's leg.

Szlotov drove at high speed over the dark streets that were uninhabited by other cars. The three of them did not speak. He did not play music or do anything except breathe. Szlotov imagined that at last he would be able to silence the reporter who thought he could tell the truth without paying the cost. The reporter lit a fire under Szlotov's business. Until this American, Szlotov had never met a reporter who was brave or fool enough to challenge the *organizatsiya*, a reporter who had a death wish or was too stupid to realize the danger.

Sarah stayed quiet in the backseat except for calling out the driving instructions as necessary. Boris put his arm on the seat back behind her and when his sweaty arm brushed the back of her head, she drew in her shoulders and leaned forward from the back of the seat. Boris bent his arm forward so his fingers just touched her blond hair.

"Bugger off, you disgusting bald bastard," she said and amplified her words with a sharp poke of her elbow into his ribcage. Boris groaned and grabbed the back of Sarah's hair. Holding a thick, golden handful of her hair, she screamed.

"Back off, Boris," Szlotov ordered. "Do not touch her again. No matter *what*." Without another word, Boris released the shock of her hair. Tears rolled down her face. Sarah turned her head and slapped Boris' cheek as hard as she could. The sound of the slap echoed off the leather interior of the BMW. Boris grit his teeth but did not retaliate. Sarah braced herself for his reply and when she saw there would be none, she began to lay a series of punches and kicks to his shins and then landed one punch to his groin, all of which he took without responding.

"All right, *stop it* already," Szlotov said. Like a kid being told to sit, Sarah calmed down. The three of them rode until Sarah swung her fist from nowhere and landed it right on Boris's throat. Boris coughed and Szlotov swerved from surprise.

"*Tikah!*" Szlotov said, using the all-purpose Russian word for 'shh' or 'watch out' or in general any place where the English speaker would use a 'head's up'. Boris held his throat and coughed. Then he got off a single punch, which by no accident landed exactly on the spot where he had stuck the hat pin in her boob. Sarah yelped and began to pant.

"Where next?" Szlotov asked her. She pointed to the right and held up her finger, trembling.

"There," she said as if exhausted. "That's the one." Szlotov stopped and parked his car right in the middle of the single-lane drive.

"That's it," Sarah confirmed. "It's the last entrance."

Szlotov could not believe it. The American reporter, Jack Land, lived in the exact same building his own mother lived in. Since none of Szlotov's business occurred here and since his mother was well guarded, having her life in the same building as the American reporter was merely a curiosity.

Szlotov opened his car door and so did Boris. Sarah got out also on Boris's side. She moved away from Boris's side of the car and moved toward the entrance to the building, which she remembered from an earlier time when she visited Jack in his apartment. It unnerved Szlotov to see the quick and ready way she entered the building where, two thin doors away, lived his mother. Sarah strode past that door without raising an eyebrow. Szlotov and Boris entered the building after her. She passed to the stairs and continued to rise until she reached the top floor. Hot on her was Szlotov, who had refrained from slowing her down because it made sense to let her get the door open for them. Sarah rapped hard on the door as Szlotov waited, out of breath, at the top of the stairs. There was no answer to the knock. Boris reached the top floor and bent over, sweating, his bald pate shiny and his hair soaked on either side. Sarah knocked for an extended time. Szlotov joined her in doing the knocking but there was no one home.

"Go to the trunk," Szlotov told Boris, flinging him his keys. Boris went downstairs. Sarah waited with a pained expression that reflected her understanding that she would not be let free until after the men got what they wanted. Boris returned with the crowbar and rock hammer. Szlotov worked the blade end of the crowbar underneath the outer door. He leaned hard on the outer door and the metal around the lock bent and warped from the stress from the crowbar. Then Boris stepped in and from the side held the rock hammer so its pointed end was lined up on the inner door's lock. With it lined up, Szlotov took a wide swing and hammered the flat end of the rock hammer, thereby transferring the impact to the lock and popping it open on the third blow. When the door opened, the inner hallway was dark. At the end of the hall, where it met a small bedroom, a light burned as if someone sat at the table and worked with headphones on, oblivious to the sound of the door crashing open, if such was possible. With his pistol out, Szlotov moved into the lit room. He glanced to the left as he passed the dark hallway leading to the kitchen. Szlotov stood next to Sarah. Boris kept an eye on the stairs. Szlotov reached the bed room and she followed him. A light was on but the room was empty. A bottle of Pepsi stood on the desk next to a glassful of ice, an American quirk anomalous in Russia, a country that looked on a cold drink as unhealthy. A laptop computer stood on the desk next to the pop bottle. A document was still visible on the computer screen. Szlotov realized he was in the home of the reporter Land who threatened to take down his entire enterprise. Szlotov saw a box on the floor. He dumped all the papers it contained on the floor. Then he gathered the piles of papers on the desk and added them to the pile on the floor. In a short time, Szlotov and Boris had gathered up the entire set of written-on documents from the apartment. Boris found a plastic sack and they stuffed everything into it. The laptop Szlotov placed under his arm.

Finished with their inspection of the reporter's apartment, and satisfied that they had found everything, the three of them approached the door to leave. Szlotov then said: "Boris, friend. One last thing I have to ask and then you can go," Szlotov said and Boris sighed as he switched from one leg to the other. "Stay here in this apartment in hiding until this reporter comes back. Get him *no matter what*." Boris shook his head with his teeth gritted and fury in his eyes.

"As you require," Boris said and stared down at the floor. Szlotov and Sarah, then, went to the first floor where they stopped and knocked on the front door of Szlotov's mother's apartment.

"Why are we stopping here?" Sarah asked when Szlotov knocked on the first floor door.

"My *mother* lives here," Szlotov said.

"*Here?*" Sarah asked with a gasp.

"Who's there?" said Szlotov's mother, behind the double doors.

"A murderer," Vladimir Szlotov answered in Russian.

"Okay, I'm opening up," she said. Sarah and Szlotov waited in the hall as his mother moved the gears to get first the inner door open and then the outer steel one too.

"Oy, Vladchik," she said and wrapped her arms around him. "I have missed you so much Vladdy."

"Mamochka," Szlotov said, leading Sarah from the hall into his mother's kitchen, which was a mirror reflection of Jack Land's apartment. His mother followed behind with the pair of *tapochkee* slippers that Szlotov had worn the last time, as a teenager, he lived with her. Disturbed by the sight of her son and his girlfriend's street shoes on her clean floor, his mother with a grunt gave Szlotov his pair of tapochkee which he put on that instant, sensing his mother's discomfort. For Sarah, his mother took a different tone, one of interest and distrust, having a long career of watching girls who came and went with her Vladdy. To Sarah, his Mamochka offered fuzzy yellow *tapochkee*, ones he had not seen since his school days when he had dated Anya Sheripotova, a blond girl with a large bust who Vladdy liked and who—therefore—his mother hated.

"Mamochka, enough with the slippers. This is Sarah. She's from *Angliyah*."

"Okay. So what?" said his mother, not even bothering to make eye contact with Sarah.

"Pleased to meet you," Sarah said in her passable Russian.

"Very," said Maria "Masha" Ilovna, her eyes dropping with great interest to the floor. "Shoes from England dirty the floor no less than Russian ones."

"Mamochka," Szlotov said, stamping his foot on her kitchen floor. His mother jumped in her chair. She stared at her son Vladimir, who returned her gaze but with a sternness that revealed his anger. Szlotov maintained his stern gaze at his mother. Her face, lips and the fingertips trembled with fright. Sarah looked first at Szlotov, then at his mother, her own mouth gaping wide open.

"Be quiet," Szlotov said, his brow pinched. "If you cannot be polite to my guest, then you must not speak."

"Forgive me," said Maria Ilovna, clutching her son's forearm. "Forgive me, Vladchik," she said. Sarah sat still with her heart racing. She watched the old woman as she went to her old Russian refrigerator and leaned back to break the magnetic hold of the door. Then, when the white steel door popped open, the wheezing old lady fought her arms up to the top shelf where she got down a tall glass jar, the blue glass reflecting the yellow, rheumy liquid it contained. Poppy seeds floated on the surface.

Szlotov and Sarah were both surprised to see his mother, using both hands, holding the liter-sized container, its outside moist and beaded with drops that accumulated on it in the fridge. Before Vladimir could intervene. Szlotov's mother Maria Ilovna pirouetted on her own left *tapochkee* and transferred, via a controlled fall, the heavy sloshing container of juice to the table. With no semblance of control, the container of liquid sloshed out a tidal wave of *kvass* or at least her personal version of the fizzy drink. Sarah reached out and steadied the old lady to keep her from falling. This simple act caused the beneficiary of her quickness to respond with a smile, a 70-year-olds curtsy, and a mumbled "*Spacibo*" as she regained her composure. Szlotov decided the waves of liquid still sloshing from side to side no longer presented a tip risk and he released his grip. With no comment other than the look on his face, Szlotov stared at his mother. She handed him an old rag to dry off his *kvass*-soaked sleeves. Acting again as if she had not almost had a near catastrophic accident, Szlotov's mother went to the cupboard before she could be stopped and returned with two glasses, which she presented to Sarah and Szlotov. His mother took a breath and put her two old hands around the glass container and was about to pour it when Szlotov barked "*N'yet.*" He stood up, took control of the container, almost dropped it himself because it was so slick. He poured *kvass* for himself and Sarah.

"Mama, do you want any?" he said, almost as an afterthought.

"No, I need nothing," she said. Szlotov sat down and took a long drink of his *kvass*. It tasted like apple cider, but with a fizzy off-taste like pomegranate. After Vladimir and Sarah each had taken a drink of the *kvass*, his mother's eyes brightened to see if they approved. Instead of telling his mother what he thought of her imitation *kvass*, Szlotov got up and poured it down the sink.

"Listen, Mama," he said. "I need to lock your door for a few days. Give me your key."

"Why?" said Maria Ilovna, the corners of her mouth and eyes drooping with sadness, as if she felt that her son was already nailing her arms in her coffin and burying her deep in the cold earth.

"It's not important why, Mama," Szlotov said, turning to face the door.

"It's necessary." She let her head drop and gave him her key. "Sarah?" he said with his eyebrows raised, as if he expected complete and thorough compliance with his every wish like Sarah were one of his fawning employees. Sarah stayed seated long enough to down all of her *kvass*.

"Very delicious," Sarah said and in reply the old lady set her lower jaw off kilter to the left in a kind of peasant's regal bearing as she performed her 70-year-olds' curtsy.

"It was nothing," replied Maria Ilovna, using the Russian phrase that gave such a reflection of pleasure and comfort in the person who used it that no English equivalent carried the same feeling. Szlotov kept his mouth closed with his arm outstretched in the air, like it was poised to drape over Sarah's shoulders. After placing her glass in the wet sink, Sarah went to the front door with Szlotov.

"Wish you well," Sarah said, hesitating at the open door.

"Let's get going," Szlotov said. Sarah walked out the door and Szlotov closed the inner door in his mother's face. Then he locked her inside and locked the outer door. Sarah headed for the street but instead Szlotov rapped hard on the door opposite his mother's.

Sergei answered the door.

"Glad to see you, Vladimir," Sergei said, smiling.

"Come with me, Sergei," said Szlotov.

"Who's going to watch your mother?" Sergei asked.

"Nobody," Szlotov said. Sergei got his things and locked up the apartment.

"Who's she?" Sergei asked, of Sarah, who stood with her blond hair and killer figure.

"A friend," Szlotov said, and Sarah didn't argue. "She's going to help us find that American." Sarah again said nothing. "Sergei, I need you to go to the Doctor. You need to get what he has for you—you will see—and transport it to Chus meats."

Sergei's entire expression changed when he heard the name of Chus meats.

"What am I moving?" Sergei said. Szlotov gritted his teeth without giving an answer. He cocked his head to the side in anger with his cheek muscles standing out.

"*Meat*," Szlotov said, spitting out the word like a bug that had flown in his mouth.

"Understood," Sergei said, distracted.

Choosing to say no more, Szlotov raised his arm behind Sarah and walked her to his own car. He opened the door and Sarah got in. As Szlotov walked around the back of his car, he decided that maybe he could take this

British girl to bed. He got in his car. Sergei drove away in his own car without nodding his head or giving any other look of acknowledgment. Szlotov decided to himself, he and Sergei were having a quarrel. As he twisted around in the leather interior of his BMW 740i, and the leather creaked and stretched beneath him, he turned toward Sarah and asked: "You hungry?"

"No, I'm tired," Sarah said, politely but with insistence. "I want to go home and go to bed."

"Maybe we could switch the order of those two things," he said and started the engine, not intending to go anywhere near her home. Rather, he drove to Prospekt Nevski and as a result of the late hour, they had the wide boulevard all to themselves. The brick buildings all the same height passed on either side of them. Szlotov looked over at Sarah and, from the way she leaned back in the plush seat, from the way she cast her gaze at the scenery passing alongside the car, from the limp posture of her left arm, resting on the center console, he knew he would have her. They reached a fork and Szlotov took the right which led them past the blue-green colored Moskovsky Vokzal, the train depot for all trains bound for Moscow. Sarah turned her head to the right and when Szlotov saw the blond flag of a ponytail flipping his way and dangling in front of his eyes, he made up his mind to have her then or else. He drove on for a short way until, up ahead of them half a block, light from a storefront streamed out into the night. Except for this 'all-night' café (that closed at 4am) nothing was still open. Patrons came out the door; girls wearing leather jackets over their long t-shirts and short skirts with legs covered only by sheer nylons up to the hipbone. The nubile girls tottered on their 10cm heels. Szlotov parked and Sarah's roving eyes arrested on the entrance of the night café.

"*I'm* hungry," Szlotov explained, getting out. Sarah sighed and joined him, preceding him into the night café. There was a polished tin counter with a glass display case next to it, showing some of the bowls of soup for sale. There were two people behind the counter, the cashier and the cook. The woman who took the money had a deep frown. She waited behind the cash register without reaching out to Szlotov. Scattered around the café were a dozen single-pole, square-topped tables. A blond woman sat at one table laughing, and with her Szlotov saw there were two tall Russian men, who knew they would get their way with her later on, when she couldn't say no anymore. An older Russian couple sipped two bowls of soup when Szlotov entered and, for whatever reason, they dropped their spoons in their full, steaming bowls of soup. The old couple left the café the moment they saw Szlotov and Sarah enter.

"*Borscht,*" Szlotov said to the cashier.

"We're all out," said the cashier, a lumpy woman with an assortment of moles on her face including one under her rounded chin, with three stiff bristles growing out of it in different directions.

"What *do* you have," Szlotov asked, his eyebrows raised.

"Cabbage soup," said the bristly cashier. "Cold," she added with a trace of a smile.

"That'll do," Szlotov answered.

"How many?" asked the cashier.

"Two," he said, with Sarah standing beside him, mute, willing to go along.

"Twenty-six rubles," the cashier said, ringing open her cash register. Szlotov gave her three ten-ruble notes and waved off the change. The cashier lost not a beat with her one hand pocketing the difference while with her other hand she passed the ticket to the cook, a stubble-faced man with the back of his hair chopped off in a way that, to Szlotov, made him look odd or perhaps deranged. The opportunity for retribution was too abundant for a deranged man with a funny haircut with a kitchen hidden away to do anything that he wished with two bowls of cold cabbage soup and any creative ideas he might have about spicing up the soup with a few of his own secretions by way of seasoning. For all these reasons, Szlotov stood and waited with queer indifference as the crucial moment for the adding of spit or snot to the bowls was a distinct possibility. Then, in a miracle all at once, the two bowls appeared on the counter, each on a larger plate and the obligatory wedge of black rye. Szlotov gave the first plate to Sarah and then he followed her with his own back to one of the unoccupied pole tables. He flicked away a speck of bread left over from the previous occupants. For the first time, Sarah and Szlotov stared across a table with their wedges of bread in one hand, their spoons in the other, moving from the surface of the liquid soup up to the rushing flood of soup into their own mouths.

"*Why?*" Szlotov asked her.

"Why *what?*" Sarah asked back, in passable Russian that still showed, from the verbal emphasis she used, that she was still formulating her question in English and then transferring the thought into Russian.

Szlotov smiled and dropped his spoon into the cold, oily cabbage soup, served in a bowl that had the obvious evidence of the previous kind of soup it had held, something based on the red beet, which would explain the dried line of borscht from the previous user of the plate. Szlotov said nothing about the outrage of the dirty crockery and instead he smiled at this British girl who did not understand most of what he meant.

"Why did you learn Russian?" Szlotov asked. "Why did you come *here*?" Sarah held her facial expression cool, as if she had faced this question many times before.

"You have the great poets, Pushkin; the great novelists, Lermontov, Dostoevsky and Tolstoy. I read Turgenev and felt what it was like to walk around the Russian countryside, stepping into the peasant taverns with Turgenev and his servant," she said.

"Always it's the novels," Szlotov said, almost to himself, as he thought about his own life and who would be interested in finding out what he thought. The lack of such a reason for a foreigner like Sarah to become interested in him made him angry and made him think that he didn't care about her. At that moment, two young—seventeen or so—girls came into the café. From the dark straight brown hair to their shoulders, the same creamy white skin and that look of common fatherhood that cast itself across each and every ingredient in their physical makeup, he guessed they were sisters. The older one went up to the counter and ordered a *chash-kuh* of coffee. The younger of the two had a rounded butt, shaped like two delicious scoops of coffee-flavored ice cream. And he found himself, though he was sitting across from Sarah, leering at the shrink and expansion of the younger girl's two scoops as she carried her coffee across the café to a table behind Szlotov. He smiled and watched the older sister, the one without the great skintight, lamb-chop hugging pants, walk across the café with her own cup of coffee, acting too as if she did not see the eyes of Szlotov—one of the most powerful men in St. Petersburg—watching her.

"You libidinous git," Sarah said, raising and then slapping her spoon on the table. "Do you want to look at birds or talk about Pushkin?"

"Birds?" Szlotov asked, puzzled. "And for that matter Pushkin is not interesting either."

Sarah said nothing and did nothing except look back at him over her soup, her upper lip curled back up in a mannered way that would have been sexy and attractive if he didn't know how much she hated him.

"Never mind," Sarah said and took a spoonful of her soup.

Szlotov took a spoonful of soup and moved it near his lips when he saw that Sarah had dunked her bread in her soup. To see a blond beauty, English, well spoken, behave in a way favored by the peasants in Russia, surprised Szlotov. He forced himself to finish the spoonful and then chewed with his mouth open and smiled at her.

"You know I'm a journalist," Sarah said, smiling at him. "You've got to admit I've been pretty good spirited about this...kidnapping you've done on me."

Szlotov smiled.

"I'm going to expect and *interview*, you know," Sarah said. She smiled at him in a way that was gorgeous.

Chapter XV

1.

GALINA rolled to the side of the asphalt and pulled up her pants, crying.

The man with the fungus-like brown hair growing on his face rolled off of her and separated his teeth as he lay on his back in the alley next to her. His dirty tongue lashed across his scummy teeth. The man wore two pairs of pants at the same time, a pair of baggy slacks over and second layer of muslin. The trouser zipper of both pairs were unzipped, revealing his pubic hair and penis, rolled over on its side and dripping juice, remnants of what he had just emptied into 8-year-old Galina Yosheva. She had been sleeping in an alley. Galina climbed to her feet and ran away while the man lay prostrate on the ground—spent. While she ran, Galina had to hold up her pants, which were not yet buttoned. She knew from the four previous times she had been raped since she ran from the American because he was going to send her back to the orphanage.

Galina ran knowing if she did not the scummy man or his friend would catch her and the rape would begin again, out in the open. They held her down while she cried and one boy or man after another came and humped on her, until her underwear was soaked.

Galina ran down the street. She ducked in the nearest alley, knowing that the scummy-teethed man might be right behind her. In the alley she stopped and buttoned her pants. The moisture from the man soaked the front of her pants but most people would just think she couldn't hold her pee. Already, Galina saw, on her back on the cold concrete, how all men and some of the boys were the same: they saw her as a girl they could fuck. It was important not to seem weak or available or vulnerable. This was how Galina felt inside her own mind, as she tucked in her ragged, dirty shirt into her torn pants. She wanted to seem as normal as possible until she could find a place to hide and sleep for a long time. She was cold all the time without her coat. She didn't even want to eat, though the only thing she found was the heel of a sandwich someone threw into the trash in such a way that it fell into the trash in one piece, with the two halves of the sandwich still laying in a stack with the thinnest triangle of Swiss cheese and a corner of cucumber and the smallest portion, a tiny ragged slip, of ham. This was her only food for the past two days. She felt a powerful tug in her stomach, which had not yet returned to deadness and quiet resignation of not expecting food and in return producing no acid.

Her stomach, at least, had not forgotten that food existed. Galina walked sluggishly down a road whose name she did not know near the Dostoevsky Metro Station. Tears rolled down her cheeks and streaked the dirt with clean stripes that did not look becoming on a young girl who had no one or anyplace to go and for whom no one took pity. She felt alone walking in the open and, by chance, she saw a conical sewer grating. It was perched atop a dirt mound with a cone on top made of concrete.

By instinct, Galina looped her fingers and lifted with her legs. She climbed down. When her face passed the plane of the lid, swirls of dust and foul smells swept over her face, the scent no sewer dweller wants to smell—rotten death. She kept going down and held her breath. As her feet hit the floor, she saw the sweat on the concrete walls. Dirt and cobwebs stuck to her fingers as she moved them down from rung to rung into the moldy darkness. The smell was overpowering. There was no question that this steam sewer had a body. Her eyes watered from the smell. She scanned around and pinched her nose until she saw a pair of white feet, with round balloons at the toes, and some thick tar oozing from them. The stench was horrible but Galina wanted to know how the *chelovek* died, whether it was murder or not. If it was murder then the entire sewer system was dangerous. All of them had one way in. The steam tunnels were an easy trap. If the kid died and there was no blood, then Galina would believe it was still safe to sleep in the steam sewers. Nothing could be worse than staying on the streets, walking and staying awake for days, always moving, until some night at 5am she would find herself a spot behind a trash bin—only to awake to some face pressed close to hers and clawing at her pants. It convinced her she needed a better plan, even if it meant become a *batonchik*.

As soon as she could stand the stench no more, she scrambled up the ladder and leaped out of the sewer without a care. She fell on the ground, was dizzy and had bloodied her cheek. She only wanted off the street, so she hurried to another concrete volcano. She climbed into it and did not, at first, smell anything. Maybe she found her place. She smelled the same peaty aroma of dried grass. The steam pipe section did not show any signs of people, either living or dead. She sat down on the muddy floor. The light from the open lid cast a bright square of golden light on the floor. Then in the light she saw on the concrete a splatter of blood dried into a splashed scab on the concrete. The blood splash, ten centimeters wide, scared her. The steam sewers were too dangerous—everybody knew about them. She lay back on the cold concrete, no longer caring if her womb touched the ground or if she herself would ever have a child. Living on the street meant she must expect some man to drag her to an alley for rape or perhaps worse. She couldn't go to the police. They would beat her or take her to an orphanage. Living in the steam sewers, she was easy to find and trap, an easy target. She needed someplace warm, someplace where nobody would bother her. She climbed out of the steam and walked on Pereulok

Kuznechnie, a broad avenue leading to Prospekt Ligovsky. She turned left on Ligovsky and followed the road to the green train station to Moscow, *Moskovsky Vokzal*. She entered the building and no one noticed or bothered her as she pushed through the double row of wooden doors. Inside, she heard the gentle squeak of the wood in the window frames and the creak of wood-on-wood joints. Her footsteps echoed off the high ceiling. She heard the din of many voices whose words wafted up into the ceiling into a muffled roar.

The walls were lined with glass-fronted cubicles, with round holes for talking and a slot to pass items to the attendant. Galina had never bought a ticket at the windows but she knew from other street people that Moskovsky Vokzal had public toilets in the basement. She had come here once for that purpose, to crouch over the holes in the brick floor on two cleats, one brick high above the brick floor. Galina remembered this foul-smelling place with the crap hole in the floor. Galina remembered, as she squatted over the hole, the updraft of fumes, a sulfurous smell of horrible filth, ammonia and—worst of all—a curiously sweet smell. These fumes rose as she squatted, doing something she wanted to do alone, with an older girl to her right, squatting over her own pair of cleats. These fumes sometimes came in a gust because the sewer went deep underground. The sewer stench blew out of the sewer that connected down deep to the underground septic sewer, the one that ran the deepest through St. Petersburg, down in the city's literal bowels. Galina stood hunched over the sewer hole. Thousands of miles of connected sanitary sewers, all led downstream. Standing up, Galina saw a white-colored roach with jointed feelers climb out of the hole. An older Russian woman with a red scarf and the thick skirt of a street woman came in and the white colored roach ran away. The old woman took her position over the cleats, and pulled her skirts up to her thighs so nothing of hers got near the floor. As the woman squatted there, clenching and holding her breath, another white roach ran out between her legs. The woman leaped away from the hole and shrieked "*Oi,*" She looked at Galina, crouched over her own hole, staring into the hole. Galina stared into the sewer hole and she saw the end of to the side a manhole cover was off. The whole time, her cleat-mate was dealing with the albino cockroach problem.

"How disgusting," the woman said to Galina. The woman noticed how Galina was standing.

"Girl?" asked the woman. "Is everything All right with you?" Galina said nothing and stared in the hole.

"Girl!" demanded the woman. "Are you normal?"

"*N'yet,*" Galina said and pulled up her pants. The old woman shook her head and Galina walked out of the womens bathroom. As Galina left, she walked into the hall and was face-to-face with the man who raped her, going to the basement.

"There you are!" the man said. He smiled widely and showed his scummy teeth. He grabbed for her arm and missed. Galina ran back into the womens bathroom. The man chased her in and the old woman screamed "Get out!" The man batted the old woman aside and all the women in the bathroom screamed as he chased after Galina, cornering her next to the cleats where she had just been standing. Galina stood by the cleats as the man approached her and then, in a flash, she jumped in the open manhole in the floor.

2.

The woman screamed and held her head. In the time it took to leap up and throw her arms over her head, Galina dropped into the brick chimney. Galina's shoulders dragged hard on the crusty accumulations on the edges of the chute. Then she felt a pair of rough hands catch her wrists. It stopped her fall. The woman screamed and the scummy-teethed man lifted Galina by her wrists out of the pit. Galina kneed him in the balls. He quickly let go and Galina fell, down toward the deep dark pool, gathering speed, making the four meters feel like forty, landing in a belly flop in the brown lake. The splash and wave echoed off the neck of the chimney. Disgusting things drenched her face on the splash back. When she went under her mouth filled with sewer water. She coughed out the horrible-tasting gravy. She was overtaken by shaking and she vomited up nothing at the sight of floating human filth.

When the waves and her own coughing calmed, Galina saw that she stood in a 3-meter-wide pipe constructed of large stones tiled together like bricks. The water was waist high. In the darkness in either direction she heard the roar of water going downstream. Spitting and fighting the current flowing toward the roar, Galina walked downstream through black water the color of beef gravy. She splashed with her thighs as she pressed onwards, downstream towards the roar. The water got higher up her chest; she felt cold and began to shiver. The water kept getting deeper and she kept walking and the stinky brown water got up to her collarbone. She shivered and hugged herself in the water. She walked toward the dim light in a room at the mouth of the tunnel. As soon as she entered the larger room, she saw in front of her a flat waterfall with random bit of debris crossing the plane of the falls. The flowing curve of water dropped into the lower pool. Light entered the concrete room from a grating along the ceiling. Under the grating ran a metal-rung ladder to a concrete platform above the sewage.

3.

Galina waded to the raised platform and, on the last few steps, the sludge reached as high as her chin but then, she reached the raised concrete platform. She did not find a ladder so she slapped her fingers on the top ledge. She pulled herself up high enough to slap her left forearm on the ledge, followed by her right. Then she saw above the platform, it was covered with laying kids. She gasped and for half a second thought of dropping herself back into the river of sewage. Rethinking that, shivering, wet, stinking of human feces, nauseous, Galina hauled herself from the water to the cold concrete slab. When she landed, dripping from the river of sewage, one of the shadowy silhouettes lying on the concrete bent up and tent-poled his arms behind to see who climbed from the *gavno*.

"Well, I'll be damned," said the boy. "Where did you come from?"

Galina caught her breath as she lay on her side, dripping. Then she sat up. Her hair hung in a single wet lock.

Another of sleeping kid sprung awake. It was a girl. She screamed and crabbed her way across the cement floor to get away from Galina and was already two rungs up the iron ladder, when a third boy, awakened by the girl's scream, jumped up and with his beefy arms, plucked her off the ladder. He held her suspended in the air like an ant stuck with a dart.

"Quiet, Dasha," said the first boy.

"I fell in the sewer," Galina said and burst into tears. She sobbed at the top of her lungs

"What did you did do, Petya," said the boy with the beefy arms.

"Shut up Tito. I didn't do anything," said Petya. "She just climbed up out of the shit." Petya swung up his arm and scratched at his head where his hair was matted and tangled and he had fleas. Galina calmed down. Tito, the beefy-armed boy turned his attention to a plastic bag in his hand. He poured a bit of syrup in the bag and started to breath in the glue fumes. His face held over the bag and it inflated and collapsed. Then, like a tree falling, the boy and his hand fell away in unconsciousness and cracked his skull on the concrete so hard it echoed. Albino cockroaches scattered. A cloud of dust was lifted by the bone of his skull cracking the concrete, and the *thwap* as his meaty arms slapped the wet concrete floor. After the dust settled, Petya crawled over on all fours. Instead of seeing to the welfare of his sewer mate, he grabbed the huffing bag and inhaled it, causing Petya also to keel over and bounce his head. Both of them lay out on the concrete. Petya had blood coming out his nose. Against the wall, the girl

Dasha wailed now that both boys were unconscious.

Two other boys lay against the wall behind her. They had not moved. Neither of them had huffed on the bag. They were unconscious or they were dead. Dasha's moan grew louder and she rocked back and forth, bashing her head on the wall. Little Dasha held a headless doll. On the side of Petya's face a jagged scar branched down from his left eye, which was missing and instead he had a jagged horizontal slit. In this pose, laying on the cement, Galina slept.

When she woke, strong light came in from the overhead grating. Galina looked behind and saw how close to the edge she had slept. The flow of water had slowed to a trickle. She looked at the floor and saw, for the first time, the skeletons and decomposed bodies of other children who had succumbed and fallen under. She realized that the two kids lying behind her were dead. They needed someone to roll them into the sewage river and to say a prayer. Galina looked at Petya. Blood oozed from his nostril. Not too long before he and Tito would get rolled in too. Dasha's cheeks were puffy from crying all night. Among the conscious there was only Dasha and Galina. Neither one of them moved nor said anything. Galina was 8 years old and Dasha said she was 7. Galina felt hungry. The soil from the sewer dried on her skin. The bodies lying piled up in the water made her understand: she had to save herself. She got on all fours and crawled to Dasha.

Dasha's eyes widened. She clenched her teeth and braced for what was coming. Without delivering the expected blow, Galina lay against the wall next to Dasha and her headless doll named *Mrs Smile*.

"Dashinka," Galina said, using the pet name for 'Dasha', which she hoped would calm her. "How did you end up here?"

Dasha lifted her eyebrows and opened her mouth. She wanted to say why. But no words came from the mouth of the 8-year-old girl who lived in the sewers and watched older kids die sniffing glue, eating and drinking nothing. The burden of answering upset Dasha and Galina patted her hand.

"What the hell," Galina said. "You're with me now, but I guess that's not so good now." Galina waved her hand over her own shit-soaked pants and shirt.

Already, having the fate of Dasha on her hands moved Galina to thoughts of Chilkovo, living with her grandmother Ludmilla. Galina remembered standing in the market with all of the other misfits who were left over after the privatization and the loss of any assistance from the government. Galina and her grandmother had not even a kopeck to buy three potatoes to feed them all for a couple of days. Her grandmother stood in the market in a line with the other people with things to sell. Most stood with things they shuttled from Ukraine or the Baltic states. Galina's grandmother sold everything. She stood selling her plastic sink stopper, held cupped in her scaly old hands, as if the sink stopper was her featured merchandise on display. Galina stood next to her. For a second after her pain of remembering her grandmother that way, Galina felt shame knowing how she had parted from her grandmother, getting on a train for St. Petersburg and Astrakhan on the promise that Galina—all of 8 years-old— would go with him and be his child wife. Galina felt embarrassed for all she had done to avoid Astrakhan.

"Dasha," Galina asked. "How fast can you run?"

Dasha smiled.

"Fast," she said. "*Very* fast."

"Are you hungry?" Galina asked then.

"Yes!" Dasha barked. "*Very.*"

Galina smiled and laughed for the first time in weeks. She got to her feet. With a reluctance born of experience, Dasha too got off the cold cement floor and rose to her full height, which was under a meter.

Galina headed for the iron ladder on the wall. As she and Dasha did so, a rock scraped under Galina's shoe. The noise opened Tito's eyes and through his bloody-nosed gaze he thrust a heavy paw on Dasha's leg. She screamed and froze with her two hands on the rungs of the ladder. Galina, above Dasha, climbed down a rung and grabbed Dasha under the arm while she kicked Tito in the head with her free leg, giving his head another good bounce on the floor. Galina hauled Dasha to the top. Galina lifted the grating with her head. The two of them felt the cool air on their faces. Galina climbed out and so did Dasha. They both lay on the ground in the warm daylight.

Galina lifted her head off the ground. She looked at Dasha, splayed on the ground, staring into the blue sky.

"Let's go!" Galina said, getting up. Dasha lifted her head with a deep frown, not knowing where and to what they were going. Galina was starving. She guessed that Dasha with her eyes in perpetual fright of what was coming next, was past being hungry. Galina jogged toward the market, a grouping of card tables held up by spindly wooden dowels. The many tin shacks were lined up in two rows, leaving an alley between them. At one end was a vendor who sold newspapers including the *Komsomolets, Sevodnya, Chas Pik, Argumenti i Facti* and all the other newspapers that flapped in the wind. Opposite the *Gazeti* stand were wooden tables loaded up with dusty potatoes. On the next wooden table were onions, dirty from being in the ground that morning. Carrots were on another card table. Galina stopped on the edge of the market. She got down on her knees to whisper to Dasha, who smiled.

"Got it?" Galina asked.

Smiling, Dasha nodded. Galina rose to her feet and walked behind the kiosk on the right. She led Dasha to the back end of the gray corrugated metal *shaverma* kiosk and its mouth-watering smell of roasting goat meat.

"Wait here," Galina said to Dasha, who creased her forehead and nodded. Galina skipped away behind the kiosks. She reappeared on the opposite side of the market, behind the kiosk that sold newspapers, each held down flapping in the breeze under bricks and stones on the top of every pile. The market was full of women with scarves tied around their heads, their arms looped in baskets with cotton drawstring sacks containing tomatoes, potatoes and onions. Around the leg of a card table stacked high with carrots, a black-and-white cat lingered with designs of its own on any scraps that might happen to fall from the adjoining *shaverma* stand. Galina went behind the newspaper stand and took a deep breath. Then, out of the blue, she screamed. Then she said "*Puh-zhar!*"

Galina yelled "Fire!" again and again. By the third yell, the market became infected with panic. Everyone rushed to look behind the newspaper vendor's flapping stall. Galina ran away but, from the direction she had chosen to run in, she was able to look over her right shoulder and observed Dasha, the short little eight-year-old girl who had run on cue from the place Galina had left her, upon hearing the word "fire" screamed at least twice. Before she had to turn her gaze in front of herself, Galina saw Dasha reach out and grab a long potato. Shifting her focus, she saw the man who stood with his back to his own vegetable stand, with his arms crossed and a severe frown on his face as he watched Galina, screaming "fire" for no apparent reason. Galina ran a block away to the spot but Dasha did not come and so Galina, after a moment, ran back to the market. Looking from behind the edge of a building, Galina saw little Dasha crying, with the fruit vendor's hand holding a handful of Dasha's hair. In his other hand, the vendor held up the potato Dasha attempted to steal. The vendor yelled at Dasha and shook her roughly. Tears streamed down her face from the dagger-like pain of the hair-pulling. The angry vendor had the dark hair and tan skin of the Cossack. He punctuated his angry comments to Dasha by jerking on her hair, which he still held. Amid the commotion and Dasha's screams, the women standing around in their faded flower-patterned dresses came to attention and shouted the same question "Why are you doing this to her?" Galina grimaced and twisted her arms together as she watched Dasha being abused. Out of the crowd, then, came a blue-uniformed member of the *Militsiya*.

"What have we here?" asked the eager, short-haired officer, speaking to the vendor, as if he was not holding a 7-year-old girl by the hair.

"A little thief," muttered the vendor.

"That true?" asked the cop, with his eyebrows raised.

"Yes, that is truth," said the vendor.

"Okay," said the officer, raising his hand to take the thief away from the vendor. The cop gripped Dasha by the neck and bent his face next to Dasha's face. "Thief, are ya?" he asked. Before Dasha could even answer, the officer thrashed Dasha around like a puppet. "Think I don't have other *bitches* to deal with?" asked the cop. Holding his mouth drawn together, the cop fumbled for a moment until he got a tight grip on Dasha. He pulled her in close to him. Then, he caught a hold of Dasha's fingers, and bent all four back until four separate snaps of her fingers were heard. Following the snapping bones, Dasha shrieked so sharply that a collective gasp came from everyone in earshot. Having broken the fingers on her left hand, the young, neatly-dressed officer released Dasha. Galina wanted to rush over to help Dasha but she was afraid she would get the same treatment.

"If I again see you, bitches," said the cop loud enough for everyone in the market to hear. "I do you worse." Dasha yowled like a dying cat. She screamed such a high-pitched shriek, punctuated by intense screams of agony, that several of women rushed up to her.

"You son of a bitch!" shouted an older woman with two broad streaks of gray flowing from the temples. The cop swung his fist in the air at the woman—just another *babushka* out of the crowd—who stood her ground and glared at him.

"Go ahead and kill me, you animal," shouted the old woman.

"Nina, quiet!" shouted a voice in the crowd.

"Does your old mother know you do *this*," continued Nina, an old woman. To punctuate the inhumanity of the cop, Nina showed Dasha's red swollen hand with the fingers that pointed in odd directions. A bone had broken through the skin. Galina, watching from a distance, saw the odd appearance of Dasha's fingers as the lady held it up. It looked like Dasha's hand had another row of knuckles.

Surrounded by the grandmothers, the cop frowned at Nina and then at Dasha, while the muscles in his sunken cheeks worked up and down, showing his rage. He said nothing more and walked. With that, a cheer of approval rose over the marketplace; the various grandmothers fell into pairs of conversations, all reveling in their combined strength over the dreaded *Militsiya*. Everyone who had gathered began to scatter, leaving Dasha and Nina standing together, the crying child and the *babushka*. Nina, the strong old lady, stood with her eyebrows arched in alarm and then she sighed and took Dasha's unbroken hand in her own. She started to lead Dasha away when Galina ran up and said: "Where are you taking her?"

Her back bent low enough to hold Dasha's hand, Nina craned her neck to see who was speaking.

"What do *you* want?" Nina said, bringing Dasha closer to herself and farther from Galina.

"She's my friend," Galina said. "We're a pair."

197

Nina flattened her lips in disgust and said: "Come on then, I've got to get these fingers between ice," Nina said.

4.

Galina walked behind the hunched-over lady, Nina Petrovna Kholota, who talked to Dasha to distract her, said she was married to Oleg Sergeivich Klolot who died in 1996 of the *Perestroika*. Nina walked and Galina followed her flat leather shoes. They went to Nina's flat and Galina followed the old lady and Dasha, whose fingers continued to swell and throb. Dasha's cheeks looked puffy and red from the torrent of weeping. Nina led them away from the sidewalk to an entrance way with the huge slab overhang. Nina opened the wood door for Dasha and then she herself entered, letting the door slam in front of Galina. Galina went in. The three of them went upstairs, first Dasha, who yelped with daggers of pain on every step up to the lobby. Nina pressed the button and the elevator door opened and Dasha stepped in, gritting her 7-year-old teeth and shielding her swollen fingers from any bump. Nina got in and allowed Galina to crowd in the tiny elevator. Dasha jerked away to avoid having her fingers touched and instead she slammed her elbow on the wall of the elevator, causing two sounds: a loud rumble of the metal box echoing up and down the 15-storey elevator shaft, and a sudden screech of agony from Dasha. It was so loud that Galina stuffed her fingers in her ears to plug them. After Dasha's shrieks calmed down, Nina jumped off and scouted the corridor. Then Galina led Dasha down the corridor in front of Nina, who opened the door to her apartment. As the inner door swung open, both Galina and Dasha gasped. It reminded Galina of her grandmother's apartment in Chilkovo but it was nicer than any she had seen. Dasha supported her arm with delicacy into the hallway with its chevron-patterned wallpaper on a yellow background.

"In the kitchen," Nina Petrovna said to Galina, leading Dasha to the kitchen table. Dasha's fingers next to her knuckles were swollen and bloody under the skin. Galina overcame her disgust and looked at the fingers. Through all the swelling, the four broken fingers tented the skin of her palm. Dasha's sweaty face and pained expression showed she was in a lot of pain. Galina looked around the kitchen, at the tea and the cookie jar. Nina came back into the kitchen and had a half-meter square patch of white cloth with a herringbone pattern in the weaving that made it appear to be the back of a man's dress shirt.

"Here," Nina said. She gave the white cloth to Galina, and placed the scissors on the table for Galina to pick up. "Cut this into long strips. No wider than her fingers are long." Nina got some playing cards and folded them into thirds along their length. Folding the card into a triangle, Nina applied a broad stroke of paste to the ends and then a short piece of Scotch Tape for strength. Like triangular hats she used the Scotch Tape to attach a long pencil to each. While she watched Nina fold the cards, Galina made a mess of the fabric with the scissors. She cut jagged strips that didn't go parallel as Nina asked but, instead, the cut ran off in another direction toward the center of the fabric. Before Nina noticed and snatched both away, Galina had not managed to generate a single usable strip despite having cut half way to the center of the cloth. Shaking her head and muttering under her breath, Nina made short cuts along the edge and then tore it the rest of the way. She rolled these into fat bandages. She opened her freezer and out came frozen slabs of sausage, a frozen jug of soup. Above the items she had just unloaded hung a thick sea-shell shaped chunk of ice, years of frost buildup. Using a wooden tenderizing mallet from a drawer, Nina hammered at the block of frost until chunks fell into Nina's hands. She delivered all of the ice to the sink and then ran cold water on top of it, so the water level rose and filled the sink with the cloudy white ice. Nina moved a chair next to the sink.

"Okay, in the sink," Nina said to Dasha. Dasha had been engrossed in her throbbing hand, swollen and red splotched with pooling blood under the skin. Now, under orders to put her fingers in the sink, Dasha panicked.

"No!" she said, shaking her puffy face.

"Girl," Nina said to Galina. "Make her put her fingers under water, until I tell you to stop."

Dasha coughed in the middle of her wail. She stared at Galina in alarm and then, seeing Galina moving toward her, Dasha backed into the cupboard. Galina pushed her forward and gripped Dasha's hand, holding it struggling under the ice water.

"It hurts!" Dasha cried. "It hurts a lot!" Nina paid no attention and continued gathering her supplies.

"Quiet," Nina said. "Cover her mouth with your hand, girl—" Nina looked at Galina's filthy hand and clucked her tongue "Wash your hand, girl! *Then*, cover her mouth." Understanding that 'girl' meant her, Galina quickly washed her hands and clapped one hand over Dasha's mouth while her other hand held Dasha's thrashing broken hand under the ice cold water. After a few minutes, Dasha stopped thrashing and instead started to collapse, hanging by her arm from the sink. Nina waved her hand to a chair by the table. Galina made Dasha sit in her chair. Dasha sat with her head slack to one side. Even after soaking in ice water for fifteen minutes, the purple flesh over the breaks was sharp with puddles of blood under the skin. Nina brought a desk lamp and shined it on Dasha's poor, broken hand. Nina examined the little broken hand, causing Dasha to cry out with a new upwelling of horrible pain. Nina addressed

Dasha's index finger. Around the unbroken tip of the finger, Nina wrapped the bandage. After the first pass, Nina placed a blue Russian pencil on top of her finger. After a few more passes, Nina unraveled the roll and slit the ends to tie together around the finger. Then, levering the pencil down to the back of Dasha's hand, Nina bent Dasha's finger straight.

"Ooow!" Dasha screamed, and a fresh wave of tears fell.

"Hold that *arm*, girl," Nina said. Galina threw her arm across Dasha's wrist—immobilizing it without resting her weight on it. Dasha roared from the severe pain. A faint crackling sound was audible as the fingers bent back straight. Nina grabbed a second blue pencil, and a strip, which she fed around Dasha's middle finger. As Nina ripped a slit in the wrap, she jerked on Dasha's finger. After four pencils were in place, Dasha lay her head on the table, sweaty, still in throbbing pain, Nina took down a glass jar of oily salve. She ladled it with a jointed stick on the skin around the breaks.

At the end, Dasha was exhausted and Nina handed her a glass of clear liquid to drink. Dasha coughed and choked. Galina recognized the smell. It was vodka. After Dasha stopped coughing, Nina made her drink the rest of the vodka in the glass which Dasha now drank like cream, expecting the burn and heat. After a few minutes, Dasha rested her forehead on the table and Nina took her shoulders while Galina took her knees and they transferred Dasha to Nina's dark green corduroy couch. Nina pulled a blanket up to Dasha's chest and placed her injured arm on top of the blanket. Dasha closed her eyes. She exhaled and a quiet fell over her. Themselves exhaling, Nina and Galina went back to the kitchen table. Before they sat down, Nina veered off toward the cabinets where she got two tea cups.

"Cup of *chai*?" Nina asked Galina without waiting for an answer. The moment reminded Galina of sitting at the white wooden table with her grandmother Ludmilla Andrievna back in Chilkovo.

5.

Now, when Galina emerged from the reverie of the memory, she focused on Nina, the old woman who stood at her own counter top, pouring grains of brown tea into an egg-shaped tin cup, chewing in silence, her brow pressed together in two puffy pillows of concern.

Nina set down Galina's cup of tea, in a thin decorated aluminum cradle around the steaming glass, but Nina drank her tea while leaning on the counter.

"You take narcotics," Nina said, matter of fact, as if she were asking if Galina liked sugar in her tea.

"No!" Galina said.

"You're a slut?" Nina continued, raising her brow and grabbing a sip of her tea.

"No, I'm not!" Galina said and looked down in sadness.

"Then you're a thief," Nina said, with final confirmation in her voice. "Or else you wouldn't be living like *this*."

Galina stared into her reflection in the half-finished cup of tea. Everyone thought she was bad. She felt small on the chair in Nina's kitchen, warm in the light of a single bulb.

"I'm hungry," Galina said, staring down at her tea. "I'm alone and so is Dasha."

"No, that isn't true," Nina said. "That little girl is going to live with me."

Galina waited to hear what was going to become of her. But from Nina no answer came. Rather, Nina's loud silence meant she did not believe Galina was hungry and alone.

"You take a girl like Dasha," said Nina, beginning a much larger argument. "And you teach her to steal." Galina said nothing. She had to admit to herself that it could be viewed that way. Although she was 8 years old, Galina knew no one would expect less. Galina did not want to live on the street but she could think of no reason for this lady to help her.

"Can I take a bath before I go?" asked Galina, raising her eyes.

"And then you'll go. I will wash your clothes," Nina said, now looking like she felt guilty for hurrying Galina back to the street and the kind of difficulties about which she could not know. Galina rose and went with a shuffling gait to the bathroom. As she peeled off her outer clothing, her underclothes were stained deep brown. Galina peeled off the crackling dirty shirt, which emitted a cloud of brown powder as she stretched it over her head.

As Nina took possession of the various pieces of clothing from Galina, she uttered a series of variants on the word "filthy", "disgusting" and "gross". Nina twisted the piston cocks and let flow the hot and cold water into the cold claw-footed tub. As the water pooled in the tub, red water from the faucet filled the tub with ruddy steaming water.

"What's this?" Nina asked, picking at a dry scab on Galina's back. The bathroom clouded with steam from the hot water. Galina stood naked and Nina examined the purple rape bruises on the insides of Galina's thighs. Nina opened the cool tap and let the tub cool off some. Galina dipped her toe and she sucked in at its temperature. Then she sat down in the water and immediately flew up.

"Too hot," Galina said but Nina placed her palm on Galina's shoulder and forced her back in.

"Stay. You need to be clean," Nina said. She used a wet rag to lather

Galina's back. As the brown water accumulated and the smell rose, Nina was forced to hold her breath. She flipped Galina around and asked her: "Girl, where have you been?" Nina waited for an answer. Galina didn't give her one—and stared at the white suds and the mist of steam, hovering off the surface of the water. Warm water was so different from cold—it almost felt like a different substance. She let herself slide back and lay. With Galina's back inaccessible, Nina flung the rag on to Galina's chest.

"Wash yourself," Nina said. She left the room. Galina lay there, not doing anything. Nina quickly returned pushing a washing machine on wheels. Nina set up the machine. Then she pulled a wide black hose off the floor and hung it over the edge of the bathtub, and connected a thinner hose to the bathtub faucet. The warm water flowing into the tub stopped and water began to fill up the white drum. Then, amidst the splashing and spraying of the water, Nina produced an electrical cord, which she plugged into the light swinging overhead. The drum began to spin with increasing momentum. While it was just getting up to speed, Nina dropped in Galina's shirt, undershirt, pants and what was left of her stockings and underpants. Nina sprinkled in some white powder from a tin can. As soon as the drum whined up to speed, a dirty flush of brown water surged out of the thick hose draining into the tub. Galina's cozy bathwater clouded with the rushing flood of disgusting smelling brown water. As the outflow rushed in and the water level crept up, brown, on Galina's chest, Nina used the small hose to spray inside the fast-spinning drum. For each douse of the hose, there was a corresponding flush of dirty water.

Galina began to whimper and Nina said "Pull out the stopper yourself." Galina did it and the clean and the dirty water went down the drain, leaving Galina shivering and with a brown residue. Since Nina had ceased to add more water, the drum spun at top speed. The motor had emptied all the water from the clothes and kept accelerating, giving out the last few droplets of dirty water. The tub drained away and Nina hosed Galina off before she shut off the tap. The last of the dirty water circled the drain and Galina felt a warm towel drop on her head. She shivered in the tub and dried herself off. Out of the washing machine, Nina fished out her damp clothing and handed the pieces in order of dressing to Galina who got dressed. She walked toward the door in her damp, heavy clothes with Nina following her. Galina stopped and looked in on Dasha, still asleep but with her broken fingers held closer to her face. Without another word, Galina went to the door of Nina's apartment.

"Wait," Nina said, running to the kitchen. She returned with a fistful of bread torn off a brown loaf of hard rye. Galina accepted the bread with the curtsy and went to the door.

"You'll be all right," Nina said. She opened the door.

Galina did not reply. She stopped on the threshold and stared back.

Without another word, Nina closed the door in her face and locked it. Galina headed for the elevator. She climbed in, went down and stepped into the night air. Her wet clothes were cold. She shivered and looked down the street at the darkness rising behind the globes of street lamps. She went to the street and sat on a granite curb. A carload of men drove past. One yelled out the window: "Girlie!"

Chapter XVI

1.

THE second Jack Land reached the landing in front of his apartment he knew something was terribly wrong. Next to the lock the door had pry marks. Jack understood his apartment had been burgled. As he stood out in the hall, he realized his knife was in the apartment, on top of his desk under a volume of 'A Sportsman's Sketches.'

Jack needed to get a stick or something from the basement. He backed down the stairs and found a flat piece of folded sheet metal, with the ends bent at 45-degrees and bolted to something. It wasn't heavy but its presence in his hand and the presence of one screw, rattling around on the tip, was just the touch that made him seize on it. Jack returned to his apartment. He transferred the club to his left hand and pulled open the door.

The inner door was itself wide open. Light from outside streamed in the balcony window. His red scarf no longer hung on its peg along the right wall. Instead, it lay on the floor with the impression of boot prints. Jack moved his left foot a step into the hallway. The floor jounced, as if it mocked his urgent need to keep quiet and stay alive. He raised his left arm and headed forward, step-by-step, over the slotted wooden floor. Jack took note that the toilet was running, from the steady hiss in the background, indicating to Jack's great alarm that the burglars who invaded his apartment had been there long enough to use the toilet but they didn't reposition the lever so the toilet wouldn't leak and make constant noise. The intruder had used the toilet and might still be there. Jack glanced into the dark hallway to the kitchen. Then he took his gamble and headed for the living room. Jack stood on the threshold of the room and the floor squeaked. He flipped on the light. Shirts, splayed hardback books, a smashed glass-bodied lamp and shade lay strewn on the floor.

The floor rug had been lifted so a foot-tall wrinkle crossed the floor.

Suddenly, the armoire flew open. Out jumped a bald man with a Hitler-like mustache. The man held a foot-long stick pin. Jack felt an adrenalin dump: "This man is going to kill me." Jack tried to run but his feet were frozen. The man rushed him. Jack fell backwards. His hand slid down the wall, flipping off the light switch. Darkness fell on the room. Jack landed on his back in the dark. The man tripped on the floor rug, and he bumped his elbows—then his hands slapped the rug. Then a sudden scream of horrific pain.

Still in the dark, Jack ran to the kitchen and grabbed a frying pan. He ran back and swung it like a golf club at the man's head, laying on the floor in the dark. The man took the pan in the face and it clanged. The man yelled like a baby again. Jack flicked on the light and looked at him, clutching his right eye where the hatpin stood. Feeling no pity for the man, Jack stood behind him and clanged him again with the frying pan. The man lay on the floor with the needle standing up, stuck in his eye. His mustache was cropped above his lip. The skin on his face was wrinkled under the eyes and with strong crow's feet at the corners. His face was contorted and blood gushed from the penetrated eye. Gelatinous mucous welled from the needle, which was buried up to the bead end.

As the man's crotch darkened with urine, Jack realized this was more than a close call.

2.

Three hours later, Jack walked up the stairs at the *Militsiya* station with his two wrists held together with hinged Russian handcuffs. With his right hand he followed the polished metal banister along the right wall as he stepped up to the second floor, where there was a grated window to the left. Behind the metal grate sat a sergeant at the wooden counter, a bright light from below shining into his face. Jack was followed by officers Oleg and Karl, who had answered the call Jack placed from his apartment. He said he had surprised a burglar who had killed himself by falling on his weapon, causing a cerebral hemorrhage to occur at the puncture site.

"What did you say?" said the sergeant to Oleg, the *Militsiya* officer to the left of Jack.

"He killed a man," Oleg repeated, skipping all the explanation.

"The murder weapon—you have it?" asked the sergeant, who had too many teeth crowding his mouth. The sergeant was confused and left his mouth open, his spit-coated teeth thrust in every direction, looking more like a bramble of branches than a set of teeth in any one's mouth.

"Have it," Oleg said, and pulled out from his breast pocket of his blue corduroy uniform a bloody stick pin as long as a butter knife.

"You're joking," said the sergeant, showing the pink of his gums with the wideness of his smile. Still beaming, the sergeant turned his gaze to Jack's face.

"Jail him," said the smiling sergeant. Not needing another second, Oleg yanked Jack away by his upper left arm.

When officer Oleg had arrived at his door, Jack made the mistake of staring at the top of Oleg's bald head. Jack stared at Oleg's bald spot a moment too long and it made Oleg dislike him.

"Beat him well," added the sergeant as an afterthought. "For the frying pan."

"It was self defense!" Jack screamed.

"Silence!" Oleg yelled and Karl grabbed the handcuffs by the hinge and then with his free hand rammed his knuckle into Jack's cheek bone. Jack felt his knees wobble and then he crumpled and fell on the concrete floor.

3.

Later, Jack woke on the concrete floor of an iron-barred cell in a Russian jail. The iron bars each had a beard-like accumulation of dirt, showing the grime of decades. His cheek was wet. A thick accumulation of dried blood lay on the floor under his nose. Rolling over, Jack caught the eye of the guard, walking along the wire catwalk outside the row of cells. The guard turned the jagged metal key in the lock. The bolts of the cell door pulled out of their catches. Jack held up his hand to block the bright light coming in the open door. After his eyes adjusted to the light, Jack saw Oleg's shiny scalp. Jack raised himself on one arm on the cold floor, and then he climbed up on the square stool bolted to the floor next to the square metal table in the middle of the floor. Along the left and right walls hung wood-slatted bunks in cast-iron edge angle-iron frames that folded up flat to the wall.

"Get up!" Oleg shouted. "We're charging you soon, and you'll need to be awake for your sentencing."

"My what?"

"You can call who you like," said Oleg. The inner door swung open. It was made of blue re-enforcing rod painted sky blue. When Jack reached the corridor he met Karl, standing like an alert bear, hunched over and wheezing, a pair of black coals in his eye sockets. Jack padded barefoot down the corridor. Oleg walked in front of him and Karl followed, as if Jack were a dangerous man. They stopped at a dial telephone, of 1950s vintage. Jack picked up the heavy receiver and dialed the number of his friend Andrei Brezhukov.

Andrei was the first person Jack met when he came to St. Petersburg. He had picked Jack up at the airport. Jack decided to move to Russia for the stupidest of all reasons: an adventure. Like all adventures, it turned into more than he planned. At first, Andrei had looked at Jack's life with much envy. Then, after Jack started to write newspaper stories that were dangerous, like the original one about the mafia, his friends began to distance themselves.

"*Da?*" answered a female voice on the third ring.

"May I speak to Andrei?" Jack said in Russian.

"*Minutitchku*," answered the female voice, Katya, his wife. After three minutes of silence, Andrei got on the line.

"I'm listening." His breathless voice told Jack that Andrei had run to the phone.

"Andrei, it's Jack," he said. Andrei exhaled deeply.

"How's it going, Jack?" Andrei said. He and heard the puff of the cigarette Andrei smoked.

"I'm in jail," Jack said.

On the other line, Andrei paused and then said: "What for? What happened?"

"For murder," Jack answered, letting a beat of silence go by.

"What happened?" Andrei asked. "Tell me you didn't go back to that mafia place—did you?"

"No!" Jack said. "A burglar broke into my place. I'm in jail until somebody—a Russian—comes here."

"Who did you kill?"

"*I* didn't kill anybody. The burglar fell on his own weapon and died in my apartment. He killed himself." Jack said, not mentioning the frying pan. In reply, Andrei growled like a Russian bear roused from hibernation. Then he repeated the noises a second time.

"Oh, my dear friend, you have a real problem," Andrei said. "I'll be right there. Where are you?"

"Thank you, Andrei," Jack said and handed back the phone to the sergeant, who explained to Andrei how to find the police station. The two officers, Oleg and Karl, now seemed to lighten in their moods. Oleg seemed elated.

"Let's now go have a chat," Oleg said, indicating by his arm which direction Jack should go. In the center tread way, even the red line had been worn away by the many criminals whose last free footsteps were along its surface. The cinder block walls were painted a turquoise and yellowy milk white in a stripe below the ceiling. Jack walked, still in handcuffs, down the corridor and then into a cell. Wide wooden slats formed the floor as well as the wooden table bolted to the wall. Sitting on the table was a Russian-style workbook with a pink cover. On the cover was the Russian word "*tetrad*" which meant "workbook". Jack knew this wasn't going to be a lot of fun.

"Sit," Oleg said, directing Jack to the seat nearer the door. Jack felt nervous because his back was facing the door. Karl did not come in the cell but stood in the doorway wheezing and whistling through his nose. Jack heard and felt Karl behind him.

Oleg sat down in the iron cell on a bench across from Jack. Still smiling, Oleg rested his elbows on the table, saying nothing.

Jack sat up straight, afraid someone from behind would kick him in the spine. Oleg reached into his breast pocket and extracted a long, blood-stained pin with a round black-beaded top.

"Your pin," Oleg said and handed the pin to the reaching fingertips of Jack, until the quickness of mind that kept Jack from getting his fingers bitten off by a snapping turtle in an Iowa creek caused him to jerk away before his fingerprints were added to the murder weapon.

"That isn't mine," Jack said, folding his hands together.

"It could have been," Oleg said, turning down the pin. From his breast pocket, Oleg took a thick wooden tube and inserted the needle into it.

Jack stared at the wooden needle case, perplexed.

"Found it on the body," Oleg said, meaning the deceased. "So, you hated this guy?" Oleg said.

"No, I never saw him before," Jack said. "He broke—"

"Liar," Oleg said and gave a single nod to someone over Jack's left shoulder. From behind, a fist slapped the left side of Jack's head, causing it to slam into the right steel wall of the cell.

"Li—" Karl added, and then fell back in a bout of thick rheumy coughs, ones that sounded like they burned.

"You seem to know a lot about this guy who lost a fight with you in your apartment," Oleg said, overflowing with pleasure at his own clumsy set up. "Maybe you two had some business together that went bad."

Sent by the mafia, Jack thought. "No," Jack said. He knew he was in bad trouble no matter what, either from the cops or the mafia. "Listen. My apartment was broken into. This man attacked me in my apartment!"

Choosing not to reply, Oleg passed a frown to Karl.

"When we investigate the crime scene, we will decide what has happened to you, based on the facts and the evidence," Oleg said, with a ceremonious flourish.

"Who was he?" Jack asked.

Smiling, Oleg said, "You know him. Why for you play this funny game like you don't know him?"

"*Please,*" Jack begged in Russian, and then again lowered his eyes.

Oleg sighed and got up to take a walk while Jack waited with his back to the door. When Oleg returned, he spoke the moment he entered the room.

"This man was Boris Leontev, a former Colonel in the Russian army."

"A soldier?" Jack said.

"Not any more," said Oleg. "No, he was a killer for the Tambov Syndicate, until *you* killed him, somehow. We're all impressed that you did, by the way. How *did* you kill him?"

"I *didn't* kill him," Jack said. "I never touched him, *except* with the frying pan."

"It's all right—we hated this man," Oleg said.

"Yes, very much," Karl added.

"Tell us how you did it. We're impressed," repeated Oleg.

"It happened just like I told you," Jack said, confused by their attitude, which reminded him that these cops could be members of the mafia.

"Why would he care about you?" asked Oleg. "Who are you that you could piss off the mafia like this?"

Seeing his chance, Jack launched into the main body of evidence for his story about what happened to the street kids, about his theory on what became of the bodies. When he had finished his most extreme litany of horrors he looked up to see how it was playing with the cops.

"That's nothing," Oleg said, rising to his feet with that reluctance of all Russians to accept a truth that reflected badly on Russia. "So what if some kids die…so a half dozen rich kids get organ transplants. At the end they throw away the child like an empty carcass."

Jack's mouth hung open in disbelief. St. Petersburg officers of the *Militsiya* knew everything. Jack looked into the eyes of Oleg to see if he was as horrified at what was happening in his country as Jack was.

"I want to tell the truth about this," Jack said. "Will you help me?"

Oleg laughed once and then said: "Not on your life."

"Why not?" Jack said.

"*Because*, is why," Oleg said, with the pale looks of the Slovak, the veined thick lips, the horse nostrils wide and flared. "What good will it do me to help you?" Oleg asked, in plain Russian, intending no nuance to his conversation.

"It's not about me," Jack said. "It's about the kids. Don't you think their lives are already hard enough?"

Without replying, Oleg rose from the bench and left the holding cell.

"Stay here," Karl said and slammed the iron door shut.

Jack listened to the echo of the blue re-bar inner bars, within the solid orange outer metal door. The cell had solid concrete walls, cold and damp, painted in light sienna, like the color of the powder on the wings of a moth. He folded down the bed opposite the door and lay on it, staring up at the unique pattern in the ceiling of the cell, painted in the same moth color but with the effects of gravity captured in the paint. Thinking that he needed sleep, Jack closed his eyes and exhaled. When the sound of his own breathing quieted, Jack devoted all his attention to the vibrations coming through the wall and ceilings. He heard a rapid pounding that rattled like a kettle drum through the corridor. He heard two deep male voices arguing in Russian with a wet angry Russian tone that made no sense to him. One of the voices rose in pitch and then a crashing sound came, followed by silence. Silence reined for many moments and then a small number of voices laughed. Jack understood Russians when they were standing in the same room with him. Understanding muffled fragments of sense was a preposterous impossibility. Jack went to sleep on the bed.

Waking, Jack heard someone walking down the corridor. A second set of footsteps followed the first, though the first set of shoes was crisp and slapped on the concrete, while the pair following seemed to skip along without a definable rhythm, slapping the ground behind the guard, trying to keep up while being horrified at the journey. Karl reached the cell door and unlocked it. About to enter the cell, Karl backed off and in stepped Andrei Brezhukov.

Andrei did not smile in the slightest. Karl closed the cell door and locked them in together. Andrei was furious. Jack wanted to say something but he was afraid of the result and so he kept silent.

"What were you thinking?" Andrei roared in English.

"He was a burglar!" Jack said.

Andrei reached in his pocket and produced a thick stack of folded gray newsprint. "No," Andrei said and unfolded the newsprint. He held the article written by Jack from the recently defunct *Nevski Novosti*. It was the article Jack wrote about the missing children. "I'm talking about this article and, how the fuck can you write this unless you have iron-clad proof. And if you have proof, give it to the cops!" Andrei frowned and crumpled the newsprint. "What you wrote got people killed!"

"I know!"

"This is *Russia*, man, not America," Andrei said, throwing the wadded paper on the floor.

"The man *in my apartment* was a burglar," Jack repeated.

Andrei smiled with a drunk's satisfied grin, slumping his shoulders on the chair, letting his lips pull back from covering his teeth. "You're fooling yourself, kid," Andrei said, his arms dangling limp from the shoulders. "That was *mafia*, about to give you some editorial commentary on your articles."

Karl reappeared and unlocked the cell door. "You can *go*," Karl said and stood back from the open cell door.

"Go?" Jack repeated. Karl nodded. Jack and Andrei exchanged glances and then they both walked out. Jack signed a document and got back his wallet, keys and passport.

Driving home, Andrei was silent. He drove hunched over with both of his hands high on the steering wheel. Jack sat with a formal posture—knees and feet together, in the middle of the floor, hands folded in his lap—as if he were riding in a taxi rather than with a friend.

Andrei took one of his hands off the steering wheel to locate his pack of *Belamor Kanal* cigarettes. Jack calmed down then, knowing the worst had passed. Andrei lurched over the pockmarked St. Petersburg roads while he steered with one hand and fished out a cigarette with the other.

Andrei wandered across every lane. Andrei swerved without signaling, expertly avoiding a patch where the road was gone and what remained was only mud, punctuated in the middle by a trench hidden by deep water masquerading as a drivable puddle.

"How is it possible that I'm out of jail?" Jack said.

"Better ask whether or not you're guilty of some crime," Andrei said, glancing over with the hurt expression of someone who played by the rules, as Andrei had, and had gotten nothing in return for his trouble.

"Maybe—then," Andrei continued, glancing over at Jack. "If you were willing to just, I don't know, work someplace without expecting to leap to the *top*."

Jack ignored Andrei and drifted off in a sea of indecision.

"I went to college eight years and then worked without status for years," Andrei said, his wrist perched on the top of the steering wheel. "And only now, I—a man of 47 years—am a *Pro* Rector. Not a full Rector. No, not even at 47 I am not—" and Andrei looked over in the middle of his speech. Jack stared out the car window, not listening to a word Andrei had said. Andrei returned both hands to the steering wheel, the only trace of his anger the bitter frown that stained his face.

"I graduated from an American university," Jack said. "What good did that do me just now? I came *this* close to spending the next twenty-five years in a Russian jail cell the size of a hamster cage."

They turned off the main road and no longer headed toward the Primordial Region, where Andrei lived in a tall apartment building with wood-fronted doors on apartments and some with the typical black padded leather with brass nails in geometric patterns. Jack recalled the look of the hallway and the stairs in Andrei's building but from the turnoff it became clear to Jack that Andrei was not taking Jack to see Katya and the kids—Yuri and Misha.

Andrei slowed down and pulled off to the side of the road. The two of them parked on the side of the road. Andrei seemed befuddled. They sat in the car, parked, on the side of the road with the Lada engine idling.

"What Andrei? You think we should just ignore these kids?" Jack asked, and then he turned the voice inward. He wondered if he was foolish to even expect these Russians to care about the children of somebody else. That was the hardest part. He loved this country but many Russians were only helping their country commit suicide. Jack thought of Russia as a land of Tolstoy and Dostoevsky, and to think that gangsters were rounding up the street children, taking their organs out and just throwing away the empty carcasses—that reached a new plane of depravity. Jack knew he had not prepared himself for any plan that included the possibility of getting killed. Jack didn't want to get killed. Jack now considered his twin options. He could drop the story and forget he had ever met Galina or he could put everything he had into saving the kids.

After a long interval of idling, Andrei throttled up the Lada and trundled off the side of the road, back into the flow of traffic but in the opposite direction, toward Novocherkasskaya Metro station. The two of them drove without talking and, as if he felt some compulsion to address the question, Andrei's crackling voice spoke up: "Maybe it's better this way—at least it solves the problem."

"I don't agree," Jack said. "And forgive me for saying it, Andrei," Jack said. "But that sounds like the exact words of Sarah Hughes—"

"Fuck Sarah Hughes," Andrei said, retaining the sneer on his face. "She is a fucking bitch and I hate her." Jack smiled and chuckled, recalling the angry exchange Andrei and Sarah had shared during a dinner party at Sarah's. "Never want to lay eyes on that bloke again," Sarah had said the next day, meaning Andrei. Andrei was pissed at Sarah for laughing at his cheap *Belamor Kanal* cigarettes. Andrei—an *Assistant* Professor of Meteorology—felt embarrassed at his low salary. To get his salary increased, he would need to get the simplest article published in a meteorology journal and he would have to get three peers to review it first. Andrei had sat drunk at the table mocking and ridiculing Sarah's ridiculous life, even suggesting that Sarah was a bottle blond.

For these sins Jack had been banished from attending any late night shindigs at Sarah's. The only way Sarah invited him over again was if he swore bloody hell not to bring that weather bastard again.

"Why do you say I'm like Sarah Hughes?" Andrei asked, irritated.

"Because she wants to do the same thing as you—ignore the whole thing," Jack said, now irritated.

"That's hardly my point," Andrei said, chuckling.

"Oh—isn't it?" Jack said. "And—if I call you up and ask for your help someday—what are you going to say?"

"You might be surprised," Andrei said, wanting to say more but declining the fight. Andrei slowed the Lada down and they were at the stop for the Novocherkasskaya Metro. Jack opened the door and noticed that the Lada's dome light did not come on. Jack pointed to it and said: "Your dome light is broken, Andrei."

"I know," Andrei said, puzzled.

"Thank you," Jack said and shut the door. Jack walked a block and reached his apartment building.

4.

The next day, Jack walked into the *Komsomolets* and got a job.

Jack had been hired on the strength of his mafia stories for the *Nevski Novosti*. His editors expected him to keep writing them. He hated writing these articles because they made him think of Galina. And now Galina was lost on the streets and probably dead. Dread of the topic made Jack feel the floor fall out from under him when Yevgeny Markov, a 39-year-old reporter on the *Komsomolets*, came into the narrow newsroom with the frosted glass windows on the doors. Yevgeny had come from the dump where the caretaker had come upon a pile of skeletons—the skeletons of children. Knowing Jack's background, Yev came to Jack.

"You said 'pile'," Jack said, throwing his knapsack over his shoulder. "How many bones are we talking?"

"I wondered the same thing," Yevgeny said. "'Piles' *is* the right word, or maybe stacks."

Jack stared at Yevgeny, waiting for him to laugh and say "Joke."

"And the worst part is," Yev said. "The heads are still on. The flesh has been stripped off everywhere but from the heads.

Jack followed Yevgeny to his car. They got into Yevgeny's tan Lada. Yevgeny took one hand off the wheel and popped a cigarette out of his pack and into his mouth. As he opened his mouth under his flat nose, Jack caught a glimpse of Yev's rotten teeth.

"The chief puzzle, in my mind," Yevgeny said as he drove his allotted 110% of the road, took a drag on his cigarette and wiggled his upper right incisor—" is to understand *why* Chikatilo ate the meat. I mean, Chikatilo is Russia's most famous serial killer yet we don't even know the most basic facts." Jack smiled to himself as he knew Chikatilo was a cult icon like Jeffrey Dahmer was in the states.

After the beat of the clock's arm passed, Yevgeny reduced it to the most basic of all questions in Russian: "For what?"

Jack was silent as he himself had not envisioned a reason.

"What do you mean 'meat'?" Jack asked.

"From the necks down," Yevgeny said. Yevgeny kept his gaze fixed in a lock on the road. "All the big muscles removed, gone."

"It just got me thinking, you know, of Chikatilo," Jack said.

"Right," Yev said. "So I'm thinking cannibals."

This time it was Jack's turn to be puzzled.

214

"Did they find the muscles that were cut out?"

"No," Yevgeny said in a hushed voice. He was a seasoned journalist who had seen plenty of death. The shortness of his reply said everything. They drove onward without conversation as the paved road gave way to a dirt road. They saw a rise in white plastic bags and paper, folded gray and dirty, lying on the side of the road. Then, tires and old rusted-out 1950s cars lined the ditches on either side of the road. From the sheer volume of garbage lining either side of the road, Jack figured they were near the dump where the skinned skeletons had been found. On the edge of the huge garbage dump was a small shack. Jack flipped open his reporter's notebook and got down a sketch of the location, of the small shack, and the tires stacked on one side of it. He noted a small path that ran from the shack out into the huge dump.

"This man—who found the skeletons—lives here. Stay away from his mouth. He bites," Yev said and smiled, exposing his own bloody gums with the swollen areas around the widely-spaced teeth.

"Does he *eat people*, I guess, is the question," Jack said.

"Maybe," Yev said and parked. They both got out with their notebooks and walked the gravel road to the shack.

As they got closer to the structure an inhuman howl emerged like a cat being stabbed with a 10-penny nail. The two reporters paused for a moment and resumed their approach toward the shack. The howl became the almost unrecognizable Russian word, "never," repeated again and again. Within two steps of the shack, Jack stopped. He saw a man with an oily face standing in a doorway, invisible except for the shiny wet whites of his eyes and shard of clear glass, affixed to a long pole like a spear. Holding the spear was a moaning man whose howl seemed a good barometer of his agitation. Yevgeny took a step back and mumbled "Quiet."

Jack did not retreat. He noted that the man looked to be in his sixties, with a tuft of hair sprouting out of the top of his head. His hands were black with the oily residue of the dump mixed with the stains of many other bits of garbage in which he plunged his hands on a daily basis.

"Man—did *you* find the bones?"

"Little bones!" replied the man, again brandishing his spear, lurching forward and darting back one instant after the next.

"Is your name Alexei?"

"Yes," the wild man, named Alexei, said.

"I gave you food before, remember?" Yevgeny said.

The man thrust out his arms and Yevgeny produced another oil-paper-wrapped sandwich, which Alexei crammed in his mouth. His cheeks ballooned on either side and the wild man turned his back and led the two of them into his hut.

After the wild man Alexei had cleared out some of the backlog in his cheeks, Yevgeny looked over and winked at Jack.

"And if you show us the bones, I have more food." Nodding, the old man ran ahead of the two reporters, his hunched back humping along parallel to the ground as his long shard-tipped spear glided along. Jack and Yevgeny had to break into a jog to keep up with him. He darted straight into the junkyard down the narrow footpath littered with broken spokes of tires and angle irons poking out. Every new path was marked by a rusted wheel-less Russian car from the 1970s. After they passed the oldest parts in the junkyard they saw large pillow-shaped mounds of garbage, covered over with a layer of clay. They reached the end where the most recent garbage was being added. There the old wild man slowed down as he picked his way through the mounds of paper food wrappers, old wooden furniture with wooden struts snapped in two. They reached the back of the pile. The wild man Alexei slowed down ahead of them. He stopped and ran his hand over the tuft of hair on his head. Yevgeny and then Jack caught up with Alexei and saw what he was looking at: laying parallel on the ground were several dozen sets of skeletal feet, sticking out of the dirt. At the place where Alexei stood were two muddy faces attached to the skeletons. The majority of the flesh was stripped from the arms, legs and chest. On another body lying on its stomach Jack saw square cuts around the kidneys but the kidneys were both gone. Again, the calf, thigh, arm and chest were stripped of meat. The entrails remained. There was a blackened, tar-like mass in the area below the rib cages of some of the older skeletons which were of varying size but all appeared to be children. Yevgeny dropped to his knees on the ground next to a child's pale, bloated face. Using a stick he found nearby, Yevgeny tried to turn the corpse's face toward him but it was stiff and would not budge. Standing nearby, Jack noticed a rank smell, making him feel like vomiting. Yevgeny, his own face inches from the arms of the uncovered corpse, used his stick to examine the edge of the arm, which looked like it had been stripped with a sharp knife cutting parallel to the length of the arm.

"Look at this edge," Yevgeny said, running the tip of the stick under the line of skin, thereby raising it above the surrounding tissue and highlighting the smooth, even line of the cuts. "This was not done by somebody having fun time," Yevgeny said, dropping the stick. "This was done by somebody doing serious business."

"Yes," Jack said. "Especially around the kidneys."

Yevgeny rose to his feet and confronted Alexei. "If I don't bring you these sandwiches, what will you eat?"

"I am hunter—hunt crows," Alexei said, brandishing his spear.

"And sometimes cannibal?" Yevgeny continued.

Alexei did not appear to know what the word 'cannibal' meant and so he repeated, "Crows—black ones with white breasts—I hunt these," said Alexei, with a relaxed delivery that indicated he was satisfied with himself.

Yevgeny was at least 60cm taller than the wild man, Alexei. Closing his mouth in a protective way, Yevgeny lurched forward and grabbed Alexei's spear.

"Stop!" yelled Alexei, squirming and whipping his arm like it was in a snare. "Let go!" Yevgeny held on to the spear with an air that seemed malicious to Jack. Another taste of a peculiar willingness to be cruel that Jack had noted in his Russian friends. Yevgeny allowed the old man to twist and strain on the spear. Not sensing that he was harming an old man, Yevgeny continued to fight on for the spear, as if his own pride and outrage at what had been done to these children could be eased if he mistreated an old man.

Finally, with a flourish, Yevgeny threw off the spear he had fought over and the old man landed on the ground, sweaty-cheeked and panting.

"Stop killing crows," Yevgeny said, himself winded.

"Go to hell," said Alexei, still lying on the ground.

Yevgeny kicked a tin can at Alexei, who did not react to the can, which missed anyway. Alexei lay on the ground, perhaps feeling more comfortable there. Jack stood between them.

"Enough," Jack said to Yevgeny. Then Jack bent down and extended his hand to the wild man on the ground. Alexei returned a suspicious glare at Jack but then he took the hand and got to his feet. Yevgeny no longer looked at Alexei, as if the old wild man didn't exist.

"When did you find these," Jack asked Alexei.

"Yesterday," Alexei said. "I see new soil. Something new is buried. Look down and its feets. Lots of feets."

"Who do you think *did* this?" Jack said. Alexei accepted the question and went into his thoughts, pondering his reply.

"You're wasting your time," Yevgeny said. "This old man isn't smart enough to have done this business. Too much work. Too much meat."

It was Jack's turn to be surprised. Usually he did not approach a problem that way, by evaluating the suspect on his sheer competence. But in his characteristic and chameleonic-like way, Jack accepted the truth of Yevgeny's point.

"Anybody new coming to the dump?" Jack asked, in a voice softened by concern.

"No one," Alexei said.

"See?" Yevgeny said.

"Though…" Alexei continued. "There *was* a man. An angry man with short hair."

Jack scribbled down the details. Yevgeny frowned in a wide scoff.

"His hands were bloody," Alexei said.

"What did he look like?"

"Angry," Alexei said.

Jack asked if he could remember anything else and then Alexei—who didn't seem all that wild anymore—just up and walked away. Jack glanced at Yevgeny, who had a big smile on his face.

"What did you expect?" Yevgeny said, not attempting to hide his smile. Jack folded up his notebook and started to walk out of the dump. Yevgeny scrambled to keep up with him. When he did, Yevgeny stood in Jack's way and leveled with him.

"Listen—it's a terrible thing that's happening in Russia when we kill our children," Yevgeny said. "But what can you do?"

"Investigate," Jack said. "In my country we have a saying: 'The truth will set you free'."

"Ah," Yevgeny said. "There is another—a better American saying. 'A sucker is born every minute.'" Being as he was oh so clever, nothing could lower the mood of Yevgeny on the way back to the paper. Jack inquired if Yevgeny was going to write a piece on the discovery in the city dump.

"For what?" Yevgeny replied. "Go ahead if you want to so bad."

5.

Jack did that. There was a change in his approach. He no longer tried to investigate it from the direction of the children and what happened to them. Now Jack knew what was going on but he still was uncertain if the cause of the problem was somehow satanic worshipers or witches. Taking the meat off of children was hard work, what with the effort it took to drag a sharp knife through the leg of a child who had lived on the street and was therefore hungry and the meat would be stringy and hard to cut. A person doing such work on the twenty-nine corpses they had found in the dump would be exhausted. An expert had taken the kidneys out of two of the 29 bodies. In the next few days, Jack took a tour of the city's meat markets. He followed the Blue Metro Line. Jack rode all the way to Zvoznaya Metro station. He exited the station named after the stars. Outside were the usual corrugated-sheet-metal kiosks. Jack walked until he found a meat kiosk. Hanging on hooks behind the oily glass front were several chunks of meat of indeterminate origin, un-refrigerated—the state it would hang in all day. One of the meat chunks was about a foot long and was darkened red color, with patches near the ends that were gray and fuzzy. They had hardly any meat to sell. Jack asked the woman in the blue smock behind the window if she knew of a larger meat store in the area.

"On Pulkova Street, in the bazaar," she said, and pointed North.

Jack went there. A large grassy field that had been turned into an open air bazaar, with piles of onions and carrots and cabbage spread out on dirty folding tables. Jack wandered through dozens of alleys made by the ragged rows of kiosks, a Tobacconist kiosk next to a bread one. Jack looked for someone who wouldn't bite off his head if Jack asked a question.

"Where can I find meat?" Jack asked a man standing on a corner.

The man was elderly with wet eyes, in pain that kept him tense the entire time Jack talked to him. In fact, 'talked' was not correct because the wincing man did not say a thing. He pointed.

"*Spacibo*," Jack said and walked in the direction the man pointed. The market was a sea of vendors seated on folding chairs behind card tables stocked with their dusty produce or tiny wares. He walked straight and, after further inquiry, he found a large meat kiosk. The entrance—in the Russian fashion— had a sign that read: "Meat". A crush of people stood in front of the white enamel, glass-front display case. The selection of meat was the same sort as the other store—stringy cuts of meat of indeterminate origin or animal. Jack looked over to the cashier, a middle-aged man with a heavy growth of beard. He looked calm and experienced.

"Where can one buy *meat*?" Jack asked.

"You can buy meat *here*, you idiot," said the man, smiling.

"No, *better* meat," Jack said.

The man did not smile this time. He stared back at Jack, sucked his gum and turned away.

"For a *child*," Jack lied. The man turned back with reduced hostility. He looked past Jack's shoulder into space. When he lowered his gaze, he spoke.

"The best meat in St. Petersburg," said the man. "would be a place called *Chus Meats*. I don't know how but Chus always seems to have a lot of meat lately."

Jack's blood ran cold. Everything became clear to him.

"Thank you," Jack said and left the meat market. He thought of Galina. "So *that's* what happened to Galya," he said out loud.

Jack thought about the children he had seen in Udelny Park so long ago. They were all eaten or transplanted by now.

6.

Jack sat on his bed and examined a package he received in the mail. It came wrapped in butcher paper and tied up with two crossing loops of twine, in the traditional Russian Postal Service fashion. Jack was not expecting a package. It occurred to him how unfortunate it would be if the package turned out to be a bomb. He shook it and from the shifting he figured it must be paper. Finding the knot, Jack untied the twine and opened wrapper. A handful of Polaroid's slipped out of a letter folded into thirds. There was a note. Jack picked up the first photograph. It showed the back end of a Russian military-style truck. A stern-faced man and several younger boys stood at the rear of the truck. One passed a limp gray-faced thing with dangling arms and legs. In the next shot, the boy who held the body was free handed. Jack was certain the boy's hands were covered in fresh blood. The next shot showed a smaller boy thrusting a bloody corpse into the back of the truck. From the way its gray head rolled on its shoulders, Jack thought he saw the face. A child. The gray smoothness of the child's face shocked Jack. His heart pounded. Next shot. The first boy passing up another bloody corpse. This one was a girl with the vestiges of blond hair beneath the dirty tangles, soaked with blood, being passed up into the truck's back.

In this same shot, Jack got a close view of the scowling man standing next to the children. Right away, Jack knew this was none other than Vladimir Szlotov, the ultimate subject of the several articles Jack had written on the abandoned kids.

Jack felt dizzy. He refused to accept that he was so perfectly correct in his guess about what was happening. "The slaughterhouse," Jack said, remembering the basement lair and the wooden cages. Then he opened the letter. It was written in bad English but readable still.

> *Dear Mr. Land,*
> *I with great interest read your story about the Mafia and the street children. I in place to know truth of such matters, as I member of such organizatsiya. I thought you might enjoy see these pictures I took. They show real face of Russian Mafia.*
> *One from in Brigada Tambov*

Jack's jaw hung slack. He finished the letter. He looked at the photos and it was clear as day the circle was complete. These were the photos. And again he thought of Galina and what had happened to her. He thought that, somehow, she lived on the streets, doing her best just to stay alive, and some Mafia thug came along and killed her.

Feeling depressed and angry, Jack sprung off the bed and went to his desk. He started to scribble on a scrap of paper.

Jack scratched: "Tambov Kingpin photographed killing 8-year-old Galina Yosheva of Chilkovo."

Jack laid out the lede and the body and shifted into the first 'graph; he knew he had no pictures of Galina, *per se*, but he was irritated with always giving the children an anonymous group name, such as St. Petersburg street kids. He wanted to accuse one Vladimir Szlotov of killing one girl, Galina Yosheva. If he could not save her life, Jack thought, he could make her death count.

7.

Jack was at work on his laptop, answering emails, writing his friend Thor, and reading the police blotter. There was a knock at his door. Though he knew he should, Jack had not moved after the attack. He'd just bent his door straight and got the lock working again.

Jack walked up to his door inside but he just listened.

"It's Sarah," came a Scottish voice from the hallway. Jack opened the door and let her in. Given the outcome of his final story for *Nevski Novosti*—the death of the Editor Alexander I. Krasnie—Jack didn't know whether or not to brace himself for an attack.

Sarah came in and non-nonchalantly sat on his couch. She glanced at his laptop. "Whatcha working on?" Sarah asked. She didn't seem angry at him, which was a relief.

"Piece for the *Komsomolets*," he said, warily. What did she want with him?

Sarah put her feet primly together and said, "I'm with *Sevodnya.* "It's a daily." She had a hint of a sly smile on her face.

"I read it all the time," Jack said. "Managing Editor again?"

"No," she said. "Just a reporter."

"Can I get you—"

"No, that's not necessary," Sarah said. She lowered her gaze to drop the idea of him fussing over her.

Jack looked at her in a way that old lovers look at each other. He wanted her in his bed again. But he knew that was over. He had a flash of Sarah, naked, on top of him, a wave of honey-colored hair being tossed with every move. Jack recalled the days of sleeping in late with Sarah, watching her as she slept, her nipples peeking above the blanket. Jack had felt as lucky as any man in the world. He remembered the jealous looks when they would show up to work late, both with the satisfied smiles of two people who had intimate secrets. Looking at Sarah how, with the controlled mood of her posture, heels together, sitting on the couch without letting her back touch it—it was enough to drive him crazy.

Sarah knew Jack was checking her out. She couldn't hate him any more. She'd already used up too much psychic energy on that. He really wasn't a bad bloke, and although she'd never sleep with him again, she felt she could trust him. As she looked around the floor at the scattered papers that Jack had not yet picked up and organized, she hugged her own shoulders as an involuntary shiver went up her spine.

Suddenly she looked up and stared him right in the eye. "It's not safe to live here, Jack. You have *no idea* what you've gotten yourself into."

"I know, the whole topic is dangerous," Jack said, breaking off eye contact.

"No! You don't!" Sarah said, shouting. "I've stepped into something dangerous myself—because of you."

"What's going on?"

"I'm interviewing one Vladimir V. Szlotov," Sarah said with a mixture of professional pride and bemused horror.

Jack's jaw dropped. It was quite a "get." Sarah got the one man Jack wanted and couldn't.

"Amazing."

"And did you know about Szlotov's mother?" Sarah said.

"What about her?" Jack said.

"She lives on the ground floor of your building."

Chapter XVII

1.

T HE most unfortunate part for everyone in his crew was that Vladimir Szlotov himself found the article by this American swine Land, who wrote a lying article about Szlotov, accusing him of killing this young street vermin. Seeing his name like he was a common street criminal compounded his anger at what Land had done to Boris, who Szlotov had known since the 1980s. For a week after the story came out, Szlotov stayed alone in his apartment without leaving. The photo that showed Szlotov and a young boy lifting a corpse into the back of a truck was not so embarrassing. But why he had used outside talent was going to be hard to explain to his regular crew. Using talent from outside the *organizatsiya* was frowned upon.

Since Szlotov had decided not to venture anywhere, Sergei was denied any travel, as there was nothing to guard against. Sergei's job was to bodyguard and so he could not go out and earn. After the story came out about Szlotov's escapades with the young criminals in the park, Szlotov was on the defensive. When Szlotov absorbed the meaning of the article written about him, an electric shiver ran up his spine and hovered above the back of his neck, as if the world had set the top of his head on fire. And the photos! Who had taken them and sent them to the journalist?

Behind the shiver passed a wave of shame. But the feeling confused him. What was he ashamed of? Killing homeless children and using their bodies for meat so that he could pay his tribute to Zortaev? Or that he got caught? No, he didn't give a shit about the children. What kind of life did they have? They were garbage. He snorted—he wasn't taking out the garbage...he was recycling. They should give him a fucking medal! Szlotov snapped back into calm control.

Szlotov remained angry that he was in hiding because of the photos, because of the article. At least the story did not mention the murder of Alexander Krasnie.

Szlotov made himself a cup of tea in the kitchen, muttering to himself about the photos, where they came from. Mentally ticking off everyone who possibly could have sent them. It couldn't have been anyone in his crew. Szlotov had gone to fresh recruits instead of using any of them. It could have been Druzhnev, he thought. He hates me, wants me out of his way as a rival. But even that made no sense—how could Druzhnev even have known was Szlotov was doing?

In the living room, nobody in his crew said a thing. They sat around watching TV with the sound down. Sergei seemed half asleep, but he was watching Szlotov through hooded lids.

Szlotov paced from the kitchen to the living room with his cup of tea. "Somebody...somebody was hiding and saw everything on the street," Szlotov said aloud. "But who?"

Sergei sat at the side with Vasya, Fyodor, Ivan and Arkady, and tried to act as disinterested. It was a big problem—was one of them a traitor who had taken the photos of Szlotov and mailed them to a reporter? Sergei wet his lips several times and looked at the floor.

"Who took those photos, Sergei?" Szlotov said, with anger in his voice.

"How should I know!" Sergei yelled back, now angry himself. "I helped you set the damn thing up but you never told me what you were doing." Sergei clamped his mouth closed and ground his teeth, taut cords standing out on his cheeks. Then Sergei leaned in close to Szlotov and said quietly. "Vladimir...what were you *doing*?" Sergei said, delivering the last word like a slap.

Szlotov remained silent.

"This is too much, even for *us*," Sergei said. "We can't keep doing this. It will end badly."

Fyodor leaned in and said, "Me and Vasya agree. This is not good business."

Vasya nodded with his rat face.

"This has got to stop," Sergei said. "I didn't sign up for this."

Szlotov took a deep breath. He agreed with them, of course, but where would this end? Either he earned money for Zortaev, or he was a dead man. One didn't retire from the Tambov Syndicate. The alternative, of course, was killing Zortaev and ending this madness. But killing Zortaev also meant killing Druzhnev. That would be tricky. It would require planning.

Four hours after the newspapers hit the stands, a copy arrived next to the half-dozen steaming links of *sosiski* and pieces of dark rye bread that was the lunch of Dmitri Zoltanovich Zortaev. And there, on the front page, was a photo that made Zortaev almost choke on sausage.

It did not take long before Szlotov's mobile phone started ringing. It was Zortaev. He answered it.

Zortaev was screaming. "What is this! What did you do! We're done!"

Szlotov had been expecting the call, and the dressing down from Zortaev. He took his medicine and sat with the phone pressed to his ear and Zortaev yelling into it. Across the room, Sergei crossed his arms and scowled at Szlotov. They could all hear Zortaev's screaming.

As Zortaev's blistering verbal attack reached its crescendo, Szlotov held the phone slightly away from his ear. He envisioned that fat, smug, crazy

225

bastard, bits of half-chewed food spewing from his lips, spittle running down the rind of his neck, his eyes bugging out of his head. Yes, Zortaev would have to go. It was the only way.

As Szlotov started at the ceiling and signed, Sergei, Fyodor and Vasya exchanged wide-eyed stares, each of them expressionless. The only sign of movement was their tongues rooting around slowly in their mouths, as if they were silently sharing opinions, making plans, shaking hands with their eyes.

2.

Szlotov's self-imposed hiding made it easier for him to continue seeing Sarah. He still believed he could have a thing with her if she did not find out he had already killed her former boss and had plotted to kill Jack Land.

Szlotov had already made a date with Sarah for that night, and so he decided to keep it. He picked her up at her apartment—meeting her at the front door instead of entering through the balcony—and planned to go to Nevski Palace Hotel, upstairs at the buffet.

Szlotov decided to eat at this restaurant, although he had not been back since Zortaev had the unfortunate incident with the lobster. As they walked in and found a table, Szlotov found himself enjoying its opulence. Sarah liked the Nevski Palace because its buffet was so varied. But she did not know any of Szlotov's history.

"So," Sarah said, the tail of a celery stalk protruding from her mouth. "What's the story on this...thing I read by that bloke Land?" she said and crunched in a few bites of celery. Szlotov breathed through his nose and returned her gaze without a scrap of shame. "Is this real?" Sarah asked. "I mean, I used to work with this bloke."

"These children were already dead," Szlotov said. "From earth flu."

Sarah let her teeth hang in the air in a big smile.

"Did you just say 'earth flu'? Let me see if I can explain this to you," Sarah said. "I know you're in the Tambovs. I know all about you. What I don't know is *why*? If you want me to keep seeing you," Sarah said. "You're going to have to give me the story and then maybe I can get out of this town and get a job with the BBC. And I'm not going to get hired by the BBC unless you stop with the 'earth flu.'"

"Fuck off," he said. She emptied her champagne glass.

"Now that's *not* the sort of talk," Sarah said. "That's liable to get you invited into a lady's pants."

After a polite interval, Szlotov smiled. He decided he would do or say

226

anything to get *invited* into the pants of this blond British lady, who smelled of *class*, who was the most beautiful woman Szlotov had ever seen. Her beauty flowed from her confidence.

"Now you are speaking 'real,'" Szlotov said and drained his own glass. Sarah laughed but with a disturbed expression. "Question is only *when* in pants, not *if*," Szlotov said.

Sarah chortled. "We'll see. Tell me your story, impress me," she said. "This bloke Land has told *his* side of your story. Why not tell *your* side of the story to me. An exclusive. Enough to jump start my career and save yours." Sarah munched on her celery. "And let's face it, your career needs saving, Vladimir, after those pictures." Sarah took a long stretch. "I know this bloke Land—*American*—and he pads his pieces. No surprise if it happened to you."

Szlotov was displeased with her reaction.

"Another thing, you can't keep on shooting editors," Sarah said. Szlotov was taken aback. He sucked in a breath. He wanted to bed Sarah but she knew enough to shorten her life. He instinctively realized that a failed relationship between he and this British girl must end in her death to sanitize her of knowledge. Prior to this moment, Szlotov had believed she could live after he was done with her.

"Nonsense," Szlotov said after a long uncomfortable pause.

"Land's story said that you killed a teenage girl, a 'Galina Yosheva,'" Sarah said.

"It's a damned lie," Szlotov shouted. "It's not true."

Sarah held back, silent.

"It is not true," he lied. Szlotov thought about the bloody dramas he had seen take place in the basement with the Doctor, the scenes of the Doctor, tired and tormented, feeling the bite of his sore gums but stripping body after body, even when his hands, his knuckles ached. Szlotov looked at the Doctor, working his way through the piles of meat, and the pain in his hands. Szlotov himself had seen the Doctor up to his elbows in the blood of these little street children. Their meet was feeding St. Petersburg as 'veal' and their organs made him rich. Well, richer. Szlotov dropped from his reverie. Sarah stared at him with great bewilderment. "Is *true*," Szlotov said, "that the man you see in these photos in newspaper was me but children were victims of plague. I was helping dispose of bodies from this plague."

Sarah stared frowning at Szlotov for several minutes and then she took a long drink of her water and decided not to pursue this line of questions any further. Szlotov was unsettled. He stared out the large window looking out of the second floor of the Nevski Palace restaurant. The evening sun was fast heading behind the Prussian-blue clouds lightened by a wash of amber and ocher.

When he looked at Sarah, she had a mouthful of pineapple, purple grapes and cut orange slices. Szlotov decided his best alternative lay not in killing the American reporter but in discrediting him.

3.

After he brought Sarah to his apartment, she went into his bathroom and took a bath. Standing in his apartment listening to the crackling fireplace, Szlotov looked around at his leather couch, his expensive Japanese stereo system and his large television. None of his money or fine things were worth a thing if his name was cast in shame. The article the American wrote was damaging. His only chance was to disprove some part of the story and cast doubt on the whole thing. While Szlotov wanted to kill this American he knew he could not. It would be attributed to him.

He opened the wide drawer above his knees and looked again at the article. On the front page was the prominent photo of Szlotov standing next to a truck where a bloody corpse was being passed in broad daylight. From the hand of one bloody child (it looked to be big Ilia on the ground) to Pavel, the crazy one, taking the body in the truck.

The article also had a second photo, following the jump to the inside page. In this second photo was shown the face of a girl, a Galina Yosheva, from the small farming village of Chilkovo, who the article claimed was killed by Szlotov himself. It irritated him. He had never seen this girl before. The children he had actually killed—so the child's blood splashed back on him—could be counted on one hand. None of those children were like this Galina, who the article said was about 8 years old, whereas all the children that Szlotov had killed were *below* 8 years of age—he was sure of it. He had never killed a teenager since he himself was a teen.

All of these thoughts led Szlotov to the jaw-setting conclusion that he was being accused falsely. With every fiber, then, he wanted to kill this American reporter Land. He wanted to smear his body under the tires of a speeding truck. He wanted to kill the American and scorch his body from the face of the earth. But he knew that plan was out of reach. Instead, he would discredit his enemy. He took the original photo of the girl from the paper and had it copied and passed around to everybody in the *organizatsiya* as a top priority: find this girl alive.

Szlotov did conclude the order with his usual caveat "if possible." This one time, they needed to find this girl 'Galina' alive. That would prove the American Jack Land a liar. Szlotov had not started this fight but he would end it.

4.

Since Szlotov stopped making his usual visits to his interests, he needed less and less the services of his old friend Sergei. The harvesting of the street children for 'veal' kept Szlotov busy, both on the harvest side and his most irritating problem, what to do with the half-stripped bodies. Also, the diversion of a small but growing number to organ transplants was the real money. Even though Szlotov didn't need him, Sergei still made his usual money but now was doomed to kill time staying in one place, in the apartment next door to Szlotov.

When Szlotov did go out, he drove alone or with the British girl. Sergei stayed behind. The weakening of his relationship with his old friend Sergei was unfortunate but inevitable as Szlotov became bored with anyone who was not the dominant player in their own life. They never discussed the real reason for their estrangement but Szlotov did not try to fool himself. Sergei disapproved of the meat and organs scheme. Sergei argued that Zortaev was crazy and that he should be put out of our misery, with the useless Druzhnev to be killed also. Szlotov knew it was a war he must win, but it was not one he was ready to start. Almost, but not yet.

5.

Szlotov was able to eliminate the first "Galina" brought in by Fyodor and Vasya. The girl, who looked about twelve, looked uncomfortable having her hair styled to match the photo. The reddish tint of her hair, raw henna dye Szlotov thought, sitting in his robe in the living room. The girl had been prepped. Standing in front of him, she had something to say without fear or hesitation.

Instead, this young imposter "Galina" stood in front of him, leaving dirty footprints on his carpeting. He stared at the square of tan carpeting and pondered how he would be able to clean it.

"How are you called?" Szlotov asked. Fyodor, who looked resigned to the rejection, stood by.

"Ilona," said the girl, raising her lip to answer the question. Without another word, the girl Ilona started to take off her pants, until Szlotov put his palm on her shoulder.

"Girl…what are you doing?" Szlotov said.

"Undressing."

"Well, *don't*," Szlotov said and waved the girl away. "No score," he told Fyodor. "Keep looking." Fyodor groaned and led Ilona away.

Later on, after many wrong girls, Arkady brought in another one. She looked like a street child with dirty, tangled hair. Her clothing was filthy, with the marks of many wet soakings and faded lines showing evaporation deposits. When confronted with the question of "How are you called?" She answered: "Galina". Szlotov allowed a smile into the corners of his eyes.

"And your family name?" Szlotov asked.

"Yosheva, of Chilkovo," the girl said and added her birth city without being asked, as if she was rehearsed to do so.

Szlotov looked at the original photo from the article and compared it to the eager dirty 8-year-old standing in front of him. There were some differences between the two. He couldn't put his finger on the reason why he did not accept the girl in front of him as the one true "Galina" that would show the American reporter *gavno* to be a liar. Then, he looked at the earlobe of the girl in the photo, *the* Galina. Szlotov had this girl stand the same way as the girl in the photo. The real Galina's earlobe was attached, while the false Galina in front of him had an *un*attached lobe.

This string of bad luck—when it came to the string of teenage girls who called themselves "Galina" went on for two days until Ivan, his backup driver found another one near the Technologicheski Institute Metro station. By now Szlotov was running out of questions that had not been coached. The girl Ivan brought in was nervous. She had no sense of triumph in her face. In fact, it looked like she had been ridden into the dirt a few too many times. Szlotov said: "Name?" The girl, after a bit of hesitation, said: "Galina."

"Family name?" Szlotov said and waited. After a delay he looked at Ivan and thought: "So, Ivan, you're so lazy you neglected to coach her?"

While Szlotov waited for the girl to answer, he brought the flat cuffs of his silk shirt into parallel alignment and fed a silver cuff link through the aligned seams.

"Yosheva," said the girl. Szlotov was about to correct her pronunciation of her own last name but then he thought: "No." Szlotov sat back in his chair. Both of his cuffs were joined by silver cuff links. He looked at the girl. She had given him a correct first and a near-close hit on the girl's last name. This girl was not eased or relieved. Rather, she stared at Szlotov. She had no idea what he planned for her.

"He's *looking* for you," Szlotov said after a long pause.

"Who's looking for me?" Galina asked. Szlotov did not offer any choices.

"The *American*?" Galina asked.

"The American," Szlotov said, gasping. Until that moment, he had been breathing. "*Vot Tak*," Szlotov said under his breath. *Bulls-eye.*

At that moment, Szlotov stood in frozen time, staring at her face, hair, hands and clothing. This girl, not older than 8, was Szlotov's salvation. On her clothing were the faded lines of some long past brown soup that had immersed her shirt and pants. Her face was a mosaic of muddy smears, touches of brown, charcoal or gray. Ivan began to smile so that his cheekbones were visible. He took a step back, smiling.

"She's the one," Szlotov said and leaned back in his chair. He turned to Ivan and said: "I'll remember this," and topped it off with a smile and a handful of Ben Franklins. Ivan left with a swagger and his cash. The girl, Galina, stood in the middle of Szlotov's apartment, uneasy and skittish. She waited while Szlotov telephoned Sergei, and asked him to come.

Szlotov sat alone with the 8-year-old girl he was supposed to have killed, looking back and forth at her face and the photo. He felt a great joy in being able to throw the entire story in the trash by showing one of the points in the article was a lie. Galina stood with her arms crossed, not knowing what Szlotov had in mind for her. No doubt, she had withstood worse in her young life on the streets.

"How did you get to St. Petersburg?" Szlotov asked her. He knit his fingers behind his head. Galina looked like a statue back at him.

"You're not wooden, are you?" Szlotov asked her. This most basic of Russian insults elicited a "*N'yet!*"

"Well?" Szlotov said.

"I rode a train to St. Petersburg," Galina said, staring off into space. Szlotov closed his eyes.

6.

Sergei walked up to Galina and she cowered. As Sergei picked her up and carried her down to the car, Galina squirmed and cried. Sergei threw her in the front seat and belted her in with her arms under the straps. As Galina slipped her arms out, he fished a pair of handcuffs out of the back seat and belted her in again. In handcuffs, Galina quieted down.

Szlotov had watched peers with neither his strength nor his smarts succeed and end up with piles of money and no dirt under their fingernails. The photos of Szlotov passing up the bodies of those bloody children counted as dirt under his fingernails that would stop him from ever escaping this life into any kind of peaceful success. This fact angered him. It encouraged him to fight back and strike down those who had sullied his reputation. The best-tasting victory could be enjoyed in the bright sunshine of day.

Szlotov walked outside and Sergei stood by the car with his arms crossed. He had a tense, angry expression on his face. Locked in the car was Galina, belted and cuffed in the front seat.

Galina looked back at Szlotov, trying to guess what he planned for her.

"Are you comfortable?" Szlotov asked her.

"Yes," Galina said and hesitated. "What do you want from me?"

"I want you to be *alive*," Szlotov said.

Szlotov took up the address book he had stolen from the editor of *Nevski Novosti* out of his glove compartment. He paged through it and then found what he was looking for, the telephone of Jack Land, that shit American reporter. Szlotov dialed the number. It rang three times and then Szlotov heard a high-pitched voice saying "*Allo*" with a bad accent.

Without hearing another syllable, Szlotov knew that he had reached the American who smeared his name for a murder he had not done.

"Sir, my name is Vladimir Vladimirovich *Szlotov*," he said. The voice on the other end of the line gasped.

"*The* Vladimir Szlotov?" said the voice.

"Is speaking a Mr. Jack Land?" Szlotov countered.

"Yes," Jack said. A long pause ensued. Neither Szlotov nor Land breathed.

"That girl you *say* I killed," Szlotov said. "She's sitting next to me."

"*Galina?*"

"Yes, the *exact* same girl you said I *killed*," Szlotov replied. "If you want her back, I'll meet you. We can trade your girl for all of those photos you have."

Jack said nothing.

"The girl and I, we come to apartment of yours."

"No, thank you. I don't care for a repeat of the last time you visited my apartment."

Szlotov found himself amused at the memory of re-decorating Land's apartment. Then that moved into thoughts of what happened to Boris and Szlotov was determined to complete his plan which involved killing the American after he admitted his article was a lie.

"The Banking Bridge...midnight," Jack said in Russian. His tortured syntax and lack of grammar made Szlotov think: "Stupid American."

"What-what-what?" Szlotov said, in the Russian manner of saying the Russian word "*shto*" three times.

"The Banking Bridge," Jack Land repeated. "You know, the one with the gold griffins. Bring Galina. I'll bring the photos."

Szlotov was about to slap down the idea on the grounds of Sun Tzu's advice regarding narrow passes but he said: "Eh, why not."

"At midnight, tonight," Jack Land said.

"I will meet you there," Szlotov said, and hung up his phone. As the phone line dropped away, Szlotov's eyes shifted from the mist in front of his mind's eye to Galina, standing with her arms crossed, frowning with irritation.

"Well, girl," Szlotov said. "You're the lucky one."

7.

At 11:48 that night, Szlotov drove his BMW 740i on Prospekt Nevski.

As they drove over the *Anichkov Bridge*, the wind sung in the wires for the trolley cars and his gaze was drawn to the wide blue waters of the Neva River. In the distance, he saw the yellow cross-tipped spire of the Cathedral of Peter and Paul, holding its own as the tallest point of St. Petersburg.

Szlotov glanced at Galina, riding in the front seat with him. He looked in the rear-view mirror at the headlights of Sergei's car following behind. Szlotov drove at full speed until he encountered the bridge crossing over the Kanal Griboedova and he applied the brakes. A second later he heard a squeak from Sergei's tires, who had not expected the brake tap.

Szlotov turned right on the far side of the canal. Szlotov slowed down his BMW until the rotation of the wheels was as slow as a barber screwing up his wooden stool. The blue canal water washed against the granite walls of the canal. Galina looked out the window. Her breath steamed the glass next to her face. Because of the fogging, Szlotov didn't see what was happening on the other side of the canal. It turned left and right after the turn Szlotov slowed to a crawl next to the griffins of the Banking Bridge, a narrow footbridge over the canal Griboedova. The bridge was supported on either end by gold-plated lions three meters tall, with their golden wings even higher. The lions held the ends of cables in their jaws, supporting the bridge's walkway.

Szlotov parked past the bridge—and Sergei parked his car so his line of sight looked across the bridge. Szlotov stayed in his car and waited. He and Sergei were the first to arrive. Szlotov appreciated the taste evident in the selection of the meeting location, even if Sun Tzu would not. No such taste was evident in the dirty Lada that drove along the opposite side of the street, facing the opposite direction. The passenger-side window was darkly tinted. There were two in the front seat at least, Szlotov thought. The Lada crept forward until its passenger-side window, dark as it was, was aligned between the granite statue bases, a meter tall.

The back door of the Lada opened up. On the far side, out jumped a tall man with shaggy, unkempt hair. After he got out, the man ducked his head back in the car and came out with a package wrapped in brown paper and twine. Szlotov noticed that the driver of the car, whoever it might be, was smart enough to leave the engine running. Regular puffs of exhaust came out of the Lada's tailpipe. Szlotov met eyes with the man who stepped out of the car. His messy hair and hunched-over posture confirmed for him without doubt that this was the American Land.

Stopping to gaze at Szlotov's BMW, parked cold in front of Sergei, the man stepped on the bridge with the complete confidence that he would not be killed with a single bullet and have his photos confiscated. The American stopped on the far edge of the bridge and waved the package he held. Szlotov sat waiting, watching how the man waved the package, and whether or not it was hard to reverse the direction of the package's movements, which would tell him its mass and whether it might contain a pistol or a bomb. Szlotov was satisfied the object the American held was light. He was not afraid of the situation. Szlotov wanted to shove the girl in the American's face and see him babble before Szlotov killed him; he popped open his door and helped Galina to the door on his side.

"Do you know him?" Szlotov asked Galina.

"The American?" Galina asked. "Yes, that's him."

"He wants you to go with him. Do you want to go?" Szlotov asked. Galina stared for a moment and said "No, not really," she said. Szlotov laughed and led her to the bridge. Jack's jaw dropped when he recognized her; she was the same Galina who had run from Sarah Hughes' apartment.

Szlotov, close-mouthed and serious, watched on the bridge with Galina. The American said, "Galina?"

"Yes," she said. "It's me. Sorry I ran. That lady scared me. I'm sorry."

From his suit's breast pocket, Szlotov took out the folded bit of newsprint and read the portion that described how Szlotov killed Galina Yosheva.

"Well?" Szlotov said. "Who gave you those pictures?"

"I must have confused her with another," Jack Land said, angering Szlotov with his non-answer.

"The photographs?" Szlotov said.

Jack Land handed over the packet tied up with string. Szlotov snatched it away and ripped it apart, dropping some pictures on the walkway of the bridge. Jack Land bent down and picked up the two that fell. As he stood up, Szlotov snatched away the photos and frowned at Jack, as if the great crime was taking the photos. The boys were covered in blood. Szlotov was relieved to see

234

that the most damning photos had *not* been published. He looked at them with horror as it was evident they would have ruined him forever in the eyes of the *organizatsiya*. He had to kill the American and the girl and kill the four boys who had helped him. Taking Galina by the hand, Jack Land turned around.

As Land and the girl stepped to their car, Szlotov stepped back across the bridge. He saw Sergei, sitting inside his car on the passenger side, ready to fire the instant Szlotov cleared. The shot was hard for Sergei since the footbridge was only two shoulders wide. Szlotov rested his hand on his pistol. Land and Galina broke into a run. As they crossed the bridge, the Lada's back door popped open. Szlotov drew and was ready to shoot. The Lada's front door popped open and out stepped an old Russian woman. The old woman stood uneasily and looked over at the bridge.

About to shoot through her, Szlotov realized who that the tottering old woman at the end of the bridge was. Not believing his eyes, Szlotov yelled "Mamochka!"

The Lada dashed off, its front door still open. Szlotov un-cocked his pistol and rushed up to get his mother.

Sergei ran out too. *"Bleen!"* Sergei roared as Szlotov's mother came toward them.

Szlotov stood immobile for a moment and then he shouted: "Fuck!"

Masha Ilovna walked by herself over the Banking Bridge. Szlotov did not imagine it was possible for him to be had. The American got everything and lost nothing. Realizing this enraged Szlotov. He wanted to kill someone right away.

"Now now, Vladdy," his mother Masha Ilovna said. "I didn't raise you to use profanity."

Szlotov put his arm around his mother and gave her a peck on the cheek.

"Sorry, Mamochka."

Sergei stood back, his face flushed in rage. He held his pistol in hand and looked at Szlotov with a dark, humorless cast over his expression. Szlotov had known Sergei his entire life. He knew what Sergei looked like when his patience was gone.

"I promise you things will be better," Szlotov told Sergei, looking him in the eye. Szlotov was now afraid to turn his back on him. "It may *already* be too late, Vladimir."

"Sergei, can you take my mother home?" Szlotov said.

"That…wasn't exactly what I had planned," Sergei said.

Szlotov detected a lack of deference and also the presence of insolence. Unconsciously, Szlotov stood behind his mother.

"Please, Sergei," Szlotov said with urgency. "She's my Mother."

Sergei's tension collapsed and he turned to his own car, his gun replaced at the crook of his back.

"Mamochka—you remember Sergei?" Szlotov said. "He's going to take you home."

Szlotov's mother seemed surprised. "What happened to that nice American man?" said Masha Ilovna.

"He won't bother you any more, Mama," Szlotov said.

"Oh he didn't bother me, Vladdy," she said. "He was quite nice, actually."

Sergei leaned over and shoved open his passenger door. Szlotov led his mother to Sergei's car and she got in. Sergei drove away and Szlotov stood alone at the Banking Bridge. He got in his car and looked over the photos again. Incredible.

Szlotov smiled the way a predator smiles before devouring its prey. Killing Zortaev would be painful, enjoyable and dangerous. Szlotov thought how to get it done.

Chapter XVIII

G ALINA sat in the dirty white Lada in the front seat, which was warm after the old lady got out.

"Andrei go!" Jack yelled.

"Where are you taking me?" Galina said.

Andrei revved the Lada and popped the clutch. The car shot forward. Galina's head pressed on the seat back. When she looked back, she saw the American riding in the back seat, looking at her and smiling. Galina looked away and flipped the latch to open the door. Galina pushed open her door against the pressure of the wind that blew at 12kph and leaned out to open the door when the American grabbed the back of her car door and pulled it back shut.

"Crazy! What the hell are you doing?" Andrei yelled and jerked Galina back in the car by her left arm, causing her to fly back in the car nearer to him and making the car lurch to the left in response to the letup in pressure on the steering wheel.

"We are your friends, idiot," Andrei barked and showed her the back of his hand. He was about to strike Galina when the American said: "Stop!" Still paying attention to his rear view mirror, Andrei turned left just to elude easy capture.

Galina stared forward in her seat and felt that she would have to accept whatever happened to her. The Lada made its way down wide Prospekt Nevski. The blue Moskovsky Train station where she had first seen St. Petersburg caught Galina's eye in a new way as she rode rather than walked past it. Andrei followed Prospekt Nevski as it headed for its crossing point of the Neva river, the Bridge of Alexander Nevski. Galina then thought in her mind's eye about Chilkovo, with a few brick buildings arranged along a central street that was narrow and paved with pitted asphalt. Galina remembered walking out into the dust in Chilkovo when she lived with her grandmother. The scent of burning birch wood and the sight of campfires dotting the hillside in front of her, smoke rising in drifting tufts that hung in the air and clotted like tangles of white-gray wool: dancing orange flames, tongues of fire and billowing smoke. Cast upon all of it, an eeriest pink glow that colored every tree, house or even the smoke itself with pink. The glow faded into a ruddy tint to the horizon.

Galina thought: "I want to go home." Her own voice whispered back: "You don't have a home in Chilkovo anymore."

The Lada turned left up Prospekt Novocherkasskaya. Galina found her gaze drawn on the left to the visible spire from the fortress of Peter and Paul. They drove up Novocherkasskaya Prospekt. Along concrete sidewalks middle-aged women carried plastic stacks of different colors and ages with grim expressions, in their cloth coats and brown wool hats. The *babushki* reminded Galina of her own grandmother back in Chilkovo. Andrei stopped at a stoplight and looked over at Galina. Galina steeled herself and knitted her fingers together and flexed them in a bit to control her fear and feeling of disgust about what was going to happen to her. The Lada turned on Yakornaya Street and then on Prospekt Metallistov. Andrei turned right off Metallistov after they intersected Bolshoi Prokovskaya Street, after a *Produkti* store. They drove off Metallistov to a dirt road. Andrei parked the Lada and Galina remembered this was the place where the American lived.

With a sense of dread, Galina got out of the car and followed the American—with Andrei behind her—into the building and up the stairs to the third floor. As they passed the landing of the first floor, Galina found her eyes drawn to the creaky wooden basement door, open a crack, as a possible place to run. Then went up the stairs and the American inserted his long toothed key into the outer door and pulled it open. The hinges squealed as he pulled and then the inner door opened. Galina heard the sound of sizzling and the smell of onions frying in oil.

"What is going on?" Galina said, aloud by accident and Andrei piped up behind her.

"I have the same question myself," Andrei said. "Every time I step into this mad house."

"It's not *mad*," the American said, using the common word to describe disorder. "It's just high spirits, right Natasha?"

"Hah!" said Natasha, her bleach-blond hair hanging limp from her head. "Completely mad," she said, wiping her oily hands on her apron.

"She took you back?" Andrei said to Jack.

"Not for long," Natasha said. Galina remembered staying in this apartment before she ran away.

The American led Galina into the kitchen where Natasha was cooking potatoes and onions. "Natasha, this is Galina Yosheva—"

"—of Chilkovo," Natasha said, finishing his sentence.

Galina whirled on Natasha: "How did you know *that*?"

"Because I'm a reporter," the American said. "I'm trained to dig. She knows because I know."

Galina lowered her eyes to the floor. She almost wished her fingers were broken so that somebody would feel sorry for her. All at once, Galina began to cry and she felt the hand of Natasha, 19-years-old, patting her back.

"Galya," Natasha said, using the pet name for name Galina, "It's okay.

You're safe with us."

Galina wrapped her fingers around Natasha's hand. She met eyes with Natasha and she felt safe. The pot of potatoes boiled over in a white suds that splashed over and flared up. Natasha pulled away her arm from Galina and tended to the potatoes. The American opened the cupboards and started to get out bowls and spoons.

"Well, that's my cue to go," Andrei said. "Glad to see you're making such a nice *communalnaya*." Natasha spun around and said "Go on, stir up trouble at home…" Galina remembered the word *communalnaya* from Chilkovo. Her grand mother lived in one of these apartments that was broken up into smaller rooms with fake walls and lots of doors added.

Andrei left the apartment and the American locked the door behind him. Galina felt better with Andrei gone. He looked at her the same way Astrakhan did.

Natasha set the table and Galina sat in front of her bowl, thick with a broth made of onions, carrots and potatoes. Galina ate her soup and felt warmth welling from her throat, sliding down with the gentle but direct taste of onion-steeped potatoes with the occasional soft bite of carrots. Galina ate her soup and ignored as she could the burning welt forming on the back of her tongue as the heat from the soup settled there.

Galina remembered feeling cold and hungry on nights when she lay in the steam sewer with the other boys and remembered the last bit of food, crust or bit of fat she had eaten.

"Good soup," the American said to Natasha, between his slurping spoonfuls. Galina ate and listened to Natasha and the American eating. The sound of them all nose breathing, slurping and swallowing droplets of the deep orange soup, filled with droplets of oil, floating together but not yet forming into larger droplets gave way to spoons scraping the bottoms of the bowls. As they dropped their spoons into their empty bowls, Natasha dropped her spoon and belched: "Pretty tasty, huh?"

"Yes," Galina and Jack said in unison.

Galina thought maybe it was possible to have folks in the world who helped other people and didn't want anything back. Galina put her bowl and spoon in the sink where the American was washing the dishes. That surprised her as she had never seen a man doing dishes before. She went in his main room and stood by the window. A large soccer field stretched out below his window.

Across the side of that distant apartment building, Galina looked at the squares of bright light streaming out of the windows. Every now and then, a tall black line would appear and move back and forth across the square of light. In other windows the light was not orange but blue and from the way the light danced and changed, Galina knew that apartment had television, something the

American did not have. Maybe he didn't understand Russian enough to make it worth while, Galina thought.

Galina took a blanket and climbed under his couch to sleep.

She awoke to the sound of the chair's four wooden legs being dragged across the wooden floor. She felt laying on top of her was a thin blanket, as she pulled it up to her head and felt the sudden cold of the air touching her feet, which were absent the shoes and those dirty socks she had been wearing when she passed between the lions on the Banking Bridge. She felt naked without them and scrambled around under the desk, looking for them. Galina saw her shoes, sitting together just beyond the desk's tablecloth. She reached out and dragged them back under the desk. The socks had been washed and a huge hole in the heel of the one had been sewn up. Galina put on her clean shoes and socks.

Galina walked to the kitchen and found Natasha cleaning the American's refrigerator. The American was gone but, not wanting to risk it, Galina asked Natasha:

"Where is he?"

"At work, at the newspaper," Natasha said. "I believe it's the *Komsomolets* now." Galina smiled and asked if she could help.

"I used to help my grandmother in the kitchen," Galina said.

"That's great," Natasha said. "I wish you were here when I had to cut onions."

"Next time," Galina said, smiling.

"Count on it," Natasha said and paused with the water in the sink running, a sponge in one hand and a scrub brush in the other.

Chapter XIX

1.

ANDREI stepped in the front door of Jack's apartment and Jack handed him a Baltika-3, which Andrei took without hesitation. Andrei paused at the doorway to Jack's room and nodded to Galina, sitting on a couch, drawing a picture with a set of colored pencils. Jack sat back at his desk where he had several long notebooks, working on a piece for the *Komsomolets*, about some grandmothers who complained that rogue police officers were invading their apartments and destroying everything.

Jack started to explain his newest piece to Andrei.

"And of course the *Militsiya* deny the whole thing," Jack said. Andrei glanced over at the couch.

"What are you going to do about this other thing?" Andrei said, inclining his head toward Galina.

"Well, I've been thinking about that, Andrei," Jack said.

Natasha came in from the kitchen with a plate of chips.

"*Priv'yet*, Andrei," Natasha said. He replied to her in Russian but then switched back to English with Jack.

"What is the plan, then," Andrei said, sipping his beer.

"Well, she has been telling us her story and it seems that she came through this guy Astrakhan—a Georgian—and that he might know the rest."

"What's that supposed to mean?"

"Her aunt," Jack said. "Lives somewhere in St. Petersburg."

"And what if she turns out to be just like the grandmother," Andrei said, ever the pessimist.

"It's a damned gamble," Jack said. He, Andrei and Natasha sat in silence, sipping their beers as Galina on the couch filled in a large patch of green.

"Let's ask Shakespeare," Natasha said and got down Jack's single volume edition of Shakespeare. This was a custom that no one in Jack's college Russian had mentioned, perhaps because it smacked of the pagan. Andrei, as the actual scientist among them did not seem to have any objections.

"Each of us will get to ask one of the three questions," Natasha said, placing the single-volume Shakespeare closed in front of her. "You can only ask three questions at a time and expect to get the correct answer. Has to be a 'yes' or 'no' question," she said.

Jack looked to Andrei for his confirmation of her depiction of the rules for Shakespeare Fortune Telling, a common Russian tradition.

Andrei smiled firmly and lifted his brow in an affirmative way, as if he had just taken part in the certification of a Doppler radar, instead of the exact process necessary to engage Shakespeare sooth saying.

"I'll go first," Natasha said, "because it was my idea. " Jack and Andrei exchanged baffled frowns. Natasha closed her eyes a moment, holding the brown "Complete Works of William Shakespeare" closed with one hand, its spine flat on the table. Having communed with her own inner pagan, her ancestors who would have lived in the time of Shakespeare in Moscow or Kiev, she asked her question:

"Should Jack and Andrei contact this Georgian bastard?" Natasha asked. She looked straight forward, said a page number and a line and opened the volume of Shakespeare to the page and then found the line. Jack and Andrei looked on, spellbound. Natasha read the line at that location:

" 'If thous didst ever thy dear father love—
" 'Revenge his foul and most unnatural murder.' "

"What does that mean?" Natasha asked, entering into the important 'interpretation' phase of the fortune telling.

"Yes," Jack and Andrei said at the same moment.

Natasha looked crestfallen, her question having gone against her preference.

Andrei grabbed the book.

"My turn," he said. He followed the same procedure as Natasha, down to holding the Shakespeare on its spine, open to no page, according to the experimental protocol.

"If Jack and I visit this Georgian, is he going to blow our heads off?" Andrei dove into the book and arrived at his page and line:

" 'Nothing will come of nothing, '" Andrei said.

"It's a 'no,' Andrei. A 'no,'" Jack said. "My turn."

Jack slid back the volume, the one he brought over from the United States in his luggage, along with *A Moveable Feast.*

Jack knew the plays in this volume well. They had entertained him for a long time. Yet, he could not really guess the page numbers for anything but a few random pages of his favorites. Jack felt the decision of which page and which line coming like an apparition, something he could not explain—it just came to him.

"Will we end up making things better for Galina?" Jack asked. Until that moment, Galina had not listened closely to what they were doing but now she was. Jack dropped his finger onto a page."

" 'How sweet the moonlight sleeps upon the bank.' "

244

Jack read it again and closed the book. Natasha looked glum, knowing once more Jack would take a risk that scared her to death.

2.

Andrei handed Jack one of the badges he wore during fire drills at the university where he taught. Though Andrei had only risen to the position of Pro-Rector in his university, as far as the fire department was concerned, Andrei was a volunteer Captain. Andrei gave Jack his old Lieutenant badge. They removed the badges from the red and orange sashes and pinned them to their lapels.

"Let *me* talk," Andrei said. "You're just the big dumb enforcer."

They were parked outside of the basement Galina had identified as being Astrakhan's. From the level of her agitation and desire that Andrei drive them away as soon as possible, Jack felt convinced this was the spot.

They got out of Andrei's Lada and both stood up straight, the posture of the *Militsiya*.

Andrei crossed the parking lot and headed for the basement with light coming around the edges of the door. He knocked hard.

No answer. Andrei knocked again, with authority and a loudness that meant "Not going away." Jack smiled at Andrei but Andrei did not return the smile, staying in character.

They heard scratching inside and then the basement door swung open and they met a hunched over, scruffy gray-haired man with a week's grown of beard on his face.

"We're looking for a man named Astrakhan," Andrei said, with full seriousness.

"I," said the man, before he stopped mute with his mouth open. "I am he," Astrakhan said.

Andrei looked in a notebook he held. He lifted up two pages with writing on them, notes about what his wife wanted him to bring home for dinner from the market, and he stared at a blank page underneath them, as if he were verifying some facts.

"Full name?" Andrei said, continuing his stern look at Astrakhan.

"Nugzar Astrakhan," Astrakhan said.

Andrei and Jack both wrote down the name. Astrakhan looked at both of the places where his name was written and he rubbed the back of his neck.

Andrei pulled out a newspaper from his suit pocket and opened it to the page with the face of Galina Yosheva on it.

On sight Astrakhan yelled at the photo with his finger.

"You know this girl?" Andrei said, truly angry, Jack saw.

Now all of Astrakhan's obstinacy softened into embarrassment and knowledge that buying an 8-year-old girl was not a good thing in the eyes of the law.

"So, you *bought* this girl, 8-years old?" Andrei said, his anger clearly visible. Astrakhan's awareness of his peril was plainly apparent to him.

Jack crossed his arms and stopped looking Astrakhan in the eye.

"Unless you can find the seller, the one who sold you this child, you're going to—"

"I've got that," Astrakhan said, elated, rushing to his chair and reading a number visible there.

"Her name is Ludmilla Yosheva."

Both Jack and Andrei wrote down the number.

"Best get your documents in order. We will be back with the FSB," Andrei said. He closed his notebook, staring at Jack. They turned and left Astrakhan standing in his doorway.

As they walked away, Astrakhan yelled:

"She owes me money!"

3.

Natasha was glad to see Jack and Andrei return so quickly.

As soon as Andrei entered the apartment, he wore a smile that could not have been wider. Jack was impressed with Andrei's performance and he was glad it had worked—so far.

"I have an idea how to get this next part done," Andrei said, with that sort of smile that people in Iowa would call a "shit-eating grin."

Natasha and Galina both sat on the couch and watched Jack and Andrei huddle near the phone. Again, the burden for the miracle fell to Andrei. He held the phone to his ear and dialed the number from Astrakhan. Then he glanced over at Galina and said:

"Your grandmother is Ludmilla Andrievna Yosheva?"

Galina sat on the edge of the couch, her hands in her lap, and she nodded vigorously and said "Da."

Andrei hung up the receiver and then picked it up and dialed on Jack's rotary phone the numbers necessary to reach the village of Chilkovo, near the town of Chudovsky in the Novgorod Oblast.

Andrei dialed the last number and then he leaned back in his chair and waited, nodding to Jack, Natasha and Galina that it was ringing. After many rings, a voice answered and Andrei said:

"*Moozh-no* Ludmilla Andrievna Yosheva?"

Andrei listened, added repetitions of a few words and then established that he was speaking to the right person.

"I am calling from the St. Petersburg School Tax Administration, and we have a student, a Galina Pyotrevna Yosheva, for whom you are the nearest living relative...I will be sending you a bill for sending your granddaughter to school..." Andrei listened and smirked at Jack.

"Yes, unfortunately, unless Galina has another blood relative in the St. Petersburg...yes, that would work. Did you say Anastasia?" Andrei furiously wrote down a number and address on a pad of paper.

"*Spacibo Bolshoi*," Andrei said. "Thank you. If we can find her, you don't have to pay."

Andrei hung up and tapped the paper. Jack felt a wave of relief but also of sadness. He looked over at Galina and saw her laughing with Natasha.

"This is the best thing we can do for her," Jack thought.

Chapter XX

V LADIMIR Szlotov stood in the cold wind and slapped his leather gloves together as he waited on the tarmac at Pulkovo-2 airport in St. Petersburg. He took out his *mobilny* phone and called up an old friend. Zortaev's ringer sputtered along and then the man himself answered.

"Allo!" shouted Zortaev. Loud Gypsy music played in the background. Then, abruptly, the music stopped. Zortaev answered in a gruff voice.

"Hello, Zortaev, it's just me," Szlotov said.

"Oh, my phone keeps making ticking noises," Zortaev said. "I'm getting a new one."

"Yes, I would hate that," Szlotov said. "I need you to come to 56 Zhukovskovo Street tonight."

"Why," Zortaev said. "I don't want to do anything."

"I've found a business that prints money."

"I like the sound of that," Zortaev said.

"Tonight then, okay?" Szlotov said.

2.

A Lear jet landed and pulled up to the hanger where Szlotov waited.

The jet taxied up, spooled down and the hatch opened. Out came a face Szlotov had not seen since his days back in Prague, working as a KGB section chief. In his unique whooping-crane stride where he folded his leg up higher than anyone else, causing his head to bob up and down, came Dr. Yakov Lezhnev, transplant surgeon, who had emigrated during the Perestroika.

Hunched over, his face unshaven and covered with patches of white hairs mixed in spots with darker hair, Yakov came directly up to Szlotov.

"Welcome to St. Petersburg," Szlotov said, his smile expressing the ironic intention of his greeting.

"Hooey to St. Petersburg," Yakov said. "Business."

Szlotov put his arm around his old friend, cantankerous as usual.

They got in Szlotov's car. Yakov wanted to go straight to the clinic. He read off the address and Szlotov, feeling sucked into another world, agreed to drive him there. The amount of money that could be earned by transplanting the organs of the homeless instead of turning them into meat was enormous and worth any small humiliation by being his old friend's chauffeur for the day.

They pulled up to an expensive medical clinic that Szlotov had never noticed since it was beyond the Fontanka canal. As they entered the clinic, Yakov kept up a monologue under his breath. All the words he said consisted of obscenity, of "*blyat*" this and "*hooey*" intermingled with the Russian. The clean clinic was the sort Szlotov had never seen: antiseptic, white, modern, with high-tech machines everywhere.

Inside the clinic, Yakov got a white doctor's coat and he was transformed in front of Szlotov from the man who had just sat in his car, cursing the dying child he was about to operate on and the parents, an old father and young wife, who had given birth to a broken kid they wanted Dr. Yakov Lezhnev to save.

In his white coat, Dr. Lezhnev looked at the chart thoughtfully with his mouth closed, wearing half-moon glasses that made him look brilliant. Standing a few feet away, Szlotov saw the parents come up and introduce themselves to Dr. Lezhnev, the father old enough to be Szlotov's father and his wife, a blond 20-something, just as Yakov had said on the ride over.

But in a miraculous transformation, Szlotov saw a deep softness in the eyes of Yakov, a sign that he cared and that seemed to comfort the old man as his bushy gray eyebrows bunched together.

The blond wife placed her hand on Dr. Lezhnev's shoulder and Szlotov knew the transformation was flawless.

They finished and Yakov threw his white coat in a hamper. He and Szlotov returned in the cold to Szlotov's BMW.

"Now let's go see the brat," Yakov said. Szlotov went directly to his building, which was not really that good looking from the side they entered. The main facade was on the front end of the hotel, facing Zhukovskovo Street, the side Szlotov and his men did not use.

"Nice quarters you have here, Vladimir," Yakov said. Szlotov could not decide if he was saying it intending to ridicule, as rich men in general do not observe any sort of social discretion and revel in blunt statements. Szlotov had noticed this same disturbing quality in himself with his own men and lately with Zortaev, especially after the photos in the *Komsomolets*. Those photos had made life harder for every *semiorka* in the city.

Szlotov waited so long trying to decide if the comment was or was not snide, he said nothing and led Yakov directly inside to the basement stairs. Two of his men, Ivan and Arkady, were eating sunflower seeds in the kitchen and they each had piles of shells in front of them. Szlotov led Yakov downstairs and the place had a new smell added to the old, and that was a case of mildew in the most extreme. Inside the wooden crates, children who were the current livestock

250

stirred in their cages.

"Show me Yuri," Lezhnev said. Szlotov turned to the Doctor.

"Get the special boy, Yuri, the one with blood group II+," Szlotov said. Dr. Mansoor nodded vigorously to Szlotov's relief and led them to a wooden cage which held the buck-toothed boy that Szlotov had almost rejected before.

"Arm," Szlotov said and the boy stuck his arm out of the cage. Dr. Lezhnev took out an alcohol swab, tore it open and rubbed down the boy's finger. He poked it and despite the boy's squirming, got a good blood sample. Szlotov released the boy's hand and Lezhnev did an analysis of the boy's blood group.

"That's it, II+," Lezhnev said. "Take him." Mansoor opened the cage and Szlotov and Dr. Lezhnev took the boy out of the basement. Ivan was surprised and gratified to see the choice had been one of his finds.

3.

Less than 90 minutes later, Szlotov stood in an operating room wearing a white gown of his own, and a face mask. However, his hands were dirty. Laying on the table was the naked boy with the buck teeth, who was called Yuri and who said he was born in Sennaya Square.

Then suddenly in his full surgical garb, in came Dr. Yakov Lezhnev. He held his gloved hands up and then he approached Yuri's back and made an incision with a scalpel. Blood welled from the incision but Dr. Lezhnev took no notice of the huge flood of blood on the table. Instead, he sawed his way through the skin to make a flap that he peeled back and then he transferred the purple kidney from Yuri to a stainless steel basin filled with warm saline. With his kidney gone, Yuri's blood gushed out in twelve seconds and the rest of his body lay gray, lifeless, spent.

As Yakov left the surgery with the kidney, he exchanged a look with Szlotov.

"Outstanding," Dr Lezhnev said, winking at Szlotov.

Szlotov dumped the overflowing bucket of blood under the lower corner of the gurney. He zipped the dead boy in a body bag and pushed the gurney out into he hall and transferred the body bag to his trunk without being noticed.

Hours later, Dr. Lezhnev emerged from the clinic having completed the surgery. The parents thanked Yakov and Szlotov took him back to the airport. It was now dark.

"Not bad for a day's work, Vladimir," Yakov said, sweaty and exhausted.

"Nope," Szlotov said. Knowing what he carried in his trunk made Szlotov feel a twinge he had not felt since he blew up the cat Grusha in his teenage years. Though Szlotov wanted to continue the Atheism that he grew up with during Soviet times, his mother always had faith in God that made him question it all and worry that perhaps these ways he found to improve his life might be building up into some bill he might have to pay back some day.

Before they parted on the tarmac, Szlotov said: "I'll send your cut to Geneva."

"My *half*," Yakov corrected.

Though he knew the deal was after expenses, he allowed the incorrect number to pass with his nod.

4.

Without going inside and asking for help, Szlotov popped his trunk and carried the body bag up the steps into his building and down to the basement, where Dr. Mansoor received the body and the bitter news that he would need to do another meat run to Chus. The men at Chus who received the large bags of raw meat never asked Dr. Mansoor where it came from—they just took the bags.

As Szlotov went upstairs to close his trunk, he spotted a large Mercedes in the parking lot at 56 Zhukovskovo Street . The driver's side door opened and Zortaev stepped out.

Szlotov had not seen Zortaev in person since the incident with the lobster. He was nauseated at the sight of the bad scar the incident had left on Zortaev's lip. The two sides of his lip had healed misaligned. It served to remove the menace from his face. Instead, he was just disgusting.

Sitting in Zortaev's car was the boss's own bodyguard, Sidon. Though the car's windows were tinted, Szlotov saw enough of an outline to recognize Sidon's slicked-down hair.

"Hello, Vladimir," Zortaev said, a greedy smile on his face. He walked up to Szlotov and shook his hand. He was eager to see the business that was printing money for Szlotov. Zortaev glanced up at the building, which now had bricks filling in the basement windows, but still looked derelict and falling apart—the back entrance of an old hotel Szlotov took from its former owner. "I love what you've done with the place," Zortaev said and smiled, causing creases in the rind on his face. In a second Zortaev bust out laughing at his own joke and he followed Szlotov down.

As they entered the basement, an unholy stench slapped Zortaev in the face, causing him to grimace and stop short. The Doctor looked up holding a meat cleaver and saw Zortaev. The Doctor slammed the cleaver into his workbench between the legs of the cadaver. He scurried over to greet Zortaev, his most famous patient. The Doctor reached out his bloody hand to shake hands with Zortaev but the latter declined and gave a pained smile and a wave instead.

Then Zortaev caught sight of the dead child on the Doctor's workbench and his brow puckered in silent alarm. He nose scrunched, his mouth formed into a deep frown, recoiling as if somewhat had shoved a dead rat in his face.

"What in hell is this?!" Zortaev shouted. He walked over the to doctor's workbench, looking at the child.

"This is why I called you here," Szlotov said. "To you, it's just *babki*. But to me, getting you that money in a poor region, means *this*."Szlotov took Zortaev on a tour of the basement, filling him in on every aspect of the money-making operation, from the high-priced organ sales to stripping the bodies for their meat, to his takeover of Chus Meats. "My father was a butcher, and he died a broken man—a poor man," Szlotov said. Szlotov told the story of his father, the butcher of Leningrad, and how he watched and learned at his father's side, and decided there was a better way than to throw your life away for nothing. Szlotov turned and stood almost nose to nose with Zortaev.

"You've turned me into my father," Szlotov said.

Zortaev listened quietly, and the only the sound heard in the clammy basement was of him breathing through his mouth. As they walked through the basement, kids in wooden cages around the perimeter of the room stirred on their litter of newspapers, rattling their cage doors. The Doctor cast his craggy-mouthed gaze around the room and silence followed it. A child in one cage continued to audibly whimper. Without a word, the Doctor went to the faucet, filled a pot with hot water, carried it over and dumped it on the cage of the whimperer. The Doctor put the pan away and returned to stand with Zortaev and Szlotov as they made their way back to the workbench.

"This is how I make this money," Szlotov said. "Turn him," Szlotov said to the Doctor, who flipped the boy's body so he lay on his stomach and the missing kidney was evident. Szlotov and the Doctor straightened up while Zortaev hunched over the body, one hand covering his mouth as if he were about to vomit. The boy's skin had a gray pallor that made it look like a black-and-white photograph.

Finally, Zortaev's urge to throw up had passed and he could stand up straight and breathe. Szlotov noted the wetness in his eyes.

"Why...?" Zortaev said. It was the first time in his life that the mobster was at a loss for words. A tear welled in his eye. "Why is this necessary? Surely you have easier ways of making money—"

"Like what?" Szlotov said. "Name one thing easier, that actually makes money."

Zortaev's eyes were wild and irrational. He was confused and unused to being challenged.. "Listen—" Zortaev started to say, with the ease of a bully.

"No, *you* listen," Szlotov said. "We started the Tambovs together. We are equals, you and I. You were the leader only in your own eyes." Szlotov waved his hand across the basement operation. "This is *my* business. If you want the *babki*, then how I earn it is none of your concern." Szlotov said. "You're lucky I still pay because you and I are equals."

"The *hell* we are," Zortaev said, his facial rind of stretched into a wince. "In my territory I am feared. People give me every bit they have. I govern by fear and receive every last *kopek*." Zortaev broke off and walked around the basement, kicking a few cages as he walked by. "You, *Vladdy*, are too busy protecting your mother. Little children like that American make you a fool."

Zortaev reached into his breast pocked at unfolded the same article from the *Komsomolets* that had made so much trouble for Szlotov. "*This* makes it my business," Zortaev said, pointing at the dead boy right by them on the table.

"The article, it was just an accident. I will not repeat that mistake," Szlotov said, angry anew at the reporter.

As Szlotov and Zortaev argued, the Doctor got to work on the buck-toothed boy from the transplant, using a long, wood-handled machete. From his hands to his feet, he flayed every bit of his skin off. The arm muscles were being removed.

Zortaev watched the gristly work out of the corner of his eye. Suddenly, he interrupted Szlotov. "You use them for transplants…and then the rest for meat?" In spite of himself, Zortaev smiled at the perfection of the scheme. "What about the bones? Oh, no no no, Szlotov, this is impossible. You must find another way. You are crazy, Vladimir. You are insane. You are unfit."

As they argued, the Doctor got a plastic sack and filled it with all the choice bits of meat that he could take off the buck-toothed kid. He hummed a tiny aire from Glinka as he worked with the knife, slicing away at the tops and bottoms of the boy's thighs to get nice square cuts. The meat stripped away easily and flopped in the sack like rubbery chicken but with a darker shade to the meat.

Zortaev stopped in mid sentence—he was trying to find a way to accept it—then he resumed.

"No, no, this cannot go on," Zortaev said with finality. "That is the *last* one."

Szlotov crossed his arms and frowned. "How then are we to pay you?" he said.

"That's not my problem," Zortaev said, allowing a smile. "Just get me my money—but not like this."

The Doctor, almost finished with the kid's carcass, reached for the short knife to go after the smaller muscles that Szlotov insisted he take.

Breathing loudly, Szlotov stared back and Zortaev. Next to them, the kid the Doctor had burned with the hot water started moaning in pain again.

"Be quiet, you," said the Doctor. Zortaev looked at the cage and frowned.

At that moment, Szlotov pulled up the cleaver from the Doctor's workbench and swung it at Zortaev's neck, hacking into the tough rind on the side. Before Zortaev could even lift his eyebrows and gasp, blood geysered from the gash. His knees collapsed.

"Perfect timing," said the Doctor. He moved the stripped boy off the table and then he dragged Zortaev closer to the drain so his blood wouldn't puddle on the floor. As Szlotov kneeled over him, foamy blood bubbled on his lips. He tried to speak, his eyes furious at Szlotov, but as the red wetness spread over his neck, the light in his eyes began to fade. Zortaev looked up at Szlotov one final time and then he was gone.

Szlotov and the Doctor lifted Zortaev's body on the table. His slack face made them uncomfortable. The dry, scaly skin of the rind was wrinkled and thick like cardboard.

"We needed to fill up that bag, anyway," the Doctor said and got to work on Zortaev while Szlotov took out the dead man's phone. From Zortaev's phone, Szlotov sent a text message to Sidon, telling him to come downstairs right away. Szlotov left the Doctor alone, using the paring knife on the body of Zortaev. Szlotov stood behind the door with the machete.

Sidon burst in the door and and as he stopped, aghast at the sight of his boss on the table, Szlotov hacked down on his thick neck from behind. It only took seconds for the high-squirting blood to trail off. Sidon's face quickly went the color of dull clay. Without missing a beat, the Doctor said: "You done with the machete? I need it."

Szlotov set the machete on Zortaev's legs and the Doctor picked it up. Szlotov dragged Sidon over to be next in line. He washed his hands in the sink. As he did so, he looked around at the eyes of the kids sitting dirty-faced in the wooden cages and it occurred to him: witnesses. Might be a problem.

5.

Szlotov had Vasya and Fyodor drive Zortaev's and Sidon's Mercedes to Lake Ladoga to ditch them. Arkaday followed in a third car. Ten minutes after they left, Szlotov called Druzhnev.

"Where is Zortaev?" Szlotov said. "He won't answer his phone."

"I thought he was coming to see you," Druzhnev said.

"He never made it," Szlotov said.

Druzhnev spat out "*Blyat!*" Then he expelled a mouthful of curses from "fuck" and "*bleen*" to "blyat."

"You think…FSB?" Szlotov said.

"Fuck!" Druzhnev shouted again. "Of *course.*"

"He knew they would get wise to the pipeline diversion—"

"Stop!" Druzhnev interrupted. "Not on the phone. I'll be right there."

6.

Sergei saw Druzhnev arrive and he called Szlotov on his cell phone. Then Sergei touched the pistol wedged in the back of his waistband underneath his bulletproof vest to make sure it was still there. Druzhnev parked, got out of his Maserati Quattroporte alone and walked in Sergei's direction. Sergei nodded at Druzhnev, flicked away his cigarette and led Druzhnev in the basement door. Szlotov went to the basement using the stairs from the floor above. He waited there while the Doctor finished up with Zortaev's corpse.

Druzhnev followed Sergei inside, then pulled up short. In front of him lay Zortaev's half-dissected body.

"What are you doing?" Druzhnev shouted and recoiled, drawing his gun. He stared in horror at the carved-up body that had been his friend.

Sergei reached around and snatched away Druzhnev's gun, which he turned on him. Druzhnev's jaw dropped and he stared at Szlotov.

"Once and for all, shut your mouth," Szlotov said and he walked around while Sergei held the gun on him. The Doctor stood aside and used one of his fingers, covered in dried blood, to wiggle his tooth. Then, he kneeled over Zortaev's corpse and picked up a knife to slice off another slab of meat from the corpse's thigh, which he put in the sack.

"You've gone insane, Vladimir," Druzhnev said, staring at his own gun in Sergei's hand. "What kind of crazy shit are you doing? You've clearly gone crazy. All of you," Druzhnev said, staring at Sergei and the Doctor. "You've gone to the devil."

"Not really," Szlotov said, completely relaxed, in his element, enjoying himself. "It's just business. You've never been in business, have you, Pavel? It's like picking grapes off the vine for you, right?" Szlotov grinned at Druzhnev,

256

stone faced, knowing his peril. "There's nothing sinister about that bag of meat," Szlotov said. "Zortaev is on his way to becoming *sosiskis*. Big, greasy sausages," Szlotov said and laughed.

"He'd be proud of that," Druzhnev said and smiled briefly.

Szlotov heard Druzhnev breathing with his mouth open and the sound alone was enough for him to end this conversation.

"Goodbye, Pavel," Szlotov said. "Say hello to Zortaev for me."

Szlotov shot Druzhnev in the temple and blood geysered from the hole in his cheek.

Sergei, who was covering Druzhnev, turned at the last second and fired twice at Szlotov. The first shot hit Szlotov in his right shoulder. The second bullet entered Szlotov's mouth, burned his tongue and exited from his left cheek. The exit wound tasted like copper and burned like he'd been stuck with a red-hot poker.

Szlotov stared at his old friend in sadness, temporarily unable to speak, and squeezed the trigger on his Glock until the clip was empty. His ears rang from the shots. Sergei took several rounds in the chest and they threw him back until he fell on several cages, knocking them over and smashing one. Druzhnev was dead from the temple shot. And while the bulletproof vest protected Sergei's heart, Szlotov had gotten him in the groin, hitting the femoral artery. Sergei was bleeding out and would be dead in seconds. The Doctor crouched behind his workbench. Szlotov lay back on the floor, his mind in a blurry daze from the two bullet holes in his face.

The Doctor peeked out from behind the table. His fingertips were bloody, as was the tip of his nose. Behind the Doctor, Szlotov saw a tiny girl with an egg-shaped head climb out of one of the smashed cages.

Suddenly the door at the top of the stairs burst open and the rest of Szlotov's men ran down, guns up and ready. They saw Druzhnev, dead, with the back of his head blown off, then rushed to Szlotov and then to Sergei. Fyodor called a "Skorry *pahmoch*" (quick help), felt Sergei's lack of pulse and then Szlotov's. Fyodor said: "You're going to make it, boss." Fyodor took off his white shirt and staunched the bleeding.

As his crew gathered in a crowd around him and waited for the ambulance, Szlotov saw the little girl with the light bulb-shaped head going around to the cages and unlocking them. Arkady arrived with a wooden board and they lay Szlotov on it before walking him up the basement steps. Szlotov felt himself going in and out of consciousness. Behind them, though only he seemed to notice, he saw several kids jump the Doctor and throw a sack over his head. The kids all dragged the Doctor into the corner. As he was carried up the stairs Szlotov saw a convergence of pikes and other sharp objects in the hands of kids, headed toward the Doctor.

Chapter XXI

1.

GALINA felt nervous as they drove across the Neva River, seeing the Peter and Paul steeple standing up, visible everywhere. Galina rode holding a bundle that was all her clothes to a place nobody wanted to talk about. The whole thing terrified her. She was scared they were going to take her back to Astrakhan.

2.

They arrived at the wooden door of a tall concrete apartment building. The door was covered in blond-colored wood strips. They entered the apartment and walked up a flight of stairs and then they stopped in front of one door. Jack, Natasha and Andrei stood in the hallway. Galina stood in front.

"Everybody ready?" Jack said. He knocked on the door. When it opened Galina's heart swelled and her skin tingled. A blond-haired woman stood in the doorway. She looked just like Galina's mother Sonya.

The woman crouched on one knee and smiled at Galina.

"Dear Galya," the woman said. "I am your mother's sister Anastasia." Galina flew at her and hugged her as she cried from happiness. She hugged her aunt and then after a few moments, Galina turned back:

"Thank you," Galina said to Jack, Natasha and Andrei.

Chapter XXII

1.

THE three of them returned to Andrei's car feeling happy but empty. Natasha and Jack sat together in the back seat while Andrei drove. Nobody talked. Jack looked out his window. Natasha looked forward and they silently held hands. Jack thought about all the other kids he had not been able to help. Had he done the right thing? Was it wrong to get involved? To fight the system? He made mistakes, deadly mistakes, but maybe this was the start of a new beginning for Russia. He knew he had pushed his luck on Metallistov Prospekt—he would have to find a new apartment.

He felt pretty good about Galina. None of them would ever see Galina again. If that meant she had a happy life, Jack was okay with that. Andrei drove them back to the apartment. Jack and Natasha got out. Still holding Natasha's hand, Jack leaned down to Andrei's window.

"Come on up—I've got a few Baltika," Jack said.

"No, I should go home," Andrei said, smiling. "Katya is waiting for me."

"No—we're a team Andrei. You need to celebrate. Okay, screw the Baltika, we'll stop and get some Jack Daniels—the real stuff." A dimple-inducing smile spread over Andrei's face. Jack saw his Adam's apple drop.

"Let me park," Andrei said. The three of them walked into the *Produkti* store and drew the attention of every woman in an orange smock working behind the counters. Jack and Andrei walked straight to the unmanned liquor counter while Natasha took some money and went for a Coca-Cola.

An irritated Russian woman with her gray hair in a bun abandoned the bread counter to help them.

"What do you require?" said the lady, her stray hairs floating like a halo.

"Jack Daniels," Jack said, pointing to the top-most shelf. The lady did not understand and she frowned and chuffed. She found a step ladder and climbed to the top of it to fetch a dusty pint of Jack Daniels Whiskey. The lady wrote down the price on a slip of paper and handed it to Jack, who ferried the price-slip to a central cashier who sat inside glass walls, higher than everyone else. That cashier took the slip of paper and enough money to pay it, which Jack covered. The central cashier gave them a receipt and they took that back to the original lady who tore the receipt half way to show that it had been redeemed before handing over the bottle.

As they walked the rest of the way back to Jack's apartment, Natasha looped her arm around Jack's arm and he felt warm. Andrei cracked the bottle and took a pull. He hissed in pain and passed the bottle to Jack.

"No, not on the street, Jack," Natasha said. Jack hesitated and handed the bottle back to Andrei, who made up for lost time. After he gasped for air, Andrei burst into song, his arms making big gestures: "The birds return back home from many distant places…"

They entered Jack's building and walked upstairs, Andrei behind still singing. When they reached his door, Natasha put her arms around Jack's neck.

"You want a child, don't you Jack?"

THE END

CPSIA information can be obtained
at www.ICGtesting.com
Printed in the USA
BVHW072228010720
582600BV00007B/207